THE
ONE
AND
ONLY
DOLLY
JAMIESON

Also by Lisa Ireland

The Secret Life of Shirley Sullivan
The Art of Friendship
The Shape of Us
Honey Hill House
Feels Like Home
Breaking the Drought

LISA IRELAND

THE ONE AND ONLY DOLLY JAMIESON

MICHAEL JOSEPH
an imprint of
PENGUIN BOOKS

MICHAEL JOSEPH

UK | USA | Canada | Ireland | Australia
India | New Zealand | South Africa | China

Michael Joseph is part of the Penguin Random House group of companies whose
addresses can be found at global.penguinrandomhouse.com

Penguin
Random House
Australia

First published by Michael Joseph in 2023

Cover design and illustration by Lisa Brewster, The Brewster Project
© Penguin Random House Australia Pty Ltd
Additional illustrations by Pavel L Photo and Video/Shutterstock.com
and OLeksiiTooz/Shutterstock.com
Author photograph by Nikita Cherry
Typeset in 11.5/16 pt Minion Pro/Adobe Caslon Pro by Midland Typesetters, Australia

Printed and bound in Australia by Griffin Press, an accredited
ISO AS/NZS 14001 Environmental Management Systems printer

A catalogue record for this
book is available from the
National Library of Australia

ISBN 978 0 14377 988 9

penguin.com.au

We at Penguin Random House Australia acknowledge that Aboriginal and Torres
Strait Islander peoples are the Traditional Custodians and the first storytellers of the
lands on which we live and work. We honour Aboriginal and Torres Strait Islander
peoples' continuous connection to Country, waters, skies and communities. We
celebrate Aboriginal and Torres Strait Islander stories, traditions and living cultures;
and we pay our respects to Elders past and present.

In memory of my grandmothers
Daphne (the Dancing Queen), whose love knew no bounds
and
Marjory (the Mysterious), always present in my heart

Part One

Chapter One

London
2019

'Good morning, Dolly. How are you today?'

Fucking freezing, if you must know.

I smile at Stacey, the senior librarian, and keep my thoughts to myself. Profanity isn't tolerated in the library. I've learnt that the hard way. 'I'm quite well, darling. And you?'

Her lips return my smile, but her eyes are steely. 'I'm fine. Just to let you know, we have an author talk at eleven so it might get a tad busy in here this morning.'

'Which author?'

Stacey seems taken aback by the question. 'A local fellow, Mike Heatherton. He's written a history of the neighbourhood. Probably not your cup of tea.'

Most of the librarians here are lovely. If I happen to miss one of the author talks or events, sweet little Jemima saves me a biscuit or a piece of pound cake, and Vanessa's always finding new novels or memoirs she thinks might interest me. But Stacey is different. She screws up her nose when she sees me coming and never has time to listen to my stories.

Stacey just wants me to go away. Of course, she can't come right out and *say* that. Her job is to serve the public. And I'm the public. So as long as I don't swear or cause a scene, she has to tolerate me.

'I'm actually quite interested in the local area,' I say. 'Is it recent history? Perhaps the author and I will have some acquaintances in common. Back in the day, Patricia Heywood – you remember her? She was a big star back in the '70s. Anyway, she used to share a flat with Eva Grant, just on the other side of the park there. They had the best parties—'

'Medieval,' Stacey says drily. 'A little before your time – or Patricia's, for that matter.'

'Never mind. I'm sure that will be interesting too.'

'Well,' she says, 'the first three rows are reserved for the historical society, so you'll need to sit in the back.'

'Absolutely fine, darling. Thank you for your help. It's been a pleasure, as always.'

She hates it when I'm overly polite. It gives her nowhere to go. She nods then and averts her gaze, making a show of looking at a pile of papers on the desk in front of her. I take my cue and continue making my way into the library, but I can't resist a parting shot. 'I'll let you know my thoughts about the author over morning tea, don't worry!'

That's when I notice her: a new woman, standing in the magazine section. She's pretending to flip through a home magazine, but really she's watching me. How utterly delightful to have an audience! I take a seat in one of the armchairs opposite the magazine racks and theatrically remove my scarf and gloves before taking out my notebook. I make a show of scribbling some notes, but I'm watching her out of the corner of my eye.

I love having someone new to observe. Mostly, it's the same old regulars in here day in, day out. Some I know by name – Glenda, who comes in to borrow books to read over the phone to her grandchildren in Scotland; Vincent, who reads nothing but crime novels; and young Erin, who still hasn't told her mum that she's dropped out of university.

4

There are others who don't like to chat too much, but we nod at each other politely, all of us pretending that we're here by choice, as we while away the hours in this sanctuary for the lonely.

At a guess, the newcomer is aged somewhere between forty and fifty. She's dressed smartly, albeit rather blandly, in expensive brands – I can tell this from the way they hang on her frame. The skirt might even be made to measure. She's carrying a Gucci tote, just like the one I used to own.

Everything about this woman screams 'money'. Her hair is ash-blonde, bordering on grey in places, and it's styled into a smooth bob. Her make-up is natural but flawless – nude lipstick and nothing heavy around the eyes. I watch as she removes her coat and drapes it elegantly over her arm. She seems completely out of place in here.

I would have assumed she was the visiting author if Stacey hadn't already told me today's guest speaker is a man. So I wonder what she's doing here. She looks like the type of woman who buys books at Harrods; one who wouldn't bother to sign up for a library card. Maybe she *is* an author, researching her next novel. Unlikely in our little community library, I think – novelists all seem to hang out in cafes these days, and the serious researchers are at the British Library or at least one of the bigger suburban branches. Still, it's not impossible. Perhaps this woman's just getting started in her career.

Oh, how lovely it would be to have another creative type in the library! Most of the other regulars are nice enough, but we have so little in common. There are only so many photos of other people's grand-children one can bear to look at. I imagine having conversations with this woman about her creative process, or even just the arts in general. What I wouldn't give to have a meaningful discussion about the theatre, or a new gallery that's opened. Dear god, even some chitchat about the latest bestselling novels would be good. It would help me to know which books I should be harassing Stacey to order for the large-print collection.

Of course, the newcomer might be a one-time visitor – or a complete bore – but there's no harm in hoping otherwise.

She catches me looking at her and I smile, but her eyes dart away. I hoist myself out of the armchair and place my notebook down on it to save my place.

She notices me approaching and this time she meets my gaze.

'Hello,' I say. 'Are you new here? I couldn't help but notice you're looking a bit lost. I'm a regular, so I know this library like the back of my hand. Is there something I can help you with?'

The sadness in her eyes leaks into her words. 'I'm afraid nobody can help me.'

Chapter Two

Geelong, Australia
1941

Marjorie Ferguson's entrance into the world was a suitably dramatic one.

Mrs Ada Ferguson wanted a hospital birth for her firstborn grand-child. Twenty-four years ago, Ada had given birth to her only son, James, in the family home on Aphrasia Street, attended by a midwife and the family physician. Although James's birth was uneventful, Ada had previously lost another child – and almost her life – after a protracted labour at home. She would tolerate no such risks for James's child. It was the 1940s and hospital births were becoming more commonplace. Ada was determined that her daughter-in-law, Eleanor, should avail herself of every modern medical intervention on offer.

When Eleanor protested that she didn't like hospitals, Ada was quick to dismiss her concerns. 'Hospital is the best place for you, my dear. Heaven forbid something should happen to that precious child of yours.'

As far as Ada was concerned, the matter was settled.

With James off fighting as part of the Allied forces in Europe, Eleanor found herself relying on her in-laws – Ada and her husband,

George – for support. She was a nineteen-year-old newlywed whose husband had shipped out barely a month after their hastily arranged marriage. James's father had welcomed her to the family, but his mother had made it clear Eleanor was nowhere near good enough for her precious son.

In his letters, James assured Eleanor that he would have married her even if she hadn't been carrying his baby, and this knowledge sustained her through the long, lonely months of her pregnancy. Eleanor knew that once he returned home and Ada saw how in love they were, she'd come around. With no family of her own, she needed to keep James's parents onside. They would be her baby's only grandparents, and she wanted her little one to experience the love of extended family, something she'd missed out on when she was growing up.

When she woke in the night with twinging back pain, Eleanor, who was completely ignorant about the realities of childbirth, momentarily wondered if this might be a sign that her baby was on its way. But it was a few weeks before her due date, the pain was milder than she expected labour to be, and she certainly didn't want to make a fool of herself in front of her in-laws, so she convinced herself that the lumpy mattress was the source of her discomfort and tried to go back to sleep.

It wasn't until a sharp pain racked her body a good three hours later that she realised what was going on. When the pain subsided, she sat up, pulled back the bedcovers and felt for the switch on the bedside lamp. She'd need her dressing gown and slippers before heading down the hallway to alert Ada the baby was on its way.

Before her feet hit the carpeted floor, another pain was upon her. This one took her breath away, and she began to feel quite frightened. There was only a momentary respite before the next one came, and then the next.

Eleanor never made it out of bed. Ada and George were awakened by her cries of pain, and they arrived at Eleanor's room just in time to see their granddaughter's entrance into the world.

●

Eleanor christened her daughter, born just as the sun was rising, Marjorie Dawn, a name Ada secretly disapproved of. Marjorie itself wasn't so bad, but Eleanor insisted on calling the infant *Margie*, which sounded common to Ada's ear. *Surely Catherine or Mary would have been a better choice?* But she was too besotted by the infant to voice her protest.

Little Margie spent the first years of her life living with her mother in a large, comfortable house in Nicholas Street, Chilwell. The house had belonged to Ada's family, and she'd inherited it upon her father's passing. When James and Eleanor married, Ada had offered them the house rent-free while they got on their feet. Her original plan had been to gift the house to James upon his marriage, but when he'd chosen Eleanor – a girl below his social standing – Ada had thought better of it.

The house was blessed with a big backyard, which featured a chook run, a vegetable patch and several climbable trees. Margie spent her days joyfully: singing to the chooks to soothe them while she collected their eggs, imagining she was a princess looking out over her kingdom from the highest branch of the oak tree, and dancing to the show tunes Mum played on their old piano after dinner.

Those early years were happy and uneventful. Uneventful for Margie, at least.

Eleanor's life was not so worry-free. She became a war widow about a year after Margie's birth. James died without ever meeting his child, which compounded Eleanor's grief. Margie's grandparents felt the loss of their son deeply. George grieved quietly, turning to his faith for comfort, whereas Ada looked to her granddaughter to fill the void in her heart.

Margie, though, was blissfully unaware of her father's absence.

For the first seven years of her life it'd just been Margie and her mum. Between the rent-free housing and the war widow's pension Mum got from the government, they managed to live a comfortable life. Mum took in a bit of sewing work from time to time to help pay for Margie's singing and dancing lessons, and if things were tight they certainly had never seemed that way. She and her mum were 'as thick as thieves', Granny used to say, and it was true. Back then Mum had seemed like a benevolent older sister. She was never too busy to play or to watch Margie perform in the endless 'concerts' she would stage in the backyard. In fact, Mum had made a set of stage curtains and hung them across the back verandah so Margie would have a proper stage for those performances. She even used her sewing scraps to make costumes for each new 'show'. 'You're my shining star, Margie,' she'd say. 'One of these days we're going to see your name up in lights. You mark my words.'

●

The first real change in Margie's idyllic childhood came just before her eighth birthday. One Saturday afternoon Margie's mum and her new friend, Mr Sheridan, took her out to the pictures and then to a cafe for lunch. The first surprise was that Mr Sheridan picked them up in his car! Grandpa had a car, but Margie rarely got to ride in it. Granny insisted that they walk to church on all but the most miserable winter days. And Grandpa's car wasn't shiny and new like Mr Sheridan's.

On the way into town, Margie could barely contain her excitement. She bounced up and down on the back seat until Mum frowned at her and told her to mind her manners. Mr Sheridan smiled in the rear-vision mirror and said, 'She's just excited, Ellie. And I don't blame her. We're going to have a great day today.'

Margie smiled back at him. She liked Mr Sheridan. He'd been to visit the house quite a few times and each time he'd surprised Margie with a little gift – a bag of sweets, hair ribbons and, on his most recent visit, a picture book. 'Now, Bill, you mustn't spoil her,' Mum had said.

'Right you are, Ellie,' he'd replied, but when Mum turned away he winked at Margie and slipped her a barley sugar. Margie laughed and winked back as she popped the sweet into her mouth.

They were going to see *Little Women*, which seemed to be very popular judging by the crowd streaming into the picture theatre.

Mr Sheridan stopped at the kiosk to purchase a bag of sweets for them to share during the picture, and while he was at the counter, Mum whispered, 'Darling, I know you are excited today, but please remember we are Mr Sheridan's guests, so you need to be on your best behaviour.'

Margie nodded her agreement but silently wondered why Mum had her knickers in a knot all of a sudden. Anyone would think Mr Sheridan was the King of England rather than just an ordinary man.

As they made their way up the stairs to the theatre, Mum took Margie's hand so she wouldn't get lost in the crowd. She was surprised when Mr Sheridan clasped her other hand. 'Don't you worry, princess. We've got you.' But the crowd didn't worry Margie at all. In fact, she felt exhilarated.

They took their seats as the lights began to dim, and when the velvet curtains parted to reveal the screen, Margie had to stop herself from squealing with excitement. (Making such a noise probably wouldn't be considered 'best behaviour' by her mother.) Some of her schoolfriends had been to the pictures more than once, but this was Margie's first time. Granny didn't approve of children watching movies. She believed Margie was too young to have her head 'filled with such nonsense'. And no matter what Mum thought, she always seemed to take Granny's advice. But now here they were, at the pictures, and Margie couldn't wait to see what all the fuss was about.

The screen flickered to life and a hush came over the audience as music filled the theatre. Margie's heart beat hard in her chest as the titles came up, then a couple danced onto the screen singing about how wonderful it was to be married. The lady had the voice of an angel and Margie couldn't take her eyes off her, not even when Mum offered her the open bag of lollies. A few moments into the musical number, the couple started singing about washing powder and Margie realised this wasn't the main event, but an advertisement for Persil! Not that it mattered. It was wonderful just the same.

The magic dissipated when the next short film – a newsreel about a rabbit plague in Victoria – began. Luckily, a Bugs Bunny cartoon followed, so Margie felt the rabbits had the final say.

The last item before the main feature showed excerpts from a movie that was coming later in the year called *In the Good Old Summertime*, which starred Van Johnson and Judy Garland. Van Johnson was very handsome, but it was Judy Garland who had Margie transfixed. If the lady from the Persil ad had the voice of an angel, then Judy was most certainly a goddess! And the way she looked in that spectacular red dress as she danced her way across the screen? Oh! Margie didn't have the words to describe it. But right then and there, she made up her mind that when she grew up she would be just like Judy Garland.

●

When the film was finished, they headed across the road to a fancy sort of cafe and Margie was allowed to choose where they sat. She chose a booth near the window so she could admire all the dressed-up ladies walking past. Margie sat on one side of the booth and both grown-ups on the other. Mr Sheridan's arm rested across the top of the seat where her mother sat, his fingertips not quite touching Mum's shoulder. He said Margie should call him 'Bill' and that today lunch was on him. 'Go ahead, little lady. Order whatever you'd like.'

Mum reminded her not to be greedy.

Once the waitress had taken their order, Bill turned his attention to Margie. 'What did you think of the film?'

'Oh, it was wonderful!' she gushed.

'What was the best bit, do you think?' Mum asked.

'All of it. And I don't just mean *Little Women*, even though that was a very good story. I loved the cinema. I loved the beautiful velvet curtains and how dark it was and how the music filled the whole place and the cartoon and—'

Bill laughed. 'I'm glad you enjoyed yourself. Perhaps we can do it again soon.'

'Oh, could we? I'd so love to see that movie they showed a little of – the one where Judy Garland dances in that red dress. She's so beautiful . . . I want to be just like her when I grow up.'

Bill looked at her fondly. 'I'm sure you will be, little lady.'

'Margie has a beautiful singing voice,' Mum said proudly. 'And she can dance, too. She's been having lessons since she was a wee tot. Last year I started teaching her to play the piano and she picked it up just like that.' Mum clicked her fingers together.

Bill looked suitably impressed. 'What a clever girl.'

'So,' Margie persisted. 'Can we go see the movie with Judy Garland in it? *Pleeease?*'

'Sure, we could do that – if your mother approves?' Bill looked to Mum for an answer and Margie held her breath. This would be the part where Mum said that today was an exception and Margie was too young to go to the cinema.

But Mum smiled. 'I don't see why not.'

'Really?' Margie couldn't believe what she was hearing. 'What if Granny finds out?'

Mum paused for a moment, as if she were choosing her words carefully. 'Granny is our elder and we must always respect her, but . . . well, some of her ideas can be a bit old-fashioned. Bill has made me realise that Granny is not in charge of us. We don't have to do *every-thing* her way.'

Crikey! Mum had never gone against Granny's wishes before. Margie briefly wondered how her grandmother would react to this little rebellion – she was a force to be reckoned with when she got mad – but if it meant more frequent trips to the pictures, Margie figured it would be worth enduring a few lectures and cutting remarks.

When Margie was midway through her Blue Heaven milkshake, Mum announced in a trembling voice that she and Bill were getting married. 'I know this will be a bit of a shock, but Bill loves you too. Isn't that right, Bill?'

Bill smiled warmly at her. 'Too right.'

'I don't want you to worry, Margie. Nothing will change between us. But now we'll have Bill to look after us. Isn't that exciting?'

Margie nodded enthusiastically. She was genuinely pleased. In fact, she was beginning to think Bill coming into their lives might be the best thing that had ever happened. First an outing to the pictures and now a wedding! This could be her chance to shine. She had visions of walking down the aisle of the church in a pink silk dress, scattering rose petals, just as Betty from school had done when she was the flower girl at her aunt's wedding. Maybe Mum would even let her sing for the guests.

Mum and Bill exchanged a smile, and Bill leant over to take Margie's hand. 'I can't wait for us to be a proper family,' he said.

The following day, over lunch, Margie excitedly told her grandparents the news. Her mother had stopped going to church years ago, but she dropped Margie off every Sunday so she could attend with her grandparents. Granny always cooked a special Sunday lunch. Mum used to come to lunch every week, even after she'd stopped going to church, but for the past year or so she'd started coming up with excuses not to join them. In some ways it was better. Mum and Granny were not exactly the best of friends, and although Mum tried her hardest to be sweet and polite, Granny was often cranky when she was there. It made the mealtime a stiff and awkward affair. Her grandmother was much easier to deal with in Mum's absence.

Margie's big announcement didn't elicit the enthusiastic response she'd anticipated. When she confessed her desire to be a flower girl, Granny pursed her lips. 'Surely your mother isn't considering a church wedding?' She sniffed. 'I wouldn't get my hopes up if I were you.'

'Ada,' Grandpa warned, and with that the subject was closed.

When she repeated Granny's words at bedtime that night, her mother hugged her and told her not to take any notice. Mum said Granny was just sad because her son – Margie's daddy – had died, and sometimes sadness could make a person mean.

'But you *are* going to get married in the church, aren't you, Mum?'

'No, my darling,' Mum replied. 'Because this will be my second marriage, Bill and I thought we'd do something different. We're going to go to the registry office in town and then we're having a party at home. Won't that be fun?'

Margie's rose-petal fantasy evaporated. It seemed Granny was right after all. 'But I really wanted to be the flower girl.'

'And you will be, my love. I'll make you a special frock. In fact, what if I make it out of the same fabric as my wedding dress? We'll be like twins!' She clapped her hands. 'You'll be like a miniature bride.'

Or a movie star! This was sounding more like it, but Margie still had one question. 'Mum, do you think I could sing for the wedding guests?'

'What a lovely idea. I'll have to ask Bill, of course, but I'm sure he won't mind.'

Margie beamed at Mum. Things were turning out even better than she'd imagined.

•

The day of the wedding started out full of promise. It was bright and sunny, perfect weather for the short-sleeved cream satin dress Mum had made for her. Mum's dress was made of the same material and, although it wasn't long or fancy like some bridal gowns Margie had seen, it did have pearl buttons and a pretty flower corsage pinned to the front. She'd never seen her mother look so beautiful.

The disappointing discovery that her mother was wearing a small hat instead of a veil was more than compensated for by her own head-dress: a flower crown! Margie admired her reflection in the mirror as Mum placed a halo of pink rosebuds on top of her freshly curled hair. For once Margie was pleased that her hair wasn't blonde, because the pink looked lovely against her dark brown hair, and the colour also made her eyes seem more blue than grey. There was no doubt in her mind she looked every bit a star.

Unfortunately, things went downhill from there. The ceremony took place in a dingy office – without an aisle to sashay down, *or* an audience – and at first the man in charge didn't even want to let Margie in. 'Bridal couple and witnesses only!' he barked. But Mum protested and Bill said not to worry, he'd fix it. He went up and shook the man's hand and spoke to him quietly. Whatever he said worked, because the man nodded and Margie was allowed to enter the room.

Not that it was worth it, to be honest. The ceremony itself only took a few minutes. There was no music, no rice being thrown, no decorations; nothing exciting at all.

The party wasn't what Margie had dreamt of either. At first the grown-ups made a big fuss of her and said how lovely she looked, but after that she was largely ignored. There were no other children invited, which made the whole thing rather boring. Even her song wasn't the triumph she'd imagined. She'd only got through one verse and the chorus when Bill started clapping and the rest of the adults joined in. Mum shushed her when she tried to say she wasn't finished yet.

Margie and her mother moved into Bill's house the day after the wedding. It was much further away from school and from Granny's than their house in Nicholas Street. Margie was shocked to discover that it was also smaller and not nearly as nice as their old place. She'd imagined a man like Bill – with his new car and expensive gifts – would have a big, fancy house, but she couldn't have been more wrong.

When she discovered that their cat, Teddy, wouldn't be coming, and that there was no room at Bill's for her piano, Margie had suggested that Bill move into their house instead.

Mum said that wasn't possible. 'We won't be here forever,' she said, brightly. 'Bill is saving to build us a brand-new home. Won't that be exciting? In the meantime, we'll just have to make the best of things.'

Margie screwed up her nose when her mother showed her to a tiny sleep-out attached to the back of the house. Mum plastered a smile on her face as she crossed the grubby linoleum floor to part a pair of tatty curtains. 'Here we are. This is your new bedroom.'

Sunlight illuminated the dust motes swirling above Margie's haphazardly placed possessions. Her bed, with its frilly pink bedspread, was shoved up against one wall. Mum squeezed her shoulder. 'Bill's place just needs a woman's touch, that's all. I'll whip up some new curtains for in here and perhaps we can get you a rug. This room will scrub up beautifully, Margie, I promise.'

'Why can't I have the bedroom up the hall? The one next to yours?'

Margie's mum took her hand and placed it on her tummy, which felt surprisingly hard. 'Can you keep a secret, my darling girl? You mustn't tell anyone. Do you promise?'

Margie nodded solemnly.

'We need the spare room for the baby that I'm growing in my tummy. You're going to be a big sister in a few months. Isn't that exciting?'

●

After the wedding Granny cut off all financial support, even refusing to pay for Margie's singing and dancing tuition. Mum explained that since she'd remarried she was no longer receiving the war widow's pension, and it was up to Bill to decide what they could afford. Bill said that, although he'd love to pay for her lessons, they were saving every penny so they could build the new house and, unfortunately, they'd all have to make sacrifices for a little while.

Even though Mum had told her not to, Margie decided she had no choice but to ask Granny for help. But it was a waste of time. 'You're too big for all that nonsense now, Marjorie. Of course, it's good for all young ladies to be able to play the piano, and you can continue to come to my house to practise that whenever you like, but I can't see the point of the dance classes. It's not as if you are going to be a ballerina. As for the singing, you can always join the church choir when you're old enough.'

Margie didn't know how she'd survive without her dance class. Miss Simpson was always telling her that she had real talent. She'd recently started keeping Margie back for half an hour after class so she could teach her new routines that were too hard for the other girls. When Margie accompanied Mum to tell her teacher that she wouldn't be back, Miss Simpson's eyes had shone with tears. 'Don't you give up, Margie Ferguson,' she'd said. 'Keep singing and dancing at home. Listen to the songs on the radio and make up your own moves.'

Margie solemnly promised she would.

Chapter Three

London
2019

'I'm afraid nobody can help me.' The newcomer cups both hands over her mouth, seemingly appalled at having spoken these words aloud. But it is too late. Her pain is out in the world now, and her face crumples with the shame of it as her chest heaves with silent sobs. She has a deer-in-the-headlights look about her. Her eyes dart around, seeking routes to make her escape, but I'm not having that.

I step forward with open arms and she allows me to embrace her. Whatever semblance of composure she's been clinging to crumbles away and her body shakes as the tears come in full force. I rub her back in the soothing way I remember my mother doing when I was a little girl. 'That's it, my darling. Let it all out. Sometimes we girls just need a good cry.'

She doesn't embrace me, but as she cries I feel an easing of the tension in her body. She gives in to her emotions and buries her face in my coat. Her aroma – shampoo, talcum powder and a light citrus fragrance – is the scent of privilege. A sliver of shame spikes me when I think of my own odour, which I fear is less than pleasant.

When the sobs finally ease, I loosen my embrace. 'I'm Dolly.'

She gives me a tentative smile. 'Jane.'

'Would you like to sit with me for a moment, Jane? It seems as if you've had a rough morning.'

Her face colours. 'No, I must go, I'm afraid. I need to collect my husband's dry-cleaning. Thank you for your kindness, though. I'm sure I don't know what came over me.' She laughs unconvincingly. 'Probably just hormones.'

'Ah. The Change. Say no more. Goodness, I remember when I was going through it, I was a wreck. Boiling mad one minute, weeping the next. But don't you worry; like all that ails us in this life, it'll pass.'

She smiles and unfolds her coat. 'Thank you again.'

The thought of her out on the street in such a distressed state worries me but, if I'm honest, my reluctance to let her leave isn't entirely motivated by concern. Her presence in the library is a welcome distraction from my mundane existence. 'You don't look well, my dear. Humour an old lady and sit for a moment.' I lower my voice. 'I know you're probably embarrassed but, honestly, you shouldn't be. No one here will have batted an eyelid at you having a tiny little cry. In fact, I doubt anyone noticed. Far more outlandish things happen here all the time, so you'll need to do more than shed a few tears to get attention.'

She gives me a look of disbelief.

I incline my head to the right. 'Gerard, the tubby one sitting at the computer over there? He strips down to his underwear on a regular basis, and Stacey has to threaten him with calling the police to make him put his clothes back on. One time, Glenda – she's another regular – got so annoyed she chased him around the library, shaking her brolly at him. It was story time in the children's section, so it caused a bit of a hullabaloo.'

She laughs, and I feel positively triumphant at having brought her a moment of fleeting pleasure.

'That's more like it,' I say. 'You're looking a little better already. Come and sit with me for a minute and keep me company. I have plenty more tales I can tell you.'

She hesitates for a second before acquiescing. 'Well, perhaps just for a moment.'

'That's the way, darling. Come on now.' I lead her back to my saved position among the comfy armchairs near the big window that over-looks the street. Luck is with us today, and there is a free chair next to mine. 'This is my favourite spot in the library. It's often sunny in the afternoons, and it's the best position for people-watching – both inside and outside.'

'Do you do a lot of that? People-watching?'

I nod. 'I find people interesting. Don't you?'

Her forehead creases. 'Yes, but . . . well, I keep to myself a lot.'

I'm fascinated by this admission and want to ask more, but I don't want to scare her off, so I start to waffle about the library in the hopes of keeping her entertained. I tell her more stories about the regulars, drawing on my dramatic skills to make the tales bigger and more enter-taining than they were in real life.

'My goodness, Dolly, what a wonderful storyteller you are.'

'It's my theatrical training, darling.'

Is that a flicker of recognition I see in her eyes? 'You were a performer?'

'It was a long time ago now.'

She smiles without commenting. Who am I kidding? Of course she doesn't recognise me. These days I look like an eccentric old bag lady, not a well-known performer. Despite my best efforts, I'm barely presentable. After all, it's not as if I can afford to get my hair set each week like I used to, or to buy made-to-measure clothes.

Everything I own now is practical. Once upon a time I never would have even contemplated such a thing. I purchased items for beauty, not function. But not anymore. Even the once-beautiful calf-length velour coat I'm wearing is showing its age. The faux fur on the lapels is slightly matted, and its peacock-blue colour has faded. It's the nicest piece I own and I use it to cover all the other shabby garments I'm forced by necessity to wear, though I'm beginning to realise the coat's almost as bad as the rest of my ensemble.

I think the loss of my shoe collection hurts the most. I never thought I'd give in to the lure of wearing shoes for comfort, but here we are. My flat lace-up boots have seen better days, but they're warm enough and at least they don't hurt my feet.

My days of glamour are long gone. When I think of how I look today, I'm hardly surprised that Jane is unconvinced by my claim. She probably thinks I'm stark raving mad – a silly old woman with delusions of grandeur.

Perhaps sensing my discomfort, Jane steers the conversation in another direction. 'Do you spend a lot of time in the library?'

'Almost every day. They're closed on Sundays, of course, so then I go to church.' I laugh at the irony of a sinner such as me attending church every week. The church is warm and welcoming, and there's always a cup of tea in the hall afterwards, but the library is my place of worship. My sanctuary.

'How do you spend your time here? Are you a big reader?'

I nod. 'I am, but the large-print collection is a bit limited and I can't read from the regular collection without glasses.' I don't elaborate on why I don't have glasses (I broke my last pair months ago and can't afford to replace them) but, thankfully, Jane doesn't ask. 'I'm afraid I've read most of the books that appeal to me. Lately I've been writing.'

'Oh?' She looks genuinely interested in this snippet of information. 'May I ask what you're writing?'

I'm not sure I quite know how to explain what it is I'm pouring out onto the page. A written confession, perhaps? A plea for absolution? I shrug. 'Just scribbling down my memories.'

'A memoir? How wonderful. Are you writing about something specific? Your childhood, perhaps? I'm sure you'd have lots of fascinating stories to tell about the way life used to be.'

The way life used to be. I know I'm old – a living relic from another time – but in my head I'm still just a girl trying to make her way in the world. I want to tell Jane that in the blink of an eye she will be me. That the years will slip through her fingers like sand, and that she will still have wants and desires and unfinished business.

Perhaps it's my wish to disabuse her of the notion that I am a mild-mannered granny, who spends her days scribbling down apple-pie recipes and memories of walking five miles to school, that causes me to blurt out a partial version of the truth. 'More like a tell-all. Confessions of a misspent youth, if you like. I worked on a number of shows in the West End during the '60s and '70s, and even had a part on Broadway once.'

Her mouth stretches into a grin. 'Really? Wow! How interesting. I'd love to read your memoir when it's done.'

Jane's enthusiasm is disarming, and I find myself wanting to keep her attention. I don't mention that my story is not meant for the world. 'Really?'

'Absolutely. I'm fascinated by what goes on behind the stage curtain.'

Jane is looking at me with curiosity. I'm sure she hasn't placed me, and she probably thinks I was just some chorus girl, not a major player, but even so, I have her full attention. For the first time in months, I feel as if my grimy exterior doesn't matter. Jane is interested in *me*.

I shrug. 'Right now it's just a jumble of scribblings, but it fills in my days.'

'Well, I hope you stick at it. Who knows, maybe one day I'll see it in a bookstore and I'll be able to claim to have met the author.'

I laugh, but nevertheless I'm chuffed that she sees me as someone who might be able to achieve such a thing. 'I'm not sure it will ever make it that far.'

'I think you should at least give it a go,' she replies as she glances at her watch. 'Goodness, is that the time? I can't believe I've been here for more than an hour. I must go, and I expect you will be wanting to get on with your writing.'

I can't remember the last time I had such an engaging conversation, and my desire for it to continue has me scrambling for ways to coax Jane to stay. 'There's an author talk at eleven. Some fellow banging on about local history. It might be good.'

'Yes, well, that does sound lovely, but I'm afraid I do need to go.'

But I'm not ready to give up. Talking to Jane is the most normal I've felt in months. Besides, I'm keen to know what brought her to the library – she doesn't seem to have any interest in borrowing a book – and what brought on her tearful outburst.

'Perhaps another time, then? They have these author talks every month. You should sign up for the newsletter thing they have. I don't have a computer of my own – I'm too old for all that internet palaver – so I don't get the newsletter myself. But I know they have one. You should ask Stacey about it on your way out.'

'It's probably on the library's website. I'll look it up when I get home.'

'Right you are. I should have realised a young thing such as you would know how to navigate the online world. I have to say, it's a mystery to me. One I'm not interested in solving.'

She laughs. 'It's a long time since anyone has referred to me as "young".'

'How old are you, then? Wait, let me guess.' She looks to be in her late forties, and she *did* mention the menopause earlier, but I shave off a few years to be on the safe side. 'Forty-ish?'

'Almost fifty.'

I grin. 'Oh, my girl, you are but a spring chicken. A baby, in fact. You have decades of life to be lived.'

The smile vanishes from Jane's face and her eyes fill again. 'Yes,' she says quietly. 'I suppose you're right.'

I don't know how to respond to that. It's obvious I've hit a nerve. Perhaps she's ill and worried that she doesn't have decades at all . . . I could kick myself for saying something so insensitive, but I can't take it back and I can't say anything of comfort without knowing the source of her grief. Instead, I reach down and open the front compartment of my wheelie case and dig around until I find the little packet of wet wipes I know is in there. 'Here,' I say. 'Take these and go to the toilets – they're right down the back on the left. You might want to fix your face before you head outside.'

She nods and stands without speaking. She's gone for quite some time – long enough that I begin to wonder if I should go and check on her. But just as I'm contemplating this, she returns with her face perfectly made-up again.

'Thank you for your kindness, Dolly. I'm sorry to have interrupted your work. I'll leave you to it now.'

'Gracious me, don't think anything of it. It was lovely chatting to you.'

She bites her lip and gives me a little nod. 'Goodbye, then.'

'Goodbye, my darling. I hope we'll see each other again.' I stand up and step forward to embrace her, and to my surprise she hugs me back.

As she loosens her hold and steps back, I reach out and grab her arm. 'Jane, take it from an old woman. It's never as bad as you think. There will be tough times – nobody gets off scot-free in this life – but whatever is troubling you will pass, or you will make your peace with it. I guarantee it.'

Chapter Four

Geelong, Australia
1955

'*Another* baby?' Granny raised her eyebrows at the news that Mum was expecting her third child with Bill.

They were seated at Granny's dining-room table, eating their Sunday lunch. Church followed by lunch at Granny and Grandpa's house was still Margie's regular Sunday routine. Since her mother had married Bill it was the only way she could see her grandparents, as, according to Granny, 'hell would freeze over' before she crossed the threshold of 'that house of sin'. Even so, Mum insisted that Margie should maintain her relationship with her grandparents out of respect for her father. 'They're your family, love, and you're all they've got. Remember that.' Margie dutifully obeyed, but some days with Granny were easier than others.

'Good grief,' Granny continued. 'I would have thought your mother would have her hands full with the three of you.'

Mum *did* have her hands full; Granny was right about that. Ronny had come along six months after Mum and Bill were married. Three years later Val was born, and soon a third sibling was to join their family.

'She's like a broodmare. That man needs to learn to keep his hands to himself.'

'That's enough of that talk, Ada,' Grandpa said, in a sterner tone than Margie was used to from him.

'I'm sorry, George, but what sort of example is that woman setting for Marjorie? Getting herself into trouble and forcing our grand-daughter to live like a pauper because of it. Having one baby with that man was bad enough, but three is unforgivable. And who knows where it will end? The two of them clearly have no self-control.'

'Enough!' Grandpa said, and Granny's face coloured at the chastisement. She said nothing more about it until Grandpa left the table to go outside with his pipe.

As they washed and dried the dishes, Granny took a different tack. 'It's going to be crowded at your house when the baby comes along.'

Margie shrugged. 'I suppose so.'

'You know, Marjorie, you don't have to live there. We have plenty of room and we'd love to have you live with us. And your piano's here. You could practise every night of the week.'

She did miss the piano. She'd long ago given up on the promised new house that would have room for it. Even her mother had stopped pretending that was likely to happen. Margie wasn't sure if Bill had ever had lots of money, or if he'd simply whittled his savings away on frivolous things, but these days there didn't seem to be any talk of moving. As long as they lived in Bill's cramped old rental house, having a piano was out of the question. But as much as she missed playing every day, Margie knew she would never leave her mother or her little brother and sister.

'That's so kind of you, Granny, but I'm needed at home.'

'No doubt,' Granny replied sourly.

And by the time baby Neil did arrive, Margie was needed more than ever.

•

Benevolent Bill – the man Margie had grown fond of before he married her mother – had grown into Bad-tempered Bill over the years.

In the beginning, he was kind enough to Margie, although it was clear to her that he saw her as an obstacle to being alone with her mother. Before Ronny was born, he could barely keep his hands off his new wife. He'd come up behind her as she washed the dishes, encircling her in his arms and rubbing his hands over her growing belly.

To Margie's disgust, her mother would giggle like a schoolgirl and say, 'Stop it, Bill. Not in front of Margie.'

'Ah, she doesn't mind, do you, love?'

Margie would shrug and head outside to feed the chooks. By the time she was done, her mother and Bill would have disappeared into their bedroom for an after dinner 'rest'. From the sound of the laughter that trickled out into the hallway, it didn't seem to Margie as if much resting was going on.

There were some benefits to Bill's desire to keep her out of the way. The portable radio he bought so Margie could go to her room and practise her dancing when her music shows came on, for one. And there were the visits to the pictures on Saturday afternoons. Bill gave her money to go every week. She'd meet up with Betty and June from school sometimes, but even if none of her friends were available, Margie never missed an opportunity to spend time with the stars she so admired. Every Saturday she slipped into fantasy land, dreaming of the day she too would light up the stage or screen.

Once Ronny was born, Margie was kept busy helping to care for her baby brother. She loved little Ronny and didn't mind, but it seemed her mother had even less time for her now. Bill was enamoured of his baby son – so long as the infant was clean, dry and happy. As soon as a new nappy was needed or a whimper emanated from the baby's lips, Bill would hand the infant off to Margie. 'Be a good girl and give your mum a break, eh?'

When Bill was happy it was a harmonious household, but when he was 'in a mood' he was prone to shouting and breaking the odd bit of china. Margie and her mother tried to avoid setting him off but it wasn't easy. Sometimes the slightest little thing – an overcooked egg or the baby crying – would be enough to start one of his tantrums. Mum said they had to be understanding. Bill's fits were due to the terrible things he'd endured during his time in the war. Margie did her best to hold her tongue, but sometimes it took all of her will not to shout right back at him when he was carrying on like a toddler.

It was one of these temper fits that cost Bill his job. He'd been a supervisor down at the cement works but was let go after an argument with one of the big bosses. After that, he took to drowning his sorrows at the local pub. Just where he went past the six o'clock closing was anyone's guess. He was a sour man after a night on the booze. He'd never hit Margie or her siblings, but the menace in his voice when he'd been drinking made her think violence from him was not impossible. Thankfully, Margie saw little of him as he often stumbled in late, long after she'd gone to sleep.

Val, Margie's darling little sister, wasn't quite three, and her mother was almost due to give birth again. Eleanor was trying to put on a brave face and kept saying how lucky they all were to be adding to their family, but Bill had given up any pretence that this child was wanted.

A month before the baby's due date, Margie sat with her mum at the kitchen table. They'd just finished the washing up and Margie was about to start on a basket of mending when Mum said, 'Leave that, love. It can wait until tomorrow. Let's have a cup of tea while there's a bit of peace and quiet.'

Once the tea was made, Mum smiled. 'Margie, love, you know Bill's not working right now.'

Margie took a sip of her tea. 'Hmm.'

'He's looking every day and I'm sure he'll find something soon, but in the meantime . . .' Her smile faded and her eyes filled with tears.

Margie's stomach churned uncomfortably. What was so terrible it would make Mum cry? Were they about to become homeless? 'What?'

'I'm so sorry to ask this, Margie. I'd do it myself, but'—she patted her protruding belly—'I'm in no fit state to be looking for work.'

Margie was confused. 'You want me to help Bill look for a job? I don't know—'

'No, darling. I need you to leave school and get a job of your own. I wouldn't ask, but I don't know what else to do. The rent is already overdue and if we don't get some money in soon . . . I had some savings from my war widow's pension, but that money's gone now.'

'Oh.' Her mother's request took Margie by surprise. She was only fourteen and, while she hadn't expected to go on to matriculation, she hadn't imagined she'd be entering the workforce so soon.

'It wouldn't be forever. We just need some breathing space to catch up. Bill will find work soon, I'm sure, and once the baby comes I'll be able to take in more mending, and washing and ironing too. It'll all work out in the end, love, I promise. You can probably go back to school in the new year.'

Margie reached over and squeezed Mum's hand. 'Of course I'll help. I'm happy to. I'll start looking first thing tomorrow morning.'

Two days later, she took a job as a machinist at the Valley Mill in South Geelong.

●

Two months after Margie's youngest brother, Neil, was born, Bill ran off with Mary next door. Margie discovered this after her mother refused to get out of bed one morning. It was a good riddance, as far as Margie was concerned, but Mum was heartbroken and didn't come out of her room for two days.

The little ones were alarmed by the sound of her weeping, and, although Margie did her best to soothe them, by the afternoon of the second day she was beginning to feel rather desperate herself. She'd had to call in sick to work and the family couldn't afford for her to lose any more pay. In the hope of getting some assistance, she put all three of her siblings down for a nap and rode her bike across town to her grandmother's house.

'Goodness, child, whatever is wrong?' Granny said as she opened the screen door.

'Bill's gone and Mum won't get out of bed. I don't know what to do, Granny.'

'I see.' There was a steely edge to her grandmother's voice. 'I'm afraid your mother has made her bed and now she has to lie in it.'

'No, Granny, that's just it. She hasn't made her bed at all. She hasn't left it since Bill went away.'

Granny's face softened momentarily, and she allowed herself a small smile. 'Surely you know that's just a figure of speech, Margie? I simply mean your mother needs to take responsibility for the mess she's made of her life. Come in and have a glass of cordial.'

Margie knew she should get home to take care of her brother and sister and the baby, and she *really* didn't like Granny speaking about Mum that way, but it was hot, and she was thirsty, so she stepped inside. Truth be told, after two days straight of being in charge of her siblings, she'd had enough. She might have been old enough to hold down a job but right now she felt like a little kid. She wanted a proper grown-up to take charge. Once Granny realised how serious the situation was, she would offer some help.

Margie followed her into the kitchen and took a seat at the table. 'I can't stay long. If the kids wake up and realise I'm not there, they'll have a fit.'

Granny gave her a sympathetic look as she poured a glass of cordial and placed it in front of her. 'You don't have to go back there, you know. You're our flesh and blood. Your father's daughter. I see his face every time I look into those eyes of yours. I've told you before that you're welcome to live here with us. What do you say?'

'Well . . .' For the briefest of moments, Margie considered how easy her life would be if she lived with Granny and Grandpa. She had her own room in their house and the bed was never cold – not even in the dead of winter – because Granny always slipped a hot water bottle between the sheets ten minutes before bedtime. There was no yelling in Granny's house, no one coming home drunk and demanding a hot dinner – although she supposed that wouldn't be happening anymore at her own house if Bill truly had run off.

The biggest drawcard, though, was the piano. The thought of having unlimited access to her beloved instrument was awfully tempting.

But of course she couldn't say yes. If she didn't go home, who would look after Ronny and Val and the baby? 'What about my brothers and sister?'

'Half-brothers and half-sister, you mean.'

Margie bit her tongue and remained silent. Her mum said there was no such thing as *halves*. Her younger siblings were family and it was as simple as that.

Granny didn't see it that way. 'Look, Marjorie, those children are your mother's responsibility, not yours.' She took off her apron, sat down next to Margie and muttered, 'And they're definitely not mine.'

Margie hung her head. It wasn't her siblings' fault their dad had run away.

Granny seemed to read her mind. 'I know it's not their fault, poor things, but their father is ne'er-do-well. I told your mother as much before she married him. But she didn't want to hear it. She was too busy being sweet-talked. I swear, your dear father would be horrified to see what's become of her. And you.'

Margie stared at her hands, hoping Granny hadn't noticed the tears stinging her eyes.

'I told your mother when she started up with that scoundrel that if she wanted to throw in her lot with his, that was her business, but she should think about what would become of you. I offered to take you in then, but she's selfish, your mum, always has been. She wouldn't hear of it. Said she couldn't bear to part with you. And as if that wasn't bad enough, then she went on to have a pack of brats to boot. I said to Grandpa at the time, "This'll all end in tears. Mark my words," and so it has.' Granny shook her head knowingly.

A bubble of rage swelled in Margie's chest at this description of her mother. Mum wasn't selfish at all. She worked hard to make sure they had enough to eat and a roof over their heads. The baby was only a couple of months old, but Mum had already started taking in washing and ironing as well as more sewing. She kept chooks and tended the vegetable garden, all while keeping the house clean and looking after the little ones. If anyone was selfish it was Granny, who'd behaved terribly ever since her mother had married Bill.

Her mother was more understanding of Granny's position than Margie. 'Your grandmother is still grieving, Margie, that's why this hurts her so much. Your daddy was her only child, and you are her only grandchild. She's just scared that we're moving on and that she'll lose you. She'll come 'round in time, just you wait and see.'

It had been five years since the wedding, and Granny's position hadn't changed. Grandpa, who was a Christian man in name and in deeds, was kinder. He always asked after her mother and often sent Margie home with a secret bag of lollies to be shared with the littlies. *No need to tell your grandmother about these.* But Granny wouldn't let Mum in the house, and she preferred it if Margie didn't mention her siblings.

'My mum's *not* selfish.'

'Hmph, well, I don't know what you'd call it, then. Getting herself into trouble not once but *twice*. It was bad enough that she trapped our James, but putting herself in a position where she had to marry your stepfather . . . well, I never. Your grandfather and I would have looked after her for the rest of our lives, if only she'd had the decency to keep herself nice.'

Margie could take no more. 'I have to go now, Granny.' She stood up and took her glass to the sink. 'Thank you for the drink.'

'Wait, Marjorie, there's no need to go. I know you love your mother, of course you do. But, the thing is, she's had a bit of a shock and she's not caring for you and those . . . your brothers and sister properly right now. I think it would be much better for everyone if we let your mum have a rest. Why don't you come here for a little stay? It doesn't have to be forever. Think about it.'

As angry as she was, Margie considered this. Maybe Granny was right about Mum needing a rest. 'Well, I could, but I'd have to bring the others with me. They're too little to look after them—'

Granny cut her off. 'Absolutely not. That's completely out of the question.'

'But they wouldn't be any trouble, Granny, I promise. I can look after them when I get home from work. Ronny and Val would be on their best behaviour, I'd make sure of it, and the baby sleeps most of the time. You'd hardly even know they were here. It would only be for a day or two. Just until Mum gets back on her feet.'

'Marjorie, be sensible. I can't have them here. There's no room, for a start.'

'But this house is enormous. Ronny and Neil can sleep in the spare room, and Val can sleep with me.'

Granny pursed her lips and shook her head. 'You are my grand-child and I love you dearly. You belong here with Grandpa and me. Your brothers and sister are no relation to me and are not my responsibility. If your mother is unable to care for them – and it seems she is – then there are places—'

'No! I'm not sending my brothers and sister to the orphanage. Shame on you, Granny.'

'Shame on your mother, more like. She's the one who's put you in this position, not me!'

As tears began to stream down her cheeks, Margie ran from the kitchen and out the front door. She jumped on her bike and pedalled furiously home. It was up to her now. If her mum couldn't look after the kids, she would work out a way do it herself. No one was going to split up her family.

As it turned out, Margie needn't have worried. The next morning, her mum was in the kitchen cooking eggs for breakfast – a rare treat. She was wearing a clean dress and her hair was done. She smiled as soon as she saw Margie. 'Good morning, my darling.'

'Good morning, Mum. Are you feeling better today?'

'I am. I'm sorry I scared you like that, Margie. I had a little turn. But I'm fine now. We're going to be all right. I promise.'

And they were.

They weren't rich, but between Margie's pay packet from the mill and the washing, ironing and mending her mother took in, there was enough to ensure they had full bellies and a roof over their heads.

Most importantly, they had each other.

Chapter Five

London
2019

I wake to the sound of a whisper. 'Dolly, can you hear me? Time to wake up.'

I open my eyes and realise I'm in the armchair at the library and sweet Jemima, the junior librarian, is gently patting my arm. 'Oh! Goodness me, I must have nodded off. What time is it, darling?'

Jemima smiles. 'Almost closing time. Stacey will be on the warpath soon, so I thought I'd give you fair warning.'

'Right you are. Thanks, my angel.'

She looks at me as if she wants to say something else, but then changes her mind. As I pick up my coat, which someone has draped over my knees as I slept, she pats me on the shoulder and walks away.

I'm not looking forward to leaving the warmth of the library, but I have no choice in the matter, so I ease myself out of the armchair and drag my case towards me. Inside, I find my purple knitted hat, a woolly scarf and my calf-skin gloves – still in reasonable nick even though they are years old. After a final visit to the bathroom, I pull on my coat and make my way to the library's exit.

'Night, Dolly. See you tomorrow.' Jemima waves goodbye as she locks the door behind me.

The autumn sun has already set, so it's dark as I step onto the street. The weather's turned from what my mum would have called 'nippy' to 'chilly', and I button up my coat as high as it will go to keep out the cold.

The high street is busy, filled with commuters on their way home. As they hurry along the footpath I scan the crowd for a familiar face, or at least someone to connect with, but not one soul makes eye contact. The mob weaves its way around me as if I am no more than an inconvenient obstacle, or perhaps nothing at all.

My interactions with others these days are few in number and often perfunctory in nature. The librarians are the only people I have any real conversation with, and although I know they do their best to be kind, they're often busy. The library is my only haven; I don't want to wear out my welcome there. Even prickly Stacey pays me the courtesy of looking at me when we're sparring. That's not something I take for granted, so I pick my battles with her and take care not to be overly demanding or annoying to the rest of the staff.

It's no wonder the conversation I had with Jane today has affected me so strongly. She's the first person in weeks I've talked to about anything significant. Since our meeting this morning I haven't been able to stop thinking about her. She even featured in my dream when I was napping. It was a variation of the same dream I always have, the one where I have lost something (my handbag, my keys) or someone (the cat, a baby . . . Julian). Today it was Jane I was looking for. I kept catching glimpses of her, but when I called to her no sound came out of my mouth.

As I amble along the high street, I wonder if I might see Jane again. She never mentioned what brought her to the library today, but it was clear she was seeking respite from something. While she's a newcomer to the library, I'm sure she's a local. She mentioned picking up her husband's dry-cleaning. That's something one usually does close to home.

There's a drycleaners right near the tube station and I find myself making my way there, as if seeing where Jane has been might bring me closer to her somehow. I'm not deluded enough to think I'll find her there – she left the library hours ago, after all – but I feel strangely compelled to retrace her steps regardless. Besides, I have time to kill. It's not as if there's anyone waiting for me at home.

As I walk, I wonder which of the nearby streets Jane might live on. I've probably passed her house many times, maybe even stopped to admire her garden.

One of the ways I amuse myself these days is to make up little stories about the people who live in all the fancy houses in this neighbourhood. I try to imagine who they are, what their lives might be like. A happy family of four – Mum and Dad and two kids, and a dog too. Mum works part time, 'just to keep her hand in', while Dad is someone important – a lawyer, a banker or doctor perhaps. The kids are enrolled at a nearby grammar or public school. They take Muffin – that's the dog – to the dog park every Saturday morning. The kids kick around a football while Mum and Dad sip lattes and Muffin yaps at their heels. They don't have a care in the world.

Of course, this is just a fantasy. Even these people with their luxury cars and central heating have problems. Money and privilege can fill your belly and keep you warm at night, but it can't cushion you from sorrow. None of us is immune from that. For many years I lived a life of pleasure, but no matter how opulent my life became, it wasn't enough to fill the void inside me; to completely black out the guilt. The best I could do was to learn to live with it.

I wonder what sadness Jane is carrying that her Burberry trench can't shield her from.

The drycleaner's window, which I'm now standing in front of, doesn't provide any answers. I turn away from it and decide it's time to get out of this drizzling rain.

The walk home takes about fifteen minutes, if I hurry, which I do tonight. Not that these old bones can move too quickly, but I don't dawdle or waste time window-shopping or admiring gardens in this weather.

It's pitch-black by the time I reach my laneway, which makes the back gate hard to see properly, and I can barely make out the latch. The damn thing sticks at the best of times, so it takes me a moment to jiggle it open.

There are no lights on in the house, which means the family must be out for the evening. This lack of light makes the path difficult to see, but at least I have no fear of being disrupted by anyone and I'm free to relax and eat my dinner in peace before bedding down for the night.

I have a feast waiting for me. Jemima brought in a thick slice of homemade meat pie, carefully wrapped in foil, and gave it to me at lunchtime. 'Maybe don't mention this to Stacey,' she whispered as she handed it over. I promised I wouldn't as I slipped the parcel into my case. As well as the pie, I still have a handful of chocolates from the freebies they were giving out at the tube station yesterday, so I've a dinner fit for Queen Lizzie herself.

With that thought warming me, I push open the creaky door to my little abode.

I step over the threshold and feel around for my torch, which I keep hanging on a nail just inside the entrance. Once located, I flick it on and shine it around to check for signs of disturbance, but there are none. Everything is as I left it this morning.

I've had a few makeshift homes recently, but this little storage shed is by far the most luxurious. For starters, the homeowners use it only for storing disused furnishings and knickknacks – they have a separate garden shed – so there are no smelly chemicals or bags of fertiliser to contend with. There's quite a lot of stuff stored in here, including a mattress and a couple of old duvets. I've made myself a proper bed out of these behind some storage boxes, so the owners won't notice it unless they move those. Of course, if they do come in here searching for something the jig will be up, but I've been here for almost two weeks now and no one has come near the place.

After I close the door behind me, I drag out the folding chair and milk crate from under the workbench and retrieve Jemima's foil parcel from my case. As I tuck in to the cold but delicious pie, I feel positively buoyant. My circumstances might have changed but I'm not down and out. I have food and shelter, which is something to be grateful for, not to mention a cosy bed. Things could be worse.

Besides, who knows what tomorrow will bring?

Chapter Six

Geelong, Australia
1959

Margie's first big break came in the late spring of 1959.

On the face of it the opportunity was a small one, but she was certain this was her chance to make something of herself. She'd heard the big news at the end of her shift at the mill, and she'd been so excited that she'd stayed late after work celebrating with some of the other girls from her section.

'And what time do you call this, young lady?' Her mother didn't turn her head to face her, but Margie didn't need to see her expression to know she wasn't pleased.

'Sorry, Mum, but I have a good excuse, honest.' She dropped her handbag – the good patent-leather one she'd saved up for months to buy – onto a chair and grabbed an apron from one of the hooks behind the kitchen door.

'Never mind your excuses. I've no time to listen to stories now, and you can take that apron off, too. Dinner's already in the oven. I've only got the gravy left to do.'

'I can do that.'

'No need. You can help me dish up when I'm ready. In the meantime, you can round up your brothers and sister. Make sure they wash up properly for dinner and lay out their pyjamas ready for bath time. Oh, and Margie, bring the washing in while you're at it, will you, love?'

'Righto.' She slipped out the way she'd come in, through the back door and onto the porch, where she cast her eyes over the backyard in search of her siblings. Margie was bursting to tell her mother the big news, but there was no point even trying when Mum was in a flap about getting dinner on the table. She'd have to wait until they sat down to eat. Never mind, it might be better that way. She'd make a big announcement and maybe they could even raise a toast with cordial. The kids would like that.

Ronny and Neil were digging in the vegetable garden. Margie hoped they hadn't caused any damage, because Mum might just go off her rocker, what with her already being in a mood. And there was no sign of Valerie at all. Always away with the fairies, that one. Sweet little thing, but not an ounce of common sense. Maybe the boys knew where she was. 'Oi, you two rascals. You need to come inside and get ready for dinner.'

As soon as he heard Margie's voice, Ronny jumped up and grabbed Neil by the hand, and the pair of them charged towards her.

'Margie,' Neil called, stretching out his chubby – and muddy – fingers, ready to embrace his big sister.

Margie laughed and stepped back, out of his grasp. 'Oh, no you don't. It's the washhouse for you two. Quick smart. Mum's in a mood, so I wouldn't muck about if I were you.'

Neil's smile disappeared. At almost five, he was the youngest and soon to be a 'big-school boy', but he still seemed like a baby to Margie. He loved to sit on her lap and snuggle into her each night when she read the boys their bedtime story.

Ronny made a face. 'Come on, Neil, hurry up. I don't want to end up being sent to bed without any dinner.' Ronny was almost nine and in the middle of a growth spurt. Their mum was fond of saying he had hollow legs.

'Has either of you seen Val?'

Ronny shrugged. 'She was playing near the chook shed last time I saw her. She reckons there's a fairy dell behind the incinerator.'

Margie's heart sank. There was all manner of rubbish at the back of the chook shed. Hopefully Val had remembered to change out of her school dress before she went off to play – there would be no time now to wash it and get it dry in time for the morning.

Before heading off to investigate the chook shed, Margie followed the boys into the washhouse to collect a laundry basket and remind her brothers to use soap on their hands. With that done, she set about finding her sister. Val appeared before Margie was even halfway across the yard, thankfully wearing play clothes, but as she came closer it became apparent that her hands were stained a deep pink.

'Margie!' She smiled. 'Is it teatime yet?'

'Nearly. What on earth have you been doing, little miss? Why are your hands that colour?'

'I've been making a potion. For the fairies. I want them to know I'm their friend.'

'I see. And what is this potion made from?'

Val's cheeks coloured. 'The boys got me some of the old veggies. Not the good ones, only things that *nobody* wants to eat. Ronny says Daddy liked beetroot and that's why we grow it, but now he's gone and the rest of us think it's disgusting.'

'Beetroot? Oh, my stars! I'm not sure what's worse – the waste of perfectly good food, or the stains on your hands . . . oh, and on your dress as well. Really, Val, you're a big girl now – almost seven years old. You should know better.'

Val's chin began to wobble.

'All right, come on then, pet, don't cry. Get those hands washed. Mind you use plenty of soap. I'll just get the load off the line and then I'll be in to help. Don't go into the house until I've checked your hands, all right?'

Val nodded solemnly and ran off to the washhouse. Poor little mite, so quick to tears. But, of course, she and the boys hadn't had the easiest life. Their dad was a scoundrel, and everyone knew it – everyone except Ronny, who steadfastly believed his dad was off 'working on the railroad'. Lord only knew where he'd got that idea. Certainly not from Margie, or their mother, for that matter. The one thing you could count on from Mum was that she never sugar-coated anything.

Things had been tough for the past few years and Mum had lost some of her softness. Margie was sad for the little ones that they hadn't grown up with the same light-hearted and whimsical mother she'd had as a child. Back then Mum was always laughing and dancing and catering to Margie's theatrical whims by encouraging her to put on concerts and plays for the neighbourhood. And Mum had never laughed at her desire to be on the stage. In fact, she'd taught Margie to believe all her dreams could come true.

Her siblings had a much more pragmatic mother; one who was more concerned with hard work and making ends meet than fostering childhood fantasies. Margie knew it was now her turn to carry the hopes and dreams for her family.

These past few years working at the mill had put a dent in her plans of being famous, but she hadn't given up. She trusted that if she kept working on her dance routines at home – carefully copying the moves she saw in her favourite films – one day her chance would come. And now it had!

As she unpegged the sheets from the line, Margie's stomach swirled with butterflies of excited anticipation. She couldn't wait to share what had happened at work. Her mother didn't know it yet, but Margie was on her way! She had the best news ever, and she just knew that hearing it would put the smile back on her mum's face.

•

Margie held off on telling her news until after the apple crumble was served.

Once the custard jug had made its way around the table, Margie clinked a teaspoon on her water glass to get everyone's attention. 'I have news! Ronny, stop poking your little sister, sit up straight and listen to me.'

Perhaps it was the shock of her stern tone, but Ronny did as he was told straight away. All four of them looked at Margie expectantly.

Mum smiled. 'Go on then, love. We're all dying to know. What is it? Have you gone and got yourself a promotion?'

'Better than that.'

'Goodness gracious me. What could be better than that?'

'I auditioned for the talent show and I got in! Just think – if I win, this could be the start of my stage career. I'm going to be a star!' At this proclamation the children burst into applause, but her mother was looking at Margie in disbelief.

'What talent show? What are you talking about?'

'Well, I didn't want to tell you, just in case it didn't work out, but remember last Monday when I told you I had to work back for a bit?'

Her mother eyed her suspiciously. 'Yes . . .'

'Well, I'm sorry, but that was a tiny fib.'

'It's wrong to tell lies,' Ronny interjected.

'Hush,' Margie said, frowning at him. 'I know that, but this was a little white lie, which we all know doesn't count.'

'What's a white lie?' asked Neil.

She let out an exasperated sigh as her mum reached over and patted Neil's hand. 'I'll tell you later, pet. Let your sister explain herself.'

'I wasn't really working late,' Margie said. 'I was auditioning. I tried out on Monday, then I didn't hear anything for days. I'd almost given up hope, but then I got a message right on knock-off today from one of the higher-ups who was on the judging panel. He said my audition was wonderful and I'm going to be part of the show!'

Her mother still wasn't smiling, and Ronny and Val had started kicking each other under the table. This wasn't going the way Margie had imagined it at all.

'Well, that's a feather in your cap, Margie, I'm sure, but you haven't told us anything about the show. When is it going to be on? And where?'

'It was all Mr Harrison's idea. You remember him, Mum. He's one of the big bosses at work, the one whose wife was so sick last year?'

'Oh, yes, I remember you talking about that. He's a nice man, isn't he?'

'Really nice. Anyway, he wanted to show his gratitude to the hospital for caring for his wife and he decided the best way to do that was by raising money. He asked for suggestions, and someone came up with the idea that some of us from the mill could put on a talent show and charge admission.'

Her mother sat back in her chair and lowered her shoulders into a more relaxed pose. 'Oh, so it's for work?'

'Yes. Well . . . sort of. It started with just the mill workers but it's now bigger than that. Because it's for charity, lots of people were happy to help. Once Mr Harrison put the word out, all sorts of wonderful things started to happen. Mr Giles said his brother is a professional director who lives in Melbourne, and he would ask him for some tips. The next thing we know, Mr Giles's brother has offered to judge the show, on account of it being for charity. And there's going to be a prize, too!'

'Well, that sounds exciting, but you won't need any time away from work, will you, love? We can't afford to lose your wage just now.'

'No. There are a couple of rehearsals, but they'll be after work. I might have to miss going to the pictures for a couple of weeks, and I'll practise on Saturday nights instead of going dancing.'

The barest hint of a smile touched Mum's lips. 'Sounds as if you've thought it all through.'

'I have, Mum, truly. It won't interfere with work at all, and Mr Harrison said all the performers will get a bonus when the show is over to thank them for their time and commitment.'

'That's fabulous, love. Truly, I mean it. I know how you love to perform. I've always felt sad that you had to give up your music and dance classes because of . . . the circumstances. I'm glad you're getting your chance to shine now. And if it means a tiny bit more money coming in, even better.'

Finally, the wide smile of approval that Margie had been waiting for settled on her mother's face.

Chapter Seven

London
2019

She's back. I'm sitting at one of the work desks, jotting down notes and losing myself in the memories of better days when I become aware of her presence. I don't have a view of the library entrance from here, so I didn't see her come in, but when I notice a light citrus scent in the air I recognise it immediately.

It's been more than a week since our first encounter. Even though the interaction was a short one, it had an impact on me. Jane is the first person – other than the librarians, who I'm sure don't take me seriously – who I've told about my scribblings. Somehow, her naming my work a 'memoir' made what I'm doing seem real. Worthwhile, even. When I started writing it was just for myself. A way to fill the long days and to try to make sense of everything that has happened in my life. Then I began to wonder if there might be another purpose to what I'm doing. I dared to think about this being my path to redemption in some way. Now, I'm beginning to believe in the possibility of my words making a difference.

Every day I've hoped that I would see her again, so I could thank her for helping me find new purpose in my work, but I'd be lying if

I said that was the only reason I wanted to see Jane. Call me a sticky-beak if you like, but I can't stop thinking about what would make a woman such as her – so obviously a reserved, affluent type – burst into tears in a public library and then allow herself to be comforted by a stranger. I've imagined dozens of different scenarios over the past week – her husband is having an affair with a woman half his age, or maybe *she's* the one having the affair and she's been caught. She admitted to being hormonal, and maybe that's all it was – the change can do terrible things to some women. Or maybe she's pregnant with a change-of-life baby that she doesn't want . . .

I swivel in my seat to find her almost upon me.

'Dolly,' she says. 'I've been looking for you. When I didn't see you in any of the comfy chairs at the front, I thought perhaps I was out of luck.'

'Looking for me?' I smile broadly. 'How delightful. I'm so pleased to see you again, Jane. I find it easier to write sitting at the desks and, thanks to you, I've been motivated to write a lot these past few days.'

'Thanks to me?'

'Yes. You're the first person I've told about my "memoir", as you called it. And now the idea is out there that my words might eventually be read, I feel committed to following through.'

She seems embarrassed but pleased nonetheless. 'Well, I'm happy to have been of some assistance, however minor. I certainly don't want to interrupt your work now you're on a roll, but I just wanted to pop by and give you this.' She places a Harrods tote on the desk beside me. 'This is for you. To say thank you for your kindness the other day. I really wasn't myself and you were such a help to me that I wanted to repay you in some small way.'

When I peer inside the bag, I see a box of shortbread, a novel and pair of soft, pink socks sitting on a mountain of other treats. 'You shouldn't have done that.'

Apparently my attempt to keep the waver out of my voice has resulted in my sounding abrupt, possibly even ungrateful, because the smile fades from her face. 'I'm so sorry. I didn't mean to offend. It's just that your kindness really meant a lot to me and I wanted to show my gratitude. I hope I haven't embarrassed you.' She puts a tentative hand on the bag, as if she is unsure whether to leave it or not.

I reach out and cover her hand with mine. This time I don't try to conceal the emotions that are flooding in. 'My darling Jane, it was you who did me a favour by spending some of your precious time with me. And now you've given me all this. I can't believe my luck.'

'It's nothing, really.'

'It's *not* nothing. It's been a long time since anyone's given me a gift. When you get to be as old as I am, sometimes there's no one left to celebrate the special days with, so this is just lovely.'

'I'm so glad. Well, I won't keep you from your work. Thank you again.'

She begins to step back but I clasp her wrist lightly to stop her. 'Wait. Don't go yet. Perhaps we could move to the armchairs, if there's space. I could open my gift and we could have a little chat. Please? It's not often I get to have a conversation with someone new and interesting.'

She laughs. 'I'm not sure how interesting I am, but thank you for thinking I might be.'

'So you'll stay?'

'How can I say no to such a flattering request? Besides, I have a little time up my sleeve this morning.' She picks up the gift bag while I gather my things and stow them in my case.

We make our way to the front of the library, only to discover every armchair is taken. 'Bother,' I say. 'We're out of luck.' I try to think of another spot where we can sit together and have a natter without disturbing anyone. There are quite a few nooks and crannies in the library, but most of them have uncomfortable seating – ottomans, bench seats, beanbags. Even if I managed to lower my arthritic old body into one of those things, I'd need a crane to haul me out again.

'Do you feel like a break?' she asks. 'I know I could use a coffee. Perhaps, if you'd like to, we could pop up to the high street and find a cafe.'

The fact that Jane is prepared to be seen dining with me speaks volumes about her. 'That would be delightful.'

We both pull on our outer garments and make our way onto the street. Today the air is crisp, but it's sunny, so our short walk is a pleasant one. We talk about the weather and how cold it's becoming. Jane says it won't be long before all the shops have their Christmas decorations out, and I agree, trying not to let my anxiety about the coming holiday season show on my face.

It's not Christmas Day itself I'm worried about. The magic of that day died with my mother. I've never really enjoyed Christmas since she's been gone. And it's not as if this will be the first Christmas I've spent alone. Julian was never in London for Christmas. He'd leave for America in mid-December to spend the holidays with his daughter and grandson. He'd always return early in the day on 31 December so we could see in the New Year together.

Now, New Year's Eve is the hardest day of the year for me. This will be the third time I've had to spend that special evening alone, and it hasn't got any easier. It's going to be strange starting the next decade without him.

A more pressing worry than beginning a new decade alone, though, is the coming winter. It's already cold out here on the streets. I'm not sure how I'll survive without a permanent roof over my head. My current situation is good enough for the time being, but how will I cope when winter truly sets in?

I force myself not to dwell on this thought. After all, the really cold weather is still some weeks away. Hopefully I will have sorted out something by then.

'Shall we try in here?' Jane asks, stopping outside the local branch of a large coffee chain. 'It doesn't seem too busy. I think there are some free tables up the back.'

'Perfect.' The tension that has been building in my shoulders eases. This isn't a place I've been moved on from. In fact, a couple of times I've even been gifted a free coffee or sandwich when I've come in to use the facilities.

Being welcomed into a store or a cafe is a privilege I once took for granted, but not anymore. When I first found myself without a permanent abode (I prefer not to use the word *homeless*, even to myself – it seems so bleak), I spent a lot of time browsing in the shops. The fact that I had no money to purchase anything didn't bother me as much as you might think. Just looking at the goods, picking them up and deciding on their various merits, was enough to keep me connected to my former life. While I was browsing, I was a normal person, just like everyone else in the store. That was back when I still looked decent enough to pass for an average middle-class grandmother. Now, my shabby clothes and, I'm afraid, possibly my body odour give me away. Increasingly, store owners have been asking me to move along. To my great shame, some have banned me from entering. But this coffee shop is one of the good ones. Here I needn't fear that I will cause Jane embarrassment by being asked to leave.

We find our way to a table at the back of the cafe. Once I'm comfortable, Jane asks what I'd like, and she heads off to order for us. It's been so long since I've sat at a table in a cafe or restaurant that I feel vulnerable at first, worried that people will be staring at the unkempt old woman I've become. But after a minute or two I realise people are too busy talking to their companions or looking at their phones to take any notice of me. I relax and take the opportunity to study the other diners.

It's mid-morning, and apart from the odd singleton peering at a laptop while their large latte cools beside them, the place is filled with trim young mothers dressed in exercise clothing. They absent-mindedly rock those gigantic double pushchairs that seem to be mandatory these days, while studiously ignoring their squealing toddlers who are playing hide and seek in among the tables. My hearing isn't quite as sharp as it used to be, but it's good enough to hear the women's loud pronouncements about how intermittent fasting has changed their lives and given them back their pre-baby bodies.

Intermittent fasting? I chuckle to myself. Seems as if I'm up on the latest trends without even trying.

Jane is making her way back to the table with a tray when she's almost toppled by an exuberant preschooler.

'Goodness me, that was close,' she says, addressing the toddler in a kind but firm voice. 'We need to be a bit careful in here because people have hot drinks on their trays. Someone could easily get hurt, so I think it's best if we don't run. Where's your mummy?'

The child scuttles off to a nearby table and climbs up on his mother's knee. Moments later, all three women at the table swivel to stare at Jane in a less-than-friendly manner. Luckily, she's busy placing our coffees – espresso for her, cappuccino for me – on the table and explaining the cakes she's chosen for us, so she doesn't notice.

'Times have certainly changed,' I say.

Jane is stirring sugar into her coffee. 'Oh?'

'When I was a girl, my mother would have clipped me over the ear if I'd been running around like that. And she would have dragged me over to apologise for any trouble I'd caused.'

Jane sighs. 'I know what you mean.'

This is my chance to find out a little more about her. 'Do you have children, Jane?'

She shakes her head and smiles sadly. 'It's just my husband and me.'

There's obvious pain in there – perhaps infertility, or an unwilling partner? I'm sorry now that I asked.

'What about you?'

'I never married,' I say, as if that settles the question. 'Should I open my gift now?'

Her face brightens. 'Yes, if you'd like to. It's up to you.'

She lifts the Harrods tote from the seat beside her and pushes it towards me. I unpack the gifts one at a time, taking care to examine each one and remark on its usefulness or beauty. I'm touched by her thoughtfulness. Everything in the bag is small and light, or consumable. There are chocolates, sweets and shortbread to eat, make-up removal wipes, a tinted lip balm, hand cream, a plush pair of socks, some pretty handkerchiefs, a large-print romance novel, a bookmark and a gorgeous red cashmere scarf. The scarf is at the bottom of the bag and I gasp as my fingers touch its silky softness. 'Jane! I can't accept this. It's too much.'

'I thought of you as soon as I saw it,' she says. 'The colour is so rich and vibrant. So full of life. Please take it. I could never pull off such a bold shade, but I think it will look perfect on you.'

I blink a few times to hold back the tears that are forming at the corners of my eyes. It's not just Jane's kindness that is overwhelming, but the fact that for the first time in months I feel truly seen by another human being. 'Thank you,' I whisper. 'I shall wear it with pride.'

She beams. 'Good. I'm glad. Now, which of these cakes would you prefer? Or shall I halve them and we can both have a taste of each?'

We agree to share the cakes, and as Jane focuses on cutting through the eclair without getting cream everywhere, I ask her the question that's been on my mind since we first crossed paths. 'I'm so glad we met, Jane, but I can't help but wonder what brought you to the library last week. I've never noticed you there before and – I hope you don't mind me saying this – you seemed a little out of place, as if you'd stumbled inside accidently.'

Jane looks up and gives me a half-hearted smile. 'You're sort of right. I certainly didn't set out to go to the library that day. I've lived in the area for many years, and last week was the first time I've ever set foot inside that building.'

'So why that day?'

She sighs. 'Richard, my husband, had asked me to pick up his dry-cleaning and it wasn't quite ready. It was cold and drizzling, and, to be honest, I was afraid that if I went back home, I wouldn't be bothered to come out again, but Richard needed his suit for the next day. I wanted to kill some time, but, as you witnessed, I was feeling a tad over-whelmed that morning. I just wanted to be inside, somewhere quiet, somewhere I could be left in peace.'

I laugh out loud. 'I certainly put the kibosh on that plan!'

Her smile deepens. 'Sometimes we don't know what we need. Talking to you was the best part of that day.'

As Jane bites into her half of the eclair, the mothers with the unruly toddlers begin to leave. Instead of heading towards the exit at the front of the cafe, the mother of the child Jane had gently chastised steers her monstrous pushchair towards our table. Jane has her back to her so doesn't see her coming, and only notices when the woman angrily addresses her. 'You've got some nerve.'

Shocked, Jane looks up.

'I don't know how you can show your face in public, let alone have the audacity to be telling off other people's kids. Here's a tip: if you must leave your house, keep your mouth shut when you do. Nobody wants your advice.'

Jane's face is beet red, but she stares into her coffee and says nothing.

'Excuse me,' I say, angrily. I glower at the woman and ready myself for a stoush. But Jane looks up and shakes her head, pleading with her eyes for me to say no more. The woman isn't listening, anyway. She spins the giant stroller around and pushes it to the exit, where her friends are waiting.

'Rude fucking cow,' I say, before I can check myself, but at least my outburst brings a smile to Jane's lips. 'No wonder the child is so badly behaved if that is the role model he has.'

Jane nods her agreement but I can see she is quite rattled. She sips her espresso quietly, and as soon as the cup is empty she says, 'Well, I really must get on. Are you fine to walk back to the library alone?'

I assure her I am, and we say our goodbyes. As I watch her leave, she seems to have shrunk a little. The despair I sensed in her last time we met has risen to the surface once more. I wish there was something I could do to help, but even if I knew what was troubling her, what use could I be? I'm a destitute old woman who's made a mess of her life. What business do I have meddling in anyone else's?

Chapter Eight

Geelong, Australia
1959

Backstage at the talent show, Lorraine Marchant grabbed Margie by the forearm. 'I think I'm going to be sick.' Lorraine didn't look sick – in fact, she looked positively radiant, but maybe the thick stage make-up she'd applied was covering a pale complexion.

'Really?'

Lorraine wrung her hands. 'I'm just so nervous. Aren't you?'

Margie shrugged. The swirling in her stomach *could* be nerves, she supposed, but it felt more like excitement. 'Take a few deep breaths,' she suggested. 'You'll be okay.'

Lorraine nodded and focused on her breathing, giving Margie the chance to concentrate on her own preparation. The song she'd chosen, 'I Don't Care', was the very first show tune she'd learnt the choreography to, from the first musical film she'd ever seen. After all these years she still loved *In the Good Old Summertime*. When she'd seen Judy Garland performing in that gorgeous red dress, she'd known immediately what she wanted to do with her life.

She'd had to pare down her routine for the talent show, as the stage was relatively small and there was no room for props, so she hoped she could do the song justice. Mum had done her best to make a replica of Judy's dress. They'd had to settle for a cheaper fabric than would have been used for the floaty garment worn by Miss Garland, but Margie felt beautiful in it just the same.

When the show's compere called her name, she was as ready as she'd ever be. She sailed out to centrestage, took the microphone and beamed out at the crowd. The hall was full to bursting with people. Margie quickly scanned the audience for Mum and the kids, but before she could spy them the band struck the song's first note, and the bodies in the crowd morphed into a single entity; a pulsing energy spurring her on. The moment she opened her mouth and began to sing, her body instinctively swung into action, the moves coming to her without thought.

It was over too soon. Following the compere's gesture, Margie reluctantly left the stage with the crowd's thunderous applause still going. How she wished she could do it all again!

Before she knew it, the show was over and it was time to take the stage once more for the presentations. There were several categories, all of which were won by other contestants. Margie smiled and clapped politely, while her heart was sinking. Perhaps she'd been a fool to hope she would win a prize. After all, many talented people had performed.

The first time Margie's name was called she didn't move. Her feet were rooted to the spot as she clapped both hands over her mouth. Had she heard right? Had she really won?

When the judge repeated her name, Lorraine, who was standing next to Margie on the stage, gave her a little push. 'Go on then, Margie, they're waiting for you to collect your prize.'

She stepped forward then and was kissed on the cheek by Mr Giles. 'Congratulations, Margie,' he said. 'You have a beautiful voice and are a most deserving winner of the overall prize.' He handed her a little trophy, then – best of all – a cheque for ten pounds. Mum would be thrilled!

She turned to face the audience, who were all clapping and cheering. This was without a doubt the happiest moment of her life so far. She didn't want the feeling to end.

As soon as Margie left the stage she was swamped with well-wishers. It took ages to fight her way through the crowd to her family. When she finally found them, her mother hugged her tight, while Ronny grabbed the trophy from her hands. 'Is this real gold?' he asked.

Val tugged on her skirt and told her she'd looked like a fairy princess up on the stage, while Neil said she was better than any of the other acts, even the magician.

When her mother finally broke their embrace, saying, 'I'm so, so proud of you, my girl,' Margie handed her the cheque.

Her mum's eyes widened. 'Margie, this is your money. You should keep it and buy yourself something nice – those heels you've been coveting, perhaps.'

'Don't be daft, Mum. I want to share it with you all. Besides, there's more than enough there for some new shoes for me and whatever you'd like to spend it on.'

An unfamiliar voice broke into their conversation. 'Congratulations, Margie. You are a very worthy winner.'

Margie turned to see who was speaking and was surprised to find Mr Giles' much younger (and more handsome) brother standing behind her.

He held out his hand to Eleanor. 'Hello, I'm Raymond Giles. I was one of the judges.'

She smiled. 'Eleanor Sheridan, Margie's mother. Pleased to meet you.'

'Likewise, Mrs Sheridan. You have a very talented daughter.'

'Thank you.'

'Mrs Sheridan, I am heading back to Melbourne at the end of this week. We're about to start auditions for a musical that I will be directing next year. Before I return, I'd love the chance to speak with you and your daughter about some potential career opportunities for her.'

Eleanor's forehead creased. 'I'm not sure what you mean, Mr Giles. Margie works here, at the mill, as a machinist.'

'Yes, yes, I know. But with a voice such as hers, she really should be on the stage. Don't you agree?'

Margie's heart leapt at the praise, but her mother's answer was guarded. 'She does have a lovely voice. Sadly, the opportunity for her to sing in front of an audience doesn't come around often, which is why we were all so excited about the talent show.'

'I can imagine. That's precisely what I'd like to talk to you both about. There might be more opportunities for a girl like Margie in Melbourne.'

Eleanor shook her head. 'Mr Giles, thank you for your interest, but our family depends on Margie's wage. She can't just go gallivanting off to Melbourne on a whim.'

'I understand, Mrs Sheridan, but I think Margie has the talent – in fact, I know she does – to perform professionally. If she got a part – even a small one – in a major musical, she'd be earning a lot more than she does as a machinist.'

Margie couldn't believe her ears! Was this actually happening? Did Mr Giles really think she was talented enough to be a professional singer? Her mother looked unconvinced, and Margie was afraid she was about to dismiss the idea. 'Please, Mum, what's the harm in talking about it?'

Eleanor's shoulders slumped. 'I just don't want you to get your hopes up for no reason, pet.'

'Mrs Sheridan, I promise you, I know what I'm talking about. I'm recently returned from directing a major production in London's West End. I know talent when I see it.'

Eleanor sighed. 'All right, then. We can talk. Why don't you come around for a cup of tea tomorrow afternoon? If you have a pen and paper Margie can write down the address for you.'

Margie felt as if her heart was going to burst. She kissed her mother's cheek and hugged her. 'Thanks, Mum.'

'Don't go getting your hopes up, you hear me? It's just a chat, that's all. I'm not promising anything.'

●

On Sunday afternoon, Margie set up a picnic in the backyard for the children and made them swear they wouldn't come inside the house unless it was an emergency. If they could adhere to that, she promised they'd be rewarded with chocolate cake after tea.

Mr Giles arrived with flowers and chocolates, which Margie knew would do nothing to change her mother's mind if she didn't agree with whatever it was he was proposing. Bill's betrayal had hardened her, and her default position had become one of suspicion.

Margie spent all morning cleaning and tidying the lounge room so they could entertain Mr Giles in there, much to her mother's chagrin. 'There's no need to be putting on airs and graces, Margie. If Mr Giles doesn't like you for who you are then there's no point to any of this.'

As it turned out, Mr Giles was perfectly happy to sit in the kitchen to have his tea. He'd brought some papers to show them, and thought it might be best if he could lay them out on the table for all to see.

He started by complimenting Margie again on her voice and asking her a raft of questions. Had she had any formal musical training? What did it feel like when she was up on the stage in front of an audience? Had she been nervous? Excited? A little of both?

When he was done with the questions, Mr Giles turned his attention to Eleanor. 'Mrs Sheridan, everything your daughter has just told me confirms my belief that she is well suited to life in the theatre. I would love for her to come up to Melbourne next week and audition for a new musical that I'm directing called *The Rose of France*. It's a wonderful story about a jewel thief named Amethyst Rose, who ends up becoming a spy. We've already signed Cara Beecham, who you might have heard of – she's a big star on the West End – to play Amethyst. I think Margie would be perfect for the chorus. It would be a great start for her.'

Margie clasped her hands in excitement, but her mother didn't seem convinced.

'She can't afford to take time off work for an audition.'

'Of course. Fortunately, we are holding auditions for the chorus on Saturday. Please let me make myself clear, Mrs Sheridan – I wouldn't be here if I didn't think your daughter had a rare talent. She's a pretty girl with a beautiful voice, and is quite a good dancer for someone with so little formal training. But it's more than that. She has something intangible about her; a star quality.' He furrowed his brow in thought as he looked at Margie, and then smiled as he addressed her mother. 'She puts me in mind of a young Judy Garland, with perhaps a hint of Debbie Reynolds, and yet she's quite unique.'

Margie gasped. Was Mr Giles *really* comparing her to her idols?

'I know it's short notice,' he said, turning his attention to Margie once more, 'but I've brought the music for a song I'd like you to learn before then, if you think you can do it.'

Margie nodded, even though she had no idea how she'd manage to learn a whole new song in such a short time without access to a piano. Perhaps Granny would let her practise after dinner each night. If not, she'd find some other way. 'Yes, I can learn it.'

'Good.' He turned his attention to Eleanor. 'Now, Mrs Sheridan, I know you're worried about pay, but I've brought this document to give you an idea of what Margie would be earning if she were to get a part in the chorus.' He pushed the paper in her mother's direction. 'As you can see, it is quite generous. And, in time, if she were to be cast in major roles, then the financial rewards can be substantial.'

Eleanor's eyes widened as she read the figures. 'That's all very well, Mr Giles, but what about when the production ends?'

'That's a prudent question. For some performers it might be tricky, but I can assure you that a talented girl like Margie will never be out of work. However, to give you added peace of mind, I have spoken to my brother at the mill, and he's prepared to guarantee Margie's job for twelve months. If she comes to Melbourne and it doesn't work out – for whatever reason – she can come home and have her job back.'

Margie looked hopefully at her mother, but Eleanor wasn't satisfied yet. 'Where would she live? Margie's young and impressionable, and Melbourne is a big city. How will I know she'll be safe?'

'There's a boarding house where lots of the young women in the chorus live. The lady who runs it, Mrs Thompson, is quite strict. An evening curfew, no gentleman callers to the girls' rooms, that sort of thing. And I'd personally keep an eye on her. I promise you she'll be kept safe.'

There were more questions, but Mr Giles had an answer for every one of them and, in the end, much to Margie's surprise and relief, her mother relented. 'Well, I suppose you'd better get practising if you're going to audition.'

●

As soon as Mr Giles left, Margie cycled over to Granny's to see about the piano.

'To what do I owe this pleasure, Marjorie? It's been a while since your last visit. We've missed you at church the past couple of Sundays.'

'I'm sorry, Granny, but I've been busy with work and helping Mum, and I've also been practising for a talent show.'

'The talent show at the mill?'

'Yes.'

'I heard something about that at church this morning. There was talk about the young girl who won. People were saying she had the voice of an angel.'

Margie could hardly contain her pride. 'That was me, Granny. I'm the girl who won.'

Granny looked surprised, but pleased nonetheless. 'You don't say? Well done, Marjorie. Why didn't you tell me? I would have liked to come and watch you perform. I don't get out much since your grandfather passed away.'

Margie's conscience pricked with shame. She'd been spending less time with her grandmother since her grandfather's passing a year earlier. Granny could be hard work on her own. 'I'm sorry. I didn't think you'd want to come to a show at the mill.'

Granny sighed. 'Never mind. Perhaps you can give me a private performance some time.'

'Yes, of course. In fact, Granny, that's why I'm here. I'm wondering if I can come around after dinner a few nights this week to use the piano. I need to learn a new song by next Saturday.'

'I don't see why not. But why the big hurry?'

'I have an audition for a part in a real musical – a proper one in Melbourne – and it's next weekend. Isn't that exciting?'

'What do you mean, a proper musical?' She looked aghast. 'On the stage? Does your mother know about this?'

'Yes, Mum knows.'

'What on earth is that woman thinking?'

'What do you mean?'

'I can't believe your mother would approve of such a thing.'

'Mum was worried at first, but Mr Giles – he's the director – explained everything, and now she's happy for me.'

'Well, I never . . . this is not a good idea, Marjorie. Being a performer – in a musical, *in the city*, for heaven's sake – isn't a suitable choice for a young lady.'

'I thought you liked my singing, Granny. I thought you'd be proud of me! Why did you encourage me to learn the piano and to sing if you didn't approve?'

'It's not the singing or the piano-playing that's the problem. Every accomplished young lady should be able to do both. It's lovely to be able to play for guests, and, as you are aware, I've always hoped you would join my church choir one day. But being a stage performer is for *common* girls, not well-brought-up young ladies.'

'Maybe once upon a time that was true, but not now. It's the 1950s, Granny, not the Middle Ages. It's a proper job and one that could earn me a lot of money.'

Granny shuddered. 'I've told you before that it isn't polite to talk about money. Good grief, your mother has been such a poor influence on you. Honestly, Marjorie, I wish you'd reconsider. No good will come of this, mark my words.'

'Don't worry about it, then. I'll see if I can use the piano at the scout hall instead.'

'There's no need to use that tone. I'm just trying to protect you. Heaven knows someone needs to. Your father would never have allowed you to become a common showgirl. I think he'd be disappointed to know you were considering such a thing.'

Marjorie's blood rushed hot with rage. She should have known better than to expect help from this bitter old cow. 'Well, my father's not here, is he?' she snapped. 'Mum has done her best in difficult circumstances, with no help from you. If my father knew how you'd treated his wife and daughter, I'm guessing the person he'd be most disappointed in is *you!*'

Chapter Nine

London
2019

The third time I see Jane, I know she's come to the library just to see me. She enters the foyer and hesitates for a moment as her gaze takes in the library proper. She's dressed head-to-toe in grey – a dove-coloured woollen dress beneath a felt coat and knitted hat. Even her ankle boots are charcoal. When she sees me, a smile lights her face and she strides towards me.

'Hello,' she says. 'I was hoping to find you here.'

'And so you have.' I push myself forward in the chair to stand, but she lays her hand on my shoulder and shakes her head.

'No, no. Don't get up.' She looks around and finds a spare ottoman, which she drags close to my chair and then sits on. She opens her handbag – a Louis Vuitton tote today – and pulls out a paperback, which she hands to me.

I look down at the book's title: *How to Write Your Life Experiences for the Page.* 'Is this for me?'

She nods. 'It was just sitting on my bookshelf taking up space. I have no use for it anymore and thought you might find it helpful.'

I'm surprised at this development, and a little embarrassed. She'd let me go on about my scribblings without mentioning anything about her writing. 'I didn't realise you were a writer.'

She shakes her head. 'I'm not. I mean, I've never written a book or anything. But I used to write about certain parts of my life for my job.' The smile leaves her face. 'That's all over now, so I thought I might as well pass the book on to someone who can use it.'

'Thank you,' I say, placing the book on the table beside me. 'I'll read it with interest.' I pause for a moment, wondering if I should pry further. Jane is obviously still burdened by something, and it seems to have to do with the job that is no more. I decide to try my luck. 'Did you leave your job recently?'

There's a hint of bitterness in the short laugh that escapes her lips. 'More like it left me.'

'Ah, I see. You weren't ready to leave?'

Her voice drops to a whisper. 'No.'

'Well, I certainly know what that feels like.'

She smiles, but there's disbelief in her eyes. 'Yes, well, I suppose I'm not the first person ever to lose a job. It's just that . . .' She pauses and then shrugs. 'I don't know . . . I guess without my business, I just don't know who I am anymore.'

So not just a job. A business. Perhaps she's facing bankruptcy? That would explain the worry she appears to be carrying.

'So, what for you now, my dear? Do you have a plan?'

She glances down at her fingernails and shrugs again. 'Honestly, I have no idea. My business was the one thing . . . the *only* thing I was good at. Or, at least, I thought I was. It turns out I was wrong about that. Now I fear I'm completely useless.' Her voice wavers.

'I'm sure that's not true. You're an intelligent woman. You could turn your mind to any number of things.'

'You're very kind,' she says, but I can see from her expression she doesn't believe me. She pats the book and stands. 'Anyway, I hope this is of use to you.'

The seed of an idea is forming in my head. 'Thank you. But you know what, Jane, I'm not much of a writer. You see, I had to leave school at quite a young age to help care for my family.'

'I'm sorry to hear that.'

'Well, it was a long time ago. Perhaps I'll write about it in my memoir. Do you really think anyone would want to read it?'

She smiles. 'I'd like to, I know that much.'

I nod as my thoughts take shape. 'To be honest, I never considered writing for an audience until you suggested it. My scribblings have just been a way to make peace with the world. You see, there are some things in my past that I'm not proud of. I guess my writing is a way of making sense of all that.'

She nods. 'Good luck, whatever you decide. I'll let you get on with it.'

'Jane, wait.'

She stops and looks at me expectantly.

My idea is an audacious one, and I can't imagine that she will agree, but if I can convince her, maybe we can help each other. 'I have a proposition for you.'

Her brow furrows. 'A proposition?'

'As I said, I hadn't considered writing for an audience before, but once you put the idea in my head the other day, I started to think it's a plan not entirely without merit. My financial circumstances have recently changed, so any potential source of income would be welcome.'

'Oh,' she says, her face falling. 'I wouldn't want you to get your hopes up. I mean, I'm sure your stories are wonderful, but there are no guarantees that a publisher would take the book. Even if it were to be published, I don't know how much money you would make. It might not be very lucrative.'

'It's not *just* about the money. I'd like to tell my story. And, besides, what else am I doing with my time?'

'Sounds as if you've made up your mind, then. But I'm not quite sure how I fit into this plan.'

'I'm no writer, Jane. Heavens, that's an understatement. I'm a terrible speller, and you could fit what I know about grammar and punctuation onto a postage stamp. I'm a good storyteller – you said so yourself, remember? – but putting the words down on paper isn't my forte. I was wondering if you might consider helping me; be my co-author, perhaps?'

She looks doubtful. 'Oh, Dolly, I don't know . . .'

Now the idea has taken root, I can't let it go. 'Hear me out. It might be beneficial to both of us. I can't pay you, of course, but we could split the profits if there ever were any. Having your help would make success a lot more likely, but, honestly, I don't even care about that. I just want to get my story onto the page in some sort of coherent fashion. I've got lots to say, but I don't think I'll ever get it out on my own. And it might be good for you, too. You did say you were at a bit of a loose end . . .' I trail off, realising just how ridiculous I sound.

Still, I can tell by the expression on her face that she *is* thinking about it. 'Well, it would certainly give me something to do with my time.' She bites her lip for a moment. 'What if I was your ghostwriter?'

'A ghostwriter?'

'Yes,' she says, clearly warming to the idea. 'You tell me the stories and I'll write them, but it'll be your name on the cover. If the book is ever published, we can worry about the money side of things then.'

I clap my hands together. 'That sounds wonderful, Jane, but your name should be on the cover too. After all, you'll be the one writing it.'

She shakes her head. 'That part is non-negotiable. I'll only do it if I can be a silent partner.'

'If that's what you truly want, so be it. So, where to from here? When shall we make a start?'

She thinks for a moment. 'Give me a day or two to do a little research. I haven't written anything like this before, so I might read up on the genre a bit and have a think about the best way to approach it. What if we meet back here at ten o'clock on Wednesday morning? That should give me enough time to get my head around it.'

I hold out my hand for her to shake. 'Deal.'

Jane grins as she pumps my hand, and I just know in my bones that this was a good decision – for both of us.

Chapter Ten

Melbourne, Australia
1960

Margie's fingers toyed with the gold key-shaped charm around her neck as she stood alone on the platform at Spencer Street station. Her mother had given her the necklace that morning, just moments before she boarded the train to Melbourne.

'Here,' she'd said, slipping the chain from her neck and pressing it into Margie's hand. 'Your father gave me this before he went off to war. It was to remind me that I held the key to his heart. You have the key to mine, Margie. I'll always love you no matter what.'

'Mum, I can't take this. It's yours.'

She pursed her lips and shook her head. 'I want you to have it. It will help you remember who you are and what I've taught you.'

Tears welled as Margie kissed her mother's cheek. 'Thanks, Mum.'

Eleanor shook her head and said, 'That's enough of that.' Her tone was brusque, but Margie could see she was fighting back her own tears. 'This is a happy day for you. Besides, tears will spoil your make-up. Now, hop on the train or you'll miss it. We can't have Mr Giles waiting around at the other end wondering where you are.'

But now Margie was at the other end of her train journey, and

Mr Giles was nowhere to be seen. She had no idea what to do. She'd never been to Melbourne alone before. Even on the day of her audition, Mr Giles had driven her to Melbourne.

She'd been so distracted by her upcoming audition that day she'd failed to take in any of her surroundings. She'd been entirely focused on the task ahead of her, determined to make the most of this amazing opportunity. The day had passed in a whirlwind. She'd been thrown in at the deep end, with the dance portion of the audition coming first. She, along with a dozen or so others, was shown the choreography for the number twice and then was expected to perform it. She got through it without any mistakes, but she feared it wasn't her most polished performance.

Luckily, she was on safer ground with the vocal audition. She'd practised the song Mr Giles had asked her to learn until she knew every bar by heart. He'd warned her that she wouldn't be asked to sing all of it, and not to worry if she was stopped before the end, so she wasn't too rattled when that happened on her first try. She was told to wait outside with the other hopefuls and she'd be called back if she made it through to the next round. After an hour-long anxious wait – during which she convinced herself she was about to be sent packing – she *was* called back, and that happened three more times before eventually she was allowed to sing the whole song. The song, 'Nothing I Wouldn't Do', spoke to her as if it had been written especially for her. Her confidence soared as she worked up to the number's powerful conclusion, and when she was done she knew before she was told that she'd made the cut.

It had been a huge day, so when Mr Giles escorted her to the Geelong-bound train afterwards, she'd been so excited that she'd failed to take notice of where they were going.

Now she wasn't even sure how far away the theatre was. Was it close enough to walk if Mr Giles didn't appear? She was wearing a new pair of heels that definitely weren't suited to walking long distances. After years of being forced to wear flats to work at the mill, she'd vowed never to choose 'sensible' shoes ever again, but already she was regretting that decision.

With her stomach churning, Margie looked in her handbag for her purse. Her mother had given her a five-pound note and some coins in case of an emergency. She was loath to use the money so soon, but supposed if it were absolutely necessary, she could catch a cab to the theatre alone.

'There she is!' Mr Giles hurried along the platform towards her. 'Sorry I'm late, doll. I went to the wrong platform and waited there for ages before realising my mistake. I hope you weren't too worried.'

Margie summoned the most grown-up tone she could manage. 'Not at all, Mr Giles. I simply thought you'd been detained at the theatre. I was preparing to get myself a cab.'

He grinned. 'Enough of that Mr Giles nonsense. You're making me feel like an old man. We're colleagues now, Margie. You should call me Raymond.'

Margie smiled and not for the first time noticed how handsome he was. 'All right. Raymond it is.'

●

The next month was exhausting, exhilarating and eye-opening for a young girl from the country.

Margie spent most of her time split between rehearsals and getting to know her housemates at Mrs Thompson's boarding house. The house itself – a crumbling six-bedroom terrace in Fitzroy – wasn't anything to write home about, but the girls were friendly enough and Margie quickly settled into her new routine. Her housemates were all performers too – three of them were in the chorus alongside her. Each day Margie and her castmates caught the tram to rehearsals together, but most evenings she came home alone to eat dinner with Mrs Thompson while the others stayed to go out to cafes together or on dates.

Mrs Thompson was an elderly woman who been on the stage herself. She expected 'her girls' to keep their rooms clean and tidy, to let her know whether they would be back for dinner and not to bring men home. That was about it. Theoretically there was a curfew – midnight, on account of the girls having to work late into the evening when they were in a show – but, in reality, they all had keys and Mrs Thompson was hard of hearing, so there were girls coming and going at all hours.

In the second week of rehearsals, Sandy Vale, who was in the chorus with Margie and who occupied the bedroom opposite hers, was home for dinner. After they'd helped Mrs Thompson wash up, Sandy said she was heading back into town to meet up with some castmates to listen to a jazz band at a coffee house. 'You should come, Margie.'

Margie shook her head. 'I need to get a good night's sleep. My voice suffers if I don't, and I don't want to be too tired to keep up with the new choreography.'

Sandy laughed. 'A couple of hours at a coffee house won't ruin your voice, lovey, and you seem to be holding your own learning the choreography just fine. In fact, you're doing so well, I wouldn't be at all surprised if you were named understudy for the lead.'

Margie couldn't believe her ears. At twenty-five, Sandy was a veteran of the chorus and knew her stuff. Even the hint of praise from her was enough to make Margie's chest swell with pride. 'Do you really think so?'

Sandy shrugged. 'I don't see why not. Your voice is far superior to the rest of the chorus. You're not the top dancer, but that's to be expected considering your lack of formal training. At the rate you're learning, it won't be long before you outshine all the others. I think they'd be mad not to pick you. Besides, you're Raymond's big discovery and he seems to have taken a shine to you.'

Heat rushed into Margie's cheeks. Was that what everyone thought – that she got the job because she was Raymond's pet? 'No!'

'And no joy lies that way, love.'

'What do you mean?'

Sandy laughed. 'You'll work it out. For now, let's just say that if you were entertaining the idea, it's not smart to get hooked up with the director. Okay?'

Margie nodded, her cheeks still burning.

'Listen, lovey, let me give you some advice. You're good – very good. I don't know quite how to explain it, but you've got that intangible quality about you. Star power.'

'Oh, I don't think—'

Sandy cut her off. 'I've been around long enough to know it when I see it. I'd bet my bottom dollar that one of these days you're going to be a leading lady. That's what Raymond sees in you and everyone else can see it too. You seem to be a sweet girl, and that's why I'm telling you this. Musical theatre isn't all sunshine and lollipops. It's hard work, long hours and, for many of us, disappointment after disappointment. It's a competitive business to be in, and while those of us who tread the boards can be the best of friends, we're competitors too. Understand?'

This was all news to Margie. In her naivety, she'd imagined the cast being one big, happy family. The thought of the chorus members being in competition with one another hadn't crossed her mind. 'I guess so.'

'What I'm saying is, this life will be a lot easier for you if you have friends. And that won't happen if you don't give people a chance to get to know you. You don't want to seem standoffish, do you?'

Margie shook her head.

'Good. If you do end up being chosen as the understudy, it will be sure to put a few noses out of joint. It'll be much easier for people to dislike you if they think you're aloof or stuck-up. You need to spend this time while we're in rehearsal making everyone love you. That way they'll be happy for you when your star begins to rise. Okay?'

'How?'

'By coming out tonight, for a start.'

●

The coffee lounge had the feel of a nightclub. It was located above a bookstore in Swanston Street and accessed by climbing a rickety set of stairs. Margie could smell the delicious aroma of coffee – a beverage she was yet to sample – before she and Sandy emerged into the dimly lit space.

She followed Sandy across the crowded room to a table where Raymond and several members of the cast were sitting. Raymond jumped up and kissed her on the cheek. 'Margie! How wonderful you could join us tonight.' He turned to the young man sitting beside him. 'Graeme, this is Margie Ferguson, the girl I've been telling you about.'

Graeme took her hand and kissed it flamboyantly. 'Lovely to meet you, darling. Ray never stops talking about you.'

Heat flooded Margie's cheeks for the second time that night. She didn't know what to say.

Graeme laughed. 'Oh, Ray, look! She's blushing. How adorable.'

Raymond rolled his eyes. 'Behave yourself, Grae.'

Graeme laughed again and stood up. He patted his seat. 'Here, doll, you sit down here. I'll go rustle up another couple of seats.' Then, to Margie's great shock, he leant over and pecked Raymond on the cheek. 'Best behaviour, lovey, I promise.'

She was dumbstruck. Had that really just happened? A man kissing another man? It wasn't something she'd encountered before and she had no idea what to make of it. It wasn't an overtly sexual kiss, just a peck, but still, it was unsettling.

Raymond patted her arm. 'Can I order you a coffee, Margie?'

She'd never tasted coffee – they only ever drank tea at home – but she didn't want to seem unsophisticated. 'That would be lovely.'

'What would you like? Espresso? Cappuccino?'

Margie hesitated. She had no idea what the difference was.

Raymond smiled and said, 'A cappuccino, perhaps? Espresso might keep you awake all night.'

She was left to her own devices for a few moments while Raymond focused on getting a waiter's attention. Sandy had left the table already to dance on the makeshift dancefloor consisting of a small table-free space in front of the band. Margie took the opportunity to look around the coffee lounge. It reminded her of the nightclubs she'd seen onscreen at the pictures, although she assumed no one was drinking liquor here. Not even pubs were licensed to serve alcohol after 6 pm.

Beverages notwithstanding, this place was nothing like the cafes she'd been to with her mother or the girls she worked with in Geelong. The walls were painted deep burgundy and trimmed in gold. Chandeliers hung from the ceiling and velvet-covered couches and chaise longues were set up in cosy corners, giving patrons an alternative to the more traditional cafe furniture such as the table where Margie was seated.

The room was dimly lit and filled with a smoky haze. As Margie's eyes adjusted to the light she noticed all sorts of oddities – men wearing flamboyant hats adorned with peacock feathers. Women dressed in men's clothing. Men wearing lipstick and false eyelashes. One scantily clad woman sitting on another woman's lap. Men dancing together! Yet, despite the strangeness of it all, she didn't feel threatened or uncomfortable. The elegance and flamboyance of the crowd entranced her. Each one of the cafe's patrons seemed to be extraordinary in the best kind of way.

Suddenly Margie felt very plain in her full-skirted dress and kitten heels.

Raymond touched her arm. 'All right, love? This place can come as a bit of a shock to the uninitiated.'

'It's wonderful.' Margie beamed.

Raymond returned her smile. 'I'm so glad to hear you say that. Carole's Coffee Lounge is an institution for us creative types. It's our sanctuary. A place where everyone is welcome and free to be themselves. This is a safe place, Margie. No one will judge you here, provided you extend them the same courtesy.'

She nodded. She wasn't quite sure what Raymond meant by that, but she felt instinctively at home among these unusual people. They were wild and confident, unafraid to be themselves and completely unlike anyone Magie had ever known. She hadn't realised it until this very moment, but deep down in her soul she wanted to be just like the clientele of Carole's Coffee House. Why settle for an ordinary life when there was so much more out there?

Graeme scrounged up two extra chairs. These were immediately occupied by Sandy and the sax player from the band. Graeme threw up his hands in mock exasperation, while Raymond laughed and patted his knee. Graeme slid in beside Margie and sat on Raymond's lap. Now she understood what Sandy had been insinuating earlier.

The evening passed in the blink of an eye. Raymond and Sandy seemed to know almost everyone in the place and Margie found herself being introduced to more people than she could hope to remember, although there were a couple who made a lasting impression, including Carole, the owner of the establishment. Carole wore a floor-length fur coat over a pair of tailored men's trousers, a buttoned-up shirt and a long silk necktie. She was breathtakingly beautiful, and Margie was almost speechless when Carole kissed both her cheeks and personally welcomed Margie to her 'home'.

Raymond's partner, Grae (as he preferred to be called), asked her to dance and wouldn't take no for an answer. She'd always prided herself on her dancing – she could copy almost any choreography she saw on the screen and was a sought-after ballroom partner at the Palais, where she went dancing most Saturday nights. But this music was different to anything she'd experienced before. It was wild and unstructured, and no two dancers seemed to be moving the same way; rather, each person was interpreting the music in their own fashion. She was hesitant at first, but with Grae's encouragement she loosened up and gave herself over to the crazy beat.

Before she knew it, the band was playing its final number – she'd been dancing for most of the night and she wasn't tired at all. If anything, she left the dancefloor feeling even more energised than when she'd arrived.

'Coffee will do that to you,' Raymond joked, but Margie knew it was more than that.

After the band wound up, Alan, the saxophone player, joined their party. 'I saw you out there on the dancefloor,' he said, looking her over appreciatively. 'You sure know how to move.'

The compliment, along with his suggestive stare, flustered Margie a little, but instead of looking away as she normally would have done, she held his gaze. 'I'm a dancer,' she said, with as much confidence as she could muster. She wanted to fit in with this vibrant crowd and she sensed there was no room for wallflowers here.

'It shows.' He offered her a cigarette, which she declined.

'No good for the voice,' she said. 'I'm a singer, too.'

He shrugged. 'Might make it even sexier.'

She wasn't sure what to say to that but he just grinned and continued. 'I know who you are. I've seen you at rehearsals. I'm a member of the band. I work here in between shows, if I can. It's good money and I like the crowd.'

'So, we'll be working together,' she said, hoping she hadn't offended him by not knowing who he was.

'Yes, how fortunate. Although, the band members don't get to mix much with the cast during the show. But everyone tends to hang out here afterwards.'

'Oh, well, perhaps we'll be seeing more of each other then.'

'I certainly hope so.'

His words made Margie's skin tingle. She hoped so too.

Sandy cut in to their little tete-a-tete. 'Time to head off, lovey. It might take us a while to get a cab.'

'No need for a cab, ladies,' Alan said. 'I have my car parked downstairs. I can give you a lift.'

'Really?' Sandy asked. 'That would be lovely, but we wouldn't want to impose.'

'I insist.'

Twenty minutes later, after Alan had dropped them safely at Mrs Thompson's door, Sandy nudged Margie as she waved goodbye. 'He's a looker, isn't he?'

Margie was glad it was dark so Sandy wouldn't see her blush for the third time that night. She didn't want Sandy thinking she was an unsophisticated country hick, even if there was some truth in the description. 'He's not bad.'

'I think he might be a bit sweet on you, Miss Margie.'

The idea thrilled her, but she tried to keep her voice neutral. 'Don't be daft.'

'I'm not. He's always at Carole's – every time I'm there, I see him – and this is the first time he's offered to drive me home. Looks as if you've got yourself an admirer.'

Chapter Eleven

London
2019

I wasn't sure if I'd live to see this morning. And, for the first time ever, I wondered if I really wanted to. But I must keep going. I might be old and arthritic, but I'm not done yet.

Last night was one of the hardest I've had since my Julian died.

Sometimes it feels as if I lost him half a lifetime ago, although it's been less than two years.

We were apart when it happened. He died in Los Angeles, thousands of miles away. He'd gone to the States early in December 2017 to support his daughter through a difficult time. The plan was to stay there for Christmas and be home for New Year's Eve, as always, but he'd had a heart attack a few days before he was due to fly home. At first it looked as though he would make a full recovery. He called me from the hospital to tell me not to fret, he'd been delayed but he'd be back in London in no time.

Sadly, he was wrong.

The following day he had another massive heart attack, and he passed away on the last day of the year, the very day I should have been welcoming him home.

I hated that I'd been robbed of the chance for a final goodbye, but such is the lot of a mistress.

The grief I felt at having lost the love of my life was quickly overlaid by fear of what was to become of me. When I had to leave our Belgravia flat – oh, my beautiful home, with its antique furniture and Persian rugs – I was devastated. Even so, I had no idea of just how hard my life was about to become. I thought I'd have to lower my standards a little, but never did I imagine I'd end up here.

It wasn't immediate, of course. It wasn't as if I went from being affluent one minute to out on the street the next, but nevertheless I was shocked at how quickly my life unravelled. The first few months, when I still had some savings, were okay. But I didn't manage my money well – at the time I had no reason to believe that I needed to. It seems ridiculous now, but I blew a load of cash in the first couple of weeks by staying at my favourite hotel and eating in fine restaurants, just as I always had. I had no idea just how expensive my lifestyle truly was. My bank balance soon dwindled and I realised I was in trouble. I managed for a while by staying with friends and spending some nights in cheap hotels. But recently I ran out of money and options. I simply had nowhere left to turn.

A few times in the first couple of nights sleeping rough I was set upon by groups of young lads on their way home from the pub. For some reason they seem to get a boost out of screaming obscenities at people like me. It was upsetting, but after a while I realised there are worse things than a bit of verbal abuse. Being spat on or urinated on is harder to take, and I had to throw away a sleeping bag I had bought from a charity shop after one charming soul vomited on me.

I tried one of the cheap hostels that exist specifically for people who would otherwise be sleeping on the street, but the other guests were unsavoury types and my mobile phone mysteriously disappeared while I was staying there. After that I was terrified of being robbed or murdered in my sleep. I figured there was no point parting with what little money I had for accommodation that provided no comfort or security. I can risk my life free of charge, thank you very much.

Since leaving the hostel I've been sleeping in whatever hidey-hole I can find that's out of sight. It's surprising how quickly one can adapt to a new situation, especially when one has no choice.

Last night was the first time in a while my plans haven't worked out. After I finished at the library, I spent some time on the high street, ducking in and out of shops to keep warm. There's a new soup kitchen set up in the church hall on Monday nights, so I headed there for a meal and to stay out of the cold for a bit longer. I stayed until lock-up, around nine o'clock, and then headed off 'home' with a full belly and a song in my heart. I was still buzzing after my conversation with Jane.

So, it came as a shock to find the garden shed I've been staying in was padlocked – someone's got wise to my tricks! Because I've been using it for a couple of weeks without any issues, I'd allowed myself to become complacent. I didn't have a back-up plan. My one saving grace was that I hadn't been careless enough to leave anything behind. My possessions were safely contained in my wheelie case.

I walked around trying to look purposeful for a while – there's less chance of being hassled if you look as if you have somewhere to be – until I remembered the alcove in the library courtyard. There's a sort of half wall beside the rear entrance that encloses a garden bed. There are a couple of bench seats in there and it's quite sheltered – it's where the librarians sneak out to have a coffee or a moment in the sun when it's quiet. Best of all, it's not visible from the street. Regular library users might know about it, but I figured the average pub lout probably wouldn't think to look there.

I was happy to see my suspicions confirmed. The alcove was empty when I arrived. It was a good choice – no overhead cover, but at least it was protected from the wind. The nip in the air suggested rain was on the way and it was already late, so I decided it was time to bed down for the night. I opened my little wheelie case and dragged out the compact but warm sleeping bag I'd purchased from a jumble sale to replace the one I'd had to throw away. It was cheap – probably because the zip no longer works properly, but that doesn't bother me too much.

I deliberated for a moment about where to set up – on top of the bench seat or underneath it – and despite knowing how hard it would be to crawl out again in the morning, I decided under was the best choice. I pulled out my thin plastic rain poncho and draped it over the bench, securing it with a couple of well-placed rocks sourced from the garden bed. Then I placed the plastic wheelie case up against one end of the seat to further protect me from the weather. I'd made myself a little cave. My coat went on the ground beneath the seat as padding against the concrete surface and to help keep the cold from seeping up into my sleeping bag, which I laid on top of the coat. I slipped on a pair of fleecy tracksuit pants over my tights and then shimmied out of my skirt, folded it carefully and put it in my case. My final bedtime preparation was to remove my blouse and pop on an old woollen jumper over my merino-wool spencer. I carefully crawled into my hidey-hole and wrapped the sleeping bag around me, feeling mildly pleased with how innovative I'd become. It wasn't The Savoy, but it would do.

My positive mood didn't last long. The coat didn't make as much difference as I'd hoped – the concrete was still cold and hard. And the poncho did little to protect me from the rain when it came. But there was nothing to be done other than to wait it out. It wasn't as if I had anywhere else to go. It took hours to drop off to sleep, and after what felt like only minutes of slumber, I was nosed awake by a fox. 'Go on, get!' I yelled, sending it scampering into the night.

I'd only just dozed off again when I was roused by the noise of breaking glass. I opened my eyes to discover a group of drunken youths had congregated in my alcove and were apparently amusing themselves by smashing empty beer bottles on the ground. I held my breath. Had they seen me?

The next bottle smashed close to my cave. One of the boys called out, 'Oi, get a load of this. There's a geezer under the bench there.'

I stayed still, barely breathing. My bones were frozen stiff. It would take considerable effort to move from my position, and even if I was upright, what hope did I have of protecting myself? There were three of them at least – hard to tell if there were more from my vantage point – and the ones I could see were big lads. My best chance was to stay quiet and hope they ignored me.

No such luck.

'Do you reckon he's dead?'

'Soon find out. Oi, geezer, are you alive then?' The hard toe of a steelcapped boot nudged me. I didn't respond.

'Look, there's a case. Pretty fancy one, too. Whatcha got in 'ere, mate?' One of them snatched up my suitcase and I heard them unzip it.

'Not a geezer then, eh? It's a woman.'

They were rifling through my things now, throwing items between them. I thanked god I was wearing my two most treasured possessions – my mother's necklace and my amethyst ring – but I was worried about my clothes, especially my beautiful new cashmere scarf.

'Anything good in there?' one of them asked.

'Nah, it's all shit. Just clothes and crap.'

I silently prayed they'd lose interest and move on.

'But let's check out this old bag. See if she's up for a bit of fun.' The speaker crouched down and dragged me out from under the bench. I tried to stand but he pushed me back down to the ground, laughing.

'Jeezus, she must be a hundred at least.' This statement was met with more laughter.

I was terrified but tried my best not to react.

'What are you doing out here, Grandma? Don't you know the streets aren't safe for little old ladies after dark? Anything could happen.' He leant over and put his face close to mine, and despite my determination not to show any emotion, tears began to leak from my eyes.

One of the others piped up. 'Come on, mate, this is shit. Grandma ain't got nothin' worth anythin'. Let's go get a kebab. I'm starvin'.'

My tormentor hesitated for a moment, staring menacingly into my eyes, but eventually he relented. 'Yeah, orrite.' He stood up and took a step back while I breathed out a sigh of relief that my ordeal was over. As the others started to move away, he delivered a sharp kick to my side as a parting gift.

I don't know how long I lay there after that. I cried for what seemed like hours, but it's hard to know exactly how much time passed. When I had no more tears, I gingerly sat up. My side hurt like hell, but I could move freely and was breathing without any difficulty, so I figured nothing was too badly damaged. I suspected I'd have one heck of a bruise in the coming days, though.

I slowly got to my feet and began to gather up my clothes, which were muddy and trodden on. Thankfully the scarf remained in my bag, unharmed. I'm grateful for that small mercy. Still, there would be no changing out of my fleecy pants today. I'd need to visit a laundromat, and perhaps a thrift shop to replace any items damaged beyond repair. First, though, I needed to find somewhere to clean up. Dawn had already broken, so I guessed it was around seven, still hours before the library would be open. There are toilets in the shopping mall that I use quite often, but I doubted they'd be open yet either.

There's one of those chain hotels (that I never would have deigned to visit in my former life) not too far from the high street with a small toilet in the foyer. It's supposed to be 'guests only', but sometimes I can sneak in there. It's often quiet first thing in the morning; new guests don't check in until later in the day, and those leaving early seem to use the self-checkout facility. The staff there don't seem too fussed about me sneaking in for a quick wash, provided I don't overstay my welcome. There's one receptionist in particular who is quite lovely. She'll sometimes slip me a little bottle of hand lotion or body wash, or sneak me a bottle of water when I'm leaving. I decided it was worth the walk even though I was feeling sore and sorry for myself.

It took me much longer than usual to make my way from the library alcove to the hotel. But I'm here now and, thank the stars, I'm in luck. My favourite receptionist – Lydia is her name – is on duty. I smile at her as I push open the glass door, and I can see by the look on her face that I must be in a bad way.

'Dolly,' she says in her strong Polish accent. 'What has happened to you? You are hurt?'

'I'm fine, my dear. I need to use your bathroom. Is that okay?'

'Yes, yes, of course. You go. I'll bring you some towels. I should call a doctor, or the police maybe? You have been attacked?'

'No, no! No police. No doctor. I wasn't attacked, it was just a fall. Everything is fine.'

A look of understanding passes between us. 'Okay. You go. I'll bring the towels.'

In the bathroom I understand why she is concerned. My hair is matted with mud and my face is grazed and ashen. I relieve myself, which takes some time as it hurts to lower myself onto the toilet, and getting back up is even worse. When I'm done, I run the water until it's warm and rinse my hands. Before I have time to inspect my injuries any further, Lydia arrives with a face cloth, towels, soap and a small bottle of antiseptic. 'Here,' she says, 'for your face. Don't rush. I will put an out-of-order sign on the bathroom.'

My eyes fill with tears. 'Thank you, my dear. I'm sorry to impose.'

She shakes her head. 'It is nothing. Take your time. The boss won't be in for another hour.'

I clean up as best I can, but even with soap, water and antiseptic, there's little I can do to improve my appearance. I have no clean clothes, my hairbrush is missing, and my face-powder compact is broken. I've washed my face and under my arms, and done my best to get the mud out of my hair. I've even salvaged a little of the broken powder to dust on my face. It doesn't cover the grazes but it gives me a slightly better colour, which is something. I coat my lips with the one lipstick I have left (the shade is Temptress, Julian's favourite) and gather up my things.

When I return to the empty foyer, Lydia is waiting for me. 'Don't go yet, Dolly,' she says earnestly. 'I have a cup of tea for you. You sit.' She gestures to an armchair covered in a drab grey fabric and I obey without argument.

Moments later she returns with a cup of hot black tea, with a slice of lemon on the side. I prefer my tea milky but I'm so grateful for the gesture that I smile and thank her for her kindness.

She leans over and says in a quiet voice, 'I've added something a little stronger to the tea. It will help with the shock. The boss comes in about half an hour, so you have time to enjoy.'

I squeeze her hand. 'Thank you.'

She smiles and goes back to the desk.

She's right. The tea (laced with whisky and honey) helps to restore my equilibrium. By the time I'm ready to leave I'm still feeling bruised and battered but I'm not as shaken as I was. In fact, I'm suddenly quite ravenous. I'll stop at the supermarket on my way back to the library to get a sandwich and a chocolate bar.

As I wave goodbye to Lydia, I say a silent prayer of gratitude for all that I have: my mother's necklace, my ring and my coat.

And the kindness of strangers.

Chapter Twelve

Melbourne, Australia
1960

As Margie stepped out of her room wearing her new cornflower-blue swing dress, Sandy caught her by the arm and then stepped back to look at her. 'Wow, that's a smashing outfit! It's too late for church, so what are you all dressed up for?'

Margie grinned. 'I can honestly say I don't know.'

Sandy rolled her eyes. 'If you don't want to tell me, just say so.'

'It's not that. Alan's taking me on a mystery date. He said to be ready at eleven and to wear comfortable shoes.'

'That explains the flatties. I don't think I've ever seen you wear shoes without a heel before.'

Margie wrinkled her nose. 'I used to have to wear sensible shoes to work at the mill every day and I swore once I was out of that place I would wear heels at every opportunity. But Alan was quite insistent I wear something I could walk a distance in. Perhaps we're going for a stroll around Fitzroy Gardens and then out for lunch?'

Sandy looked at her with concern in her eyes. 'I hope you're not getting too serious about him, Margie. I haven't noticed you dating anyone else for weeks. Maybe even longer. I know he's dreamy, but he's also a bit of a player. If you're having a good time, that's great. Just don't get too involved. Remember, he's not the only fish in the sea.'

Margie waved away her concern. She wasn't worried. They'd been dating exclusively now for almost two months and Alan had been the perfect gentleman.

But this wasn't the first time she'd been warned about his reputation. A couple of the girls in the chorus had even repeated some ridiculous rumour that he had a wife and baby tucked away somewhere in the country. Alan had laughed that one off when she'd asked him. He said the rumour had been started by a girl in a previous show who he'd gone on one date with and not asked out again.

'Don't worry, Sandy. I know what I'm doing. I best get downstairs. I don't want to keep him waiting.'

She made her way out of the house just in time to see Alan's cherry-red Morris Minor pulling up out the front. She waved as he got out and came around to open the passenger-side door for her.

'Aren't you a sight for sore eyes?' he said as he stepped forward to kiss her cheek. 'You look gorgeous.'

'Thank you.' As she climbed into the car, she spied a picnic basket on the back seat. She clapped her hands. 'A picnic! I love picnics and I haven't been on one in ages.'

Alan grinned at her as he started the car. 'Glad you approve. I thought we could make the most of this warm weather while it lasts. I know a nice secluded little spot where we can sun ourselves. It's a bit of a drive but worth it for the views, I think. Are you up for it?'

'I'm up for anything.'

'That's what I like to hear.'

The conversation came easily as they headed out of the city. Alan was great company, and in between pointing out pretty houses and commenting on the rural landscape he entertained her with funny anecdotes and gossip from the orchestra pit. The further they got from the city, the more spectacular the scenery became. They were climbing now, the little Morris chugging in protest at the winding ascent.

After about half an hour of navigating the winding roads, Margie began to feel carsick, so she was enormously relieved when they came to a wide clearing on the side of the road and Alan pulled over.

It seemed an odd place to stop. 'Are we having the picnic here?'

He laughed. 'No. I just wanted to show you the view.'

She felt so poorly that the scenery was the last thing on her mind. In fact, she'd had her head down, focusing on her breathing to prevent herself from being sick. But now she looked up and took notice. 'Oh my goodness! Alan, this is breathtaking.'

'Isn't it just? Come on, let's take a closer look.' He jumped out and sprinted to her side of the car so he could open the door. When he offered her his hand, she took it with a smile.

They walked to the safety barrier, where Margie marvelled at the spectacular sight of the gorge in front of them and the rolling hills beyond. 'How did you know about this place?'

'I grew up around here. When I first got my licence, I'd drive out here whenever I felt a bit low. This view would always cheer me up. If you squint, you might just be able to see my parents' old farm.' He leant forward and pointed, but Margie yanked him back in fright.

'Careful! You could fall.'

He laughed and stepped towards her, circling his arms around her waist and pulling her close. 'It's okay. The barrier's quite strong. I won't fall, I promise. It's nice to know you care about me so much, though.'

'I do care about you,' Margie blurted out, and immediately regretted having said too much.

But Alan looked at her with tenderness in his eyes. 'Sweet Margie, I care about you too.' He reached up and cupped her cheek with his hand. 'You are so beautiful, how could I not? You've bewitched me.' When his lips met hers there was such tenderness and honesty in his kiss that Margie felt light-headed. Could she actually be falling in love? Could he?

He stroked her hair and then broke their kiss. 'Come on. Let's get going. I can't wait to show you the picnic spot and we're nearly there.'

A few minutes later they pulled off the main road and onto a tree-lined gravel track. They drove on for about ten minutes, and the further they went, the thicker the bush around them became. 'I hope you know where you're going,' Margie said. 'I'd hate for us to get lost out here.'

'Don't worry, my darling. I know this land like the back of my hand.'

My darling. Margie's heart began to beat double time. It felt as though something had shifted between them today. Up until now, Alan had been fun and affectionate, but completely proper with her. They'd kissed a few times, and she knew he found her attractive, but today he was showing her she was more to him than just a flirtation. He'd brought her here, to his home turf. He'd told her he cared about her and then kissed her in a way that demonstrated he was telling the truth. Now he was calling her 'my darling'.

It went without saying that she was head over heels in love with him. She'd been too afraid to say the words out loud before, barely daring to even think them. It was too soon – she was far too young to be in love, according to her mother. (Eleanor seemed to conveniently forget that she'd met Margie's dad when she was around the same age as Margie was now.) But in her heart, she just knew. When she was with Alan, she felt beautiful and confident – like a real woman and not a little girl. If Alan felt the same way, then . . .

She allowed her mind to go there just for a second. She hadn't thought marriage was something she'd wanted – at least, not yet – but maybe she'd been too hasty in dismissing the idea altogether. She couldn't think of anything better than sharing her life with a husband who understood how important performing was to her. As a member of the theatre world, Alan knew the stage was part of who she was.

But would he want children?

He didn't seem the type. She didn't see motherhood as something that was in her future – she'd helped raise enough kids for one lifetime – but if Alan was adamant, she'd consider it. Perhaps one baby wouldn't be so bad. But not straightaway. She needed a chance to make a name for herself on the stage first.

The car came to a stop, rousing her from her thoughts. Margie looked around. There was no picnic ground, just dense bush on both sides of the road.

'We need to walk from here.' Alan was already halfway out of the car.

Margie got out before he could open her door. 'Through the bush?' She feared her voice revealed her concern. She was a girl who liked lipstick and heels. Hiking wasn't part of her normal repertoire.

He grinned. 'It's not far, I promise. Just down that little track there, see?' He indicated a dusty track not far from where they'd parked.

She gave him a tentative smile. 'Okay.'

'That's why I insisted on the comfortable shoes. It's worth the effort, you'll see. I'll just get the picnic basket and then we can head off.'

Less than five minutes later Margie heard the sound of running water. 'Are we near a river?'

'A little creek. We're just on the edge of the state forest here, but hardly anyone ever comes in this way. There are picnic grounds on the other side of the park, near the main entrance, but they can get busy on a sunny day. No one seems to know about this spot, so we'll have it all to ourselves.'

As he finished speaking, the creek came into view. There was a small clearing on the bank – a perfect spot to set up for the day. 'Oh, Alan, this is so romantic. I thought we were going for a walk in the gardens followed by lunch in a restaurant, but this is so much nicer.'

Alan squeezed her hand. 'I'm glad you think so. And just wait till you see what I have in store for lunch. It's a feast fit for a queen.' He pulled her towards a grassy spot on the bank, which was shaded by a giant eucalypt, and pulled out a rug from within the wicker basket he'd been carrying. He spread it out and beckoned for her to sit, and, once she was comfortable, he began to unpack the remaining contents of the basket. Cheese and pickle sandwiches, cold meatloaf and a salad consisting of lettuce, tomato, cheddar cheese and boiled eggs were lovingly laid out before her.

'You've gone to so much trouble,' she said.

'It was no trouble at all. But I'm not done yet. There's still more.' He pulled out a bottle of wine and a small leather case, which contained a set of aluminium tumblers.

Margie had only ever had wine once before and it had gone straight to her head. 'Oh. How lovely. But I'm not sure I should be drinking wine with lunch. I fear it will make me quite silly.'

'Nonsense. You could never be silly. Besides, a little won't hurt. I find a small glass with a meal helps me to relax and enjoy myself even more. Won't you give it a try? It's not as if we have to work.'

He'd gone to so much effort, it was hard to say no. 'Go on, then. Pour me one – just half a glass.'

'That's my girl.' He poured a small amount into a tumbler and handed it to her, before pouring another for himself. He stretched out beside her on the rug. 'This is the life, eh?' He raised his cup and clinked it against hers. 'Cheers.'

'Cheers.' She took a small sip. The wine was sweet and acidic at the same time. It wasn't awful, but she wouldn't exactly call it pleasant either. She had to concentrate to stop herself from wincing at the bitter aftertaste.

Alan was looking at her eagerly. 'What do you think?'

'Very nice,' she lied.

Seemingly satisfied with her response, Alan lifted the plate of sandwiches and offered it to her. 'Have something to eat. It'll make the wine go down more easily.'

He was right. After a couple of sandwiches and a piece of meatloaf, she found the taste of the wine more acceptable. And she felt deliciously lighthearted. Alan was regaling her with funny stories from the orchestra pit and she found herself laughing like she hadn't in years. When he offered her a top-up, she found herself agreeing. 'I guess a little more won't hurt.'

'There's still cake in the basket, and a flask of tea too.'

Margie patted her stomach. 'I'm full for now, but I'll take a tea later.'

'Righto. It'll be there when you're ready.' He settled back next to her so that his arm was positioned behind her, and his thigh was pressed against hers. He took a large swig of his wine and then carefully placed the tumbler beside him on an empty plate so it wouldn't fall over on the uneven surface. 'I think the cook deserves a kiss,' he said lightly, turning his face towards her.

She laughed and pecked him on the cheek.

'I'm sorry, that just won't do.' He pushed his mouth onto hers and kissed her, softly at first and then more urgently than he ever had before, rolling his body over and easing her down so that he was half on top of her.

Her pulse was thumping hard against her chest wall as she closed her eyes and sank into bliss.

He pushed his hand into her hair and cradled her head, deepening the kiss, before momentarily drawing back and whispering her name. His hand moved from her head to her neck and then slid lower, finally coming to rest on her breast.

Margie's eyes shot open. She should have anticipated this – Alan was a man, after all – but she hadn't. She should ask him to stop. It wasn't proper. His hand was fully cupping her breast now, gently squeezing, and, to her horror, she felt her nipples responding to his touch, hardening against the stiff material of her brassiere. 'Alan, stop.'

He immediately withdrew his hand and sat up. 'I'm sorry. I thought you were enjoying yourself.'

She pushed herself up to a sitting position. 'It's not that . . . I just don't think we should get too carried away. I mean . . .' She looked around self-consciously. 'What if someone should see us?'

'No one is going to see us here. We'd hear someone coming long before they saw us.' He leant in and kissed her tenderly. 'You're so beautiful, Margie. Don't you know what you do to me? I just want to be close to you. To touch you. To make you come alive with my touch.' He kissed her neck. 'I just want to make you happy,' he said.

'Oh, Alan, I want to make you happy too.'

'Do you trust me?'

She nodded. 'Of course.'

'Then show me.' He fingered the top button of her dress and looked at her pleadingly.

She should refuse. They weren't married and he hadn't even told her he loved her – not really. But he appeared so vulnerable right now and she did so want to please him. If she refused, maybe he'd realise she wasn't a real woman after all – just a silly little girl playing at being in love.

She gave him a tentative nod.

He smiled as he began to slowly unbutton her dress, his fingers ducking under the fabric and sliding teasingly over her bra as he did so. Her nipples tingled with a strange sort of pleasure, and she found herself leaning into his touch almost involuntarily.

When she was unfastened to her waist, Alan pushed the dress from her shoulders and sat back to look at her. 'Oh, god,' he breathed, 'you're exquisite. I want to see you in the flesh. Take off your bra.'

Margie shook her head shyly. No one had seen her completely naked since she was a child – not even her mother. The other girls in the chorus had teased her about her modesty when they'd first started rehearsals – she blushed every time she had to strip down to her underwear for a fitting. Now the show had started she'd become accustomed to the wardrobe people seeing her in her bra and knickers, but what Alan was asking was a step too far. 'I . . . I can't.'

'Don't be shy, my darling. This is what love between two adults looks like. We shouldn't be ashamed in front of each other. Would it help if I went first?' He began to unbutton his shirt without waiting for an answer.

His bare chest was toned and lightly tanned. He took her hand and placed it over his heart, which she could feel pounding. 'It's all yours, Margie. It beats for you.'

Emboldened by his vulnerability, she reached behind herself to unclasp her bra and then leant forward so it dropped off her shoulders.

'Oh god, Margie. Oh god, oh god.' He lurched forward and took both breasts in his hands, circling her nipples with his thumbs.

The sensation took her by surprise. This was wrong, but his touch felt remarkably right. A soft moan escaped her lips, which seemed to excite Alan even further. He kissed her passionately and then moved his mouth to her neck and finally her breasts. He took a nipple in his mouth and Margie gasped with shock . . . And inexplicable pleasure. She'd had no idea she could feel like this, that her body could respond in such a way to a man's touch.

As he teased her with his tongue, she found her breath coming in short pants. Alan's hands roamed all over her body, which felt as if it was on fire. She moaned again and he responded by sliding a hand under the skirt of her dress, and sliding it up her thigh until it reached the place that pulsed between her legs.

She froze. This was too far. 'Alan, no, stop. We can't go any further.'

'Come on, Margie, you like it, I can tell.' He began to stroke her over her underwear.

She clamped her legs together and he withdrew his hand with a frustrated huff. 'What's the problem? You were enjoying yourself a minute ago.'

She felt like such a child. 'It's just that we shouldn't without . . . I haven't . . . what if we make a baby?'

He laughed. 'Oh, darling, I promise you that won't happen.'

'I mean it, Alan. If there was a baby, we'd have to . . . I'm not ready to be a married woman yet.'

'Sweetheart, we're on the same page, believe me. Relax, I know what I'm doing.'

'It's not just that. I haven't ever. . . .' She dropped her gaze, unable to look at him.

'That's okay,' he said, his voice tender and cajoling now. 'I'll show you what to do and I'll be gentle, I promise. It might be a little uncomfortable at first but that won't last. I know how to show a girl a good time.'

Margie hesitated. 'I don't know if I'm ready for that.'

But Alan wasn't taking no for an answer. 'Baby, please, don't be a tease.' He took her hand, placed it on the front of his trousers and groaned. 'Feel that? See what you've done to me? I need you, Margie. I thought you cared about me. You're not just leading me on, are you?'

Tears pricked the back of her eyes. 'No. I didn't mean to. I do care about you, Alan. But I can't give myself up to someone unless . . .'

'Unless what?'

'Unless they love me.'

'Oh, baby, of course I love you. Would I ask you to do this if I didn't? The question is, do you love me too?'

She nodded. 'I do.'

'Well, then, show me how much. Be a good girl and open your legs.'

Chapter Thirteen

London
2019

'Madam, I'm afraid I must ask you to leave the store.' The young male voice comes from behind me. His tone is harsh, perhaps in a misguided attempt to convey authority.

I ignore him and continue perusing the sandwiches in the chilled goods section.

'Come on, now. Don't make me call security.'

I roll my eyes and turn to see a pimply-faced boy who has a plastic 'Manager' badge attached to his store uniform. 'I'm sorry, are you talking to me?'

'You know I am. I'm sorry, but it's time to move on. We don't want our paying customers being harassed.'

'Who am I harassing? I'm just trying to choose a sandwich.'

'You're blocking access to the chilled items.'

'Now you're just being ridiculous. How am I blocking access? I'm not a large woman.'

He wrinkles his nose and then blushes such a deep shade of red that his skin tone almost matches his acne.

And that's when I realise he's referencing my odour. The heat of shame stings my cheeks and I'm momentarily dumbstruck. The boy-manager and I stare at each other for a moment while I decide what my options are. I'm indignant at being asked to leave when I have the money to pay for a sandwich. I decide that if I'm not leaving here with something to eat, I will instead satisfy myself by having the last word. 'Listen, you snivelling little arse—'

'Dolly?'

I turn to see Jane striding up the aisle towards me with a bright smile plastered on her face and a look of steely determination in her eyes.

'Are you all right?'

I try to conceal my humiliation and smile at her. 'Jane, how lovely to see you.'

She glances at the boy-manager and then looks at me with real tenderness in her eyes. 'What's going on here? Is everything okay?'

'This *gentleman*—' I raise my eyebrows and nod in the direction of the manager '—seems to have some issue with me being in his store. All I want is to buy myself something to eat.' I hold up a plastic triangle containing a limp-looking egg and lettuce sandwich.

Jane pats my arm as if to say *Don't worry* and then turns her attention to the perplexed manager. 'This lady is with me, and I'd appreciate it if you'd show her the respect she deserves and let her shop in peace.'

'But—'

'But nothing,' Jane says firmly. 'Where are your manners? Didn't your parents teach you to respect your elders?'

He opens his mouth to speak, but Jane stares him down. He shrugs and walks away without uttering another word.

Jane shakes her head. 'Young people these days. I don't know . . .'

Now that the boy has backed down, the adrenaline that has been pumping through my veins begins to subside. I've got what I wanted – the chance to purchase a meal – but I don't feel victorious, I feel humiliated and ashamed. I need to get away from Jane before the tears begin to fall and I embarrass myself further. 'Thank you, my dear. That was very kind of you. I'd best get on and pay for my sandwich before that uppity boy changes his mind.' I turn and begin to hobble towards the checkout.

'Dolly, wait.'

I hesitate. Maybe I should pretend I haven't heard and just keep walking. I can't bear for her to see me this way. She seems to have formed the opinion that I'm an eccentric but interesting old lady. Perhaps she's wondered about my state of dress but dismissed it as a sign of senility. Now she will know the extent of my shame, and perhaps she will reconsider her offer to help me write my story. I don't want to contemplate that right now. I just want to go somewhere quiet and eat my sandwich.

'Dolly,' she says again, and there's a pleading tone in her voice.

I turn to face her. 'Yes, dear?'

'Are you okay? Please forgive me for saying this, but you don't look your best this morning.'

An involuntary sigh escapes my lips. Part of me wants to tell her the truth – that under these rags I call clothes I am battered black and blue. That I'm old and tired and almost at my wits' end. But what would be the point of that? No one ever solved a problem by wallowing in self-pity. I pull back my shoulders so I am standing up as straight as my arthritic spine will allow. 'Just one of those days. Perhaps I got out on the wrong side of the bed.'

She smiles weakly, clearly unconvinced by my false bravado.

'Things are looking up now,' I say brightly. 'Thanks to you I have my sandwich, and I'm headed to the library for the day, so all will be well.'

Jane nods. 'Okay. Good. It's just that, well – I'm not having the best day myself. You see, my husband is away and, to be honest, I'm a little bit lonely. I know you have plans to go to the library, but would you consider joining me for brunch at my place instead?'

I glance in her shopping basket and notice it's loaded with luxury items – a wheel of brie, water crackers, chicken liver pâté, two different types of dip and an expensive-looking tub of boysenberry swirl ice cream. 'Not planning a party, then?'

'What . . .?' Her gaze follows mine and she laughs. 'No . . . well, yes, actually – a pity party for one. But not until tonight. I'm definitely free for brunch. Why don't you put the sandwich back and I'll grab some eggs and bacon, and maybe some croissants?'

I have no doubt her offer comes from a place of charity, and usually I'd be too proud to accept, but today the thought of a warm house and decent food is simply too hard to knock back. I turn and shove the sandwich on the shelf behind me – in between the packets of shortbread and Jaffa Cakes – and grin at Jane. 'That'll give Mr High-and-Mighty something to do.'

She grins back at me. 'Right. Let's get ourselves some food and get out of this place.'

Chapter Fourteen

Melbourne, Australia
1960

As she ran to the centre of the stage for her final curtain call, the crowd roared. They were already on their feet and the sound of the applause was thunderous. Out here, everything was perfect. She felt like a star. Everyone loved her and all her problems melted away.

The past few months had been tumultuous, to say the least. Right now, she should be having the time of her life. On the surface she was living her dream. Sandy was right in her prediction that Margie would be chosen as Cara's understudy. Three weeks after opening night, Cara caught her heel in a tram track and ended up with a broken ankle. Margie tried not to be too delighted at her leading lady's misfortune, but Cara's broken bone was literally the break Margie had been waiting for her whole life.

She couldn't help but be excited. She intended to make the most of the opportunity, and so far that had been working out just fine. The reviews had been glowing, which kept the producers happy, and Raymond told her she should look for an agent because soon the offers would start rolling in. She was on her way!

Or, she would be, if not for the black cloud that hung over her every moment she wasn't on stage.

Sandy popped her head into the dressing room as Margie brushed out her hair. 'We're off to Raymond's flat for a nightcap. Are you coming?'

Margie shook her head. 'No, you go on without me. I've got an early start tomorrow. Raymond's given me a few days off.'

'Lucky you! Anything special planned? Have you got a new beau? High time, if you ask me. I know Alan seemed like a good sort, but there was something slippery about him. Can't say I was sorry to see him move on from the show. Besides, best not to get too hung up on any one bloke at your age, I reckon. It's much more fun to play the field. So'—she raised her eyebrows suggestively—'is there a new fella on the scene?'

Margie's stomach churned at the mention of Alan's name, and she had to focus on her breathing for a moment to quell the nausea. 'No, not a new fellow, I'm afraid. My mum's not well, so I'm heading home for a few days to help her with the kids.' Margie hated lying to her friend, but she thought it best to keep her story consistent. Less chance of being caught out that way.

Sandy looked aghast. 'Oh, love, I'm so sorry. Anything I can do?'

'No, she'll be fine, I'm sure,' Margie said, forcing some lightness into her tone. 'I'll be back in a couple of days. That's if Julie doesn't outshine me as leading lady – Raymond may not want me back.'

Sandy laughed. 'As if that would happen. Everyone knows you're the star of the show now.'

It was hard to believe, but what Sandy said was true. The show was winding up its Melbourne run at the end of the year and heading to Sydney. Not only was she cast in the lead role for the Sydney season, but two weeks ago Raymond had proposed she consider taking a bold next step in her career.

'Australia isn't big enough for a talent such as you, my girl. The world is your oyster, Margie. After we finish up the Sydney season I'm going back to England. Why don't you come with me? I really think you have what it takes to make it in the West End . . . Broadway, even. Think about it, won't you, lovey?'

Margie had nodded eagerly, and true to her word she gave it some thought. In fact, she'd barely thought about anything else. There was so much to consider. The West End and Broadway were what dreams were made of. She could barely believe she was being offered the opportunity. She'd be mad to say no. But what about her family? How could she leave them behind? And now there was this new problem, the one she was racing home to deal with. She needed to see her mother.

Margie boarded the train and took a window seat in an empty compartment. If the train wasn't too crowded, she might be lucky enough to have it to herself for the entire journey. She was not in the mood for small talk today. Normally she was excited to be making the trip home, but today her stomach was filled with butterflies.

An older man wearing a suit entered her compartment and doffed his hat. 'May I?' he asked, indicating the vacant seat opposite her. She gave him the barest of smiles. Hopefully that would give him the hint she wasn't up for any friendly chatter. She needn't have worried; he pulled out a newspaper and buried his head in it, leaving Margie to her thoughts.

There was no one to greet her when she disembarked at Geelong station. She hadn't told anyone she was coming. It felt strange, though, getting off the train and hailing a taxi alone. Normally Mum came to greet her.

Now that Margie was earning decent money, she'd talked her mother into letting her buy a car for the family. It wasn't as if she were rolling in cash, but she could afford to buy a small one second-hand.

Mum had been reluctant at first. 'What would be the point? We've managed fine without one until now. Besides, I'm not sure I remember how to drive. Bill only made me get my licence so I could ferry him and his mates back and forth from the pub. I haven't driven since he left and took the car with him.'

But Margie wouldn't take no for an answer. 'You'll be fine. It's like riding a bike – you'll remember once you get started. It'd be great for me to have a car to drive when I'm here, and it'd be so much easier for you. You could drive the kids to school on wet days instead of them having to walk in the rain. And imagine not having to lug the shopping up the hill. I'd feel so much happier if I knew your life was just a little bit easier. I worry it's all getting too much for you.'

Mum had laughed. 'Don't be silly. I'm fit as a fiddle, and we're all used to walking and catching the bus.'

'But it would be much more convenient. It'd help you get more mending work, too. You could charge more for a drop-off and pick-up service.'

She'd considered this, but then shook her head. 'The thought of it scares me, to be honest. So many accidents.'

'Not if you're careful, which you would be. Please, Mum, I'd love to do this for you. Give it some thought.'

It had taken a few weeks, but eventually Margie got her way. These days Mum seemed to be constantly behind the wheel of 'Herman' the little Hillman. Any excuse for a drive. She'd be cross when Margie turned up without giving her the opportunity to collect her, but Margie had feared if she'd phoned ahead her mother would guess something was wrong. She didn't want her mum worried for a moment longer than she needed to be.

It was just after ten o'clock when the taxi pulled up out the front of her childhood home. The kids would all be at school and hopefully her mother would be ready to put her mending or ironing aside for a few minutes so they could share a pot of tea. Difficult conversations never felt quite so terrible with a cup of tea in hand.

She walked up the driveway, noticing the slightly overgrown grass between the two concrete strips leading to the garage. She'd have to have a word with Ronny. It was his job to mow the grass and keep the garden neat.

'Yoo-hoo! Anyone home?' she called as she let herself in through the back door. The last thing she wanted to do was to scare her mother half to death with her arrival.

Mum rushed in from the living room. 'Margie! My goodness, what a surprise. What are you doing here? Is everything all right? They haven't put you off, have they?'

Despite her queasy tummy, Margie laughed. 'No, Mum. Nothing like that.'

'Just a day off, then? What a lovely surprise. Put the kettle on, would you, love? I'll just go and turn off the iron and we can have a nice cup of tea. Goodness – it's almost as good as Christmas morning having you here so unexpectedly.'

Margie's heart sank as she filled the kettle and put it on the stovetop. Her mother's joy would soon be shattered.

Once they were settled at the kitchen table, the tea drawing in the pot between them, Margie could no longer bear the strain of keeping her secret to herself. 'Mum,' she said, 'I came home today for a reason. There's something we need to talk about.'

'What's that, then?' Her mother's eyes momentarily met hers and then, as if she'd read her daughter's mind, her gaze lowered to Margie's stomach. 'Oh, no. Tell me it isn't true.'

Margie's eyes filled with tears. 'I'm so sorry, Mum.'

'And the father? Will he help?'

What was left of Margie's composure crumpled. 'It's over between us.'

'He left when he found out about the . . . your situation?'

She nodded without comment, not wanting to put her mother through the pain of listening to the sordid details. Alan wasn't going to be around, that was all she needed to know.

Her mother lowered her gaze and swore softly. 'Bastard.' After a moment's silence she looked up from her tea, her eyes glassy with unshed tears. 'Marjorie Dawn, how could you do such a thing?'

'I didn't mean for this to happen. Things just got out of hand somehow. It wasn't as if I wanted . . .' She trailed off, humiliated. How could she tell her mother she had unwittingly placed herself in a situation where her beau wouldn't take no for an answer? She opted for a slightly more sanitised version of the truth. 'He told me he loved me,' she continued. 'I . . . I was a fool. I believed him, but soon after . . . After he got what he wanted he told me he thought it would be better if we didn't see each other anymore.'

'How did you meet him? Is he part of the production?'

Margie sobbed. 'He was. He's gone now. I'm so sorry, Mama. I thought he loved me. I thought he was the one.'

Her mother's face softened. 'Oh, my darling, what a ratbag.' Eleanor stood up and went to the sitting room, returning with a freshly pressed handkerchief, which she gave to Margie. 'Here you are.' She bent down and lightly kissed the top of her head. 'Don't worry, my love. We will work this out together.'

Margie wiped her eyes and blew her nose. 'Mum, I can't have a baby. The Sydney season starts right after we finish up in Melbourne. That'll run for about six months they think, and then Raymond has asked me to go overseas with him.'

Her mother sat back on the chair with a thud and proceeded to put her head in her hands.

'Mum?'

She raised her face to look at Margie. 'Raymond? Isn't that going from the frying pan into the fire? He must be twice your age.'

'It's not like that. Raymond doesn't like . . .' She tried to think of a delicate way to explain that Raymond was not attracted to women, but decided she'd shocked her poor mum enough for one day. 'Let's just say he's not the marrying type. He's not trying to race me off. He thinks I have what it takes to make it to the big time. He's looking out for opportunities for me on the West End.'

'As in the West End in *London*? In your condition? You can't be serious!'

'Well, I wouldn't be pregnant then. He's talking about next year. After the Sydney run is over.'

'By then you'll have a newborn baby. I'm sorry, Margie. You are going to have to face facts. You need to forget about a career on the stage, I'm afraid. In fact, you may as well call your director right now and tell him you won't be coming back. Lord only knows how we will cope without your wage, not to mention another two mouths to feed around here, but we will. In this family we look after our own.'

103

Margie's voice trembled as she spoke the next words, terrified of what her mother's reaction might be. 'Perhaps there is another way.'

'Whatever do you mean? Even if the director would allow a pregnant woman on stage – which of course he won't as soon as you begin to show – I can assure you you won't be physically able to keep singing and dancing the way you do once you're a bit further along. And once you've had the baby, working on the stage will be out of the question. You need to do the right thing by the production and let them know as soon as possible so they can find a suitable replacement.'

'But what if I wasn't pregnant?'

'It's too late for that. You are.'

'But what if I *wasn't*? I've heard talk. One of the chorus girls, she . . . there was a rumour she was pregnant, but now she's not. I could ask—'

Her mother threw up her hands in horror. 'Do not even *finish* that sentence. I will not abide that type of talk in my house. You were naive and made a silly mistake – that is something I can understand and forgive. Lord knows I'd be a hypocrite if I didn't. But now you must accept the consequences of your mistake. Because to suggest anything else is blasphemous. I know I haven't brought you up to be particularly religious, but I thought I'd taught you right from wrong. Like it or not, you are a mother-to-be. The child in your belly is real. If you take any action to deliberately cause harm to that child, let alone . . . Well, that is a sin so great I'm not sure how I could forgive it. Do you understand me, Margie? If that's your choice, then you can no longer call this your home.'

Chapter Fifteen

London
2019

Jane's house is apparently close by, but last night's ordeal has taken its toll and I'm hobbling along at a snail's pace.

Jane walks slowly, stopping from time to time to give me a rest. When we get to the park we sit for a few minutes on a bench to watch the ducks on the pond, and once we get going again she takes time to pause and admire little things along the way, such as a colourful display of winter jasmine. She makes it seem as if this is the most natural thing in the world and that she is in no hurry to get home, which I appreciate.

Eventually we stop in front of a semidetached house with a manicured garden. 'Here we are,' she says.

I follow her through the gate and up the path to the glossy black front door. She opens it wide, stoops for a moment to pick up the post from the doormat and then stands aside and beckons for me to come in.

The hallway is bright and airy, and I can see a formal sitting room through the open double doors to my left. The room is decorated in a modern yet classic style – a pale-coloured sofa and two matching armchairs are strategically placed so that the ornate fireplace takes centrestage. A vase of flowers adorns the glass coffee table, and the table itself sits in the middle of a plush Persian rug.

'Let me take your coat,' Jane says.

The thought of exposing the extent of my dishevelment is too much. I shake my head. 'Thank you, dear, but no. These old bones do feel the cold.'

'I have the central heating going and I'll light the fire in the sitting room for a bit of extra warmth. The living areas do get quite warm, sometimes too warm for me.'

I hesitate. I don't want to be rude, but neither do I want Jane to see my shabby appearance and pity me more than she already does.

'I promise I'll take good care of your coat. We can hang it in the hall cupboard. I think you'll be more comfortable without it.'

Heavens, she thinks I don't trust her with my belongings. 'I have no doubt my coat will be safe, it's not that. It's just, well . . . this is embarrassing, but I'm not dressed to be visiting anyone today. I had a bit of . . . let's just say it was a rough night. This morning I was hungry, so I popped up the street to get a sandwich and that's when I met up with you. I'm not dressed for brunch.'

'Oh, goodness, don't worry about that. You're among friends here.'

There's such warmth and kindness in her eyes that I decide to take a chance. 'If you're sure you don't mind?'

'Not at all. You are perfectly fine just the way you are, Dolly, but if you are really bothered by your outfit, I could loan you some clothes. In fact'—she puts her hand to her waistline and looks thoughtful—'I've gained a few pounds lately and have some clothes that no longer fit. I was going to donate them. You'd be doing me a favour if you took them off my hands.'

Jane is by no means overweight and I wonder if she is fibbing. 'You must have been positively skeletal if this is you after gaining a few pounds.'

She waves away the comment. 'Oh, it's just a pesky few pounds around my middle. I dress to disguise it. But I've definitely gone up a size or two. I'm sure my old clothes would fit you.'

My desire to have something decent to wear overrides my shame at accepting this charity. 'I suppose if you have no use for them, I could take them off your hands.'

'Wonderful. Come and I'll show you to the guest suite. You can use the bathroom in there to change. We might as well leave your bag in there too, in case you need something from it.' Jane wheels my suitcase across the foyer and beckons for me to follow her up a set of stairs. After taking two steps up she stops and turns to look at me. 'Can you manage the stairs? There's a powder room downstairs, but the bathroom in the guestroom is much larger and I think you'll find it easier to get changed in there. But if you'd rather not endure the stairs . . .'

'No, I'm fine. Just slow, that's all.'

The stairs do present a bit of a challenge, but it's only one flight and I get to the landing without incident. I follow Jane down a long, carpeted hallway.

We pass several closed doors before Jane stops in front of one. 'Here we are,' she says, opening the door to a spacious bedroom. 'The ensuite is just through the sliding door. Feel free to freshen up if you'd like. There are clean towels in the cupboard. Please help yourself to toiletries, and there's a hairdryer under the sink if you need it. I'll just pop down the hall and get some clothes for you. Back in a jiffy.'

As soon as she leaves the room I open the ensuite door and take a moment to drink in the pure luxuriousness of my current situation. The bathroom is almost entirely white apart from the gigantic slate-grey floor tiles. There's a large freestanding bathtub and a separate shower as well. A low oval-shaped sink rests on a marble-topped vanity, which houses a wide set of drawers as well as two cupboards. This ensuite is every bit as nice as (and a good deal more modern than) my old bathroom in Belgravia. If this is the guest bathroom, what must the main one be like?

I open the cupboard under the sink to find a stack of fluffy white towels and wicker baskets filled with high-end toiletries – lotions, soaps, deodorant and toothbrushes, all still in their packaging. There's even a basket with assorted cosmetics.

I grab two towels from under the sink and place them on top of the vanity, and then turn on the shower. I undress while I wait for the water to heat up, leaving my filthy clothes in a pile on the floor. I wonder if Jane would be so kind as to let me use her laundry while I'm here. Perhaps I can say my machine is on the blink? Or maybe I could just tell her a version of the truth – that I'm between permanent abodes at the moment.

Who am I kidding? Jane has guessed the truth by now, I'm sure. I can see it in her eyes. She may not know the extent of my desperate situation, but she's certainly figured out I'm not simply some eccentric old retiree who likes to hang around the library.

I step into the shower and let the water run over me, closing my eyes for a moment to savour this pure bliss. I can't remember the last time I had a proper shower. There was one at the hostel I stayed in a few weeks back, but it was a communal bathroom and the lock on the door was broken. I was so worried someone would burst in on me that I couldn't relax. And the floor of the shower was grimy with mould.

I open my eyes and am ashamed at the brown water swirling down the drain. How has my life come to this? Not that long ago, I had my own beautiful bathroom. I chose my clothes for style and didn't have to think too carefully about how durable or costly they were. I had a soft, warm bed made up with high-thread-count Egyptian cotton sheets and a down-filled duvet. And I showered daily.

I pump a dollop of shampoo into my hand, lather my hair and gather my thoughts. Right now, I am okay. I am getting clean and will soon be dressed in fresh clothes. A meal is being prepared for me. None of these are small things. There are others out there on the streets who'd give anything for any one of them. Right now, I am safe. I need to focus on enjoying these gifts. I'll worry about what comes next when I get to it.

When I'm done showering, I wrap myself in a towel and spend ten minutes blow-drying my hair, and then twist it up into a low bun. I can't believe the difference it makes – I feel more like myself than I have in months. I brush my teeth with a new toothbrush and then dig around in the cosmetics basket to see what I can find. I discover a bottle of liquid foundation. I prefer a powder compact usually, but this will do just fine. It's darker than what I'd normally use, but when I pat it on with my fingers it covers the grazes reasonably well and I'm quite happy with the result.

I move into the bedroom and notice several garments laid out on the bed. My eyes prick with tears of gratitude when I see the quality of the outfits Jane's left for me. These are not old clothes fit for the rag bag, but beautiful, quality pieces.

The sheer delight of having new underwear is hard to describe. Once upon a time I took knickers and tights for granted. Now I'm thrilled to be putting on these new items over my freshly washed and moisturised skin. The bra is slightly too big – the girls aren't what they used to be – but it's clean and soft. So much better than the threadbare old thing I've been wearing. I choose a pretty pink blouse; silk – oh my stars! The fabric floats around me like a cloud. Jane has teamed the blouse with a grey woollen skirt, a little staid for my liking, but it's well cut and, besides, beggars can't be choosers. At this point I'm grateful for any item that is clean and dry.

I step into the skirt and suck in my breath slightly as I fasten the waistband over the tender bruise blooming on my skin. There are shoes, too, beautiful low-heeled courts, but when I try them on they're a little tight. I try on a pair of black, block-heeled mules instead and have better luck. For the finishing touches I go to my case and retrieve my lipstick and my necklace.

There.

I look like a middle-class grandmother, but I'm clean and present-able, which is something.

I follow my nose back to the kitchen and am rewarded with a delighted gasp from Jane.

'I *knew* that blouse would suit you. You look lovely, Dolly.'

'Thank you for the clothes, and for the use of your bathroom. I . . . well, let's just say I'm not living at my usual address right now, for various reasons, and I've missed having all the little luxuries of home.'

Jane nods but doesn't press any further. 'Brunch is almost ready. I've set the table in the breakfast nook – it's the sunniest part of the house.' She indicates a small round table in a glass alcove just beyond the kitchen. 'Why don't you go and take a seat and I'll bring in the food in just a moment.'

'Can I help with anything?'

She smiles and shakes her head. 'It's pretty much done. The bacon and croissants are in the warming drawer. I just need to scramble the eggs. It'll all be ready in a jiffy. There's juice and a pot of tea on the table. Feel free to help yourself.'

The table is set with Royal Doulton china. I recognise the pattern, Epiphany, because I used to own the same set. Or, I thought I did. As it turns out, the china – like everything else from my previous life – belonged to Julian. It's nice to see it again on Jane's table, though. Funny that of all the possible patterns for a breakfast set we both chose the same one. It's probably silly, but seeing the china makes me relax. I'm not out of place here – anything but. Jane and I are more alike than we are different. I might have had a few rough months, but I'm no ruffian. I still know how to breakfast like a civilised person.

I pour myself a cup of strong black tea and add a decent serving of milk. My first sip elicits an involuntary sigh of satisfaction just as Jane arrives carrying a basket of warm croissants.

She smiles. 'Good tea?'

'Just how I like it.'

She places the basket in the middle of the table. 'I'll be right back with the bacon and eggs.'

The food is not just warm and filling, it's restaurant-quality delicious. So good that I'm momentarily overwhelmed. I think about all the meals like this I have taken for granted. All the times I screwed up my nose and pushed food aside because the bacon was not crispy enough, or the eggs were too dry, or too runny. I think of all the small comforts I enjoyed without sufficient gratitude – central heating, warm slippers, tea in a fine china cup.

Jane is prattling on about what a beautiful sunny day it is, something about how she hadn't thought it would turn out so well. To my horror my eyes fill with tears that I can't stop from spilling down my cheeks.

She puts down her fork and reaches out to touch my forearm. 'What's the matter? How can I help?'

I shake my head. 'I'm fine. Just being silly. You've already helped so much. I'm just overwhelmed by your kindness.' I wipe the tears away with the back of my hand.

She jumps up and disappears into the large butler's pantry at the rear of the kitchen. When she returns she hands me a small packet of tissues. She sits down again and looks me in the eye. 'Dolly,' she says, 'you can trust me. There's obviously a lot going on in your life right now. If you want to talk about it, I'm more than happy to listen. You know what they say, a problem shared is a problem halved.'

'Don't mind me. I'm just a silly old woman in a bad situation of my own making. I don't expect a respectable person such as yourself would understand my plight – indeed, at times I find it quite unbeliev-able myself.'

'You might be surprised. I know quite a bit about bad situations.' I wait for her to elaborate, but she lowers her gaze and says no more.

As much as I want to understand what is causing her pain, I know how hard it can be to open up about the things that ail us. I straighten, pull back my shoulders and force myself to smile. 'I think we can both agree that right at this moment we are enjoying a lovely meal and decent company. Let's enjoy ourselves and not sully the moment with talk of sad times.'

She stares at me for a moment and then nods. 'You're right. Let's just focus on a wonderful brunch.'

I lift my glass of juice in salute. 'Cheers, Jane.'

She laughs and clinks her glass against mine. 'Here's to a beautiful new friendship.'

Chapter Sixteen

Geelong, Australia
1961

She still had a week to go and Margie had gone from dreading the birth to wishing it would just hurry up and be over. Not that she was looking forward to having an actual baby – the thought absolutely terrified her – but she was looking forward to getting her figure back, to sleeping on her stomach again and to this first part of the ordeal being behind her so she could get back to doing what she loved – performing.

Despite her mother's initial disappointment at Margie's 'condition', now that the birth was imminent Eleanor couldn't conceal her excitement. The new arrival was all she could talk about. Last night she'd been keen to discuss Margie's feeling about whether she was carrying a boy or a girl. 'It will be lovely to have a new baby in the house again,' she'd said as Margie eased herself into a chair to have her pre-bedtime cup of tea. 'Our Val would love a baby girl. The babe will be more like a sister than a niece to her.'

'The baby *will* be her sister or brother. Once it's out it's all yours, Mum. Isn't that what we agreed?'

'Well, yes, I'll be raising the baby *initially*, but I've been thinking;

once the kids and I join you in Sydney, there will be no need to conceal the baby's parentage. It's not as if anyone up there will know us. We could just say your husband has died. No one will be any the wiser.'

'You seem to forget I'm joining the show up there. I don't want anyone in the theatre to know.'

'But won't most of the cast be new?'

'Mum, the theatre world is small. If people got wind of the fact I'd had a baby out of wedlock it could kill my career, and then where would we be? If you want me to keep putting bread on the table, it'll be best for everyone if we just stick to the story. You'll raise the baby. I'll help as much as I can, but – girl or boy – it'll be your child.' She hoped her mother wasn't having second thoughts. Margie had no desire to raise this child as her own.

'Yes, well, that's certainly the plan for now, but I want you to know you can change your mind at any time. You don't know how you'll feel once the baby is born.'

Margie didn't reply. They'd had this conversation many times since Margie had first floated the plan with her mother.

Having Eleanor raise the baby was Raymond's idea. She'd delayed telling him for as long as possible, but once her waistline began to thicken she knew it was time to confess she was leaving the show and that she wouldn't be able to take on the lead in Sydney after all.

'Oh, darl, what a mess. You're committed to having it, then? Because I know a place—'

She shook her head. 'My mother would never forgive me.'

'Oh, love.' Raymond reached inside his jacket and dug out a pressed handkerchief, which he offered to her. 'So, what's the plan?'

She shrugged. 'Go home. Have the baby. Get whatever work I can to help make up for my lost income. I can go back to the mill, at least until the baby is born. After that I don't know. Luckily, I have some savings, so that should tide us over for a little while.'

He shook his head. 'And give up your dream? You have the most talent of any young woman I've ever worked with, Margie, and I'm not just saying that. You could have it all.'

113

'It's too late for that. Even if I wanted to . . . to get rid of it, I'm too far along. No doctor would do it.'

Raymond rubbed his chin. 'Just how far along are you?'

'Four months already.'

'Hmm, I wonder . . .'

'What is there to wonder? I've made my bed and now I must lie in it. I'm so sorry to let you down like this.'

Raymond shrugged. 'I don't know. Maybe there's another solution. You wouldn't consider adopting out the little one? I mean, he won't have a father and without your stage career it'll be hard to make ends meet. Perhaps it'd best for everyone to let the little fellow have a fresh start with someone else. There are plenty of childless families dying to adopt.'

It wasn't as if this idea hadn't crossed her mind, but her mother had warned her against it. 'You don't know what it feels like to be a mother,' she'd said. 'Your child comes from you, is part of you. Giving your baby to a stranger will be like giving away your soul. The shame of being an unwed mother will pass in time, but the damage done by giving away your child might never heal.'

Not having any other experience to draw on, Margie took her mother at her word. She didn't feel any attachment to the baby so far, but Mum said that was because she hadn't felt it move yet.

She shook her head sadly at Raymond. 'I don't think I can do that.'

He wasn't ready to give up on finding a solution. 'What about your mum?'

'What do you mean?'

'She's still pretty young, isn't she? I remember thinking that when I first met her.'

'So?'

'Couldn't she take the little one off your hands? She could look after the baby while you worked to support the whole family.'

'I don't think so. My mum's got enough on her hands with my siblings. I can hardly expect her to look after my illegitimate child while I swan off having a lovely time of it. I wouldn't ask her, even if I thought she might say yes.'

'Just think about it, would you? Honestly, doll, with your talent it won't take long for you to be a star on the West End, maybe even Broadway. I'm talking to producers about a new show which would premiere in the West End year after next. They want me to direct. I can get you in – maybe not as the lead but definitely in the chorus. I don't know how long the show will run, of course, but you could come for a few months and see what you think. Once you're established, you could bring your whole family over to stay if you'd like. It'll be decent money. Think about what a difference that could make to your baby's life. To your whole family.'

Margie had dismissed the idea out of hand, but on the day of her final performance, Raymond had pressed her again. 'Come on, love. Don't give up on us. We make a great team. We can make this work.'

As crazy as the idea sounded, she was becoming increasingly worried about how her family was going to survive once her savings dried up. Before this had happened she'd been dreaming of a better life for her siblings. Neil was a smart little fellow. So clever that she'd dreamt of him being able to attend university, if that's what he wanted. And she didn't want Val having to leave school early like she'd had to. Ronny loved all things mechanical; she'd hoped maybe one day he could have his own garage or workshop. But none of that could happen now and it was all her fault. She owed it to her family to at least run the idea past her mother.

Mum was more amenable to the idea than she'd imagined. 'I have to say, I had been worried about where the money was going to come from to feed two more mouths once your savings are gone. I didn't tell you this sooner because I didn't want to worry you, but the landlord is making noises about selling this place next year. Says he's going to retire and wants the money to build a big house in Queensland. It might be hard to find something to rent if we don't have a dependable income.'

'Oh, Mum. I'm so sorry. I can't believe I got us into this mess.'

'I don't blame you, love, truly I don't. You were naive and made a mistake. What's done is done, we just need to find a way forward. Maybe this plan of Raymond's isn't so crazy after all.'

And so they'd made a pact. Margie would leave the show and go home to have the baby. Once she was sufficiently recovered from the birth she'd head to Sydney – hopefully in time to rehearse before opening night. Eleanor and the children would follow a month or two later; that way it would be easier for Eleanor to pass off the baby as her own. Margie would be spared the stigma of having an illegitimate child and there would be no impediment to her career. If all went well, she might even be able to continue on to London after the Sydney season.

Margie was thrilled with this arrangement. Her only concern was her mother bearing the brunt of the gossip that would inevitably accompany the baby's arrival.

'What about your reputation, Mum?'

Her mother had laughed. 'I'm a woman with an absent husband and kids to two different fathers. Don't tell me people 'round here aren't already talking about me.'

'But you haven't done anything wrong.'

'Margie, I'd much rather people's tongues wagging about me than you. You've got your whole life ahead of you. It's better this way for us all. Believe me.'

Margie had been home for a couple of months now and felt as if she could barely wait another day to get back to her real life. So far, the maternal feelings her mother had predicted had not eventuated. She couldn't imagine being a mother and, rather than growing more attached to the infant as its arrival grew closer, she found herself feeling resentment towards it.

She hated how her body had changed, and sometimes at night, when she felt the child moving inside her, she was transported back to that day on the banks of the creek. When she thought about this child's conception she was filled with revulsion. She couldn't wait to expel it from her body.

It wasn't the baby's fault, she knew that. But she very much doubted she would ever be able to love the child the way it deserved. She didn't want it. And if she was being honest with herself, she regretted not getting rid of it when she'd had the chance. She should never have told Mum. She should have confided in Sandy instead and taken care of the matter herself. It wasn't as though she didn't have the contacts or the money. But it was no use dwelling on that now. The baby would be here soon and her mother was the perfect choice to raise it.

The baby kicked her under her ribs, causing her to wince in pain. It was as if the child knew it wasn't wanted and was doing its best to make her life miserable. Last night had been particularly uncomfortable. It'd been blistering hot in her bedroom and her back was aching. Which was no surprise given all the weight she was carrying. Her stomach was the size of a gigantic watermelon. It was so big it threw her off centre and made her walk funny. She waddled around the house like a giant duck.

Despite her fatigue, Margie dragged herself out of bed to help the kids get ready for their first day back at school after the summer holidays.

Mum looked up from the bread she was buttering and smiled as Margie entered the kitchen. 'You look tired, love.' Her mother's face was lined with concern. 'Why don't you go back to bed? I can manage this lot on my own. They're all getting bigger now and can do most things for themselves.'

'I like to help,' Margie said, and it was true. She was grateful to her mother for giving her the opportunity to return to the theatre and she wanted to show her appreciation.

'There's not much to do. I think everyone's just about ready. Looks as if there's a storm coming, so I think I'll drive the kids to school this morning. If you want to help you can do these dishes for me. Take your time, I won't be back for a while. I'm going to stop by Dickens and get a few things for dinner while I'm out.'

Margie smiled. It pleased her no end to see her mum making use of the car. She helped finish packing the lunch boxes and then rounded up the little ones, planting goodbye kisses on Val's and Neil's heads, but Ronny dodged her, saying he was too big now for 'all that sissy muck'. She waved them goodbye and waddled her way back to the kitchen.

Once the dishes were done and the floor swept, the cool change blew in from the south. Margie opened all the windows to let in the cool breeze and then decided to try to make up for some of the sleep she'd missed out on the night before. It didn't take her long to drift off.

Sometime later the sound of the screen door slamming startled her awake. Either it was the wind, or Mum was home. While she was sleeping the rain had started up. She could hear it clattering on the tin roof above. She eased herself out of bed to investigate.

In the kitchen she was startled to find not her mother but Granny pulling down the window sash. As far as Margie knew, Granny had never set foot in this house before. Why was she here now? 'Granny?'

Her grandmother jumped in fright and then swung around to look at her.

'Marjorie! You scared me half to death. I didn't know you were . . .' She stopped speaking as her gaze rested on Margie's protruding belly. 'Lord, give me strength.' She stumbled forward and grabbed the back of one of the kitchen chairs to steady herself, and for a moment Margie was worried she might be having a heart attack.

'Granny, are you all right?'

Her grandmother gave a small shake of her head as she seated herself at the table. She took a couple of deep breaths and then looked at Margie. 'No need to ask why you are home. How far along are you?'

'I'm due any day.'

Granny dropped her head into her hands at the same moment as Margie's cheeks began to burn.

'Granny, I know this looks bad, but it's not the end of the world. No one knows – well, hardly anyone – and Mum's going to pass off the baby as her own. She'll raise it while I go back to work. Nobody needs to find out.'

Granny lifted her head and, to Margie's shock, her face was tear-stained. She couldn't remember seeing her grandmother cry before – she was stoic even at Grandpa's funeral.

'Sit down, Marjorie.'

'I'd rather stand, if you don't mind. My back feels better when I'm on my feet.'

'Margie,' she said in a kind but firm tone. 'I have some news to tell you, and I think you should sit down before I do so.'

Slightly bemused – her grandmother had never once called her anything other than Marjorie – Margie did as she was asked. 'What's the news?'

'There was a terrible accident this morning up on Pakington Street, not too far from my house. A truck collided with a car and all the occupants of the car were killed instantly.'

'Oh, Granny, that's awful. Did you see it happen? Is that why you're upset?'

Granny shook her head. 'No, I didn't see it happen, but a neighbour came to fetch me.'

'Why did they do that?' Margie's brow creased in confusion.

Granny's face was ashen. 'The driver of the car was your mother, my dear.'

It took her a moment to comprehend her grandmother's words. As their meaning slowly dawned on her she felt the air being sucked from her lungs. 'You mean . . .?'

He grandmother nodded. 'They're gone. Your mother, your brothers and your sister were killed instantly. The one consolation is that they wouldn't have suffered. May their souls rest in in peace.'

Chapter Seventeen

London
2019

I sip my tea, occasionally pausing to dab the corners of my mouth delicately with the crisp linen napkin. Maybe it's overkill, but I want Jane to see I'm a civilised person with manners, despite my current state of misfortune.

Our conversation is light but nevertheless erudite. I ask Jane what she likes to read and I'm delighted to discover we have some favourites in common. I describe my old library in the Belgravia flat and pity seeps into her eyes, so I laugh and say there's no need to hoard books when I have an entire public library at my disposal.

She smiles at me. 'Would you like to move to the sitting room? We can make ourselves comfy in there and settle in for a nice chat.'

This is my cue to leave. Jane is too well mannered to say so, but I've overstayed my welcome. 'I should go. I don't want to hold you up.'

It's Jane's turn to laugh awkwardly. 'Hold me up? Not at all. I have all the time in the world. In fact, having you here is a treat. My husband is away, and . . . I'm not sure when he'll be back.' A defeated sort of expression settles on her face. 'To be honest, I'm at a bit of a loose end and I'd love some company.'

Perhaps we're getting closer to the source of Jane's secret pain. I'm intrigued. Besides, I'm in no hurry to leave the warmth and security of her home.

I nod. 'The sitting room it is, then.'

We settle ourselves in the beautiful room at the front of the house. She ushers me into an armchair and implores me to put my feet up on the ottoman and make myself at home. I take her up on this suggestion, sliding the borrowed slingback mules off my feet and placing them on the floor beside me. The abundance of riches I've been afforded this morning – the shower, clean clothes, a full belly and now this wonderfully comfortable chair – have had a soporific effect and I find my eyelids becoming heavy.

Jane busies herself with the fire for a moment and then settles on the sofa. 'I'm so pleased you're here,' she says. 'I have something I want to talk to you about.'

'Oh?' I say, curious.

'I'm afraid I have a confession to make.'

My drowsiness instantly vanishes. Perhaps she's going to tell me what is bothering her and why her husband has taken off. 'Go on, then.'

'It's just that . . . well, the first time we met at the library, I had the feeling we'd met before, but I couldn't place you. A few days later, I was watching an old episode of *The Neighbourhood* and I saw a woman who looked like a younger version of you. I looked up the cast on the internet and I discovered the name of the actress who played Mrs Mackin is Dolly Jamieson. I kept researching and discovered that, in her younger days, Dolly Jamieson starred in several West End musicals. Dolly isn't a name you hear every day, and you'd already told me you'd had a career in the theatre, so I was almost certain . . . but then—'

I cut her off before she can say it. 'Then you thought it couldn't possibly be true. How could an old bag like me have been an actress on the TV?' I laugh to show that this is perfectly understandable.

Patches of crimson appear on the apples of her cheeks. 'No, that's not it at all. It's just that they were quite old episodes, and people change, so I couldn't be sure, and I didn't want to embarrass you by asking. But looking at you today – with your hair done and some make-up on – the resemblance is uncanny. You're her, aren't you? You're Dolly Jamieson.'

'The one and only.'

Jane clasps her hands in delight. 'I knew it. Oh, Dolly, this is amazing! What stories you must have to tell. Now I know who you are, I'm much more confident that we'll be able to sell your book to a publisher.'

'Do you really think that's possible?'

'With a bit of luck, maybe it is. People are always interested in the backstory of famous people. Who knows, you could be sitting on a bestseller. Wouldn't that be nice?'

It would. I assume Jane's thinking of the money, which of course I am too, but I'm thinking of the readers as well. Or, more specifically, the one reader I really care about. 'Let's not get too far ahead of ourselves. We have to write the thing first.'

Jane smiles. 'It's going to be wonderful. Just you wait and see. I'd be happy to start today if you'd like?'

I stifle a yawn. It seems the events of the past twenty-four hours have suddenly caught up with me and I'm exhausted. If I head back to the library, I can get a few hours' kip in my favourite chair before nightfall. 'I'm sorry. I didn't sleep well last night. Perhaps I should get going. We can meet at the library tomorrow as planned and make a start then.'

'Of course. That's fine, whatever suits you. We don't have to work on the book today, but I was rather hoping to encourage you to stay a little longer. It's so nice having you here. In fact, I was wondering if you might stay on for dinner? It would lovely to have someone to cook for.' She shakes her head and drops her gaze to the floor. 'Sorry. You're probably beginning to think I'm some weird stalker. It's just that Richard – my husband – often works late. It's barely worth cooking for one, so half the time I sit in front of the telly, stuffing my face with junk instead of eating a proper meal.' She's talking quickly now, seemingly embarrassed to admit this. 'And now he's away for goodness only knows how long. So, if you have no other plans, I'd love to make you dinner. If you're worried about making your way home after dark, you'd be welcome to spend the night in the guestroom. But please don't feel obliged. I'll completely understand if you don't want to.'

The thought of a warm bed for a whole night is irresistible. 'I would absolutely love that,' I say.

Jane visibly relaxes. 'Great. Lovely. Now, you said you were tired. Would you like to go upstairs now and take a little nap?'

I shake my head. 'I feel content right where I am. I'd just as soon stay here, if you don't mind me nodding off in your sitting room? I fear that I won't be able to keep my eyes open much longer, no matter how much I want to keep chatting with you.'

'Perfect.' She beams. 'You stay right where you are, and I'll go and start planning what to make for dinner. I'll be in the kitchen if you need me.' She stokes the fire and pops on another log before leaving me to it.

●

A baby is crying. Somewhere. I can hear him, but I can't find him. I run through my childhood home, looking in every room. In my bedroom I hear cries coming from inside the wardrobe and fling open the door. My cat, Teddy, springs out and startles me.

'Chicken! Get out of there.'

I awaken with a jolt. For a moment I can't get my bearings and I wonder if I'm still asleep, but then I remember I'm in Jane's home. I have no reason to be unhappy and yet I feel decidedly melancholy.

'Sorry, Dolly, if that blasted cat woke you. He's not mine. He belongs to one of the neighbours, but he slides in here any chance he gets.'

I shake my head and smile, attempting to push my blue mood away. 'I'm fond of cats. I was dreaming of my old boy, Teddy, in fact.'

'Well, this boy is going outside. Please go back to sleep if you're still tired.'

I sit up properly and remove the blanket Jane must have placed over my legs. 'I'm feeling quite refreshed, thank you. What time is it?'

'Just after three.'

'Good grief. I've slept half the day away.'

'You obviously needed it.'

'Well, I'm all caught up now. But don't mind me if you have things to do. I'm used to entertaining myself.'

'Nothing to do but enjoy your company. I've done all the dinner prep and have popped a bottle of champagne in the fridge to chill, so we're all set for this evening. I think it's about time for afternoon tea, unless you have a better idea.'

I think about my muddy clothes heaped on the floor of the guest bathroom. 'Afternoon tea would be lovely, but before we get to that I have an enormous favour to ask.'

Jane beams as if she can't think of anything more delightful than doing a service for me. 'Name it.'

'The accommodation I've been using recently doesn't have laundry facilities and I'm wondering if I might use yours, if it's not too much trouble?'

There's a brief flash of pity in her eyes but she does her best to pretend otherwise, which I appreciate. 'Yes, of course. I'll put a load on for you.'

I baulk at the thought of her handling my tattered and putrid garments. 'Oh, goodness, there's no need for that. I'm happy to do it myself. Just point me in the direction of your washing machine and I'll sort out the rest.'

Thankfully she doesn't argue, but instead shows me to the laundry room, which looks out over the garden. She says she's going to organise a platter of nibbles for afternoon tea. I head upstairs to collect my clothes from the spare bedroom. When I reach the landing, I stop to give my creaking knees and throbbing hip a rest. I hate to complain about old age when I know it's a privilege not everyone is given, but when I think of how easily my body once moved compared to now, it's difficult not to feel a twinge of longing for what used to be.

I make my way along the hallway, trying to recall which of the many doors leads to the guestroom. I remember it was on the right-hand side, but other than that I'm not sure. I choose a door halfway down the corridor and try the handle. The door swings open and reveals a bedroom, but not the one I was in earlier.

This room clearly belongs to a teenager, and it has a distinctly masculine feel. There's a single bed made up with black-and-white linen, and a grey patterned rug covers the floor. A framed photo of a sportscar hangs above the bed and there's a guitar propped up against the wall beside it. Shelves above the corner desk house books and trophies.

I'm taken aback by this discovery. Jane has not mentioned a son. In fact, she denied having any children when I asked her. For a moment her denial makes no sense, but as I continue to stare into the room, it becomes apparent. The room isn't lived in. The pristine bedlinen, the excessively neat desk, the carefully placed trophies and ornaments give me the sense that this room hasn't been used for a long time. Perhaps the boy is off at university and his room is left like this for him to use during semester breaks. But there's a chill in the room that suggests otherwise.

Perhaps this room is the key to the pain in Jane's eyes. My heart aches for her at the thought, but somehow in my bones I know my fear is true. Jane's boy is lost to her.

Chapter Eighteen

Geelong, Australia
1961

In the days after the accident, Margie spent as much time asleep as she could. It was her only respite from a grief so intense she feared it might suffocate her.

Granny had been wonderful. She'd taken Margie into her home and cared for her like she was a small girl. Granny had also organised (and paid for, Margie presumed) her family's funeral. Margie didn't attend, choosing to stay in bed instead. Granny hadn't tried to persuade her otherwise. 'It's probably for the best considering . . . well, let's just say the fewer people who know about your condition, the better. I'll tell everyone you are too distressed to come. No one will question that.'

Margie didn't care what people thought. She couldn't see the point of singing hymns, saying prayers or weeping over an open grave. None of that would help. It wouldn't bring her family back.

All she wanted to do was sleep.

The evening after the funeral, Granny brought Margie's supper to her in bed. She'd been surprisingly undemanding since delivering the heartbreaking news of the accident, but Margie suspected that wouldn't last forever. Tonight, rather than leave Margie to pick at her meal in peace, Granny hovered by the end of the bed. 'Margie,' she said. 'I know this is hard, but we need to have a conversation about what will happen after . . . after the birth.'

Margie couldn't bear to think about it. 'I don't care,' she said. It shamed her to say this, but it was the truth. She couldn't think about this baby with anything other than regret.

With a pang she heard her mother's words in her memory. *We look after our own.*

Giving up on her child felt like a betrayal of her mother, but what could she do? Right now, she wasn't sure she could care for herself, let alone a baby. 'Do whatever you like. All I know is I can't look after a child.'

Granny didn't seem too shocked at this declaration. 'A wise choice, I think. I'll see what I can find out. Judging by the size of you, we haven't got a lot of time to organise things.'

Granny made some discreet inquiries through her church, but nothing had been finalised, so when Margie went into labour – a full week after her estimated due date – the child's fate was yet to be decided.

She laboured in the very room in which she'd been born, but this time the home birth was planned. Easier to keep the child's arrival quiet that way, Granny said.

Margie was shocked at the violence of it all.

Mum had tried to explain labour to her, but she'd glossed over a lot of the details. Such as just how painful and primitive the whole thing was. Margie had no idea she'd sweat and pant and grunt the way she had. When the pains had first started, she'd railed against them, not yet ready to face the consequences of her labour, but there was no stopping it. Her body pressed on regardless.

Granny mopped the sweat from her brow and told her when to push. She wasn't exactly sympathetic to Margie's plight, though. 'Stop wasting your precious breath making that awful noise,' she said when Margie screamed out in pain. 'Use that energy to push instead and it'll all be over before you know it.'

Margie tried to do as her grandmother instructed. All she wanted was to get this thing out of her. When the next pain took hold she closed her eyes and focused on pushing, and as she did so, she felt a burning sensation between her legs.

'That's the way,' Granny said. 'Concentrate on bearing down.'

But Margie was far away; back on the riverbank with Alan's sweaty body thrusting into her. She opened her mouth and let out a blood-curdling scream.

Granny slapped her face. Hard.

She opened her eyes in shock but there was no time to protest. The next pain was upon her already and this time she kept her eyes open.

On and on it went, Margie silently crying through the injustice of it all. Eventually, after a final searing pain that caused Margie to truly fear she was being split in two, the baby slipped out into her grand-mother's steady hands. 'A boy,' Granny announced matter-of-factly. She covered him with a clean towel and laid him on the bed until the afterbirth came (another thing Margie had known nothing about). Granny snipped the cord, tied it off and then took the baby to bathe and swaddle him.

Margie rolled onto her side to face the wall. When her grand-mother returned and asked if she wanted to see the baby, Margie shook her head. 'I'm tired,' she said. 'Take him away.'

'Yes, I think that's probably for the best. You get some rest. I'll put him down in my bedroom and come back to change the sheets.'

Hours later, Margie woke feeling ravenous. She realised she hadn't eaten since early that morning, and it was now quite dark – past dinner-time, she presumed. She eased herself out of bed, found her dressing gown and slippers and headed to the kitchen to make a sandwich.

Granny had her back to the door and didn't notice Margie enter the room. She was sitting at the kitchen table, rocking the swaddled infant and talking to him in a tone Margie had never heard from her. Her voice was soft and gooey as she stroked the baby's face and said, 'Who's a handsome fellow, then? Yes, you are. Just like your grand-daddy. You're the spitting image of my James, little one. Yes, you are.'

'Granny?'

Her grandmother swung her head around to look at Margie. 'Oh. There you are.' The soft tone was gone, but Margie noted her eyes were shiny with unshed tears. 'He was a bit unsettled, so I've fed him some sugar water and I was just going to put him down again. He's not due for a proper feed for another hour. I'll put him back in the basket now.' She cleared her throat and stood up.

Margie couldn't help but sneak a glance at her son's face as her grandmother took him from the room. She wanted to see this remarkable baby, the one who had the power to turn her iron-willed grandmother into mush.

Margie couldn't see any resemblance to her father. She hadn't known him as an adult, let alone a newborn baby. As she looked at the infant's face she was reminded of someone, though. A vision of Alan's red face, beaded with sweat as he tore her underwear from her, flashed before her eyes.

Margie turned her head away and resolved not to look at the child again.

•

Two days later, Margie was jolted awake by a wailing sound. Usually, the infant's cries were short lived, but when the noise continued for several minutes, Margie reluctantly got out of bed to see what was going on. She hadn't seen much of the baby since the day he was born. Granny had been caring for him, insisting Margie take her time to recover. Margie hadn't argued and had tried to stay as far away from the child as possible.

After some investigations and advice from the minister at her church, Granny had chosen an adoption agency. The baby was to go to some sort of babies' hospital, where the woman in charge had assured Granny he would quickly be placed with a new family.

Margie slowly made her way to the kitchen. Her private parts were still tender, and she felt battered and bruised all over. If that wasn't bad enough, overnight her breasts had swollen to the size of bowling balls, and two wet patches had appeared on her nightie. Her milk must have come in properly while she slept and now the baby's cries were causing her breasts to throb. When she didn't find her grandmother in the kitchen, she searched the rest of the house – even looking in the garden – without luck.

The wailing was becoming louder and harder to ignore. Margie went back to the kitchen and shut the door behind her, but she could still hear him. Defeated, she plonked herself down on a chair at the kitchen table. There was a note propped up against the fruit bowl.

Gone to the butcher. Back at eleven.

The adoption people are coming today so please make yourself presentable.

Margie began to cry. It was ten-thirty now and she didn't think she could bear another half an hour of listening to the wailing. What if she took herself off for a walk? Perhaps the baby would just cry himself back to sleep. But what if the adoption people arrived and there was no one home? She couldn't risk that. The sooner they came and took this squalling infant away, the better.

Perhaps if she picked up the basket and put it in the garden he'd be happier. And if he wasn't, she'd at least be able to eat her breakfast in relative peace. She made her way out of the kitchen and up the hallway to her grandmother's room, where the baby was in the carry basket her grandmother had borrowed from one of the church parishioners. Apparently, Granny had told them she was caring for a sick relative's baby for a week or two. As Margie bent to pick up the basket, the infant's squawks became louder still and – to her horror – milk began to drizzle from her left breast.

'Shh,' she said. A thought struck her. Perhaps his nappy needed changing. As a baby, Neil would often cry inconsolably when his little bottom was wet. Reluctantly, she lifted the child from his carrycot to check. To her surprise, the infant quietened. Instinctively she pulled him closer and began to rock him. Perhaps this was all he needed to get him back to sleep. She cradled him in her arms and began to gently pat his still-dry bottom. The baby, quiet for now, nuzzled into her bosom and began moving his head from side to side. Without warning he let out an ear-splitting cry. Margie was left in no doubt about what he wanted.

'No,' she said, more to herself than to the child. 'I can't. I won't.'

But with her breasts aching and the child screaming she found herself wondering if it would really be so bad to relent and feed him. Her grandmother had been feeding the baby some sort of infant formula, which Margie had no idea how to prepare. Her mother had always breastfed the babies when they were newborns, so Margie had no experience with bottles and special preparations. She couldn't bear this screaming for one minute longer, and her breasts were crying out to be drained. 'All right, all right. You win,' she said gruffly to the red-faced tyrant in her arms.

Still standing, she cradled him using one hand, while she loosened her robe and pulled open her nightie with the other. The baby knew what he wanted and needed little encouragement to find her nipple. He opened his tiny mouth wide and she manoeuvred his head with her hand until he was in exactly the right spot. He clamped his mouth closed, causing a moment of exquisite pain before he began to suck and her body was flooded with unexpected euphoric pleasure. Carefully, she made her way to the armchair in the corner of her grandmother's bedroom and eased herself into the seat.

At first she was lost in relief as the pain in her breast subsided, but after a little while she began to focus on the baby himself. As he suckled, a tiny thread of attachment began to form. She studied his little face and, when he opened his eyes, she fancied she could see a trace of her sweet baby brother Neil in them. Perhaps, if she tried very hard, she could forget all about the child's father and love him for himself. Her mother had managed to love the children Bill had fathered, even though the man was an utter scoundrel. Maybe she could do the same. If she could just put that awful day behind her, somehow block out the moment her virginity was torn from her, perhaps she could learn to love this little one.

Once her left breast felt more comfortable, she detached her son, who took no time in demonstrating his disapproval. She quickly offered him the other side and within minutes her child was drifting off into a milky sleep, his suckling becoming more lethargic with every second that passed. To her surprise, Margie found she didn't want him to stop. She didn't want this moment to be over. She knew she should detach him and put him back in the basket on the floor, but she couldn't bring herself to do it. This was likely the only time she would feed her son. She wanted to take some time to remember.

It wasn't supposed to be like this. Yes, she'd got herself into trouble, and she'd never expected having a baby would be easy. Mum had promised she'd be there to help and that Margie needn't be afraid. She said she'd be there every step of the way.

The plan had been for Margie to go back to work – they needed the money, after all – but Margie wasn't going to be completely separated from her child. Not forever, at any rate. The way Granny was talking, it was as if she expected Margie to go back to the theatre and just forget that she'd ever had a baby.

And that was what she wanted too, wasn't it?

Suddenly, she wasn't so sure. Perhaps this little child was a chance for a new start? The chance to create her own family now that she'd lost her mother and siblings.

'What on earth do you think you're doing? Get away from him right now.' Granny's voice seethed with anger as she swooped in and snatched the baby from Margie's lap.

'He was crying. I didn't know what else to do.'

'Babies cry, Marjorie. It doesn't hurt them. You know what does hurt them? Being brought up by wanton women with no morals. You're a prime example of that misfortune. My James made a big mistake when he planted his seed in your mother's belly. She wasn't worthy of him, but she seduced him and then you were on the way, so he had no choice but to marry her. He could have had his pick of fine young women, but she caught him out. It breaks my heart to say this, but you've turned out to be just like her. I won't have you taint this poor little man the same way. He's the last link I have to my James and I simply won't allow you to ruin his life.'

The baby was crying again, and Margie found herself unable to hold back her own tears. The accusation about her morality stung. She'd always thought of herself as a good girl, but Granny was right. She'd been foolish. She should never have let Alan touch her the way she had without having a ring on her finger. This was all her fault. 'I'm sorry.'

Her grandmother swayed back and forth now, trying to soothe the baby. When she replied, her voice was quiet but determined. 'In a few hours someone from the agency will be here. You will sign the papers without a word, do you hear me? For heaven's sake, Margie, do you think I *want* to give away my great-grandchild? Of course I don't, but there's no choice. Not if he's to have the life he deserves.'

Hot tears blurred Margie's eyes. She knew Granny was right, and she certainly didn't want to be saddled with a child all on her own, but when she'd fed the baby just now she'd felt something, an attachment she wasn't sure she was ready to give up on just yet. 'What if he ends up with a family who neglects him? I'd never forgive myself.'

'I won't let that happen. I've thoroughly vetted the agency and offered to pay for the boy's education myself, provided I'm kept up to date on his progress twice a year. This is the best outcome for us all.'

'I'm not sure—'

'For pity's sake, girl, think of your child. What other choice is there? If you raise him as your own, he'll always be illegitimate. How can he ever rise above that? If you truly care for him, you'll think about his future and not your own selfish wants.'

Margie didn't have an answer to that.

'There's one more thing I've been meaning to say, Marjorie. I'm not a monster – I won't kick you out onto the street – however, I think it would be best for all of us if you leave here as soon as you are well enough.'

Chapter Nineteen

London
2019

In the light-filled laundry room I stand in front of the washing machine and contemplate how I might ask Jane if she has a son. Part of me wonders if I should even attempt it. She's clearly avoided talking about him before, so maybe she's not ready to discuss what happened – if, in fact, anything did happen. Perhaps my gut feeling is wrong, and the boy is simply away backpacking. There could be any number of explanations for why he's not living here.

And perhaps it's not my place to meddle. But Jane seemed so distraught that first day in the library, and even though she's tried her best to hide it ever since, I can still see the pain in her eyes. If I'm right and she's lost a child, perhaps it would do her good to talk about it. After all the kindness she's extended to me, the least I can do is provide a sympathetic ear. Sometimes it's easier to share your troubles with a relative stranger – there's less to lose that way.

She appears in the doorway. 'How are you going in here? Finding everything you need?'

'Yes, thank you. It took me moment to work out your machine but I got there in the end.'

'Good. Ready for a cup of tea, then?'

'Lovely.'

I follow her to the dining room, where I discover a beautifully set table. A different china setting to the one we used at brunch – a classic Wedgwood pattern – is laid out on a crisp linen cloth. A vase filled with white chrysanthemums adorns the middle of the table and next to it is a tiered cake stand with finger sandwiches and little quiches on the bottom, homemade biscuits and slices on the next tier, and pastel-coloured macarons on the top. Jane pulls out a chair and indicates for me to take the seat opposite.

'My goodness, Jane, this looks wonderful. I feel as if I'm in the Diamond Jubilee Tea Salon.'

She looks chuffed. 'Oh, it's nothing. I do love to entertain, but I haven't had a chance since the . . .' She trails off and there's a fleeting look of pain on her face. But she recovers immediately. 'I haven't had much of an opportunity to do so lately, so it's absolutely my pleasure.' She diverts the conversation back to me. 'Have you been there? To the tearooms at Fortnum and Mason?'

'Oh, yes, many times. These days it's full of tourists, but I don't mind. The tea there is second to none, and I'm rather partial to their fruit scones.'

She nods. 'I know what you mean. Not that we've been for ages. Richard thinks it's pretentious.' The smile leaves her face momentarily. 'Shall I be mother, then?'

Her choice of words delights me. I haven't heard anyone use that saying in ages. 'Please.'

Jane rotates the pot and pours for both of us, remembering from this morning how I like my tea. 'There you are.'

'You are the perfect hostess, Jane.' I turn my attention to the plate of sandwiches and try not to salivate as I make my selection. 'It's a shame you don't have more opportunities to show off your talents. Does your husband not enjoy entertaining? Is that why you don't do it often?'

She sips her tea before answering. 'He used to. We both did. Once upon a time we were known for our dinner parties. Richard is a good host. I'm queen of the kitchen, but Richard is charming and loves to make people happy. He certainly knows how to show guests a good time.'

I wonder if perhaps Richard has shown some of his guests *too much* of a good time, and that's why he's not here now, but Jane doesn't elaborate. Instead, she asks, 'And what about you, Dolly? I imagine you might have had the chance to host your fair share of glamorous parties in your day?'

I chuckle. 'Me? No, not really. Although I've certainly been to a few in my time. I much prefer to be a guest than a host, so I'm in my element today.' I bite into the cheese and pickle sandwich I've selected, and for a moment I'm lost in the pleasure of consuming freshly prepared food.

'I'd love to hear about some of them. Goodness, I imagine you've rubbed shoulders with some interesting – not to mention famous – sorts in your time.'

'I suppose that's true. Although, that life doesn't seem real to me now. In a way it never was.'

'What do you mean?'

'The fame, the money – all of that is fleeting and it doesn't change who you are inside, and it doesn't fill any voids. You find that out pretty quickly when it all goes away.'

'Yes,' she says, and I can tell by her tone she understands exactly what I'm saying.

'Still,' I say in a brighter voice, 'it was fun while it lasted.'

'And it will make good reading. Great content for the book. Do you have many photos from those days? I suspect a publisher would kill to see any previously unpublished photos of the glitterati in their heyday.'

I think of my photos, all taken away with the rest of my worldly goods. Shipped to America, as far as I know. I packed a couple of albums, along with some framed photos of Julian and me, in my luggage when I first left the flat and went to The Savoy. No one at the hotel had batted an eyelid at my steamer trunk, two suitcases, three hatboxes, beauty case and cabin bag when I checked in. I soon realised, though, not only could I not afford to stay at the hotel indefinitely, neither was I going to be able to move around with all that baggage.

My old friend Adnan had come to the rescue. Adnan and I go back a long way. We were introduced by a wardrobe assistant when we were both young and ambitious. Adnan's shop in Notting Hill was known for high-quality vintage garments and was frequented by many in the business. He's still trading, although these days the shop isn't the going concern it used to be.

'I don't have many photos left, unfortunately. But I have a couple of albums in storage over in Notting Hill. I can go and collect them if you think they'll be helpful.'

'No rush, but yes, I think having the photos would be very useful indeed.' She picks up a sandwich and begins to nibble at it.

'Maybe I'll head over to my friend's shop on Sunday. He was kind enough to store some of my possessions for me. I could go get the photos after church. Adnan's wife visits her sister on Sunday afternoons, so there's no chance of running into her then and causing problems.'

Jane's eyebrows shoot up in surprise. 'Were you and Adnan a bit of an item at some point?'

I laugh at the thought. 'Goodness, no, never. In fact, in the early days I thought he was gay. Maybe he is . . . In any case, there was never anything more than friendship between us. But his wife isn't very understanding of our friendship, so it's better for everyone if I visit when she's not there.'

'I see. Perhaps you can come for dinner on Sunday night after you've been to Adnan's? We could go through the photos together then.'

'What about your husband? Will he mind me crashing your Sunday dinner?'

A strange expression settles on her face. 'Who knows if he'll even be back by then. And if he is, it'll be fine. In fact, he'll be pleased to see I've made a new friend. He's always telling me I need to get out and do more with my life. I expect he'll be thrilled to find I have a new project to work on.'

'In that case, I gratefully accept your invitation.'

Jane beams at me.

I return her smile and take a small sip of my tea before continuing. 'Now that we are friends and you are going to find out all manner of things about me, I think it's only fair we spend at least a little bit of time talking about you.'

Jane wrinkles her nose. 'Oh, there's nothing to tell. I'm quite boring.'

'I'm sure that's not true. I'd love to know more about you. Do you have some family photos you'd like to share with me? I didn't notice any on display.'

The smile disappears from her face. 'Oh, I'm not really the sentimental type,' she says.

'What about a wedding photo of you and your husband? Surely you have one of those.'

She shrugs. 'Yes, probably. I'll see if I can find one to show you later. We painted the house last year and redecorated. I put the photos away then and haven't got them out again.' She nods at my empty cup. 'Another?'

'Yes, please.' I slide my cup across the table so she can pour. 'It's just the two of you, then?'

She nods.

'Has it always been that way?'

The lid on the china teapot rattles and I realise Jane's hand is shaking. She places the pot back on the table and stares at me. 'What would make you ask that?' Her cold tone takes me by surprise.

'I'm sorry. I didn't mean to pry,' I start, but then stop. I am prying and I did mean it. This woman is the first person to show me any real care in months. She deserves my honesty. 'Jane, I am sorry. I *was* prying. But not with ill intent, I promise. It's just that earlier when I went upstairs to collect my laundry, I accidently opened the wrong door. It was a mistake – your house is large and I lost my bearings. I promise I wasn't snooping. In any case, I could be wrong, but it seemed as if the room I saw belongs to a young man. Or at least it did at one time.'

Jane's shoulders sag and the colour drains from her face.

'That's Tom's room,' she says. 'He's . . . I mean, he was . . . my son.'

Chapter Twenty

Melbourne, Australia
1961

Essendon Airport was daunting. There were people everywhere and constant announcements about flights arriving and departing. Raymond had booked and paid for Margie's flight and told her to go to the TAA ticket counter to collect her documentation. 'The airline staff will show you where to go from there, lovey. I promise everything will be all right,' he'd said.

Raymond might have sorted out her ticket, but he wasn't a magician. Even he couldn't fix this mess. Still, there was nothing left for her in Geelong now that baby Jamie was gone, so she might as well be in Sydney.

As she left the check-in counter she heard the cries of a newborn and saw a young woman walking towards her, cradling a tiny baby. Margie's breasts began to tingle. She had to race to the ladies' room and line her bra with clean handkerchiefs to mop up the milk that had started to leak from her breasts. It had been more than forty-eight hours since she'd fed her son for the first and last time. The pain in her breasts was starting to ease, but she feared the pain in her heart never would.

It wasn't ideal to be travelling in her condition. The bleeding hadn't stopped yet and she was still so tender from the birth that sitting for long periods was uncomfortable. She felt like a leaky, bloated cow. This was hardly the triumphant return to the theatre she'd been fantasising about for months.

She'd left her grandmother's house the evening before last. As soon as the people from the agency had taken the baby, she'd wasted no time packing her bags. The taxi arrived within half an hour of her covert call and, on hearing the toot of its horn, she slipped out of the house without a word to her grandmother. She left in the dark without looking back.

At Geelong station she'd used the payphone to call Mrs Thompson, who said she could most certainly put Margie up for a few nights. In fact, her old room was currently empty, so she'd feel right at home.

With her immediate accommodation organised, she set about planning what to do next. The only living person she truly wanted to see was Raymond. She knew he was already in Sydney, staying at the new Hilton Hotel. Mrs Thompson had a strict 'no trunk calls' rule, so she'd have to find a payphone to call the hotel. Maybe a telegram would be more efficient. That way there would be no risk of her running out of coins. She was sure Raymond would know what to do.

And she was right. Upon receipt of her telegram, he'd called her at the boarding house and told her not to fret; he would organise for her to come to Sydney. He called again in the evening, telling her to make her way to the airport and that a ticket was waiting for her. He would collect her at the other end.

So, now, here she was, boarding an aeroplane to take her far away from all her problems, making her way to a new life.

Apart from some fleeting panic on take-off, Margie was untroubled by the flight. It was her first time in the air, but once the thrill of leaving the ground wore off, the whole experience became quite mundane. If it wasn't for the presence of the air hostesses, she might have believed she was taking a bus or a train trip. The lack of excitement was a pity, really, because she'd been counting on the novelty of the flight to distract her from the terrible regret that had plagued her ever since she'd left her grandmother's house.

Despite everything – her unreadiness for motherhood, her feelings towards the baby's father and the desire to be back performing – she couldn't help but wonder if she'd made a mistake. It had all happened so quickly.

'Granny, I'm not sure I can do this. I need more time. Tell them they can't come,' she'd pleaded.

'More time for what? Think about what you're saying, Marjorie. The sooner the child finds a permanent home, the better. We've been through all this. If you keep him, our darling Jamie will be a *bastard*.' As she whispered the word '*bastard*', Granny's mouth turned down at the corners, as if she'd tasted something sour. 'You're a mother now, Marjorie, and mothers make sacrifices for their children. If you stay here you will ruin your reputation and spoil any chance Jamie has of living the life he deserves. Honestly, this is the best outcome for everyone. You get to keep working, and Jamie will get a decent and respectable upbringing.'

No matter how much she thought about it, Margie couldn't come up with a better idea. Her grandmother had made it clear she would give her no financial assistance if she chose to raise Jamie herself. As much as she wanted to keep him with her, she had no idea how to make that happen. She couldn't take him to the theatre with her. Even though Raymond knew her secret, it was important that nobody else find out. There was no doubt in her mind that the scandal would kill her career before it had even started.

She'd thought about quitting the theatre for good and looking for another job, but what? She'd only ever worked in the mill and her wage there hadn't been huge. Even if she could get her old job back, she didn't think it would pay enough to feed and house her and Jamie. And who would care for him while she was at work?

If only her mother were here. If only she hadn't bought the family that stupid car. Mum hadn't wanted it, but she'd insisted. She'd thought it would make her family's life just a bit easier. And, to be honest, she'd been big-noting herself a little. When she'd paid for it, she'd imagined the neighbours looking at the car with envy and her mother proudly proclaiming, 'It was a gift from my daughter.' What was the saying about pride coming before a fall? But she wasn't the one who'd paid the price for her arrogance. Her long-suffering mother and innocent siblings had paid her debt to the universe.

Who was she kidding? Granny was right. She had nothing to offer a child. She wasn't fit to be a mother. Sending the baby off to a good home *was* the perfect solution. If only someone could make her broken heart understand.

●

As promised, Raymond was waiting to greet her at the airport when she arrived in Sydney. He embraced her, kissed both cheeks, European-style, looked her up and down and then whistled. 'You look amazing.' He dropped his voice. 'No one would ever guess.'

'This dress is hiding a lot.'

There was sympathy in Raymond's eyes. 'How are you, doll?'

She tried to smile. 'I'm okay, I guess. It's been a rough couple of months.'

'I know, lovey. I'm so truly sorry about everything that's happened. I know how close you were to your family, especially your mum. And these past few days – leaving the way you did – must have been simply awful. But you're here now and your theatre family will take care of you, I promise.' He linked his arm in hers. 'Let's get your luggage and get out of here. I can't wait for you to see the hotel we're staying in. It's really quite spiffy.'

They collected her suitcase and headed out of the terminal to find a taxi. Raymond squeezed her hand. 'I know it might not feel like it, but you've made the right decision. I promise you, Margie, your life is just beginning.'

Margie shrugged. 'Right now, all I want to do is sleep.'

Raymond squeezed her shoulders protectively. 'That's perfectly understandable. You should be resting after what you've just been through. Don't worry, you'll have everything you need at the hotel. Your castmates are aware of your arrival, but I've explained about your recent bereavement. No one is expecting you at rehearsals yet. You can rest up, safe in the knowledge no one will suspect that you've just . . .' he paused for a moment and then whispered behind his hand, 'given birth.'

Margie couldn't help but smile. She understood Raymond was trying to be discreet but the sight of him whispering behind his hand so the taxi driver wouldn't hear was somewhat comical. 'Thank you, Raymond. You've been such a sweetheart about all of this. I truly don't know what I would have done without you.'

'It's my pleasure. Honestly. I just want you to rest and recover. Then, when you feel up to it, we can work on getting your career off the ground. I know it's hard to imagine, but one day this whole sorry mess will be behind you. You won't have any regrets when I make you a star.'

Margie was grateful to Raymond for his help, but she couldn't honestly say she believed she would ever recover from what she'd been through. She tried to smile but she couldn't stop tears leaking from the corners of her eyes.

Raymond took her hand and squeezed it. He continued to hold it for the remainder of the cab ride to the hotel. He tried to distract her by pointing out places of interest, and became particularly animated when discussing the new opera house under construction. 'They say it's going to be one of the finest in the world. Imagine that! Who knows, maybe one day you'll get to perform there, my darling.'

She loved him for his confidence in her. She had no idea if she would ever become the type of star he was imagining, but she did know she couldn't imagine her life without the theatre. She was desperate to be back onstage again. When she was performing, she thought of nothing but her role. When the curtain went up she was somebody else, and right now she'd rather be anyone other than Margie Ferguson. She knew once she was back treading the boards, the ever-present hole inside her would be filled, at least temporarily.

143

'Mark my words,' Raymond was saying, 'one day the whole world will know the name Margie Ferguson. Men will worship her, and women will envy her.'

Margie sighed. 'Honestly? I'm bloody well sick of Margie Ferguson. I'd rather be anyone but her.'

Raymond grinned. 'So be someone else. Now's your chance, doll. You're in a new city. You can be whoever you damn well please.'

Chapter Twenty-one

London
2019

The look of distress on Jane's face as she whispers the word 'son' sends a shard of pain through my heart. What was I thinking? Here we were, having a perfectly pleasant afternoon, and I had to go and spoil it by cracking open a wound Jane clearly wanted left alone.

'I'm so sorry, my dear. I shouldn't have forced the subject. We don't have to talk about this if you don't want to.'

'Richard wants to pack up his room,' she says. 'He wants to pretend Tom never existed. Perhaps he thinks if there are no reminders, he'll be able to forget he ever had a son. I suppose he thinks it'll be less painful that way.'

I nod but don't speak, afraid that any interruption might deter her from continuing.

'But I can't forget. Even if I wanted to – which I don't – I could never forget that Tom was here. He was my baby, my little boy . . . I gave birth to him, I raised him. I tried my best. I did what I thought was right, and then . . .' She shakes her head. Just when I think she is finished speaking, she goes on. 'Then he was grown up. But not really.' She looks at me with disbelief in her eyes. 'Eighteen is an adult in the eyes of the law but he was still just a child. A silly little boy, in some ways. He played video games and watched cartoons – anime, they call it, but that's just another name for cartoons. Just a child . . .' She trails off, shaking her head once more.

'And then?' I ask gently.

'Then he was no more.' Her tone is flat, almost completely devoid of emotion, but I recognise the distress behind her words.

I hold off on responding in case she wants to say more, but she is silent and her gaze is unfocused, making me wonder where her memories might have taken her.

Eventually I say, 'I'm so sorry, Jane. The loss of a child is a terrible thing to bear.'

She stares at me and there's anger in her eyes. 'Don't,' she says sharply. 'Don't you dare give me those empty platitudes. I don't want to hear them. You have no idea what I've been through. What I'm going through.'

Her ire takes me by surprise. Nevertheless, I'm pleased to see a spark of *something* in her. Anger is better than despair. 'That's true enough. I don't know how you feel or what you've been through.' I pause for a beat to ready myself for what I am about to say. I wonder if it will only serve to increase her fury. Perhaps she will be so incensed that she will kick me out and refuse to work on my story. But I must tell her. She will find out soon anyway, and if I don't confess now she will judge me even more harshly for withholding the truth. 'I do know how *I* felt,' I say. 'How I still feel.'

'What do you mean?'

'I lost my son, too. It was a long time ago and I've learnt to live without him, but I still feel the loss all these years later. In fact, the older I get, the keener my pain. I'm riddled with regret, you see.'

The sharp lines of her expression melt away as her anger dissipates. 'Oh, Dolly, I'm so sorry. I didn't know.'

I shrug. 'How could you?'

She looks a little shamefaced. 'As I said, I googled your name. I might have downplayed exactly how much research I did on you. But none of my searches mentioned a child – or any other personal relationships, for that matter. There were some oblique references to a "special friendship" with Julian Barrows but nothing else.'

I inwardly flinch at the mention of Julian. Good grief, what other information is out there about me? I really must get my head around this googling business one day.

'I'm sorry,' she says again. 'What happened with Tom changed me. I never used to be such a terrible person.' A hollow laugh escapes her lips. 'Maybe that's not true, either. Maybe I was never a good person. I mean, everyone thinks they're the good guy, right? But it seems I was kidding myself.'

I'm not sure what she means by this, but it's clear her words are coming from a place of guilt – somewhere I'm all too familiar with.

'Jane, I don't know what happened to your son, but I do know you are not a bad person.'

'You don't know that.'

'I do. Look at how kind you've been to me. Maybe you've made some mistakes in your life – who hasn't? – but that doesn't make you a bad person.'

She laughs mirthlessly. 'Maybe I was just a bad mother . . .'

I don't have the facts to dispute this, so I say, 'Not as bad as me, I'll bet.'

She smiles. 'Oh, Dolly, you don't have to say that. Truly. What's done is done. I'm sorry you lost your son. It's a terrible thing for us to have in common, but perhaps it explains why we've bonded so quickly. I hope you don't mind me saying that?'

I return her smile. 'Not at all. Perhaps we were fated to find each other. Although, we may not have as much in common as you think.' I have to tell her now. There's no more putting it off. My stomach churns and I place a half-eaten mini quiche back on my plate. I look her in the eyes and say, 'I lost my son too, that's true, but he didn't die. Well, not that I know of . . .'

'I'm not sure I understand.'

'I gave up my son for adoption when he was just a few days old. I was unmarried and very young.'

147

'Oh,' she says, but there's sympathy mingled with the surprise in her voice. 'That must have been awful.'

'It was. At the time I thought it was for the best – for him and for me. I thought there was no other choice.' Now I've said this much, I may as well explain. I tell her the whole story – the accidental pregnancy, the plan for my mum to raise the baby and all that happened next.

Jane's eyes glistened with tears as I described the terrible accident that claimed the lives of my mother and siblings.

'I know it's not the same thing,' I say. 'I'm not trying to pretend I have suffered the way you have. But I do know what it's like to spend every day missing a child. I hope you won't think too badly of me. Times were different then. There wasn't the support for single mothers there is now.'

She slowly shakes her head from side to side. 'Think badly of you? No, of course I don't. It sounds as if you had no other choice.'

I place my empty teacup back on its saucer and sigh. 'At the time it seemed that way, but to be perfectly honest, I didn't try. After my mum died, I just sort of gave up. I was in shock, I suppose, and I let myself be talked into giving Jamie up for adoption.'

Jane smiles. 'Lovely name.'

Tears prick my eyes. It feels strange – but also wonderful – to be talking about my Jamie. 'Named for his grandfather,' I say. 'I never got to meet my dad, but my grandmother said my little one looked just like him. James Robert Ferguson was Granny's only son, so I named my boy after him.'

'Your grandmother couldn't help raise him?'

'No. I begged her, but she wouldn't hear of me keeping him. She said it would bring shame to the family and my son would suffer because of it. She made me think he would be better off without me, and so I let him go.'

There's no judgement, only sympathy in Jane's eyes. 'Do you know what happened to him?'

I shake my head again. 'Granny organised the whole thing through her church. A woman from an adoption agency took him. The day that happened I left my grandmother's house and I never saw her – or Jamie – again.'

Jane's brow furrows as though she is deep in thought. 'But surely that wasn't legal?'

I shrug. 'It was the early 1960s. Adoption laws weren't what they are today. And I did sign papers relinquishing him, so . . .'

'Dolly, I'm so sorry.' She slumps back in her chair. 'This is such a heartbreaking story. Have you ever tried to find him?'

I nod. 'A couple of times. I first tried about four years later, when I'd started to make some decent money. I hired a private detective in Australia to track him down, but he had no luck. I wonder now if that detective just took me for a ride. Even at the time I was a little suspicious. But I had no way of proving it, and I needed discretion, so I didn't want to make a fuss. Years later, Julian—'

'Julian Barrows?' She raises an eyebrow.

'Yes,' I say without further explanation. One secret at a time. 'Julian encouraged me to try again and, dear friend that he was, he put me in touch with a lawyer who he thought might be able to help. The lawyer was quite optimistic, but after several months of looking and exploring a few promising leads we ended up at a dead end. I gave up hope after that. Until now, that is.'

'Oh?' Jane sits up straight in her chair, her eyes flashing with interest. 'Has there been a new development?'

'No, not really. But I have hope that if I write my story, perhaps my son will read it one day and understand. That is, if you're still happy to work on the book with me now you know the truth.'

'I absolutely want to work on your story, Dolly, but I'm not sure how it will help you find your son. Even if he happens to read the book, how will he know it's about him?'

My shoulders slump. It's not as if this thought hasn't crossed my mind, but my story is all I have left, so I've been clinging to the idea it will somehow reconnect me with my child. 'I don't really know. I just know I feel compelled to write it. Now more than ever.'

'What do you mean?'

'At first I started writing down my memories out of boredom. The days in the library can be quite long when you don't have a purpose.'

Jane laughs. 'Don't mention boredom to that snitchy librarian. I'm sure she'd be insulted that the library's extensive collection isn't enough to keep you entertained.'

I grin and reach for a piece of lemon slice. Now that I know Jane isn't going to judge me for my past, I feel my appetite returning. 'Stacey would be less than impressed, I'm sure. And I do love to read, but I also love to have a purpose. I've been a working woman for most of my life, although, granted, not the past few years. Still, even when I wasn't working I had things to occupy my mind – meals to cook, friends to visit. You know how it is . . .'

Jane nods. 'Yes,' she says, and I detect a note of sadness in her voice.

'So, I started writing about my life to fill the hours. Increasingly, my thoughts turned to my pregnancy and my little boy, and I realised I was writing to explain myself – to justify my actions, if you like. I was telling Jamie the story of his birth and letting him know he was loved. That even though I didn't choose to get pregnant, I didn't just throw him away. I wanted him to know I gave him up for his sake, so he would have a better life than the one I could give him.'

'I'm sure he knows that.'

I frown at her. 'How would he know? He doesn't know who I am.' She gives me a sympathetic look and I continue. 'My scribblings have been cathartic, that's for sure. In the beginning that's probably all I hoped to achieve, but then I met you. Your encouragement made me think maybe others might be interested in what I have to say. Then, when I discovered you were a writer, I felt as if the universe was sending me a sign. I know it's a long shot, but I'd like to give it a try.'

Jane nods slowly. 'Well, that's not a terrible idea. It's definitely worth a try.' She bites her lip, deep in thought for a moment. 'If we can find a publisher, then the publicity surrounding the book might provide us with some leads. This is the sort of human-interest story newspaper and magazine editors love. We could even appeal to the public to come forward if they have any information about the adoption. If nothing else, it might increase the book sales, and if we're very lucky it might lead to some new information on Jamie's whereabouts.'

I'm excited now, my mind racing with possibilities. 'You mentioned before about googling me.'

Jane makes an embarrassed face. 'Yes, sorry about that. I should have just asked you.'

I wave my hand in the air dismissively. 'Oh, I'm not worried about that. I was just thinking, if you know a bit about that sort of thing – the internet web thing – that might be helpful to us.'

'Yes,' she says, and I can tell from her voice that she's trying hard not to laugh. 'The internet might be very useful indeed. We can use it to find all sorts of things – dates of the stage shows you performed in and TV shows you've worked on. Goodness, I can't wait to hear about all that.'

'Yes, yes,' I say impatiently. 'That all sounds good, but it's not what I mean.'

'Oh? What do you mean, then?'

'As you've probably figured out, I'm not exactly a whiz with the new technology. Lovely Jemima at the library helps me read my emails once a week. Julian used to . . . well, I didn't get too many emails before, but Julian would help me log in every now and then. I'm terrible at remembering passwords and the like. Anyway, I've noticed quite a lot of talk among the young ones about this Facebook thing. And there are other things like it. We had a woman come to the library and run a Computing for Seniors workshop. I went to it but I didn't take much notice of all the palaver about the Facebook. It seemed to be more for those who wanted to look at photos of their grandchildren, and I don't have any so I couldn't see the point.'

Jane chuckles. 'I don't think you're missing much, to be honest.'

'Probably not, but it does seem to be all the rage.'

'How does this relate to your book, Dolly?'

'Maybe you could help me put the word out using Facebook and the other whatevers. We could probably reach a lot of people that way.'

Jane visibly blanches. 'The internet can be a strange and scary place,' she says. 'I'm not sure it's the right approach.'

'Oh,' I say, disappointed. 'That's a shame. I thought I was onto something there.'

'How about we focus on getting the book done first?' She smiles. 'We can worry about how to get the word out later.'

'Yes, that's a good plan,' I say. 'We should make a start first thing tomorrow.'

When Jane stands and begins to clear the table, I realise we have spent ages talking about my Jamie but barely a word has been uttered about her Tom.

'Jane, before you do that, is there anything you want to say? We started talking about Tom and got sidetracked. I want to hear all about your boy.'

She shakes her head as she picks up a plate. 'I should get a start on dinner. And I'm sure your load of laundry will be done by now. You might want to put it in the dryer.'

'Are you sure? I know I prattle on a bit, but I can be a good listener when it's required.'

'I'm sorry, Dolly. Not today. We're having such a lovely time. I just. . . .'

I stand and pick up the used napkins from the table. 'I understand,' I say. 'Now, shall I pop these in the laundry?'

I can see the relief in her smile.

Part Two

Part Two

Chapter Twenty-two

Sydney, Australia
1961

'Dolly Jamieson' entered the world on a warm February evening in 1961. Her friend, Raymond Giles, marked the occasion by opening a bottle of expensive champagne and sprinkling several droplets on Dolly's head to 'christen' her.

'Stop it, Raymond! You'll ruin my hair.'

'I have to say, Doll, you were always a knockout as a brunette, but you're a total bombshell as a blonde.'

Dolly touched her carefully styled and sprayed hair. 'Do you really like it? I figured I might as well have a change of look to go with the new name, and there's the bonus of not having to wear that damned wig on stage.'

Grae chuckled. 'The hair is amazing. And let me say again how much I *love* the new name.'

The newly christened Dolly smiled. Perhaps it was the actress in her, or perhaps it was because Raymond had been calling her 'Doll' since they first started working together that made the transition so easy. Being called Dolly seemed perfectly natural already. She'd let go of Margie Ferguson, but she hadn't been able to let go of her son – not completely. Jamie's name formed part of her new surname. That way she would always have a little piece of him with her.

'Are you ready to make your re-entrance into society?'

It had been three weeks since Raymond collected her from the airport. She'd barely left the hotel since. The first week was spent almost entirely in bed. Raymond visited twice a day – before and after rehearsals – to make sure she was eating. Sandy, who'd come up from Melbourne to be lead chorus, came each day too. She encouraged Dolly (Margie insisted on everyone calling her by her new name at all times) to take a shower and put on a fresh nightie each day. Dolly had tearfully confessed the whole truth to Sandy on the day after her arrival, but Sandy had sworn to keep her secret. The only other person Dolly had seen these past two weeks (apart from the hotel staff) was Raymond's partner, Grae.

Grae came every day while the others were at rehearsal and regaled Dolly with theatre gossip and outlandish tales. She'd surprised him that morning by being up and dressed when he arrived.

'Well, look at you!' he said approvingly. Then in a softer, more tentative tone, 'You look better, love.'

'I feel better.' It was true. Sort of. She was all alone in the world and there was nothing she could do to change that. Her beautiful family was gone and she couldn't bring them back. Her son had been taken from her and, as painful as that separation was, it was probably for the best.

After weeks of wallowing, she realised she had two choices. She could give up and end it all, or she could get up out of bed and fight. In her heart she knew what her family would want her to do.

There would be no more self-pity. She'd been gifted with a talent – so many people had told her so – and she would make use of it. She would never have a family, never be a mother. Instead, she would dedicate her life to her career. Margie Ferguson belonged to another time, another world. In the new world, Dolly Jamieson was going to be a star.

'Darling, you've been cocooned in this hotel room for far too long. Should we do something fun today?'

156

Dolly nodded. 'I've decided I'm ready to go back to rehearsals tomorrow, so I'm thinking maybe I could use a trip to the salon.'

'Ooh, that's a wonderful idea. I mean, we can't have you meeting the cast with your hair as it is.' He wrinkled his nose. 'You are always gorgeous, of course, but if the cast is going to accept you as their leading lady, they'll want to see a bit of star power. Leave it with me.'

Thanks to Grae's connections, half an hour later they were on their way to one of Sydney's top hair salons. The idea to go blonde had come to her on a whim in the cab when Graeme was talking about launching her onto the Sydney scene. She was an unknown here. What better opportunity to start afresh and leave Margie Ferguson and all her troubles behind? Today she would embrace Dolly Jamieson in all her glory. She would forget the past and go boldly into her future.

Now, back in her room for pre-dinner drinks, she had no regrets. It really was the beginning of a new era.

'Here you go, Doll,' Raymond said, handing her a glass of champagne. He took the tray and offered a glass to Grae and one to Sandy.

'Thank you, Raymond.' Dolly raised her glass and looked at her friends. 'Thank you all. I don't know how I would have survived the past few weeks without you.'

Sandy smiled. 'You would do the same for us.'

'It's been a pleasure, my love,' Graeme added.

'I know you've been through a lot these past few months, Doll, and we can't take the place of those you've lost, but I hope you know we're here for you now and we always will be. Your theatre family loves you.'

A lump formed in Dolly's throat as she heard these words. Raymond was right, no one could take the place of her mother and siblings, or her precious baby boy, but it helped to know there were people in the world who truly cared about her. There were no words that could adequately express her gratitude to her friends so instead she raised her glass and said, 'Cheers to you all!'

Grae glanced at his watch. 'We'd better down these and get going soon. The table is booked for seven-thirty, and I'd hate to lose our reservation.'

'Ah, don't worry about that, Grae. I told them I'm bringing a VIP to dinner tonight; Australia's newest star.'

Dolly nearly choked on her champagne. 'I hope you didn't say that.'

'I did indeed. And why not? It's the truth.'

Dolly shook her head, but Sandy touched her arm and said, 'You *are* a star, Dolly. I knew it the first time I saw you on stage. I told you as much, remember?'

Dolly chuckled. 'I just thought you were being kind to the new girl.'

Grae snorted. 'Ha, as if that's how it works in theatre circles!'

Raymond rolled his eyes. 'You old cynic, Grae.'

Sandy drained her glass. 'You're on the cusp of stardom, Dolly, mark my words. Don't you forget the little people when your name is up in lights on Broadway.'

'Too right!' Raymond said. 'But one city at a time, eh? Ready to take Sydney by storm, my lovely?' he asked as he helped her into the new red satin evening coat Graeme had insisted on buying her that afternoon.

She laughed. 'I'm not sure dinner in the hotel restaurant counts as taking the city by storm.'

'It's a start, lovey. And I, for one, am excited to see where you go from here.'

•

Opening night came around in the blink of an eye. Once Dolly was back at the theatre, she easily slipped into her leading-lady persona. She took it easy for the first couple of days of rehearsal, but after that she realised the more she worked, the better she felt. When the curtain went up for the premiere performance, she couldn't have been more ready. With the spotlight trained on her, she began to sing, and with every note she left Margie Ferguson further and further behind.

On stage she transformed. She *was* Amethyst Rose, cunning jewel thief turned World War II spy. She was brave and confident. She had no fear.

When the curtain fell, there was a mighty roar from the crowd. Dolly knew then that, just like Amethyst, she would be fine in the end.

After the opening-night party, Dolly went with a few of the cast to Raymond's suite to await the reviews. Don Balham – the show's male lead – was there, along with Sandy, a couple of the chorus and the producers. Grae had brought along two friends, which Raymond seemed unusually testy about. 'It's hardly an intimate group now, is it?' Dolly overhead him whisper tersely to Grae as they were organising drinks for everyone.

'What's wrong with him?' she asked Sandy when Raymond huffed off to the bathroom.

Sandy laughed. 'Just opening-night jitters, that's all. You know what he's like.'

Dolly shrugged. She hadn't been the leading lady when the Melbourne show opened, and she hadn't stayed long at the party afterwards. She didn't recall Raymond being particularly testy that night, but perhaps she'd been too green to notice.

Despite Sandy's reassurance, her stomach knotted in fear. Raymond had taken a significant risk in casting her as the lead and if the reviews were critical of her performance, maybe he'd reconsider his choice. Or, worse still, what if the entire show flopped because she hadn't been good enough to wow the critics?

'Was I terrible? Be honest. I know he took a risk casting me as the lead. Melbourne was one thing – I inherited the role, and it couldn't be helped, but here . . . well, that's a whole different story. I couldn't bear it if I'd let him, or any of you, down.'

Sandy squeezed her arm. 'Hush. The reviews will be great, I'm sure. Raymond is always like this before first reviews, no matter how good the performance. You were spectacular, everyone said so – even Don, and he can be a bit of a downer. Loves himself so much that he never thinks any of his leading ladies come up to scratch. But I overheard him telling Pam that you had perfect pitch and it was nice to be working alongside someone who matched his talent.' She rolled her eyes and Dolly laughed.

'He didn't?'

'He did. Watch out for that one. He has a keen eye for the ladies, and with all that glowing praise, I'm willing to bet he has you in his sights.'

Dolly plucked out the toothpicked strawberry floating in her Pimm's and lemonade and pointed it at Sandy. 'Don't you worry about that. I'm done with Lotharios.' She wrinkled her nose in distaste. 'Besides, he's old enough to be my father.'

'Pfft,' said Sandy, laughing. 'As if that'll stop old Don. Honestly, he thinks he's god's gift to women.'

'Well, not this woman. I'm not interested in him, or any other man.'

'You need to let him down gently, though. Donny boy has a fragile ego and a mean streak, which is not a good combination. You don't want to get on the wrong side of him.' Sandy winked. 'If he makes a move, perhaps tell him you bat for the other team.'

'What?' She had no idea what Sandy was going on about.

'You said you'd sworn off men. Perhaps you could make him think you prefer ladies instead.'

Dolly felt heat in her cheeks and Sandy laughed at her obvious discomfort.

'Oh, come on, Doll, I can help if you like.' Without warning she grabbed Dolly around the waist and drew her close, kissing her on the lips as she did so.

Dolly pushed her away playfully. 'Get out with you. Since when do you like girls?'

Sandy shrugged, laughing. 'I don't know. I'm an adventurer. I'll give anything a go once. And I tell you, Doll, if I was going to change teams, you'd be my first pick.'

A knock on the door put an end to any further tomfoolery. Graeme answered it and collected the tray of papers from the hotel's concierge. 'I wanted to deliver these personally, sir. Please send Mr Giles my very best wishes.'

Graeme nodded and handed the man a sizeable tip. 'Thank you, Murray. Mr Giles will be very grateful, I'm sure.' With that he took the tray and headed for the bathroom. He knocked twice on the door. 'Ray, they're here.'

The door opened, and Dolly saw a pale-faced Raymond beckon Grae inside. The mood in the suite became subdued for several minutes until a whoop sounded.

'Thank god,' Sandy said as Raymond emerged, triumphantly waving the paper above his head.

'Someone call room service and order more champagne,' he called, making a beeline for Dolly. 'We have a hit on our hands!' He threw the rolled-up paper to Graeme before hugging Dolly and lifting her up off the ground. 'Read it out to everyone, Grae.'

Grae stood on the coffee table, cleared his throat and began to read.

'*Tonight's premiere performance of* The Rose of France *was a triumph for director Raymond Giles. The show's Melbourne season, while moderately successful, was beset by problems, including the loss of West End star Cara Beecham early in the season.*

'*Giles took a risk with the Sydney cast, casting all Australian leads. Don Balham is well known to Australian theatregoers, having taken on major roles in several productions, including a spectacular performance last year in* West Side Story. *Tonight, his execution in the role of Gerard was flawless and he solidified his place as a true Australian talent.*

'*However, the night's standout performance came from newcomer Dolly Jamieson. Giles's casting genius was on full display from the moment Miss Jamieson took to the stage. The audience was mesmerised not only by her sweet yet powerful voice, but by her stage presence. Miss Jamieson has that rare ability to draw the audience in and make them truly believe they are living inside the character's head.*

'*Ladies and gentlemen, let this reporter be the first to announce: a star is born!*'

A cheer went up around the room and Grae proposed a toast. 'To Dolly!'

Dolly was so overcome with relief that his words barely registered. Not only was it important to her not to let down Raymond and her castmates but, she suddenly realised, without this show she would have nowhere to go. Her savings from the last show were all but gone. She'd bought that blasted car and then had to pay out the lease on her mother's house. She had a little bit in the bank, but it wouldn't last long if she wasn't working.

Thankfully, it seemed she wouldn't have to worry now.

'To Dolly!' the room echoed and then a huge cheer went up, before toasts were made to Don, Raymond and the rest of the cast.

'I'm going to call it a night,' Dolly said to Raymond. 'I don't want to break up the party, so I might just slip out quietly. Tell Grae I said thanks for the lovely party and the toast. I appreciate all the support.'

Raymond nodded. 'It's been a big day. I'm sure you need your rest.'

'Thanks, Raymond, for everything. I'm not sure what I would have done—'

'Oh, Dolly, I'm the one who should be thanking you. This show – your performance – is going to open doors for us, you mark my words. Broadway, here we come!'

Chapter Twenty-three

London
2019

I'm floating on a soft, warm cloud, and as I slip into consciousness I wonder if perhaps I have died in the night. But then I open my eyes and realise I am in Jane's guestroom, having spent the night between silky sheets and warmed by a down-filled duvet.

The bed is soft, almost too soft. My body has become unused to such comfort, and when I go to rise my old bones are uncooperative. It takes me a while, but eventually I coax myself out of bed with the promise of a hot shower. Two showers in two days. What luxury! I don't even feel dirty, but I'm not passing up the opportunity to soothe my aching bones under the hot spray.

When I'm done, I wrap myself in the terry-towelling robe hanging on the back of the door – just like a five-star hotel! – and head to the wardrobe, where I've hung Jane's hand-me-downs. These new-to-me clothes put all my other clothing to shame. I dress in a navy woollen skirt and team it with a cream blouse and navy cardigan. It's a more subdued look than I would normally wear, but I'm grateful to be wearing clean, comfortable and well-made garments. There's a pair of tan loafers that won't look too bad with this outfit. Better than my lace-up boots, at any rate. I look longingly for a moment at the sling-backs I wore yesterday, but they won't be any good for walking in, lovely though they are. The loafers aren't perfect, but they'll have to do. I'll wear the red cashmere scarf Jane gave me when I leave here – that'll give the outfit a lift.

I spend a few more minutes doing my hair and using Jane's cosmetics to fix my face. The result is quite pleasing, even if I do say so myself. Once I'm satisfied that I'm presentable, I make my way downstairs. I can hear Jane clattering away in the kitchen and as I get closer I smell something delicious cooking.

Jane turns from the stove to greet me. 'Good morning. Did you sleep well?'

'Like a baby. Thank you again for inviting me to stay last night.'

'The pleasure was all mine. Are you hungry?'

'I honestly don't how I could be after that feast we ate last night, but whatever you're making smells so enticing I don't think I can refuse.'

She grins. 'I'm using up last night's leftover salmon to make omelettes. But I can do bacon and eggs, pancakes; whatever takes your fancy.'

'An omelette will be perfect.'

'There's freshly squeezed juice and some cut-up fruit in the breakfast nook. Go through and I'll be with you in a moment.'

I pour myself a juice and sit, basking in the glorious autumn sunlight that warms the room. Last night was the most I've enjoyed myself in ages. Possibly since Julian died. Free from the worry of where I would sleep, and with a full belly to boot, I was able to relax and enjoy Jane's company. She was keen to hear all about my days performing in the West End and, after a glass or two of bubbly, she convinced me to perform a couple of show tunes for her. Jane was very complimentary about my crackly old voice, telling me I hadn't lost any of my talent. It was a wonderful evening. One I won't forget in a hurry.

'Here you are.' Jane places a plate in front of me. A fluffy omelette topped with smoked salmon, capers and crème fraîche sits at its centre. I feel as if I'm back at The Savoy.

'This looks simply scrumptious,' I say.

Jane's delight at my words is obvious in her smile. 'It's just so lovely to have someone to cook for. Even when Richard is here, he never has time for a cooked breakfast. He gulps a coffee and is out the door. Sometimes he's gone before I wake up.'

'What does he do?' I ask.

'He's a lawyer – a criminal defence lawyer,' she says. 'He's a partner at a big firm in the city.'

'That must keep him busy.'

'Yes, more so than ever. There's some travel, too. He gives guest lectures, that type of thing. I thought by now he might start to ease off a little but ever since . . .' She pauses for a moment, seemingly lost in thought. 'He isn't here a lot these days, it seems.' She lifts the juice jug. 'More?'

I shake my head. 'I'm fine.'

'Anyway,' she says brightly, 'as you can see, I have plenty of time on my hands, which means I can devote myself to working with you on your book. Shall we get started today?'

'I'd love to.'

'We can begin right after breakfast if you'd like. I'm happy to accompany you to the library. Or we could work in my office if you'd prefer?'

This house is so lovely that I'm afraid every minute I extend my stay will make it harder for me to leave. 'Thank you, but I think the library is best. That way I can keep working and you can come and go as you please.'

Jane opens her mouth as if to speak and then closes it again. Finally, she nods. 'Yes, okay. As soon as we're finished up here we can get going. I'm eager to start.'

Half an hour later, we're standing in the entry hall. Jane retrieves my coat from the closet and I feel my cheeks redden at the sight of it. I'm not sure how I have kidded myself that this shoddy old garment made me look halfway respectable.

Jane notices my discomfort. 'It looks as if your coat was damaged when you fell yesterday.'

'Yes,' I say, grateful that she allows me to save face by not questioning my lie.

'I have the best drycleaner. He truly is a genius. I'm sure he could clean and repair this and make it as good as new. What if I lent you one of my coats for the day and we can drop this off at the cleaners on our way to the library? It's not far out of our way.'

Another kindness that I wish I didn't need to have extended to me. But perhaps there will come a time when I can repay Jane. 'Thank you. This coat has sentimental value. I'd love to see her restored to her former glory.'

'Good. I'm sure Harish will do a good job. He loves working with fragile garments and bringing them back to life. I promise you he'll take good care of it. Let me just pop upstairs and find another coat for you to wear. I think I have just the thing.'

Moments later Jane reappears with a double-breasted red and navy chequered coat that is clearly designer made. She opens it up for me to slide on and I'm thrilled when it fits like a glove.

'What do you think?' she asks.

'Perfect! I'm all set.'

'Yes, it looks great, as if it was made for you. You know, I never wear that coat. It was given to me – once upon a time I used to get given all sorts of things because of my work. Anyway, it just never looked any good on me. It's never been worn. If you like it, you can have it.'

'Jane,' I say scoldingly, 'you can't keep giving me things. At the rate you're going, you'll have nothing left to wear.'

She shrugs on her coat – the beige Burberry trench she was wearing the first time we met – and laughs. 'You should see my wardrobe. Richard says I have an obscene amount of clothing and he's probably right. As I said, designers and brand managers used to send me sample garments. I have a ton of stuff that's never been worn. You should take a look sometime and see if there's anything you'd like.'

'That's very kind, but I can't keep accepting gifts from you.'

'It's just going to waste sitting up there in my closet. I keep meaning to sort through it and take what I don't want to Oxfam. I'd be very happy to see you making use of them.'

'Perhaps I will take a look one day.' How can I tell her my wheelie case is the only storage I have and I'm already struggling to fit in the first lot of clothes she's so generously gifted to me?

'Good. Ready to go, then?'

I grab my case, which Jane has already brought downstairs for me, and we make our way out the door and down the path. Jane is just closing the iron front gate behind her when she is addressed by her next-door neighbour, who is hovering by her front fence, trowel in hand. I note the tool is conspicuously free from dirt and immediately identify the woman as a busybody.

'Good morning, Jane!' she calls in an overly cheerful voice.

Jane's face takes on the look of someone who is about to endure a great trial. 'Good morning, Mrs Sturgeon. How's the gardening going?'

'Sorry? Oh . . . yes, good. Just pulling out a few weeds. You know how it is.'

'Hmm. Well, we must be off. Good to see you.' Jane's tone implies it is anything *but* good and I have to suppress a laugh.

'How are *you*, Jane?' She cocks her head and adopts a sympathetic look.

'Oh, I'm *fine*. Great, in fact.'

A look of surprise crosses the neighbour's face. It's fleeting, though. 'That's the way. No use letting Negative Nancys get you down, that's what I always say,' she chirps brightly. 'Although'—she drops her voice now—'I did happen to see that piece on *What Katy Says* the other day. I thought it was very unfair. I mean, who's to say why things happen the way they do? Everyone's always so quick to blame the mother. Not me. I blame the schools. And the video games, too. Puts ideas in young people's minds. And the economy, too. With all the mothers working these days is it any wonder they can't keep track of what their kids are thinking? I'm forever grateful I was able to be a full-time mother. Of course, in my day we were happier with less. Didn't need all the mod cons the way people do these days. But that's progress for you. You can't stop it.'

Jane looks uncomfortable. 'Right. Well, nice to see you, Mrs Sturgeon. We must—'

'Aren't you going to introduce me to your friend?' Mrs Busybody is openly staring at me now.

'I'm sorry. How rude of me. This is my friend, Dolly. Dolly, my next-door neighbour, Mrs Sturgeon.'

Mrs Busybody's eyes narrow. 'Have we met before? You seem familiar.'

I wave my hand dismissively. 'I doubt it. I'm new to the area and a recent acquaintance of Jane's. We're working on a project together and are due at a meeting at the local library. I'm afraid we don't have time to stand around nattering all day, so if you'll excuse us . . .'

'I've got it! You used to be on the telly. I was sure I knew you from somewhere.'

I glare at her. 'As I've just explained, we're very busy. I'm afraid I don't have time for idle chitchat with'—I pause and wrinkle my nose—'*fans*. Perhaps another time.'

Mrs Busybody's mouth drops open momentarily before she says coolly, 'Don't let me keep you.'

Jane links her arm with mine and we move off down the street as quickly as my creaky old legs will let me. As soon as we're a safe distance away, Jane bursts out laughing. 'You certainly put that old battleaxe in her place.'

I giggle like a conspiratorial schoolgirl. 'Did I? Well, good! I know her type. All that false concern when the real intention is to make you feel small.'

'Very astute observation, Dolly. She's always been painful but since . . .' She hesitates for a beat and then shrugs. 'Lately she's been more intolerable than ever.'

From this and the conversation I just overheard, I presume Mrs Sturgeon's nosiness has become more pronounced since the death of Jane's son. What type of a person seeks to make a mother feel worse about the loss of her child? But Jane seems to have shrugged off the hurt – at least for now.

We walk through the park to the high street, chatting and laughing all the way. I realise I almost have a spring in my step today – a far cry from yesterday's painful hobble. It's amazing what a difference a good sleep and some decent food can make.

We stop near the pond to watch some children feeding the ducks. 'When Tom was little he was terrified of the ducks,' Jane says. 'It annoyed Richard. "They won't hurt you, Tommy," he'd say, but Tom would just squeal and hide his face in my skirt while Richard kept feeding them.'

'I'm not a huge fan of ducks myself. Or any birds, really. Once, when the work had dried up a bit, I took a job acting in a panto-mime. There was a pirate character in the show, and he had a live parrot sitting on his shoulder throughout the performance. It was a vicious thing and I was terrified of it. Luckily the job paid well.'

Jane laughs at this, and we continue on.

At the drycleaners, Jane introduces me to Harish, the owner of the business. 'Pleased to meet you, Mrs Jamieson. Any friend of Mrs Leveson's is a friend of mine. How can I help you today?'

Jane hands over the shopping bag containing my coat and Harish removes it. 'Oh my goodness! This is just wonderful.' He looks at me. 'Givenchy, 1968, am I right?'

'Yes!' I say, delighted by his keen eye. 'It's definitely Givenchy, but I'm not sure of the year. I bought it second-hand in the 1970s.'

He's laid out the coat on the counter and is looking at it lovingly. 'I'm almost certain this was part of the '68 collection, but I will check online before you pick it up.'

'You can clean it, then?' Jane asks.

'Most certainly. That won't be a problem. I see some of the stitching has come undone in the lining – I can fix that too, and take care of any other small areas of damage if you'd like?'

'That would be wonderful,' I say.

'How long will you need, Hari?'

'I'll get started right away. You can collect it tomorrow morning.'

I'm walking on clouds the whole way to the library; the aches and hurts of yesterday have disappeared. I have a full stomach, new clothes, my beautiful coat is getting a spruce up and, best of all, I have made a new friend.

At the library Jane asks Stacey if there is a meeting room available for use today and Stacey smiles her good smile, the one she usually reserves for visiting authors, and checks the computer. She nods and says for us to follow her so she can unlock the room, smiling all the time. Jane must have the magic touch, because this smile has never been directed at me before.

'I'll leave you to it, ladies.'

I return her smile. 'Thank you, Stacey.'

She does a double take. 'Dolly? I didn't . . . Well, you look so . . . I didn't realise it was you.'

'Really?' Jane says incredulously. 'Goodness, I'm surprised, considering how often Miss Jamieson works here at the library. Perhaps you need new glasses.'

I bite back a laugh as Stacey's cheeks colour, and she scuttles away.

The hours pass quickly as I tell Jane all about my early years. She doesn't take notes but rather records our conversation on her phone. The wonders of modern technology!

I tell her about the days when it was just Mum and me in the Nicholas Street house. 'My mum was often sad. She must have been lonely after my dad died, and while my grandparents helped out financially, I don't think my grandmother would have provided much moral support to my mum. Of course, I didn't understand any of that back then – all I knew was sometimes my mum would look sad, and occasionally I'd hear her crying in the night.'

'That must have been hard.'

I shrug. 'In a way I have that time to thank for my love of performing.'

'How so?'

'I learnt I could make my mum smile if I sang. I started putting on regular concerts for her. It became quite a big deal at one stage. Mum made stage curtains that we could rig up on the back verandah and we'd pop some folding chairs on the lawn so the neighbours could watch as well. Mum was so proud when anyone complimented me on my voice. She was always my biggest fan.'

Jane asks questions about my mother, my grandparents and my siblings, which of course leads us to Bill. I've talked more in the past few hours than I have in many months. So much so my voice is becoming hoarse. 'Goodness, I think I've just about talked myself dry.'

Jane looks at the time on her phone. 'Is it any wonder? It's well and truly lunchtime. I'm sorry, Dolly. We should have stopped for a bite to eat an hour ago.'

'It's not your fault. I'm the one who's been talking like a threshing machine.'

She pauses the recording on her phone and smiles. 'It's chilly out there. What if I go grab us some sandwiches and a cup of tea and bring them back here? Unless of course you feel like a walk to the coffee shop?'

I hate to admit it, but the walk from Jane's and then the extra hike to the drycleaners has taken it out of me a bit. I don't usually bother with lunch. If I can't snag a free cup of tea and a biscuit from a library event, I make do with cups of water from the bubbler outside the ladies'. 'You go get yourself some lunch, dear. I'll catch up with a few of the regulars while you're having a break.'

'All right, then. I'll be back as soon as I can. Unless you want to call it quits for the day?'

'No, not at all. I'm itching to get this book done as quickly as possible. I'm not getting any younger, you know.'

Jane laughs and heads off while I close the meeting room door and take a wander to see what's going on in the rest of the library today. It's all rather dull. I see Glenda in one of the reading chairs in General Fiction. She gives me a strange look when I sit down next to her. 'How was your granddaughter's birthday?' I ask. 'Did your daughter-in-law approve of the book you sent?'

She clasps her hand to her chest. 'Dolly! I'm sorry, I didn't recognise you for a minute. I was worried when you weren't here yesterday. I asked Vincent and he said you hadn't been in today either, so I was quite concerned. But now here you are, and looking a million dollars, I might add.'

'Thank you.' I know Glenda is probably curious about my sudden transformation, but I'm not sure how to explain it, so instead I repeat the question about her daughter-in-law and then she's off, telling me all about her little granddaughter's birthday and how the daughter-in-law is such a fusspot. 'There's a problem with everything I choose,' she complains. 'I'm not allowed to buy her pink things because that's not "PC", or something. No sweets because they're not good for her teeth. What's a grandmother to do? I thought it was my job to spoil the grandies, you know? But it hasn't worked out that way. Even the books I send have to be vetted by the mother in case they have "sexist undertones".' She rolls her eyes. 'I tell you, it's a whole new world out there, Dolly.'

I smile and make sympathetic noises, but all the while I'm thinking how lucky Glenda is to have family, even if they do drive her batty.

Jane returns carrying a large paper bag and holding a tray containing two takeaway cups. She doesn't look in my direction as she makes her way back to the meeting room. 'You'll have to excuse me,' I say to Glenda. 'Jane and I have work to do.'

Glenda looks in Jane's direction. 'Is she the woman who burst into tears in the magazine section?'

'Yes,' I say. 'We've struck up a bit of a friendship.'

'I'd be a bit careful with that one if I were you.'

'Oh?' I say in a defensive tone. 'Why is that?'

'I overheard some of the story-time mums talking about her that day. Apparently, she was involved in some sort of internet scandal. Fraud of some type. Didn't quite catch it all, and it's not as though I know enough about the internet to make heads nor tails of it anyway, but you should watch yourself. I'd hate to see you being taken advantage of.'

'I think they must have the wrong end of the stick,' I say, surprised at the depth of my loyalty to Jane, when in truth I hardly know her. But my gut tells me there's not a dishonest bone in her body.

'If you say so. Just be careful. Don't give her your bank account details or anything.'

I laugh at this. It's not as if I have anything to lose. But, nevertheless, I'm touched at Glenda's concern. 'I promise I'll be careful, but I'm absolutely sure there's nothing to worry about.'

Back in the meeting room Jane has unwrapped two packets of sandwiches. 'I got egg and lettuce because I know you like that, but there's chicken on this one if you prefer.' She pushes a disposable cup across the table to where I'd been sitting before. 'I got us tea too.'

'I didn't expect you to buy me lunch.'

'It was my pleasure. Now, I've had some thoughts about how we can structure the book. Shall we talk about that while we eat?'

I sip my tea and nod, and Jane launches into a discussion of the merits of a linear timeline versus a circular one. By the time we've finished eating she's decided on a book in three parts – early life, the theatre years and then a smaller later years section. She thinks we should try to collate some pictures to go with each part. I tell her I have some of my childhood, but not many of the theatre days, although there may be a few in storage at Adnan's.

'We can probably find some online,' she says. 'I can help you navigate the internet, but let's not worry about that too much right now. I think we need to focus on getting the basic framework down.'

I haven't got the foggiest idea of how to make this all come together so I simply eat my sandwich and nod my agreement.

Jane pulls out a spiral-bound notebook and starts constructing a timeline of my life, asking me for pertinent dates – when I was born, when and where I went to school, when I first started in the theatre and so on. I can remember most of the dates pretty well, although some things are a little foggy.

'Just do the best you can,' Jane says, encouragingly. 'We just need a starting point. I can do online research to verify anything you're unsure of.'

We talk for at least another hour as Jane tries to piece together an outline of the major milestones in my life. She's heavily focused on my life in Australia for the moment and is making a list of things we will need to research further. Once we get to my job at the Valley Mill, I find myself stifling a yawn.

Jane looks at her watch and her eyebrows shoot up. 'It's nearly three o'clock. We've been at this for hours. Maybe it's time to call it a day.'

'The time has just flown, and I've thoroughly enjoyed myself, but I have to admit I am getting a bit weary.' I tap my head. 'I haven't had to use the old grey matter so much in ages.'

Jane laughs. 'I still have some time to kill, so I'm going to do a bit of research. Shall we reconvene here tomorrow at ten? I'll see if I can book the meeting room before I leave.'

'Lovely. I'll see you then.' I grab the handle of my wheelie case and make my way out of the room. I haven't got anywhere to go, but I don't want Jane to feel as if she has to stay with me, so I wave goodbye and head off to browse the magazines. I don't have the slightest interest in reading about celebrities or five easy weeknight meals, but I like to take a couple of magazines to the reading area so I can have an afternoon kip. Stacey can't complain about me sleeping in the chairs if I pretend I've accidentally nodded off while reading. I am an old lady, after all.

●

I wake to the sound of Jane's voice. 'Dolly, are you okay?'

The sunlight has gone. It must be getting late. 'Yes, I'm fine, thanks.'

Jane crouches down beside me. 'The library's about to close. I've been researching for a couple of hours and was just about to leave when I noticed your case sitting here. I came to see if perhaps you'd left it.'

'No. To be honest, I often have a little sleep here in the afternoons. Jemima knows to check for me before she locks up.'

'It's just that . . . forgive me for asking this, but . . . Dolly, do you have somewhere to stay tonight?'

Jane is my friend and I find I can't lie to her, even though the shame of my truth burns my cheeks. 'No, I don't.'

She nods. 'Then, would you consider coming home with me?'

Chapter Twenty-four

London
1964

The doorman at The Savoy Hotel greeted Dolly by name. 'Lovely to see you again, Miss Jamieson.'

'And you too, Phillip. Is Mr Giles here, do you know? I'm afraid I'm running quite late for our luncheon.'

'No doubt you are worth waiting for, Miss Jamieson. I believe Mr Giles went through a little while ago.'

Dolly loved this hotel. It was her favourite in all of London. She still pinched herself sometimes when she thought about how much her life had changed in the past three years. After the successful Sydney run of *The Rose of France*, Raymond had told her she was ready to try her luck on the world stage – starting with the West End.

She'd followed Raymond and Grae to London and waited tables for months while attending auditions. Eventually she decided it was her Australian accent holding her back, so she took a job singing in a Soho nightclub and took acting and elocution lessons during the day.

When she'd first arrived in London she'd been completely over-whelmed by the city. She'd somehow imagined that her time in Sydney would have prepared her for living in one of the world's busiest cities, but she was wrong. Everything was different. The fashion, for starters. Her clothes – considered stylish back home – weren't a patch on what she saw the women wearing here. She almost felt frumpy compared to the local girls, who were wearing shorter hemlines and bolder colours than she'd seen before.

It wasn't just the fashion, though. Life was lived at a faster pace than she was used to. She was terrified of the traffic, and the crowds made her claustrophobic. Raymond and Grae laughed at her attempts to board public transport. She waited patiently while others pushed in front of her. 'You need to hold your ground, Dolly,' Grae told her. 'Otherwise you'll get eaten alive by this city.'

Two years on, she was an old hand at pushing through queues and she was no longer a wide-eyed ingenue.

She had the club to thank for that. It had an electric energy that attracted all sorts of people, including some decidedly shady characters. Performing while there was a drug deal going on at the bar or a fistfight in the back helped toughen her up. She took her cues from the barmaids and soon figured out how to breezily fob off the unwanted advances of drunken patrons.

In the end she learnt to enjoy it; the experimental music, eccentric personalities, irreverent fashion, even the whiff of danger all contributed to her London education. Still, she was happy when she landed an ensemble part in *Blitz* and was able to leave her nightclub days behind.

A few months after her first performance she was promoted to the role of Elsie and received a modicum of critical praise in the theatre papers. That led to a part in *Carnival*, and then to the part of Gloria in *Gentlemen Prefer Blondes*. She'd held that role for the whole London season and got plenty of attention from the critics. So when Raymond finally got backing to stage *The Rose of France*, she was no longer an unknown, and that helped to convince the producers she should reprise the role of Amethyst.

The production was due to wind up in a month after a stellar run of more than a year. When the show closed, she was going to take a few weeks' break before starting rehearsals for *The Matchgirls*.

She rushed through the foyer and made her way as quickly as she could to the hotel's restaurant. Raymond was already seated. 'Sorry I'm late, darling. I was on a call with Maurice and you know how he can be. I thought I'd never get him off the phone.'

Raymond gave her a half-smile. 'At least you can't complain that your agent's inattentive.' He paused for a second, a frown settling on his face. 'He didn't say . . . I mean . . . did he have any news for you?'

'No. It was truly a call about nothing. He was rabbiting on about me being his top client – which I know isn't true. He clearly wants something.'

A waiter in a full dress suit brought a bottle of Moët to the table for Raymond's approval.

Raymond waved his hand dismissively. 'Yes, yes, that's fine. Just open it.'

It wasn't like him to be ungracious to waitstaff. Dolly smiled at the waiter. 'Thank you so much.'

Raymond took the hint immediately. 'Sorry, old chap. Didn't mean to be brusque. I have some good news to share with the lady and I'm eager to get on with it, that's all.'

'Not at all, sir. Shall I pour?'

'Please.'

'Good news? What is it?'

Raymond waited until the waiter had backed away from the table before raising his glass. 'Here's to the latest star of Broadway.'

'And who might that be?'

'It's you, Doll. Or it will be soon.'

'Me? I don't understand.'

Dolly could see Raymond's eyes twinkling even in the muted hotel light. 'I was worried Maurice might have spilled the beans, and I wanted to be the one to tell you. I've just had confirmation that *The Rose of France* is getting a run on Broadway, and they want me to direct and you in the lead role.'

Dolly gasped. 'Good gracious, really?'

'Really. Here's to us, Doll. Isn't this what we've always dreamt of?'

'I truly can't believe it! When does it open?'

'March next year. You'll need to be there in late January to start rehearsals. They're insisting on an American male lead – they have Julian Barrows lined up. You'll like him, Doll. He's a gentleman and he was actually born here, I believe, so you'll have a translator.' He laughed and Dolly rolled her eyes. 'The American producers have already put out a casting call. Liddy and Simon are heading over to help with auditions.'

'But I've just signed on to do *The Matchgirls*.'

Raymond shrugged. 'So?'

'I've got a contract. I've committed.'

'Maurice will get you out of it. They've still got plenty of time to recast the role.'

'I hate to go back on my word like that.'

'Doll, this is big. If this is a hit, it will cement you as one of Britain's biggest stars and it will open the door to more work in America. If you say no to this, you might never get the opportunity again.'

Dolly sipped her champagne and thought about what Raymond was saying. He had worked so hard for *The Rose of France* to have a West End run. It wasn't easy getting an Australian production off the ground in London, but thanks to Raymond's tenacity and the flexibility of the show's writers, he'd eventually found producers who were willing to give it a shot.

Dolly knew she'd only been placed in the leading role due to his persistence. The producers had wanted an established star, but Raymond had argued that they had Ricky Morgan in the male lead as a drawcard, and that Dolly was a huge talent who would be the making of the show.

It was a gamble that had paid off for all of them. *The Rose of France* had opened to rave reviews, and Dolly was heralded as a star in the making.

Everything about the experience was wonderful. Dolly loved working with Ricky – who was a rare combination of talent, wit and generosity. If he'd been interested in women she would surely have fallen in love with him. The public were unaware of Ricky's preference for men and it didn't take long for the press to mark him and Dolly as an item. The pair had great fun playing up to the rumours, which suited them both. For as long as it was widely assumed she and Ricky were together, Dolly didn't have to fend off other suitors. Their make-believe affair helped to raise her profile while leaving her free to focus on the one thing that truly mattered – her career.

Her hard work was beginning to pay off. Recently, a recording of the show's major numbers had hit the charts and her agent, Maurice Quinn, was currently in discussions with the record label about a possible solo album for Dolly. *The Rose of France* was due to close just before Christmas, so she'd jumped at the offer to star in *The Matchgirls*. Maurice had said it was a natural progression and that if the critics liked her performance it would solidify her place as a bona fide star of the West End. She didn't want to put any of that in jeopardy. But, then again, Raymond was right: Broadway had always been her dream.

She put down her glass. 'What if I take the role and *Rose* is a flop on Broadway?'

Raymond laughed. 'Oh, ye of little faith. It won't flop. It'll be a huge success. *Rose* is a special musical and a perfect showcase for your talents. Working in this industry is a gamble – we all know that – but, honestly, this is the opportunity of a lifetime. You'd be mad not to grasp it with both hands.

●

From the moment her feet touched the ground at the newly christened John F. Kennedy International Airport, Dolly knew she'd made the right decision. This was *the* place. The atmosphere was electric, filled with the hopes and dreams of all those who found their way here. If she could make it here, she would truly be a star.

She adored London, but New York was something else. She didn't know how to describe it. The city had a pulse all of its own. It excited her in a way she'd never felt before. She loved everything about it – the fast pace, the accents, the yellow taxi cabs and most especially the thriving theatre scene.

Rehearsals started a week after her arrival and she'd been nervous on the first day, worried the local ensemble would resent an outsider being cast as their leading lady. The introductions were polite, but Dolly felt a distinct frostiness in the air until Raymond let it slip both he and Dolly were from Australia. The sheer exoticism of their origins broke down some barriers and Julian Barrows – *the* Julian Barrows – took a particular interest then. He said he was fascinated by Australia and wanted to go there one day. He begged Dolly to join him for lunch after rehearsal so she could tell him all about Sydney and Melbourne.

That was when her real love affair with New York began. In the weeks before opening night, her life fell into a pleasant rhythm. She'd start the day with a light breakfast in her room and then walk the few blocks to the theatre for rehearsals. When rehearsals were done she'd have a late lunch with some of the other cast members, and then they'd take turns showing her the various highlights of their beloved city. By the end of the second week, she'd visited the Empire State Building, the Metropolitan Museum of Art and the Guggenheim (such an amazing building), and shopped at some of New York's finest stores on Fifth Avenue.

Sometimes she needed to pinch herself to make sure she wasn't dreaming. Little Margie Ferguson had had big hopes of being a star back in Geelong, but when she'd ended up working in the woollen mill, it had been hard to see how she could ever make that dream come true.

Now, instead of wearing homemade clothing, she was shopping in some of the world's most famous stores. When she'd first arrived in London, she'd been blown away by the fashion scene – all the young women wearing Mary Quant's bright colours and tiny hemlines had been so different to what she was used to. Once she'd adapted to the London scene, she'd whiled away whole afternoons browsing the King's Road fashion boutiques, although back then she hadn't been in a position to buy anything. Now she was able to shop on Fifth Avenue!

If only her mother could see how things had turned out for her.

During the third week of rehearsals, Julian Barrows asked her if she could skate.

'I'm afraid I never learnt. Ice skating isn't a common pastime in Australia. It just doesn't get cold enough for there to be much ice.'

'Well, there's no time like the present to learn. I'm sorry to say I can't join you and the others for lunch today as I have another commitment, but how 'bout I make it up to you by taking you skating at Rockefeller Center this evening? We could have dinner afterwards, if you'd like.' Julian's tone was casual, as if he were inviting her to split a sandwich at the local deli, but Dolly's stomach flipped regardless. Dinner. Just the two of them. It felt like a date.

As soon as the thought crossed her mind, she batted the idea away. Julian was married. Everyone in the world knew that. He'd married Sondra Radley in a lavish wedding about a year ago. Sondra was one of Hollywood's biggest stars, practically American royalty, and was completely glamorous, so of course her husband wasn't flirting with Dolly. He was just being friendly. A good castmate, like the rest of her colleagues. And if he was being flirtatious, then she would most definitely set him straight. She wasn't the type of girl to knowingly fool around with another woman's husband.

These were the lies she told herself as she pondered what to wear. She'd packed her Kiki Byrne little black dress and a pair of black patent court shoes in anticipation of date nights, but she could hardly skate in a dress. And, besides, this was absolutely *not* a date. It was an outing with a colleague. Nothing more.

An hour later she met Julian in the lobby of her hotel wearing a pair of tight black trousers and a black turtleneck under her leopard-print coat. She'd slipped a pair of kitten heels into her oversized Dior handbag so she could change out of her fur-lined booties for dinner.

He greeted her with a low whistle and kisses on both cheeks before whispering in her ear, 'You look stunning.' He took her by the hand. 'Let's go knock the socks off everyone at the Rockefeller Center.'

And so the deception began.

He held her hands as they took to the ice, skating backwards so he could steady her. At first she felt like a toddler taking her first steps, but under Julian's tutelage she eventually got the hang of it, moving forward in tentative strides across the rink. Once she'd found her balance, Julian released her hands and skated beside her. 'You're a natural,' he said.

She laughed and glanced at him. 'Hardly!' As if to prove her point, she wobbled and braced herself to hit the ice. As she fell, Julian swooped in and caught her in his arms, pulling her up so they stood face to face, their chests pressed together. She hoped he couldn't feel her heart thumping, but judging by the look in his eyes as he gazed into her own, she suspected he felt *something*.

'Perhaps that's enough skating for one night,' he said, gently releasing her from his embrace.

'I think you might be right.' She turned and shuffled inelegantly towards the exit of the rink, ignoring Julian's chuckles behind her.

He took her by the arm as they walked briskly towards the restaurant. 'After seeing your form on the ice, I think you'd better hold on to me. The ground is a little slippery tonight.'

She socked him on the arm playfully. 'Shut up, you. I think I did well for a first-timer. Maybe I should challenge you to do something I'm good at.'

'I'm all for it. What would you have me do?'

She thought for a moment and then grinned. 'How about at rehearsal tomorrow you dance the first number of the second act in a pair of high heels?'

He guffawed. 'I don't think so! I mean, I can't even imagine how that's possible.'

'I do it every day.'

He grimaced. 'Touché. I'll lay off about the skating. Anyway, here we are.' He stopped under the awning at the entrance to a very grand-looking restaurant.

'Oh, we're here already? I need to change my shoes. I can't go in wearing these.'

'Once we're inside, I'll have the waiter show you to the restroom.'

She shook her head. 'Oh, no. I don't want to walk through such a fine restaurant dressed for skating! This outfit will be passable with heels, but without . . . no, I just can't.'

'Well, then, Cinderella, let me help you.' He crouched down. 'Give me your shoes.'

'What?'

'I presume you have the shoes in that giant handbag? Give them to me, and I'll put them on for you.'

She laughed and shook her head but he wasn't taking no for an answer, so she relented and did as he said. Julian unzipped the boots and then told her to put a hand on his shoulder for balance as he lifted her feet one at a time to pull off the boots and slide on her kitten heels. Other diners had to walk around them to get to the door, but none seemed to mind. One cheeky fellow even quipped, 'Looks as though you've found yourself a real Prince Charming, there.'

The restaurant itself was breathtaking, thanks in large part to the huge floral arrangements decorating the space. The maître d' greeted Julian warmly and ushered them to a cosy corner table.

'I must say, you seem much more at home here'—Julian cast his hand around to indicate the opulent decor of La Grenouille—'than on the ice rink.'

She laughed. 'Really? I'm obviously doing a good job of hiding my roots, then. I was only thinking this morning how gobsmacked my mother would be if she could see how luxurious my life is now. Once upon a time this place – the menu, the table setting, even the gorgeous flowers – would have completely overwhelmed me. I came from very humble beginnings, you see, and when I first started in the theatre I was a wide-eyed innocent afraid of making a mistake, or of being found wanting. Back then, I'd never even been to a restaurant! My naivety made me vulnerable, and I made some terrible decisions. Some so catastrophic that I . . .' She paused and then waved her hand as if to clear the air, not wanting to veer into the darkness that had ensued after her relationship with Alan.

'Anyway . . . I got my first big break as the lead in the Sydney production of *The Rose of France*. Actually, before that I'd been the understudy for the show in Melbourne and the lead fell into my lap after Cara Beecham broke her ankle, but in Sydney, I was chosen in my own right. I was picked to be the star! When that happened, I decided I was going to grab the opportunity – and everything that went with it – with both hands. Since then, I've made it my business never to shy away from an experience, even if the idea of it is intimidating.'

'Is your mother still . . .?'

'No. She died years ago. I like to think she's watching over me, though.'

'I'm sorry for your loss. I'm sure she'd be proud of what you're achieving.'

'Thank you.' Dolly smiled, trying to steer the conversation in a lighter direction. 'She'd certainly be impressed by the flowers here, but I'm not sure what she'd think of the escargot.'

Julian grinned and then whispered, 'To be honest, I'm not a fan of the escargot myself, but please don't tell anyone. I have an image to maintain.'

She threw back her head in laughter and he joined her.

'Are all Australians like this, or are you one out of the box?'

'Like what?'

'So refreshingly honest. So easy to be with and talk to.'

'Am I?'

'You are. I guess in this business everyone is always so busy trying to impress each other that it's rare to have a *real* conversation with anyone. Sometimes I feel as though my whole life is one big performance. I don't feel like that when I'm with you.'

'I'm glad,' she said. 'I feel very comfortable with you. You've been a great friend to me from the moment I arrived here.'

He smiled and raised his glass in a toast. 'To new friends.'

'Friends,' she said, clinking her glass against his.

Chapter Twenty-five

London
2019

We walk briskly – or as briskly as I can manage – back to Jane's house, hurrying to get out of the evening chill. Jane is as animated as I've ever seen her, her breath forming clouds as she talks about her ideas for the book and how, now that she's heard some of my childhood anecdotes, she thinks the story could be framed. 'It'll make a wonderful "rags to riches"–type tale,' she says. 'Not that I think you had a terrible childhood, by any stretch of the imagination, but people love the fairytale of an ordinary person made good.'

I laugh. 'Rags to riches and back to rags again!'

Jane looks mortified. 'Oh, Dolly. How insensitive of me. I'm sorry.'

'No need to be sorry. It's the truth. Perhaps it will serve as a cautionary tale.'

'Or perhaps it will have a surprise happy ending,' she says hopefully, and I smile at her optimism.

As we open the front gate, I notice light streaming out from an upstairs window.

'Richard must be home,' Jane says.

I've intuited that all is not well between Jane and her husband. 'Perhaps it would be better if I didn't come in after all.'

'No, not at all. Richard will be pleased to have a guest. He's always saying we should entertain more.'

I *am* curious to meet this husband of Jane's, so I nod. 'If you're sure?'

'I am. Come on.'

When we enter, the house is warm and there's a spicy aroma wafting from the kitchen.

'Jane?' a male voice calls as we enter the hallway. 'I'm in the kitchen. Don't faint, but I'm making dinner.'

I follow Jane to the kitchen to find a tall, dark-haired man stirring a pot of something – smells like curry – on the stove.

'Richard, I'd like you to meet my friend, Dolly,' Jane says. There's no warmth in her voice.

He swings around, spoon in hand, and little mustard-coloured droplets flick onto the countertop and the floor.

'Oh,' he says, clearly surprised, but he quickly recovers. 'I'm sorry. I didn't know we had a guest.' He rests the wooden spoon on an empty plate and steps forward with his hand outstretched. 'Richard Leveson,' he says cordially. 'Pleased to meet you.'

I take his hand and shake it firmly. 'I'm so sorry to barge in on your homecoming dinner.'

'No, not at all. Any friend of Jane's is a friend of mine.' His tone is polite but neutral. I can't tell whether he's truly fine with my presence or not.

'I didn't expect you,' Jane says, and there's an awkward pause for a moment.

He looks shamefaced. 'I'm sorry. I should have called to let you know my plans.' He glances at me and then back at Jane. 'I finished my business early and thought I would surprise you. I arrived a couple of hours ago and discovered you weren't home, so I popped up to the Indian place on the corner and got us a takeaway. Thought I'd save you the trouble of cooking.'

'Right. Well, as you can see, I've invited Dolly for dinner, so—'

'Oh, don't worry, there's plenty. I couldn't decide, so I got chicken korma and lamb rogan josh, and there's naan. I've just put it on to reheat and I'm cooking rice, too.' Richard wears the proud expression of a child who has just learnt to tie his shoelaces.

Jane nods. 'Good.' She turns to me. 'Would you like me to help you take your things upstairs?'

'No, I can manage. I'll leave you two to catch up for a bit.'

'Dinner won't be long. About ten minutes,' Richard says.

'Thank you. I'll be back in a jiffy.'

I've left my wheelie case in the hallway, so I retrace my steps to collect it before making the slow trek up the stairs. As I haul the case up one step at a time, snippets of Jane and Richard's conversation carry through to me. I can't hear every word but it's clear from the tone that an argument is brewing.

Where have you been . . .?

Never mind about that. Where did you meet. . .?

You're the one who wanted . . .

. . . could be an axe murderer!

My ears prick up. They're talking about me! As quietly as possible I make my way back down the stairs and edge into the foyer, getting as close to the kitchen as I can without being noticed.

'Honestly, Jane, have you completely taken leave of your senses? You can't just invite random strangers home to stay. Especially when I'm not here. Good god, anything might have happened.'

'Don't be so melodramatic, Richard. As you can see, I'm perfectly fine.'

'That's hardly the point.'

'No?'

'The point is you know nothing about her. She could be anyone – a violent criminal or a petty thief. For all you know she could be a spy from one of the tabloids.'

Jane laughs at this. 'For heaven's sake, have you looked at her? She's a sweet, vulnerable old lady. She's not a criminal or a spy; in fact, she's had quite the career on the stage and even been on TV. Not that it matters. She's my friend, and that should be good enough for you.'

'Your friend?' Richard scoffs at this. 'You've known her for, what, two whole days?'

'Longer than that, actually. I'm not sure why you are so put out by this. Aren't you the one who's always telling me I need to find new interests, meet new people?'

'I meant take up golf or join a bridge club, not collect strays,' Richard says in an exasperated tone. 'Jane,' he says in a softer voice, 'I love that you are so kind-hearted, truly I do, but I'm worried about you. You're not making good decisions. It's understandable after what we've been through these past few months, I know, but I can't help but worry. I wish you'd consider going back to Dr Keller.'

'You didn't seem too worried when you took off two days ago and didn't give me any indication of when – or if – you were coming back.'

'I'm sorry, I just needed a break. I told you that. I didn't realise you thought I might not come back. I thought you understood, but obviously we're not communicating effectively right now. Kate – I mean, Dr Keller – says—'

'Fuck *Kate* and fuck you, Richard.'

This isn't about me anymore, so I shouldn't be eavesdropping. Nor should I be here. Jane's husband clearly loves her and is rightfully being protective of her. I know I'm not the cause of whatever is wrong in their marriage, but I don't want to add to the tension.

I back away quietly and make my way to the front door. I open it as noiselessly as possible and slip out into the night.

●

Jane arrives at the library right on ten, the time we originally agreed on.

I almost didn't come today. I was certain she'd turn up as planned and I didn't want to face her after last night. But where else was I going to go? I had to be out of the hotel by ten anyway. After what happened the other evening I'm afraid to spend another night on the street, but by the time I left Jane's it was too late to even bother trying for a bed in one of the shelters. Instead, I made my way up the street to the hotel where Lydia works and booked myself a room. It's a three-star hotel, and once upon a time I would have considered it cheap, but these days I'd call it a splurge. One I can't afford, of course – it's almost cleaned me out of cash – but I've decided I'm going to sell my treasure and then I'll have something to live on.

It breaks my heart to think of selling the amethyst and diamond ring that has adorned my right hand for so long. Adnan tried to convince me to sell it ages ago, after I'd relented and sold off a few of the vintage dresses he was storing for me. He knew I was struggling then, not that I'd ever told him the full extent of my troubles. I knew he'd want to help somehow and I also knew his wife would not be happy about that. It was better for him to think that money was tight but that I wasn't desperate.

'The dresses will fetch you a few hundred quid and keep the wolf from the door, but the ring is something else. A Tiffany original, of that era,' he'd said, 'mark my words, Dolly, you'll get a fortune for it.'

At the time I wouldn't hear of it.

The ring is the closest thing I have to a wedding band and it seems traitorous to part with it. But now it seems I have no choice.

Last night, having made my decision (and safe in the knowledge that cleanliness and the new-old clothes gave me a veneer of respectability), I booked into the hotel and slept safely for the second time in a week. This morning, after the briefest deliberation, I made my way here. I suppose I knew Jane would come and that I would have to explain myself. I'm hoping she's not too upset and that we'll still be able to work on the book together. Now the husband's back in the picture, though, I'm not counting on it.

Jane walks towards me. She has a dry-cleaning bag folded over her arm and a relieved expression on her face.

'I wasn't sure if you'd be here,' she says.

I shrug. 'Where else would I go?'

'Dolly, about last night . . . I'm so sorry. I—'

'Jane, please, there's no need to apologise. I was imposing and as soon as I realised that I took my leave. Forgive me for not saying goodbye, but I didn't want to give you the opportunity to talk me out of it. You've been so kind to me and the last thing I want is to put you in an awkward position.'

'You obviously overhead my conversation with Richard.'

I don't insult her intelligence by pretending otherwise. 'I did, but don't worry. I understand. He was concerned to come home and find you'd been harbouring a stranger. I don't blame him for that.'

'But you're not a stranger. You're my friend.'

'Yes, I feel that way too. But, in reality, we haven't known each other long. And one can't be too careful these days. Your husband was just looking out for you.'

She sighs. 'Yes, I suppose that's true, but sometimes his care feels suffocating. We haven't seen eye to eye since . . . well . . . since we lost Tom.' She shifts the dry-cleaning bag to her other arm.

'Shall we go to the meeting room and talk there?' I say. 'We have it booked, after all.'

She nods. 'Yes. Yes, that would be great. Why don't you make your way down there and I'll get one of the librarians to unlock it for us.'

By the time I reach the meeting room, Jane has caught up to me. 'It's Stacey's day off,' she says, 'so Vanessa just gave me the key and told me to hand it in at the desk when we're done.'

I smile at Vanessa's tiny rebellion. Stacey would have a fit if she knew. She's such a stickler for the rules. Jane unlocks the door and I follow her inside, dragging my case behind me.

Jane places the dry-cleaning bag at one end of the table.

'Do you want to talk about it? About you and Richard . . . and Tom?'

She shakes her head. 'Not yet. I want to give you something first. I collected your coat.' She gives me an apologetic smile. 'Call it a peace offering.'

'Oh!' I say, clapping my hands together in anticipation. 'Let's have a look.'

As she unzips the bag and removes the coat from the wire hanger, my eyes immediately mist with tears. It's the coat I fell in love with all those years ago. Just looking at it takes me back to the first time I saw it in Adnan's shop.

'Oh my stars. I don't believe it. It looks brand-new.'

Jane nods her agreement. 'Hari's done a great job. If you look closely there's still some wear and tear, but he's mended all the major damage and it's cleaned up a treat.'

I take it from her and hug it to my chest, breathing in its fresh, just-cleaned scent. 'Thank you, Jane. This means the world to me.'

'Try it on. See how it feels.'

'Ooh, good idea.' I slide off Jane's old tartan coat and hang it on the back of the chair. Jane helps me into my coat and I feel more myself than I have in months. I step back and give a little twirl, so she can appreciate the total look.

She laughs and says, 'Very nice indeed. It's not just the coat that has a new lease on life.'

I grin and spin around one more time, as if to prove her point, and then I say, 'Okay, enough of this. Time for us to get to work. That is, if we're still working together on the book?'

Her cheeks flush pink and I fear now is when she will make her excuses.

'I'm more than happy to,' she says. 'I'm so glad you haven't been put off by what happened last night.'

'Pfft, as if I'd be put off by such a trifling matter as that. My dear, you'll have to try harder if you want to get rid of me.' I wrap my arms around myself, hugging my coat to me, before sliding it off and passing it back to Jane, who is holding the hanger.

'Good,' she says as she rehangs my coat and zips the suit bag up. 'Now, on a somewhat related topic, I want to talk to you about your accommodation.'

I glance at my beautiful ring for just a second. 'No need to worry about that, my dear. I had a little hiccup, but that's all about to be sorted.'

'Oh, really?' I detect a note of disappointment in her voice, or perhaps it's disbelief. 'Well, good for you. I truly am pleased to hear your problem is sorted, but I'd be lying if I didn't admit it's a tad disappointing for me.'

'I don't know what you mean.'

'I was hoping you'd give us another chance to show you some hospitality. Richard felt terrible after you left – he even went out and walked around to see if he could find you, but you were long gone.'

'Honestly, Jane, it's fine. There's no need for either of you to feel badly.'

'It's not about that, I promise. I like having you around, and seeing as we are working on the book together I thought it would make sense to have you as a house guest for a little while. That way we can work whenever we want, not just when the library is open.'

'That's a kind offer, Jane, but I don't think it would work.'

'Because of Richard?'

'I don't want to be a source of tension between the two of you.'

Jane takes a seat at the table and sighs. 'Richard and I have different ideas about things. About grief and moving on. Any tension between us isn't caused by you.'

'Still, he made it clear he was concerned about having a stranger in the house, and I don't want to make him feel uncomfortable in his own home.'

'Well, that's just the thing. Richard has changed his mind about that. After you left last night we had a long talk, and once I told him who you are and explained the project we're working on, he felt quite embarrassed about his reaction to you. I showed him some old YouTube clips of you on the stage and he was very impressed. He's right behind me working on the book with you.'

After what I overheard last night, I find this hard to believe. 'Wonderful.'

Jane laughs. 'For an actress, you're not a very good liar. You obviously don't believe me, but it's true.'

I shrug. 'Jane, it's okay. We can just work on the book here. That was the original plan and it's a perfectly good one.'

'Okay, but just hear me out before you make up your mind. I know the change of heart seems sudden, but Richard – for all his faults – just wants what's best for me. Once he realised how passionate I am about telling your story he was completely on board with the idea. I know you said your accommodation is sorted, and if that's true then I'm happy to hear it, but if you were just trying to spare me some embarrassment then please consider my offer. I'd love you to stay with me for a while. I think we could get a lot more work done if we were sharing a house, but, more importantly, nothing would make me happier than being in your company.'

My thumb rubs the back of my ring, an action I repeat countless times a day. I try to imagine what it will be like to find that finger suddenly bare. 'Well, nothing's set in stone yet.' I smile inwardly at the unintentional pun. 'It could be a week or two until my arrangements are finalised. I was just going to stay in the hotel on the high street until then.'

Jane's face shines with hope. 'How about this? Why don't you come for dinner this evening? Richard will be delighted to see you, I promise. If you feel comfortable then you can stay on until your new accommodation is sorted. If you feel at all unwelcome, I'll call a cab to take you to the hotel. Deal?'

I extend my hand to her to shake on it. 'Deal.'

Chapter Twenty-six

New York City
1965

Dolly told herself she was not falling in love with Julian.

She had sworn off love a long time ago. There had been plenty of romantic liaisons, of course. Her body had been ravished aplenty but her heart had remained deliberately indifferent. She chose her lovers carefully; men who wanted what she did – a good time, with no strings attached. That way she was in no danger of jeopardising her one true love. Her career was the centre of her life, her talent and ambition wholly reliable. Men, she had come to learn, were not fit to be relied upon to provide happiness.

But more and more she found herself thinking about the charming Mr Barrows.

After their skating and dinner excursion, the friendship had gone up a notch. The day after their 'date' he'd donned a pair of heels to perform the first number of the second act, as she'd challenged him to. He wobbled about the stage, sending the cast into fits of hysterical laughter, and eventually Raymond insisted on the shoes' removal before someone got hurt. Julian then conceded defeat, saluting all the female members of the cast. Not only did this act endear him to Dolly, but it set off a chain of practical jokes among the cast members, which made rehearsals even more fun than they had been before. Dolly and Julian were the ringleaders, and despite Raymond's grumblings about professionalism, even he seemed to recognise that the backstage levity was helping the cast to bond.

In this atmosphere it was easy for Dolly to tell herself that the chemistry she and Julian shared on stage was the result of good acting, and that the flirtatious smiles he gave her when no one else was looking were just a bit of friendly fun. None of it meant anything.

When he'd held her hands as he taught her to skate, she was sure he was just being chivalrous. When he'd told her how unique she was that night at La Grenouille, she knew he was speaking as a friend. He'd even said as much.

Tonight, when he'd fed her a piece of delicious Steak Nino during a candlelit dinner at The Drake Room, she told herself he was being hospitable. When he'd gazed into her eyes and told her she was beautiful, she kidded herself that this type of hyperbolic praise was just the way of Americans and he didn't really mean it.

But, just now, standing in front of her hotel-room door as he kissed her fully on the lips, her heart cracked open.

She kissed him back.

And then good sense prevailed. She placed her hand on his chest and pushed him, hard. He stepped back until he was pressed against the door to her hotel room.

'I can't do this. You need to leave,' she said.

He put his hands in the air in surrender. 'Dolly, I'm sorry. I must have misread the signals. I thought you liked me. I thought there was a spark between us.'

'I do like you, but there's a big problem. You're married, and I don't fool around with other women's husbands.'

Julian began to laugh.

Fury bubbled up inside her. 'I hardly think it's a laughing matter.'

'I'm sorry. You're right.' He shook his head. 'It's just that . . . well, I assumed you knew. Everyone else in New York seems to, at least everyone in the New York theatre world. But you're new here, so I suppose it makes sense.'

'Knew what? I have no idea what you're talking about.'

Julian put his finger to his lips as a room service waiter approached, wheeling a table filled with empty plates and glasses. 'Good evening, Mr Barrows. Miss.'

Julian nodded at him. 'Evening.' He waited until the waiter had entered the lift at the end of the hall before continuing. 'Do you think we could continue this conversation in your room, where we'll have some privacy?'

'I don't think that's a good idea. Whatever you have to say for yourself, you can say it here.'

'Very well. I know what it looks like, but my marriage to Sondra is not real.'

'Really? I've seen the photos.'

'Yes, we had a big fancy wedding, but the marriage is a lavender one.'

'I don't know what you mean.'

'It's a sham.'

'You mean it's not legal?'

He sighed and shook his head. 'It's legal enough, but it's just for show. I don't love Sondra and she doesn't love me. The marriage suited both of us for different reasons.'

'Julian, forgive me, but this doesn't make sense. Both you and Sondra are big stars in your own right. Surely you could marry whoever you want.'

He gave her a despairing look. 'There's not a hope in hell of Sondra marrying the person of her choosing. She's very much in love with her personal assistant.'

There was a *ding* at the other end of the hall and the lift doors opened. A couple got out and made their way along the hallway towards Dolly and Julian.

'So? This is 1964, Julian. I don't think anyone would think less of her for falling in love with her employee.'

'Can we please go inside to talk?' he asked. 'I don't want to risk us being overheard.'

She hesitated, not wanting to give him false hope. She was no virgin, but she drew the line at fooling around with married men. And, as trustworthy as Julian seemed, her experience with Alan had taught her that sometimes even the nicest-seeming men could turn out to be complete bastards.

'Please, Dolly. I swear to you I'm telling the truth. I want to explain it all to you but there are things that could ruin my career and Sondra's career if they got out. Can't we talk in private?'

'Oh, all right,' Dolly said in an exasperated tone. 'But just to talk. Do you understand me? Nothing else.'

Julian nodded as she retrieved her room key from her handbag and opened the door.

Once inside, Julian took a seat on the chintz-covered couch and Dolly sat in the armchair opposite.

'Well, go on then. Explain it to me.'

'Sondra's assistant is a woman.'

'Oh . . . Oh, I see.'

He shifted uncomfortably in his seat. 'Dolly, that knowledge is private. There are those in the industry who know, and even more who suspect, but if it was made public, it would be the end of Sondra's career. I have no business even telling you, I just couldn't bear for you to think of me as some sort of cad who cheats on his loving wife. I need you to promise you will keep this to yourself. Please. I'm not asking for my sake but for Sondra's.'

'Sondra's secret is safe with me,' Dolly said coolly. 'But I still don't quite understand why you would marry a woman you don't love. It's a big sacrifice to make; one most people wouldn't make just out of the goodness of their heart.'

He rubbed a hand over his face. 'You're right. I had my own reasons.'

She stared at him silently, waiting for an explanation to follow.

'I'm not sure how much you know about me – about my previous relationships?'

She shrugged. 'I read. I remember you being linked to a few of your co-stars, especially that girl from *Sandy Point*.'

'Helena Shaw. Yes. We met when filming the movie. She was from the Midwest and she seemed so sweet. She was out of her depth in Hollywood, and I tried to take her under my wing.'

Dolly raised her eyebrows. 'Do that often?'

'I know what you're thinking, but, honestly, I was just trying to be nice. And then we got to know each other a little and I liked her. One thing led to another, and then . . . well, things got out of hand.'

'What do you mean?'

'We became an item for a while and at first I was happy, but then I realised we were very different people. The movie went well and Helena got a lot of attention. We got invited to a lot of parties. She started drinking a lot, and more.'

'Drugs?'

'You guessed it. Instant fame can do things to people. Helena didn't cope with it very well. She had these terrible mood swings. Sometimes she was the life of the party but other times I'd find her crying on the floor of the bathroom. She started filming another movie, but her behaviour was pretty bad. She was often late to the set and she didn't always know her lines. The director was threatening to sack her. Life with her was like being on a never-ending roller-coaster. I couldn't take it anymore, so I broke up with her.'

'And you married Sondra on the rebound?'

'No.' He smiled sadly. 'It wasn't that. I was relieved to be free of Helena, but she didn't take the break-up so well. One night I got a call from her. It was obvious she'd been drinking. She'd booked herself into a hotel and was threatening to jump from her balcony if I didn't come right away.'

Dolly gasped. 'How awful.'

'When I got there she'd trashed the room and was throwing things from the balcony.'

'Oh my goodness.'

'Yes. Fortunately I was able to stop her before anyone got hurt, but she was screaming so loudly that the police were called. When they arrived they found the room smashed up, the two of us struggling and a whole lot of cocaine. We were both arrested.'

'I don't remember any of this being in the papers.'

'No, it wasn't. That's where Sondra comes in.'

'I'm not following you.'

'Sondra and I share an agent. There were rumours flying around about Sondra's sexuality and he'd decided the best way to put an end to that was for Sondra to marry another star. He thought the big celebrity courtship followed by a wedding with all the trimmings would do the trick. He knew the studio bosses would be thrilled about this, so he was sure if I agreed to marry Sondra then the head of the studio would see to it that my arrest was hushed up.'

'But that's ridiculous. You didn't do anything wrong!'

'That's the last thing anyone cares about once the press gets hold of a story. The scandal could have killed my career then and there.'

'So you married a woman you didn't love? That's a terrible price to pay.'

He shrugged and held up his palms to face the ceiling. 'It's not so bad. I like Sondra. We're great friends. We have a beautiful home in Beverly Hills. It's huge – we each have our own wing and we essentially live our own lives. I spend a lot of time here in New York and some time in London as well. Sondra prefers LA.'

'You see other people?'

He nodded. 'Discreetly, of course. Maxine, Sondra's partner, lives at the house, but she's an employee, so nobody questions her presence.'

'So, how long will this arrangement last?'

'We signed an agreement to stay together for five years. After that we can renegotiate or end the agreement. We must spend at least three months of every year together – but it doesn't have to be consecutive – and we are bound to accompany each other to public engagements, awards nights and so on. She'll fly out here for the premiere of our show. We'll play the loving couple for the night and she'll fly home the next day.'

'Is it worth it? Living your life this way?'

'Honestly, until recently I would have said absolutely. My star was on the rise when I met Sondra but I hadn't made it to the big time. Marrying her made me a household name overnight. I've been given opportunities I would never have had without our union. Until a few weeks ago I would have said it was the best decision I've ever made.'

'What happened to change your mind?'

'I met you.'

Dolly didn't know what to say.

'I know this is unusual. I know I'm asking a lot, but, Dolly, I'm falling for you big time. Just give me a chance. Sondra and I have been married for a year already. Four years will fly past and then I can ask her for a divorce.'

'Whoa . . . hold on a minute. One kiss and you think I want to *marry* you?'

Julian laughed. 'Okay, maybe I'm going too fast. All I know is I want to be with you, Dolly, and I hope you can look past my circumstances and allow me to be part of your life.'

Dolly moved towards him, seemingly drawn by a force outside her control. Perhaps she would regret it later, but right now all she wanted was to feel Julian's touch. She sat beside him on the couch and drew him into her arms. 'Let's try this kissing thing again and see how it goes from there.'

Chapter Twenty-seven

London
2019

Jane and Richard are the perfect hosts. After apologising for his 'unforgivable outburst' the evening before, Richard is completely charming, serving hors d'oeuvres, filling my glass with bubbly and offering to take my case upstairs. 'You will stay, won't you? At least for tonight?'

I can see why Jane fell in love with him. He's witty, engaging and attentive. He seems to anticipate his wife's every need. I watch him respond to her sigh when she opens a cupboard to find the bin overflowing by removing the offending rubbish without being asked. He fills her drink, helps to chop the vegetables for dinner and generally makes himself useful. I try to imagine Julian being so at home in the kitchen and the thought makes me laugh.

Despite the cosy domestic scene, last night's tension hasn't completely gone – there's an air of forced cheerfulness between them – but they're both genuinely warm and welcoming to me. Their marriage might be in trouble, but I'm not the cause of their problems and, who knows, perhaps the distraction of a geriatric roommate will ease the friction between them.

'Thank you, Richard. I will stay, if you're sure I'm not imposing?'

'Not in the least.' He beams. 'I'll pop your things upstairs before we head into the dining room.' He looks at Jane. 'How long until we serve up?'

'Couple of minutes. The soup's almost done.'

'Right. Back in a jiffy, then.'

Richard collects my case from the entry hall where I've left it, and we hear him padding up the stairs.

'You see?' Jane says, looking at me with optimism. 'There's absolutely no reason not to stay for as long as you'd like.'

I hate to rely on charity, and I've been forced to more than once these past months. But somehow this doesn't feel like charity, it feels like friendship, or maybe even fate. 'Thank you. You're both very kind. I will stay until I can get my other arrangements in order.'

'Excellent. Shall we go through? The soup's ready to serve. I'll get Richard to bring it in when he comes down.'

Richard reappears from the hall. 'Did I hear my name?'

'Oh, good. We're heading to the dining room. Would you carry the tureen for me?'

The soup is cream of mushroom – rich and delicious. Jane's cooking is restaurant-quality. 'This is scrumptious, Jane. You are a stellar cook.'

Richard nods enthusiastically. 'Isn't she? I keep telling her she should try out for *MasterChef.*'

'Yes, because that's just what I need, more public exposure,' Jane says in an acid tone.

Richard winces at her sarcasm. 'Yes, of course you're right. Sorry, I wasn't thinking . . .' He drops his gaze and takes another spoonful of soup.

Jane has the decency to look embarrassed. 'Sorry, that was uncalled for. I apologise.' She looks at me. 'I'm a little touchy on the subject of publicity since . . . since we lost Tom. He . . . well, it's just that—'

'Our son's accident attracted some media attention,' Richard explains. 'As you can imagine, it was difficult for us both.'

I nod, thinking back to the day in the coffee shop when that horrible woman verbally abused Jane. Perhaps her outburst was somehow connected to the news coverage of what happened to Jane's son. I've certainly had my share of experience with negative media stories over the years, which is part of the reason Julian and I were so careful to keep our relationship private. I'm desperate to know more, but this is the first time Jane has given any detail about her son's passing, so I don't want to push her. 'That must have taken a toll.'

'Yes,' Richard says, putting down his spoon. 'It was awful. The media were relentless—'

'Let's not dwell on this tonight,' Jane says. 'I don't want to ruin Dolly's first night here with tales of woe. And, as you're constantly reminding me, Richard, that's all in the past now. We need to move on.' Jane's tone is pleasant enough, but Richard looks suitably rebuked.

'Yes, you're right.' There's an awkward silence for a moment and then Richard speaks again. 'Jane tells me the two of you are working on a book together. That sounds wonderful.'

'Yes, I'm excited to have Jane's help with the project,' I say. 'I have lots of memories but I'm no writer. It's hard for me to work out what's of note and what's not.'

'I'm sure readers will be fascinated by your life story. I haven't had the pleasure of seeing you onstage myself, but I know you were a star of the West End back in the 1960s and '70s.'

'Not just in the '60s and '70s,' Jane interrupts. 'Dolly's worked for a good portion of her life.'

Warmth floods my chest at Jane's attempt to honour the whole of my career and I smile at her appreciatively before turning my attention to Richard. 'Certainly my younger years were the most successful. But I did have a few smaller parts as the years went on.'

'Not to mention starring in a long-running TV show,' Jane says.

Richard looks embarrassed. 'My apologies. I don't really get to watch much telly.'

I laugh. 'No need for apologies. I'm not sure *The Neighbourhood* would be your cup of tea. I know Julian . . .' I hesitate. I haven't told Jane about the relationship with Julian yet. 'My friend, Julian, watched it once or twice, just to be supportive, but in the end pronounced it "utter tripe".'

Richard laughs but Jane says, 'That doesn't sound very supportive.'

I shake my head. 'I didn't mind. He was right. And we never could lie to one another.'

'Well,' Jane insists, 'I certainly enjoyed it and I know it was very popular not just here in England but in many other countries too.'

'You're right about that. The show had fans worldwide. Oh, the fan mail I used to get – and my fair share of hate mail, too!'

Richard swallows a mouthful of soup and then cocks an eyebrow at me. 'Really? Hate mail? Wow. How did you cope with that?' He steals a glance at Jane, but she's looking right at me.

'It never really bothered me.' I shrug. 'Mrs Mackin was a character. She wasn't me. The hate wasn't personal.'

Jane's shoulders slump just a little. 'Yes, I can see how that would make a difference.'

'In any case, I think you'll have loads of readers lining up to buy your book,' Richard says brightly. 'What prompted you to want to tell your story now, all these years after leaving the spotlight?'

'I had no intention of writing a book until I met Jane. I was just scribbling down my memories to pass the time. It was Jane who suggested other people might be interested in what I had to say.'

Richard beams at her. 'Jane has a good head for that sort of thing. Knowing what people will find interesting.'

Jane smiles at him and for the first time I notice a sense of tenderness between them. Up until now it's seemed as if they were playing the parts of a happily married couple, but now I feel as if I've caught a glimpse of something real. Or, at least, the remnants of a love that once was.

'At first I was reluctant, but then I realised writing the book might help me to achieve my greatest wish in this life.'

'Oh,' says Richard, as he stands to clear our empty soup plates, 'and what's that?'

'To be reunited with my son.'

Richard stops clearing the table for a moment. 'Well, I have to admit, I didn't see that coming. I assumed you were keen to find a new source of income.'

'Richard!' Jane looks alarmed. 'Ignore him, Dolly. You don't have to talk about this.'

Richard clears his throat. 'Sorry, that was very rude of me. It's none of my business.'

I laugh at them both. 'If I'm going to stay here for any length of time, you two are going to have to relax a bit. I'm not easily offended, and I wouldn't have brought up the topic if I didn't want to talk about it.' I look at Jane. 'Clearly you have worked out I'm in a bit of financial bother – I assume that's why you offered to put me up?'

Jane nods silently as Richard sits back down at the table.

'And obviously you've discussed this with Richard, so it's a fair enough assumption for him to make – that I'm writing the book for the money. And, of course, nothing would please me more than being financially independent again. As lovely as you both are, I hate relying on "the kindness of strangers", as Tennessee Williams would say.' I laugh at my weak attempt at a joke to try to lighten the mood, but they're both looking at me with pity in their eyes. 'Don't worry, I have a plan for financial freedom – with or without the success of the book – so you won't be stuck with me for long.'

'You're very welcome here, no matter how long that takes,' Jane says and then frowns. I can't be one hundred per cent sure, but I think Richard may have just kicked her under the table.

I wave away her offer. 'That's very kind, but I promise I will be sorted out soon. I've been waiting on an inheritance that has been held up by some legal issues. I thought it would be well sorted by now but seeing as it isn't I've decided to sell off some assets. All will be in order soon, I promise.'

Richard opens his mouth as if to speak and then closes it abruptly. A return kick from Jane, perhaps?

'You have a home here in the meantime,' Jane says, and Richard nods his agreement.

I'm not sure if he means it or if he is merely trying to keep the peace, but I'll take his concurrence at face value for now.

'Forgive me if this a dense question, but I'm curious how the book might reunite you with your son. Is it a peace offering of some sort? Are you estranged?' Richard asks.

Jane looks as if she's about to chastise him again but before she has the chance, I cut in. 'It's not a dense question at all. Jane asked a similar thing.'

Jane has the good grace to look embarrassed.

'I haven't seen my son since he was a few days old. I had him when I was very young and I gave him up for adoption. Over the years I've tried to find him, without any success, and I'd given up hope of ever meeting him, but when Jane suggested writing the book it sparked fresh optimism in me. Perhaps there is still someone out there who knows something about my son. Perhaps if they read the book, my story will entice them to come forward with some leads about his identity.'

'It seems rather a long shot.'

'Richard, for heaven's sake.'

'It's all right, Jane, I don't mind. Richard's right, it *is* a long shot. I know that. But after exhausting every other possibility, it's the only option I have left.'

Jane shoots Richard a warning look and he stands. 'Well, I should be clearing this table so we can enjoy the next course.' He collects the plates and disappears into the kitchen, which gives Jane the opportunity to apologise again.

'You must forgive Richard. It's his lawyer brain. He's always asking inappropriate questions. I don't think he even realises he's doing it.'

Richard returns with a bottle of red wine in hand, which he places on the table. 'I thought this would go well with the main course.'

Jane looks at the label and nods. 'Speaking of which, I might check on the potatoes. The meat's resting, so we should be just about right to serve up.'

'Shall I come to carve?' Richard asks.

Jane shakes her head. 'The vegetables might still need a few minutes, and I have to make the gravy. You stay here and entertain Dolly. I'll call you when I'm ready to serve.'

Once Jane is out of earshot, Richard leans in and speaks in a low voice. 'Forgive me for being forward, Dolly, but I'm just wondering what other methods you've used to try to find your son. If you don't mind me asking, that is.'

'Not at all.' I give Richard a precis of everything I've tried so far, including the leads that Julian's lawyer friend turned up.

'How long ago was that last attempt?'

'Oh, ages. Fifteen years ago at least, maybe longer. I gave up after that, you see. The hope and then the subsequent disappointment was too much to bear.'

'But now?'

'Now I'm an old lady and I've come to realise life isn't endless. I want my son to know my story. Even if the book doesn't lead to a reunion – and I agree with you that it is unlikely – at least I will have given it one last shot. And I will have left something behind for him. It will comfort me to know my story is out in the world and that one day my son might read it and understand why things happened the way they did.'

'I see. Well, I think the book is a splendid idea for many reasons, but what if there was another way to get in touch with your son? Would you be interested?'

'Absolutely, but, as I said, I think I've exhausted all the options.'

'Right, yes, of course. Well, perhaps the book will yield the answers you're looking for.'

'I hope so. There's no harm in trying, right?'

Richard looks doubtful but he smiles and says, 'None that I can think of.'

Chapter Twenty-eight

New York City
1965

Dolly woke to sunlight streaming in through her hotel room window. Every night, after Julian had slipped out and retired to his own bed, she pulled back the drapes so she could take in the bright lights of Manhattan before she drifted off to sleep.

She wanted to make the most of every moment, because life surely couldn't get any better than this. It felt almost too good to be true: here she was, in a fancy hotel in New York City, about to make her Broadway debut.

The final rehearsals and previews had gone well. Of course, they wouldn't truly know if they had a hit on their hands until tonight. Tonight! Opening night at last.

Being the leading lady in a Broadway musical was everything she'd ever dreamt of, and yet the universe had seen fit to give her even more. These past few weeks she and Julian had been as inseparable as two people engaged in a secret love affair could be. Julian said they needn't worry too much – many in the theatre world either knew or had guessed his marriage to Sondra was not the real deal. 'But we need to be careful the press doesn't get hold of the story, so I'm afraid there won't be too many candlelit dinners at fine restaurants, at least for the next little while.'

Dolly didn't mind. Not really. Now she knew the truth of the matter, all she cared about was that Julian loved her. And she had no doubt that he did.

That first night, he hadn't left her room until daybreak. Nothing had happened between them other than a couple of passionate kisses. Not that Dolly would have rejected any advances Julian made that night – in fact, she would have gladly welcomed him into her bed. But he was a perfect gentleman, telling her, 'You made it clear when you let me in that we would do nothing but talk and I'm going to stick to that promise.'

She'd laughed. 'I'm not going to hold you to that now.' But he'd made up his mind.

He told her about growing up in London and then Connecticut, and how he'd come to New York to go to college and stumbled into acting from there. His parents had been against the idea – so much so that his father disowned him. It'd been hard to pursue his dream against their wishes, but he felt he had no choice. 'I tried to walk away from acting more than once, but the theatre kept calling to me.'

Dolly had never felt more connected to another human being.

She told him all about her life in Australia. About her childhood and about losing her mother and siblings in the crash. He held her hand and told he was so sorry she'd suffered such a great loss, and she could tell by the look in his eyes that he meant it.

And then she'd taken a deep breath and told him all about her baby boy.

He listened carefully as she recounted her feelings for Alan and her belief he felt the same way. She glossed over exactly what happened on the riverbank, merely saying that one thing had led to another.

'And when he discovered you were pregnant?'

She shrugged. 'He told me to get rid of it, but, well . . . in the end I couldn't do that. My mum and I planned that she would raise the child, but then . . .'

'Oh, my darling, you have had too much sorrow for one lifetime. If I could take some of that away from you I would.' He kissed her gently on the top of her head and promised he would try never to be the cause of any more pain in her life. 'I will do my best to make your life as joyful and happy as possible. I wish I was free to love you openly, Dolly, but that just isn't the case right now. I am free to give you my heart, though, and you can be certain you have that.'

She'd kissed his lips and they'd held each other close.

'We won't have to keep our secret forever. Just four more years, and then I can ask Sondra for a divorce. I know that seems like a lifetime, but you're still young. There'll be time for us to have a family of our own, if that's what you want.'

This statement had stopped Dolly in her tracks. She'd never wanted children, but then Jamie had come along and she'd wanted nothing more than to be *his* mother. She'd been robbed of that chance and she knew in her heart she could never have another child. How could she play happy families with Julian when somewhere out there her firstborn was being raised by someone else? If Julian had his heart set on being a father, then they needed to put an end to this before it went any further.

'I can't have any more children,' she said.

'Oh, my love, are you sure? Modern medicine is wonderful and we have the best doctors here in the States. If you want—'

'No, that's not what I mean. I *won't* have another child. I had a son and I failed him. I could never bring a new baby into this world with that on my conscience. I didn't ever want children, but when the universe intervened and delivered me a son I should have risen to the challenge. Instead, I blew it. I had my chance and now it's gone. The theatre is my life now. I'll understand if that means you want to end this before we get in over our heads.'

He laughed. 'I don't know about you, but I am already way out of my depth. I couldn't give you up now if I tried.'

'I'm serious, Julian. I won't change my mind. If you want children, you'd best walk away from this now.'

'My darling, darling girl. All I want is you. I want whatever you want, full stop.'

Since that moment they'd spent every minute they could together. Dining together just the two of them wasn't a good idea in case it generated interest from the press, so most of the time they saw each other as part of a loud and jolly group made up of cast members and their friends. Most nights they'd end up dancing at Shepheard's Nightclub, which was not only the hippest venue in town but also conveniently located in the very hotel where they were staying. At some point in the evening Dolly would say her goodbyes and retire to her room. After a decent interval, Julian would follow. They'd spend most of the night together, but Julian would eventually retire to his room three floors up.

Sadly, there would be no such rendezvous tonight. After the performance there was to be a private party hosted by the producers in Shepheard's Nightclub to celebrate the (hopefully) successful opening night. Sondra was flying in from LA to be with Julian at the event. She was due in just after lunch. Dolly knew she had no right to be jealous, and Julian had reassured her Sondra posed no threat, but she couldn't help feeling nervous about meeting her lover's wife. 'It'll be fine,' Julian had said last night. 'Sondra knows about us. She doesn't mind. Honestly, this is all business to her. You have to think of it that way too. When you see us together tomorrow night, remember, it's just a performance.'

Dolly knew he was right, but nevertheless it stung that she couldn't spend her night of nights with the man she loved.

Still, she wasn't going to let that ruin her day. Raymond had assured her that by tonight she would be the toast of Broadway. And, tomorrow, Sondra would be gone.

A loud rap at the door caused her to throw back the bedcovers and pull on her robe. 'Who is it?' she called.

'Bellhop, miss. Special delivery for you.'

She opened the door to find the young man's face almost totally obscured by the bouquet of red roses he was holding. She thanked him and asked him to set them down on the coffee table while she collected her purse for his tip.

'That's not all, miss.' He presented a silver tray with a white envelope and a small blue box tied with white ribbon at its centre.

'Goodness, I am spoilt.' She took the gift, handed the boy his tip and saw him out the door, and then took the parcel back to bed. Before she could open the card, the telephone rang on the bedside table.

'Hello?'

'Good morning, my darling,' Julian's voice crooned. 'Did my gift arrive?'

'Is it from you? I should have guessed. I haven't opened it yet.'

'I wanted you to have a memento of today. I considered giving it to you last night, but I thought it would be a nice way to begin this special day.'

A lump formed in Dolly's throat. He truly was the most thoughtful man on earth. 'That's so kind of you. The roses are gorgeous. You needn't have got me a gift as well.'

'Nothing's too good for my girl. Open it now, while I'm on the phone. Don't bother with the card, you can read that later.'

Dolly giggled like a schoolgirl. 'Oh, all right. Just give me a moment.' She tucked the receiver under her chin, untied the white satin ribbon and prised the lid from the box. Inside sat a gold ring set with a spectacular oval-shaped amethyst. Three rectangular diamonds sat either side of the glittering violet stone.

Dolly gasped, speechless, and Julian laughed gleefully on the other end of the phone. 'Do you like it?'

'Like it? Oh my god, Julian, it's the most beautiful thing I've ever seen.'

'It's a promise ring, Doll. My promise to you that, no matter what happens, no matter what obstacles we have to overcome, I will always be yours.'

'Oh, Julian, thank you. It means the world to me.' The lump in her throat returned as her eyes filled with tears.

'How about we breakfast together downstairs today?'

'I'd love nothing more – but is that wise?'

'Well, if we were both in the restaurant around nine and we happened to bump into one another, I think it would be downright rude of the leading man not to ask his leading lady to join him.'

She grinned. 'Good thinking, Mr Barrows. Perhaps I'll see you there.'

•

The rest of the day passed in a blur. Despite 'bumping into' Julian in the restaurant and being invited to join him, they'd had very little time on their own. Several well-wishers dropped by the table, and then Raymond and Grae appeared. It was all very exciting and festive, but not particularly intimate. It didn't matter. Dolly had Julian's ring on her finger and that was enough.

The afternoon was taken up with opening-night preparations. The producers had organised a backstage photo shoot, which required her hair and make-up to be done and then undone so she could be made up properly for the performance. She saw Julian only briefly, when the photographer asked for a few shots of them together. After that she was kept busy by reviewing the script and choreography to make sure her performance was step-perfect.

Dolly was aware of Sondra's arrival, but only because she'd overhead the girls in wardrobe talking about it. She must have come to the theatre to surprise Julian, but Dolly was occupied all afternoon and didn't get the chance to see her before the show. Perhaps it was just as well. What if Sondra resented her in some way? Julian had insisted it wasn't the case and she trusted him, but . . .

Now was not the time to worry about that. With five minutes to curtain up, Dolly had to focus on becoming Amethyst. Tonight was the most important performance of her life – the rest of her career depended on it – but the only way to make sure the performance was a good one was to put that thought out of her mind. For the next two hours she needed to inhabit her body and be at one with her character.

Her first scene with Julian was not until after the end of the first number, so she was surprised when he sidled up to her just as she was about to take her place on stage.

'Break a leg, my love,' he whispered in her ear and then he was gone. Moments later, the curtain rose and Dolly launched into her first song.

●

A round of joyous applause greeted Dolly as she entered Shepheard's Nightclub on Raymond's arm. The reviews wouldn't be in for a few hours yet, but she had a feeling they'd be good. Raymond seemed only slightly nervous, and he'd hugged her after the show and told her she was 'simply perfect'. In Dolly's opinion, the whole cast had given a flawless performance, and the audience seemed to agree. There'd been a long standing ovation at the end of the show that resulted in several curtain calls.

With opening night and her Broadway debut successfully behind her, it was time to relax. However, there was still one hurdle to overcome – meeting Sondra.

She didn't have to wait long. The maître d' greeted them as they entered the club. 'Miss Jamieson, Mr Giles, welcome. Mr Barrows is already here and would be most honoured if you would join him and his wife for supper.'

Dolly smiled but didn't trust herself to speak.

Fortunately, Raymond answered for them both. 'We'd be delighted, wouldn't we, Doll?'

'Absolutely.'

The maître d' nodded. 'Very good. If you'll follow me.'

Sondra was every bit as beautiful in real life as she was on the screen. Maybe even more so. She and Julian stood to greet Dolly and Raymond as they approached the table. Sondra was petite – the top of her head only just reached Julian's chin – but her presence was huge. She wore an elegant, black velvet floor-length gown with a high empire waist. Dolly immediately regretted choosing her knee-length, buttercup-yellow shift to wear to the afterparty. What had seemed fun and festive in her bedroom now seemed frivolous and lacking in class.

But if Sondra found Dolly to be unstylish, she hid her opinion well. Her signature chocolate-brown eyes, framed by dark eyeliner and perfectly sculpted eyebrows, exuded warmth as Julian made the introductions. Dolly found herself starstruck and speechless for a moment, but recovered enough to mumble, 'Pleased to meet you.'

Sondra tucked a strand of her glossy brown hair behind her ear and smiled. 'Gosh, me too. Jules has been raving about you ever since the first week of rehearsals. I've been simply dying to meet you.' She tapped the chair next to hers. 'Come sit by me so we can get to know each other a little.'

Dolly did as Sondra requested, her mouth suddenly dry. Was this going to be some sort of interrogation? But from almost the second she took her seat, Sondra made it clear there was no animosity on her part. She laid her hand on Dolly's forearm and said, 'I just love your dress. It's like a burst of sunshine. I feel very dull in comparison.'

Dolly shook her head. 'Oh, goodness, there's nothing dull about you. I was just thinking how elegant and stylish you looked.'

Sondra laughed. 'Then we shall have to agree to disagree.'

'What are my two favourite ladies disagreeing on?' Julian cut in.

'That's between us,' Sondra said teasingly. 'You boys go back to talking about golf or cars or whatever it is that floats your boats.'

Julian raised his hands in a surrendering motion. 'Okay, okay. I'll keep out of it.' He winked at Dolly and she smiled to let him know everything was fine.

In fact, things turned out better than fine. Sondra couldn't have been nicer. She gushed over Dolly's performance in *The Rose of France*, batted away compliments about her own stellar career and engaged in some very light and harmless gossip about a couple of her co-stars. Dolly was charmed.

Julian ordered champagne for the table, and once it was poured he made a toast. 'To the two leading ladies in my life. It's so lovely to have you both here tonight.'

'And to *Rose*,' added Raymond. 'May her stay on Broadway be a long and successful one.'

'I'll drink to that,' said Sondra.

It didn't take long for their little party to become a merry affair. Dolly and Julian were frequently interrupted by well-wishers, and others wanting a photo or a quick word. Dolly loved every minute of it. Here she was sitting next to a real-life movie star and people were asking to take her photo! Sondra had her fair share of admirers too, but she graciously declined any photos that didn't include Dolly or Julian. 'Miss Jamieson's the star here tonight,' she said on more than one occasion.

They'd been seated less than twenty minutes when Grae arrived, kissed Dolly and begged her forgiveness at dragging Raymond away to 'show him off' for a bit. Five minutes after that, Julian was called away by one of the producers.

'Now that I have you all to myself, I can be frank with you,' Sondra said. 'I hope you'll forgive me for being so forthright when we've only just met, but who knows how long we'll have before we're interrupted again.'

Dolly's mouth went dry. Was this the part where Sondra warned her off? She smoothed her dress and took a deep breath. 'Of course. Please feel free to say whatever you need to.'

Sondra laughed a little. 'Oh, Dolly, there's no need to feel anxious. I'm not going to reprimand you. In fact, quite the opposite. I know all about you and Julian and I just want you to know I'm delighted for you both.'

Heat crept from Dolly's neck up into her cheeks. This was one of the strangest conversations she'd ever had.

'I can see I've embarrassed you, but you needn't feel ashamed. I love Jules – he's my family – but I'm not *in love* with him. Do you know what I mean?'

Dolly nodded. In many ways their arrangement was no different to her sham love affair with Ricky, except she and Ricky hadn't stood up in a church and taken vows.

'I want Julian to be happy and he wants the same for me. I've found the love of my life, and I very much hope that Julian has too.'

'Oh!' Dolly said. 'Sondra, thank you. I'm not sure I'm the love of Julian's life, though. It might be a bit early to make that call.'

Sondra poked her arm playfully. 'From everything he's said to me, I'm pretty sure I'm right. The man is hopelessly in love with you, Dolly. You needn't doubt that.'

Dolly reached for Sondra's hand and squeezed it. 'It's incredibly kind of you to say all of this to me. I can see why Julian cares about you so deeply.'

Sondra waved the compliment away. 'Not at all. But, Dolly, if you truly love him in return, I need you to know that it's not going to be easy. It's fine now while you're both here in New York, but sooner or later Julian will be offered a movie part he can't resist, or maybe you will. You'll have to endure being apart and keeping your relationship a secret at the same time. I will be on his arm at every opening night and award ceremony, and there will be photos of us looking lovingly at each other in all the magazines. That will be hard on you. It's hard on my Maxine.' She glanced at Dolly and for the first time that evening seemed unsure of herself. 'Jules did tell you . . .?'

'He did.' Dolly smiled to reassure her.

'All I'm saying is, it won't be easy, and there may be times when you doubt the relationship or feel jealous of me. I'm telling you now that you have no reason to.'

Chapter Twenty-nine

London
2019

Staying with Jane and Richard is complicated. On the one hand, I'm grateful for the comfort and safety of their home, but on the other hand, I feel as if I'm in a tenuous position.

Jane's been unfailingly kind and welcoming, and tells me daily she loves having me in her home. Richard has been polite but distant. There's tension in the air whenever he is home. I can't tell if this friction is due to my presence or if there's more going on. He does seem happy that Jane is engaged in the writing project and appearing more animated, although Jane doesn't seem to appreciate his comments of support.

'For heaven's sake, Richard. We're working a significant project, not "keeping busy"', she said last week when he mentioned how nice it was to see her occupied again.

'Yes, of course. My apologies,' came his stiff reply.

Maybe the frosty atmosphere in the house has nothing to do with me, but, even so, I'm not sure Richard fully trusts me yet.

I'm doing my best to fit in without getting in the way. The last thing I want is for either of them to regret their invitation to host me until I can sort out my finances. A situation, I'm ashamed to say,

I have done nothing about. It's hard to sacrifice my ring when there's no immediate need.

And things are going along well enough here, for the time being at least. Jane and I have been working on the book together in the afternoons, but we go our own way in the mornings. I still go to the library almost every day. I like to see the other regulars and the librarians – even Stacey, who has warmed to me considerably now I am no longer (visibly at least) one of the great unwashed. But the main reason I leave the house is to give Jane some breathing space. We've been getting on so well, but I don't want to push my luck. Sometimes she comes to the library too, but most days she prefers to work from home.

Richard works long hours and isn't always back for dinner, but he tries to make sure he spends Saturday and Sunday evenings with Jane. I make myself scarce on Saturday nights, taking a light supper up to my room, to give the two of them an evening together.

On Sunday mornings I head off to church, as usual. It's a funny thing: if you'd asked me two months ago if I was a believer, I would have laughed at the very idea. I would have said I only attended Sunday service because I had nowhere else to go when the library was closed. Now there's no need for me to pull myself out of my safe, warm bed early on Sunday mornings. And yet I do. Maybe it's out of a sense of gratitude for my recent good fortune, or perhaps it's fear that god might punish me and take it all away if I don't keep fronting up. Maybe it's just habit. I don't know, but it's where I'm off to now.

I pop my head into the kitchen to find Jane making pancakes and Richard frothing milk for coffee. 'I'll be off now. See you both in a few hours.'

'Have you eaten?' Jane asks, like a worried mother, making her way to the fridge.

'Yes, thank you. I had some fruit and toast with my tea earlier.'

She opens the fridge door and grimaces. 'Damn, I forgot to get cream for dessert.'

Since I've been staying here, Jane has made a big deal of Sunday dinners. I'm not sure what she's making tonight but it's sure to be delicious. 'I can stop at that little supermarket on the high street on my way home,' I offer. 'I have to walk right by it anyway.'

Richard nods his head to the near-empty milk bottle beside him on the counter. 'We need milk too, and perhaps some apples.'

'Dolly won't be able to carry all that, Richard.' Jane looks at me. 'Don't worry about the cream. Seeing as we need a few things, Richard can pop down to Sainsbury's later in the car.'

Richard, who is still in his pyjamas and robe, looks less than excited at this idea. 'Hang on.' He disappears into the hall for a moment and returns with his wallet. 'What if I give you my card, Dolly? That way you can pay and then grab a cab home. There are always plenty around on the high street.'

Jane frowns, but before she can protest I jump to accept. This is a big show of trust from Richard, and I'd like to prove to him that I'm worthy of it. 'Yes, that's a great idea. Sometimes I get tired on the walk back from church and I have to stop for a bit to rest, so I'll enjoy the cab ride. Thank you, Richard.' Jane can hardly object now.

He shrugs as he hands over the card. 'Anything to get out of a trip to Sainsbury's.'

●

The usual vicar at St Stephen's is away today and one of the curates is leading the service. Poor thing is so nervous his voice is shaking, which makes it hard to concentrate on what he's saying. I tune him out, my thoughts drifting to my shopping expedition on the way home, which I'm quite looking forward to. Not only will I have the chance to prove to Richard that I can be trusted with his bank card, but it'll be nice to wander around the shop and not be under threat of being asked to leave.

It's amazing the privileges a clean set of clothes affords one. I can now safely browse in any shop I like – even ones I've previously been banned from. Most of the shopkeepers don't recognise me as the old bag lady they used to shoo away. Browsing is one thing, but today I will

be able to make a purchase and know without a doubt I have sufficient funds to pay. It's not my money I'm spending, and I'm relying on
charity to enjoy this small pleasure, but even so, it does feel as if my life
is getting back on track. I'm determined to be grateful for and to take
pleasure in each small opportunity that comes my way.

After communion, I exchange some brief pleasantries with the
curate and a couple of other members of the parish before taking my
leave. Today I'm keen to get on with my shopping, so I don't stay for a
cup of tea and biscuits in the church hall like I usually would.

It's a crisp and sunny morning, so I enjoy the short walk from
St Stephen's to the high street. I take my time getting to the supermarket, stopping to look in the windows of several smaller stores on
the way. Even so, it doesn't take me long to get there. I select a trolley
and begin to amble up and down the compact aisles although I only
need a few items. It's not a giant store, so after twenty minutes I'm done.

I wheel my trolley to the checkout, where the young girl serving me
makes polite conversation. To say I am delighted is an understatement.
When the time comes to pay, I pull out Richard's card with a flourish.
It's a bit of a novelty, to be honest. Both Julian and I preferred cash for
everyday items, only using cards to pay for high-end restaurants and
hotels. I offer the girl the card and her face clouds in confusion. 'The
machine's right there,' she says, pointing to it.

'Oh,' I say. 'Sorry. I don't often use a card.' I look at the box in front
of me for the place to swipe the card.

'You just tap it on the top,' she says with an encouraging smile.

I lay the card flat on top of the machine, but nothing happens. The
man in line behind me huffs impatiently.

'Would you like me to try?' the girl asks kindly.

I smile at her. 'That would be lovely. Thank you, dear.' I hand her
the card, which she flips over and glances at.

Her smile disappears. 'Is this your card?'

I feel myself blushing. 'Well, no. It belongs to my friend. He asked
me to buy him some things.'

'Is your friend nearby?'

'He's at home, I think,' I say, feeling increasingly flustered. 'I'm not sure. Maybe he's gone to play golf or something. I don't know. I've been at church, you see.'

She gives me a sympathetic look. 'I can't put these through if it's not your card, I'm afraid.' She picks up the handset beside the cash register.

I nod, trying to keep my cool. The last thing I want is to cause a problem for Richard. 'Look, never mind about the groceries. You can just give me back his card and I'll tell him he'll need to come and pick up these things himself.'

'Just one moment,' she says. 'I'll see what I can do.' She turns her body away and speaks quietly into the handset. When she's done, she says, 'If I could ask you to wait there for the time being, the manager will be along in a moment to help you.'

'Oh, for Pete's sake!' the fellow behind me says as he gathers up his shopping and heads to another checkout.

My cheeks are burning. 'I'm sorry to be the cause of such a fuss. I should have insisted he give me cash. I'm not great with all this new technology. Perhaps it would best for all if we don't worry about the shopping. If you could just give me my friend's card . . .'

She smiles at me but doesn't hand over the card. 'The manager will be along shortly.'

'I'm here now.'

I turn and my heart sinks. It's the same pimple-faced boy who tried to turf me out of here the day Jane came to my rescue. He's eyeing me suspiciously, and I wonder if he recognises me.

'This lady was trying to pay for groceries with a card that isn't hers. She says it belongs to her friend. I've explained that's against store policy.'

The boy-manager doesn't take his eyes off me. It's as if he's expecting me to do a runner. Not much chance of that – these arthritic old bones wouldn't get me far if I tried. 'Thank you, Emma. You can close off now and take your break. I'll handle this.' He holds out his hand and she gives him the card.

The girl looks at me apologetically before taking her leave. Something tells me I'm in real trouble now.

'I'm afraid I'm going to have to ask you to come to the office with me.'

'The office? Why?'

'Store policy. We take credit card fraud very seriously. You're going to have to speak to the police, and they can decide what happens from there.'

'The police?' This can't be happening. I haven't even been asked for my side of the story. 'This is ridiculous. There's no need to call the police. You can call Richard, the card owner. He'll verify my story.'

'I'm afraid that's not how it works. If you'd please follow me.'

My fear gives way to rage. How dare this impertinent young man treat me – or anyone – like this? 'No. I'm not going anywhere,' I say, raising my voice. 'Call the police if you must. Let your customers watch a little old lady being harassed to tears. See what that does for your public image.'

'As you wish.' He stares at me coolly. 'I was only trying to give you the chance to deal with this privately, but if you want to have your affairs aired in public'—he throws his hands up in front of him—'so be it.'

People are looking at me now, and one cheeky sod seems to be taking photos or maybe video on his phone. Perhaps my rebellion wasn't so smart after all, but I've dug my heels in now, so I stand my ground and say nothing.

It takes an age for the two young constables to arrive, by which time I am desperate for the loo. The male constable talks to the boy-manager while the young woman comes to speak to me. 'Let's start with your name, shall we?' she says impassively.

The pain of having to stand for so long combines with my anxiety about needing the toilet, so that when I open my mouth to answer a gulping sob emerges instead of my name.

'Are you all right there?' she asks, in a more sympathetic tone. 'Feeling okay?'

'I need the toilet urgently,' I say quietly.

She looks across to where her partner and the manager are conversing. 'The lady needs the toilet. I'll take her through to the staff facilities

223

and meet you two in the office.' She turns to me. 'Come on, let me show you the way.'

Perhaps apprehending shoplifters and the like at this store is a regular occurrence, because the officer seems to know where she's going. She takes me by the arm and confidently leads me through a swinging door into a sort of storeroom and then through another door marked *Staff Only*. We make our way down a poorly lit corridor until we reach the toilets. 'There you are. I'll be waiting right here for you.'

I race into the single cubicle, not worrying about the faint odour of other people's urine or the wet pieces of toilet paper left on the grey linoleum floor. I've used worse these past months and, besides, all I'm concerned with right now is getting my pants down without wetting them. Somehow, I manage to make it onto the loo in time. I'm so relieved not to have wet myself that I momentarily forget the predicament that brought me here. Once my bladder is empty, though, I feel my eyes filling with tears. I don't fear the police – I know I haven't done anything wrong – but this will be a major blow in my campaign to keep Richard onside. Instead of demonstrating my trustworthiness, this expedition has just proven that I'm nothing more than a thorn in his side.

I stand up, wash my hands and head outside to face the music.

The young constable smiles at me. 'Now, let's start again, shall we? I'm Police Constable Brewer. May I ask your name?'

'Dolly.'

'Come on then, Dolly, let's get to the office and get this sorted out.'

We head back down the corridor, and as we walk she asks me to tell her what happened with the card. I give her a quick rundown of the story, saying that I am staying with friends and they asked me to pick up some groceries for them on the way home from church.

'So this fellow whose name is on the card, he'll verify your story?'

'Yes, of course,' I say.

'Right, well, I'll have a word to my partner and we'll try to get this fellow . . .' She raises her eyebrows questioningly.

'Richard,' I offer.

'Right. Richard. We'll see if we can get Richard down here to sort this whole mess out.'

She stops outside a door marked *Manager* and knocks twice before pushing it open. The other police officer and the boy-manager are already inside. PC Brewer leads me to a chair and tells me to make myself comfortable, then she looks at her partner. 'Can I have a word outside?'

The boy-manager leans back in his chair and eyes me suspiciously, as if I'm about to knock off the pen jar or pocket the pads of sticky notes on his desk. I return his stare.

Fortunately, it doesn't take long for Brewer and her partner to return. She addresses the boy-manager. 'We think it's better if we can resolve this matter here, rather than at the station.'

The boy-manager huffs but says nothing.

'Dolly, do you have Richard's number?' she asks gently.

I shake my head, thinking how guilty this makes me seem. 'I'm sorry, I don't have a mobile phone and I never thought to write it down.'

'Right, well, it might take us a bit of time to track him down, but we'll manage.'

I suddenly remember I have Jane's number tucked away in my coin purse. 'I have his wife's number. Would that do?'

PC Brewer smiles. 'It's a start.'

I open my handbag – one of Jane's cast-offs – and find the coin purse. I hand over the slip of paper and Brewer passes it to her partner. He turns to the boy-manager. 'Is there somewhere private I can make this call?'

Once they've left the room, Brewer makes small talk with me, asking where I'm from and if I've known Jane and Richard long. She doesn't seem to find my answers suspicious, but as this is my first encounter with the law, I can't be sure if she's just chatting or if this is some type of covert interrogation. The others seem to be taking forever to return and I'm starting to worry that this might not be over as quickly as I had hoped. A lump has formed in my throat, and the tears I've been holding back are threatening to fall.

Just as I'm afraid I can't keep my composure any longer, the door opens and the young constable smiles at me. 'Mr Leveson is on his way. He has verified your story, Ms Jamieson, so it's just a matter of checking his ID. And then you'll be free to go.'

This is welcome news, although the thought of Richard seeing me detained by the police does not overly cheer me.

Brewer tries to keep the mood light by chatting away, which I appreciate, but the minutes tick by slowly nonetheless. She suggests to the boy-manager that he can leave us if he has more pressing work to attend to, but he declines, saying that keeping the store free from theft and fraud is of the utmost importance and nothing could be more 'pressing' than that.

I suppress the urge to roll my eyes, and a surreptitious glance at Brewer's face makes me think she feels the same way.

After what seems like hours, but in reality is probably less than ten minutes, there's a knock on the door and a young supermarket employee ushers in a worried-looking Jane and an irate-looking Richard.

Jane rushes to my side and clasps my hand. 'Are you all right?'

I nod and turn to Richard. 'I'm so sorry for all this trouble, Richard.' Try as I might, I can't keep the waver out of my voice.

Richard is staring furiously at the boy-manager. 'Are you proud of yourself? Putting an old lady through an ordeal such as this? Do you even know who she is? I have a good mind—'

'Richard!' Jane admonishes.

Brewer makes a placating motion with her hand. 'Sir, are you Richard Leveson?'

Richard swings around to address her. 'Yes, that's correct.'

'Let's keep our cool, shall we? Before we go any further, Mr Leveson, we need to see some photo ID.'

This mollifies Richard somewhat. 'Yes, of course. My apologies, constable.' He fishes in his inside coat pocket for his wallet and quickly produces his driver's licence.

Brewer nods. 'Right. Now, sir, is this your card?'

The other police officer hands over the card and Richard nods. 'It is.'

'Can you explain to us what this lady was doing with it?'

He looks at the male constable. 'We went over this on the phone.'

'If you wouldn't mind repeating it one more time, sir,' Brewer insists.

'Right, well, this lady, Ms Jamieson, is my guest. She was on her way to church this morning and I asked her if she could pick up some things on her way home. I didn't have any cash on me, so I gave her my card to use.'

'You're aware that bank cards are intended to be used only by the named card holder?' Brewer says.

'Well, yes, of course I am. But who hasn't given their card to a family member to use at some point? Everyone does it. It's hardly a hanging offence. In any case, if someone is in trouble here, it should be me, not Ms Jamieson. She was only doing what I requested.'

My heart leaps at his defence of me. Maybe things will be okay after all.

Brewer smiles. 'Oh, I don't think anyone is in trouble here, Mr Leveson. Just a misunderstanding. Perhaps it might be best if you kept your card for your personal use in future.'

He nods. 'Yes, of course, constable.'

Brewer looks at her colleague, who flips his notebook shut in response. 'Right,' she says, addressing me, 'you're free to go, Dolly. It was nice to meet you.'

Jane helps me to my feet and links her arm with mine. 'Let's get you home.'

I smile at PC Brewer and thank her. Richard opens the door for us and pats me on the arm as I pass. He hands his car keys to Jane. 'Take Dolly to the car, would you? I'm not quite done here.'

Concern flashes over Jane's face, but she simply nods and leads me out. Richard obviously overestimates my walking pace or under-estimates the volume of his voice, because we are only a few feet away when I hear him shouting at the boy-manager.

'Do you know who that woman is? She's a national bloody treasure, that's who! Dolly Jamieson – look her up some time. How dare you treat an old lady this way. Calling in the police and frightening her, when a simple phone call could have solved the whole issue. How would you feel if someone treated your mother or your grandmother with such disrespect?'

I stop walking and turn to face the office.

'Come on, Dolly. Let's go.'

I shake my head. 'Let's wait here for Richard,' I say. 'Just in case . . .' I don't need to finish the sentence, because although Jane sighs, it's clear she knows exactly what I mean.

'Sir, I think it would be best if you left now,' the male constable's voice interjects.

'I'm going,' Richard says and the door swings open. 'But I will never spend another cent in this store, and I will be advising everyone I know to do the same.' He emerges from the room and looks surprised, then a little shamefaced, when he realises we overheard the whole exchange. 'Sorry,' he says.

Jane raises her eyebrows, and he shakes his head.

'I know, I know. But I simply can't stand bullies. Now, let's get home and get our Sunday back on track.' He links his arm through mine and I begin to chuckle.

'What's so funny?' Richard asks.

'*National bloody treasure.* That was laying it on a bit thick, don't you think?'

'Oh, be quiet. I was trying to make a point.' Richard nudges me good-naturedly and joins in my laughter.

'You're *our* treasure, Dolly,' Jane says. 'And don't you ever forget it.'

Chapter Thirty

New York City
1965

Central Park was alight with the colours of late spring blooms. May was such a gorgeous month. It wasn't yet too hot, but the city was warm and vibrant. Everywhere Dolly looked there were signs of new life – from the thick green grass carpeting the park's open spaces to the tiny ducklings waddling after their mother at the edge of the Pond. There was even a marching band ahead of her, apparently practising its choreography for an upcoming event. It was as if the city sensed her happiness and was celebrating right along with her.

The past couple of months had flown by in a dreamlike wonder. The show had opened to rave reviews and was playing to a packed audience at every performance. That fact alone would have been enough to make her heart sing, but incredibly there was more. Her relationship with Julian, although still fresh, was magical; far beyond any fantasy she could have concocted for herself. He was kind, funny and adorably attentive. They were discreet in public, but several trusted members of the cast and crew now knew they were together, which was nice. It meant they could enjoy socialising at private dinner parties without fear of being exposed to the press.

Nevertheless, they were careful. Publicly, he was charming and effusive towards his co-star, but he was like that to everyone. When they were alone, however, an onlooker might have mistaken him for her servant, so eager was he to make her happy.

At first the lovemaking made her nervous. There was no doubting her desire for Julian – she felt it in every fibre of her being – but it was a want tinged with fear.

She was worried about pleasing him. Obviously, a man such as Julian had taken many lovers and she couldn't help but wonder how she compared. Was she as beautiful as some of the other women he'd bedded? Was her performance up to scratch? Despite having had many lovers herself, she had no idea whether she'd lived up to their expectations. It had never really mattered to her before. Sex had just been the inevitable outcome of having someone take her to dinner or accompany her to an event. Occasionally she'd enjoyed the act, but more often than not it left her cold. Now, going to bed with a man she loved, she wanted their union to be filled with passion. What if she wasn't enough for him? Even more than that, she worried about getting pregnant.

But she shouldn't have worried about any of it. Julian was a patient and generous lover. He made her feel things she didn't know were possible. Did things to her she'd never imagined or even heard of. Things with his hands . . . And his tongue. Last night he'd taken her to such heights that her body had rocked with an explosive pleasure that had paralysed her in the aftermath – much to Julian's delight. She felt herself blush at the memory of it. Strangely, she hadn't been embarrassed in front of Julian. The way he'd looked at her – as if she were some sort of goddess – made her feel beautiful, and powerful.

He took care of the contraception. They'd used rubbers every time so far, but Julian had also mentioned that if she wanted to go on the birth control pill, he knew of a doctor who would be obliging. It was early days yet in their relationship, but he showed no signs of being perturbed by her unwillingness to have children. In fact, he kept talking about a bright and rosy future in show business for the two of them, a future that left no room for offspring.

The grief she carried with her every day of her life had gone from being a gigantic boulder that weighed her down to a tiny pebble in her pocket. It was always with her still, but it wasn't the burden it had once been. For the longest time she'd wondered if she'd been born under an unlucky star – cursed never to be truly happy. Now she knew that wasn't the case. She'd had her fair share of tragedy, but the universe had finally decided to cut her a break. Spring was well and truly here, and her life was in full bloom.

It was such a glorious afternoon and her heart was so full that she didn't even mind the fact she had spent her day off alone. Julian had taken an early flight to Los Angeles this morning and wouldn't be back until late tonight. He'd raced off to an urgent meeting with his agent and the studio boss regarding a film they wanted him to star in later in the year. Dolly didn't want to think about a time when they wouldn't be working together, but Julian had promised they'd make it work.

Now the sun was getting lower in the sky and the breeze had a slight nip in it, signalling it was time to make her way back to The Drake. It'd been so warm when she'd set out earlier that she hadn't brought a jacket, and she couldn't risk getting a cold.

Raymond and Grae had invited her to dine with them, but she'd declined, telling them she wanted an early night. She was planning a luxurious night on her own. Room service, a bubble bath and a decadent treat that she would never indulge in when Julian was around – a box of chocolates and a stack of gossip magazines. She stopped by the newsstand near the park's entrance to stock up on mags. The chocolates – a gift from a fan – were already waiting in her room.

●

After a long soak in the tub, Dolly dried off and slipped into the soft terry-towelling hotel robe without bothering to dress. There was no one she needed to please, and if Julian happened to arrive back before she went to sleep, he'd be more than happy to find her naked beneath her gown. She smiled at the thought and set herself up in bed with the magazines and chocolates, fanning out her contraband so she could make her choice. Copies of *Modern Screen*, *Movie Mirror*, *Confidential* and *Hollywood Tell-Tale* all called to her with their sensational headlines:

Annette's private wedding and honeymoon photos
Liz sells out her country! The shocking reason
Frank Sinatra: His love for a woman he can never have
Hollywood baby bonanza: Which stars are expecting babies this fall?

First cab off the rank was *Hollywood Tell-Tale*. She wanted to skim this one and then tuck it out of sight before Julian showed up. He had no time for gossip sheets and particularly disliked this one. 'That rag is full of trash,' he'd said when he noticed her reading it backstage one day.

'It's just a bit of harmless fun. I don't take it seriously.'

'Harmless? Tell that to the people whose marriages have broken up because of it, or who lost roles because of the stupid rumours it published.'

She'd closed the magazine and changed the subject, making a mental note to indulge her appetite for industry gossip only when Julian wasn't around.

He wasn't due back for hours yet, so there was plenty of time to get her fill. She popped a caramel-filled chocolate into her mouth and began to flick through the pages. It was a juicy issue, filled with scandal and innuendo involving the biggest stars of the day. Poor Liz Taylor got more than her fair share of attention and Jackie Kennedy had plenty of column space dedicated to her, too. Dolly was halfway through the magazine (and a quarter of the way through the chocolates) when she turned the page to see Sondra staring back at her.

The headline above Sondra's picture took her breath away.

Pregnant stars: Get ready for a celebrity baby boom this fall

Sondra? Pregnant? There had to be some sort of mistake.

But when she looked at the photo of Sondra it did look as if she were expecting. Dolly's pulse thrummed in her temples. Could it be trick photography? Sondra hadn't looked pregnant when she'd attended the opening night, but she had been wearing that gorgeous empire-line gown. That waistline could hide a multitude of sins. Or perhaps she wasn't pregnant then.

Dolly scanned the article for more information.

Sondra Radley and husband Julian Barrows will welcome their first child in the fall, according to a source close to the couple. No official announcement has been made, but with Sondra beginning to show, Hollywood Tell-Tale *expects the couple to go public with their happy news any day now.*

It was unconfirmed, then. Maybe Sondra had simply worn an unflattering dress and the reporter had put two and two together and got five. That must be it. She did look pregnant in the photo, but these gossip magazines were not known for their accuracy. It was best not to get too out of sorts until she'd spoken to Julian. If this story were true, he would have said something – she was certain. Or maybe Sondra was pregnant but the baby wasn't his. Perhaps that's why he hadn't mentioned it.

Maybe he didn't even know himself. As far as she knew, in the months since Dolly and Julian had been together, the only time he'd seen Sondra was on opening night. The two of them had shared his hotel room that evening, but she was sure Julian wouldn't have slept with Sondra then. Not after he'd given Dolly the promise ring that morning, and Sondra had given them her blessing the very same evening. She couldn't believe they would betray her trust that way.

She would know soon enough. As soon as Julian arrived home, she decided, she'd show him the magazine and see what he had to say for himself.

She closed the lid on the chocolates and placed the magazines in a neat pile on the nightstand, her appetite for both now non-existent.

●

The moment Julian walked through the door she knew it was true. He forced a smile as he greeted her but his face was pinched with worry, or maybe it was shame.

She didn't say a word, just held up the magazine.

All the remaining colour drained from his already ashen face. 'So you know, then. I hoped I'd have the chance to explain before you saw it.'

'It's true?' She couldn't keep the growing feeling of hysteria from leaking into her words.

'It's not what you think.'

'The baby's not yours?'

His shoulders slumped. 'It is, but—'

'Fuck, Julian! How could you?' she shouted, hitting him with the magazine. 'I trusted you. I *loved* you.' She hit him again as tears began to stream down her cheeks.

'I'm so sorry,' he said, stepping back out of her reach. 'My darling, please, come and sit down. Let me explain.'

She wanted him to leave, but if she threw him out then it would be over, and she'd be all alone in the world again. It was inevitable, but she didn't know if she was ready to face that reality right away. She stood motionless for a moment and then allowed him to lead her to the couch, where she sat while he fixed them both a stiff drink.

Finally, he sat beside her and began to talk. 'Sondra is pregnant, due in October. The baby is mine.'

Dolly took a large swig of whisky, welcoming the burning in her throat and chest as a momentary distraction.

'It was just one stupid night. Before I met you. I would never, ever cheat on you, Dolly. I hope you know that.'

Dolly shrugged. 'It seems I don't know you as well as I thought I did.'

'Back in January I was in California for a few days. Sondra and I had agreed to do some photos and a feature article for *Modern Screen*. We went out for dinner and got tipsy on too much champagne. Sondra was upset because she and Maxine were fighting. She said Max was feeling invisible and had decided they needed to spend some time apart. We were drinking, and I hadn't been with a woman since the split with Helena. Sondra can be very persuasive when she wants to be, and . . . well, one thing led to another, and now here we are.'

Dolly took another sip of her whisky while she let his words sink in. 'Here we are indeed. How long have you known?'

'Just a few days. Sondra got wind the photos were being published by *Hollywood Tell-Tale* and she called me. She swears she's only known for a week or so. She thought her growing waistline was the result of indulging in too many sweets. She tried dieting for a few weeks and exercising more, but it seemed to make no difference. When she started to think about it, she realised she'd had a tummy bug that lasted for a couple of weeks in March – just after she'd been here, in fact.'

'Morning sickness?'

He nodded. 'She said once she stopped to think about it, she couldn't believe she'd missed the signs. A doctor confirmed it last week. That's when she called me.'

'So, there was no urgent meeting with the studio? You went to see her, didn't you? Christ, I can't believe this! I've been such a fucking fool.'

He reached for her hand, but she snatched it away. 'I'm sorry.'

'What about me? What about my feelings? After everything we've shared, everything I've told you, did you even think about how deceiving me like this would make me feel?'

'Like I said, I only just found out myself. I'm sorry I lied, but I needed time to process the news.'

'I honestly can't believe this is happening.'

'Dolly, please. It's not ideal, I know, but it's doesn't have to change things between us.'

'Oh, Julian. Don't be so bloody naive. You're going to be a father. The pretend marriage was one thing, but this . . . this changes everything. A child isn't something that can just be forgotten or glossed over. I'm sorry, Julian, I can't be a part of this.'

'What do mean by that?' he had a panicked look on his face.

'I mean that I've had a wonderful time with you, Julian, and I had high hopes for us, but I see now that what we had was too good to be true.'

'Dolly, don't say that, please. We're not over. We're fine. This doesn't make any difference! Sondra and Max will raise the baby. I mean, I'll

235

be part of his or her life too, of course, but I don't need to be there every day. The child will be cared for and loved. I will contribute financially and spend time in California as I have always done. Nothing has to change.'

Dolly raised her eyebrows, distracted for a moment by the mention of Max. Right now, she was probably the only other person in the world who could understand what Dolly was feeling. 'What does Maxine have to say about all this?'

'She was furious at first, and I can't say that I blame her. She's still upset with Sondra, but she's warmed to the idea of a baby. Maxine has always wanted to be a mother and this pregnancy will give her the chance to do that. Officially, she'll be the child's nanny as well as Sondra's assistant, which will give her a plausible excuse to be with Sondra and the baby all the time – at home, on vacation, whatever. It will make their lives a lot easier in some ways.'

'Well, that's convenient for Sondra. I'm glad it's worked out for them.'

'It can work out for us too, Dolly.'

Dolly shook her head sadly. 'Julian, you are the only man I have ever truly loved, and it breaks my heart to say this, but I have to let you go. If we stay together you'll be torn between wanting to be in California with your family, and wanting to be with me. You'll end up resenting me.'

'I won't. I promise.'

'You can't promise that. A child changes everything, and that is how it should be. You don't know yet. You've never had a child. But when he or she comes along the world will be a different place. I know you don't think so now, but when you become a father, you'll forget about what we had. You'll realise how insignificant this relationship is in the scheme of things.'

'That's just not true. My love for you is the most important thing I have in my life.'

'I don't doubt that's how you feel right now, but it won't be – or, at least, it shouldn't be – once you become a father. You have to put your child first; that's not up for debate.'

He stood up and began to pace the room. 'I won't accept it. We'll find a way to make this work. There's no reason you can't be part of the child's life too. In time you'll be the baby's stepmother. It's just these next few years we'll need to negotiate, but we'll figure it out.'

'For god's sake, Julian, don't you see? I don't *want* that. I don't want to stick around and watch you raise a child that isn't mine, and I certainly can't let myself feel any attachment to another baby when my own child is being raised by strangers. You can't ask me to do that. It's not fair.'

He stood still then and looked at her, with tears streaming down his face. 'You're the love of my life,' he said.

'And you're mine. But I'm afraid this is just not meant to be.'

•

In the morning, Dolly rose early and packed up her things. She had the bellboy call her a cab to take her to the airport. Raymond would be furious at her for breaking her contract, but she had to go. She couldn't risk staying here and falling back into Julian's arms. New York had been wonderful, but now it was over. It was time to go home to London and start all over again.

Chapter Thirty-one

London
2019

Once we're in the car I repeat my apology to Richard, who won't have a bar of it.

'None of this is your fault, Dolly. If anyone's to blame, it's me. If I hadn't been so damn lazy this would never have happened. I should be apologising to you.'

Jane makes noises as if she's agreeing. I hope this incident doesn't cause more friction between them.

'Well, let's get home and put this whole sorry incident behind us, shall we?' Richard says, swinging the car out of the car park and onto the main road.

Jane turns in her seat to look at me. 'I have a special dinner planned for tonight. And a dessert I'm trying for the first time. Hopefully that will make up for this morning's ordeal.'

They're both being so kind that it's hard not to start feeling cheerful. And it's not as if I haven't suffered far worse things than this morning's little debacle. In a way, it may even have a silver lining. It feels as if something has shifted between Richard and me.

When we arrive home, Jane insists I go upstairs and relax. 'You've had quite the morning. Have a bath, if you'd like, or a nap. I'll bring you up a tray for lunch.'

I realise I am quite hungry, which is unsurprising given it's long past lunchtime. 'That would be lovely, Jane. Thank you.'

Richard mutters something about having work to do and disappears into his study while Jane rolls her eyes at his back.

The afternoon passes pleasantly enough. After a light lunch, I take Jane's advice and have a bath and then a nap. It's almost five when I wake, so I dress for dinner and head downstairs. Jane doesn't want me in the kitchen because of the surprise dessert she's making.

'I've put some canapés out in the sitting room. Richard's waiting there with the bubbly. Go on through and I'll join you in just a few minutes,' she says.

Richard seems pleased to see me. 'How are you feeling? Recovered from all this morning's excitement?'

'Completely. It's but a distant memory. Or, more precisely, an amusing anecdote to include in my memoir,' I say with a grin.

He beams. 'Good to hear.' He lifts the bottle of champagne. 'Shall I pour you one?'

I nod. 'Please.'

Richard offers me a plate filled with tiny delicacies. I select a mini toast topped with smoked salmon and cream cheese, and a mini mushroom quiche. 'The prawn thing is good,' he suggests, and I add one of those to my plate too.

We're both quiet for a minute while we enjoy the food, then Richard looks at me sheepishly. 'I owe you an apology.'

'Richard, we've been through this. It's fine. I blame that horrible little upstart of a manager, not you. But, in any case, it's over now.'

He shakes his head. 'Not for this morning. Just in general.'

'Oh?' I put my plate down on the coffee table.

'When Jane first invited you to stay, I was concerned.'

I laugh. 'You mean you were worried about your wife bringing an old vagrant woman into your home? I can hardly imagine why.'

He smiles, but his eyes are tinged with sadness. 'I was worried about her sudden friendship with you, yes, but it wasn't about you.'

'What was it, then?'

'Look, I'm not sure how much Jane has told you about the past year or so . . .' He trails off and takes a gulp of champagne.

'I know you lost your son,' I say in a low voice. 'I can only imagine how terrible that must be, for both of you.'

'Yes, it's been awful.' He drops his voice, so it's barely more than a whisper. 'Losing Tom was unspeakably painful, but the circumstances in which we lost him made everything so much harder to bear. For Jane especially. She didn't just lose her son, she lost her whole identity.'

I nod sympathetically. If anyone can relate to this, it's me. I am a mother without a child. Do I even have the right to call myself that – a mother? But, of course, Jane and I are not the same. She raised her son for many years before he died. She is a proper mother, worthy of the title and entitled to her grief.

'After it happened, she barely left the house. She only got out of bed to go and sit on Tom's bed and cry. She stopped cooking. Said she couldn't see the point for just the two of us. At first she ate very little, but when her appetite returned – Jane has always loved her food – she started ordering pizzas and all manner of other junk food, which she'd consume in bed while watching TV. I thought it would pass, but when the weeks turned into months, I asked the grief counsellor I've been seeing to make a home visit.'

'Did that help?'

'Not at all. In fact, it made things worse.' He shakes his head sadly. 'Jane was furious at me for bringing Kate into the house. She accused me of not caring, of wanting to forget that Tom ever existed. She told Kate she didn't want to "move on", that she didn't deserve to, and that she welcomed the grief because it kept her connected to Tom. "My grief is all I have left to give to our son now, and you will not take that away from me," were her exact words.'

'Oh dear.' My heart is aching for my lovely Jane.

'I didn't know what to do after that. I suppose, if I'm honest, I gave up a bit. I withdrew and left her to it. For the past few months things have been largely the same. I've got on with things – work helps, in that regard – and Jane has pretty much stayed home and mourned.' Richard's eyes are moist now, and I feel enormous sympathy for what he's been through.

'It's such a difficult situation,' I say. 'I feel for you both.'

'Thank you, Dolly. So, before Jane met you, there had been a few small signs of improvement. She'd started getting dressed some days and leaving the bedroom. Occasionally she could even be persuaded to go out for a walk. I tried to encourage this by giving her errands to run – asking her to pick up my dry-cleaning and so forth. Anything I could think of to get her out of the house. Sometimes I'd think she was showing signs of progress, but then she'd hole herself up in the bedroom again for days on end. I was at my wits' end.

'Every time we tried to talk about Tom it ended in an argument, so I began to avoid the topic altogether. Some days she'd seem fine and others she'd be almost catatonic. It was completely unpredictable. When I came home to find she'd suddenly made a new friend, a friend many years her senior – if you'll pardon my saying so—'

I wave away his concern.

'—I just didn't know what to think,' Richard concludes.

'That seems perfectly understandable.'

'Jane's decision-making has been impaired since we lost Tom, so I had to wonder if she'd simply lost her marbles.'

I laugh, and Richard smiles awkwardly.

'Sorry,' he says. 'But, Dolly, I want you to know how wrong I was to think that. Inviting you to stay with us has been the best decision Jane has made in a long time. Your presence and friendship seem to have brought her back to life, and I can't thank you enough for that.'

A lump of emotion forms in my throat but I am saved from having to respond by Jane's appearance in the doorway. 'What are you two nattering away about?'

'I was just asking Dolly how the book is coming along,' Richard replies smoothly.

Jane's eyes sparkle. 'We've got a couple of rough chapters under our belts now, haven't we, Dolly?'

241

'Yes.' I turn to face Richard. 'Jane's prompts have brought back memories of my childhood I didn't know I still had.'

A flash of concern crosses his face. 'I hope that's a good thing?'

'Mostly it is. But some of the things I plan to share will be painful, I can't shy away from that. Not if I want to tell the truth, which I do. It's the only hope I have of my son understanding why I made the choices I did.'

Richard inhales and looks as if he is going to say something before changing his mind. 'Well, I for one can't wait to read it.'

Jane nods. 'It's coming along very nicely. Of course, there's a way to go yet.' She accepts the glass of champagne Richard is holding out to her. 'The entrée won't be long. Perhaps we could move into the dining room?'

'Good idea.' Richard extends his hand for me to take. As he helps me out of the chair, I notice Jane smiling at him and there's a look of love in her eyes.

Dinner is roast lamb and vegetables, complete with homemade mint sauce and gravy. This is a dish that takes me back to my childhood. Earlier in the week, I'd mentioned the Sunday lunches we would eat at my grandparents' house in the days before Mum married Bill. Every Sunday, without fail, Granny cooked roast lamb with all the trimmings. I'm touched Jane has gone to so much to trouble to recreate it for me.

Richard keeps our glasses filled with a delicious shiraz, and as the wine heats my blood I find myself reminiscing about my early life in Australia, entertaining the two of them with stories of exotic childhood foods such as fairy bread, chocolate crackles and honey joys.

Jane is so delighted by my descriptions that she whips out her phone and types some notes to add to the book while Richard clears the plates. The tension between them has eased. So much so that, when it's time for dessert and Richard offers to accompany Jane to the kitchen to help with the final preparations, instead of batting away the offer and saying she's perfectly capable, *thank you very much*, she smiles warmly at him and accepts.

Dessert is a showstopper: pavlova topped with freshly whipped cream, pomegranate seeds and pistachios. A glossy red syrup has been drizzled over the top.

'Oh my stars!' I say when Jane proudly places the dish at the centre of the table.

'I'm sorry it's not a more traditional rendition,' she says. 'I know your grandmother always used strawberries, but they're not in season, so I thought pomegranate might make a reasonable substitute.'

Richard places a small crystal jug beside the pavlova. 'Extra pomegranate syrup,' he says.

'I love pomegranate.' I beam at the two of them. 'This is a beautiful surprise. A perfect blend of old and new. Thank you.'

Once we've all had a chance to sample the melt-in-your-mouth deliciousness, Richard looks at Jane. 'You've outdone yourself, my dear. This is truly splendid.' Jane responds to the compliment with a warm smile, which Richard returns awkwardly, like a shy teenager. It's adorable to watch. 'I hope you won't think I'm trying to steal your thunder, Jane, but I actually have a surprise of my own,' he continues. 'I have some news for you, Dolly, that I hope will make up for this morning's mishap.'

Jane's forehead creases. It seems as if this is news to her too.

I laugh to break the unease I sense seeping back into the room. 'There's no need, Richard. This morning is already a distant memory.'

'Nevertheless'—he clears his throat—'I've been thinking about your . . . situation for some time now. I thought perhaps there was something more that might be done.'

'Richard, what are you talking about?' Jane asks impatiently.

'Sorry. Dolly, I do hope you don't mind, but I took the liberty of making some inquiries about finding your son.'

My stomach lurches and my hands begin to shake. I place my dessert fork down on the plate. 'You've found Jamie?'

He shakes his head. 'No, no, not yet. But I have some information I think you might find helpful.'

'Go on.'

Jane is staring at him incredulously and he shifts uncomfortably in his seat. 'After our discussion about your son, I asked one of my colleagues about adoption laws in Australia. She wasn't fully across them but she said it would easy enough to find out more. As it turns out, each state in Australia has different laws, but I knew from talking to you that the adoption took place in Victoria. You told me the last time you tried to find your son was more than ten years ago, correct?'

I nod. 'Easily.'

Richard smiles. 'The law has changed significantly since you last tried to track down your son. In 2013, the Victorian state government brought in changes to allow birth mothers to have access to their children's records. There's a bit of a process involved – you'll need to prove who you are and have an interview with a counsellor before any information will be provided to you. If there was an official adoption agency involved, the adoption information service can tell you whether they're still operating, and can help you contact the agency or access the records. There's no guarantee you'll be able to contact your son, but you should be able to find out what happened to him.'

Tears spill from my eyes. 'I don't know what to say.'

'Oh, Richard,' Jane says in a tremulous voice.

I glance up to see her looking at Richard with real affection. One hand is over her heart and she's using the other to wipe away tears that are dripping down her cheeks.

Richard's face flushes with colour and he smiles at me. 'When you're ready, Dolly, I'll just need to see your identification documents – passport, birth certificate, whatever you have – so I can get the paperwork in order.'

'Ah,' I say, suddenly crestfallen. 'That might be a problem.'

Chapter Thirty-two

London
1971

'No audition? Really? Come on, Cecil, what's the catch?' Dolly couldn't believe what she was hearing. Parts didn't come her way that easily these days – not parts worth having, anyway.

Her spectacular departure from the Broadway production of *The Rose of France* had sullied her reputation, and it seemed these days she had very few contacts in the industry who were willing to go out on a limb for her. Raymond, who'd eventually forgiven her for leaving, was now permanently based in New York and the few friends she had left in the West End were just like her – devoid of all power.

When she'd first arrived back in London six years earlier, Maurice had begged her to go back to New York. 'It's not too late to fix this, Dolly. The producers have announced that you've had to return to London temporarily for a personal bereavement. I get it. You're exhausted. I blame myself, really. We've worked you too hard these past couple of years. Have a few days off, then pull yourself together. If you can get back to New York by next week, no one will be any the wiser.'

Personal bereavement. They'd got that right. She was grieving. Mourning the life she'd allowed herself to hope for. How could she have been so stupid? All these years of protecting her heart and focusing on her career had come undone in mere months. She'd been duped. Charmed by a smooth-talking actor.

She tried to tell herself that it didn't matter. She'd been a Broadway star (albeit a fleeting one) and she could build on that. She'd focus on the West End for a while, and another Broadway part would come along eventually. She didn't need Julian Barrows or any other man. She would focus on her work, just like she'd done ever since she'd lost her family in one fell swoop. But right now, she needed to recuperate.

'I can't go back, Maurice. I just can't. Tell them I'm sick or something, whatever you want, but I need you to get me out of that contract. I simply cannot work on that show.'

'Rest for a day or two, Doll. I'm sure you'll change your mind.'

But she didn't.

As the days turned into weeks, she spent her time taking baths and playing sad songs on her record player while she fantasised about what could have been. She couldn't eat, couldn't sleep and most definitely couldn't entertain the idea of going back to work.

At first Maurice called daily to try to get her to come out for lunch or dinner, to meet with producers about upcoming roles, and when that failed, he tried simply to get her to come out for a walk. But she steadfastly refused and eventually stopped answering the phone.

From time to time her girlfriends called by, but she was terrible company. She knew that if she didn't snap out of this funk her friends would eventually give up and move on.

Sal, one of her castmates from the London production of *Rose*, brought pastries one morning and made her a pot of tea. 'My god, Dolly, you look positively skeletal. Eat up.'

Dolly smiled weakly and picked at her croissant. 'I just don't have any appetite.'

'Geez, that bastard really did a number on you. What you need is to get out of this bloody flat. Get back out there and find yourself a new fella. What's say we go out tonight?'

Dolly shook her head. 'I don't want a new man. I just need to be alone for a while. To rest.'

'Rubbish. Moping about never helped anyone. I'll come by tonight around eight. Make sure you're ready.'

True to her word, Sal was back that night and wouldn't take no for an answer. They went to a new licensed club in Soho, so at least there was alcohol to numb Dolly's pain. After downing almost a whole bottle of champagne on her own, she allowed herself to be persuaded to get out on the dancefloor. 'See?' Sal said. 'I knew you'd be okay. Things will get better, Dolly. You just have to keep putting one foot in front of the other.'

Maybe Sal was right. What other choice did she have?

After her hangover subsided the next day, she'd called Maurice. 'I'm ready to go back to work.'

Maurice was delighted. '*Hello, Dolly* is being staged in December. You're too young for the lead, and I hear they've signed that American actress, Mary Martin, anyway. But there are a couple of other good roles that haven't been cast yet. Let me see what I can do.'

When she was offered the part of Irene Molloy, Maurice had taken her out to celebrate. 'This will be great, Doll. I know it will. Think about the publicity! "Dolly shines in *Hello, Dolly*." Honestly, I think it's a sign. Only good things ahead for you, my love.'

Dolly wanted to believe him. It *was* a good part, one that gave her the opportunity to show off her vocal talents. But it wasn't the lead.

She trudged through the rehearsals, feeling like a failure. A few months ago she'd been the star of the show. Now, Mary Martin had the best dressing room and the ear of the director. Everyone, including Mary, was kind to her, but she couldn't help feeling that this role was a backwards step. Yes, she could work hard and build on it to make something bigger happen. She'd done it before and there was no reason to believe she couldn't again. But she was tired of having to fight for every little scrap of success.

And what was it for, anyway? She had no one who cared. Not really. No parents proudly watching on, no siblings bragging about her success. No husband, or even a lover, to squire her about town boasting about being the 'luckiest man alive'.

When she'd lost her family, she'd vowed to make a success of herself to honour them, but now she realised how futile that oath had been. What was the point, when they weren't here to see her triumphs?

She confided in Sal, who told her things would be better once the show opened. 'You just need to be back in front of an audience.' And Sal was right. Sort of. She *did* love performing for a crowd. But when the curtain came down, nothing in her shitty life had changed.

To keep the darkness at bay, she turned herself into the ultimate good-time girl – drinking champagne by the crateload, dancing in clubs until dawn and sleeping with any man who took her fancy. It didn't make her happy, of course, but at least there was less time to think about how desperately lonely she was.

Eventually her lifestyle started to impact her work. Her lack of sleep and the hangovers took their toll. She was frequently late to make-up, and then angry when the girls took too long and failed to adequately cover the damage to her appearance. She loudly complained to anyone who would listen that they were incompetent and made her look ten years older than she was. Her fear of failure and feelings of inadequacy made her impatient with the rest of the cast. She demanded perfection from everyone else but required tolerance of her own missteps, expecting her castmates to cover for her when she fluffed a lyric or missed a cue.

Looking back now, she could admit that she'd been a nightmare to work with. One night she'd actually passed out onstage. That was the final straw for the director. Five months after opening night, she was sacked.

Maurice pushed her to record an album. There'd been an offer from EMI the previous year and Maurice was sure he could resurrect the deal. So far, her departure from *Hello, Dolly* had been framed as her leaving to pursue other creative projects. If the record deal came off, that might help quell the rumours of bad behaviour on Dolly's part.

Somehow Maurice pulled it off. The terms of the deal were not as favourable as she'd originally been offered the year before, but Maurice said that wouldn't matter if the record was a hit.

Unfortunately, being in the recording studio brought her no joy at all. There was no audience to feed off and Dolly found the work tedious. Her fear of the album being a flop led her to obsess over every detail, which in turn led to arguments with the producer. By the time the record was released it was way over budget and the relationship with the label had soured. The record debuted at number 45 on the charts, but never climbed any higher. The following week it was in the seventies, and the next week it didn't even make the top one hundred.

Two years had passed since she'd left New York. Two years and two failures.

Maurice declared there was nothing more he could do for her. He left, helping himself to a large chunk of her earnings that he claimed he was entitled to. Dolly had no idea if that was true, but she didn't have the wherewithal to fight him.

Being dumped by the record label was the kick in the pants she'd needed. With most of her money gone and her reputation in tatters, she realised she had two options – work her guts out to get her career back or descend into obscurity and poverty. She had no skills to work outside the theatre, and no desire to be someone's wife, so she figured she had no choice other than to sober up and work harder than she'd ever worked before to repair the damage she'd done.

It hadn't been easy. She'd swallowed a large dose of humility and gone back to auditioning, taking on every bit part that was offered to her. She'd cut right back on the booze, started eating better and attended dance classes to show potential directors her commitment to improving. She was on time for rehearsals and fittings, and took every note given to her by a director with grace.

But it hadn't really helped. She could still get parts, but six years after she'd walked out on *The Rose of France*, nothing major was on offer. She was a West End hack, her star no longer on the rise.

Last year, she had managed to get Cecil Bainbridge to sign her on as a client. As agents went, he was a small-time hustler – not a patch on Maurice – but he genuinely cared about her, and occasionally he came through with something that earned her a bit of cash.

'Come on, spit it out, Cecil. A major part with no audition. Are all the scenes topless or something?'

Cecil shrugged. 'You were recommended for the part, apparently.'

'By whom?'

Cecil looked thoughtful. 'Well, they've already cast Julian Barrows, so . . .'

Julian.

She hadn't seen him since she left New York. Not that Julian hadn't tried. He'd called, had sent letters to her via Maurice and even made the flight across the pond, in the hope of talking her around, she supposed, but she'd refused all his overtures. She couldn't see him; she didn't trust herself not to fall into his arms, and that simply wouldn't do.

But now she needed a break, and *Godspell* had the makings of a hit. Could she really afford to knock back the offer?

She sighed. 'I don't know, Cecil. I mean, it's not even playing in the West End.'

'Now you're being silly. Chalk Farm is hardly the sticks, Dolly, and The Roundhouse is a big theatre. I can tell them no if you'd like, but, honestly, offers like this aren't exactly pouring in right now. If I were you, I'd think about that.'

Cecil was right. She was practically skint and couldn't afford to be looking a gift horse in the mouth. But how could she face Julian after all this time? How could she look into his eyes and not be overwhelmed by her emotions?

She'd seen the photos of him with his daughter, and every picture of him lovingly looking at his little girl confirmed for Dolly she'd done the right thing. She had no business taking him away from his family. She'd frequently comforted herself with that fact, but it hadn't made the loneliness any easier to bear. Six years had passed and she hadn't fallen in love again. Oh, there'd been men – she'd bedded more than she cared to remember – but no one could fill the gaping hole left by the loss of Julian.

Could she work with him without her heart being broken all over again? What if he wanted to rekindle things? Or maybe after all these years he'd have no interest in her. She didn't know which would be worse.

'I'm sorry, Cecil. I don't think I'm right for the part. Please tell them thank you for the offer, but I'll have to pass.'

●

Two days later, Cecil knocked on the door of her one-bedroom flat. 'Big news. I'm sorry to show up unannounced, but I wanted to tell you in person.'

She ushered him inside. 'What is it?'

'The producers of *Godspell* have made you another offer – one I don't think you can afford to refuse. They've doubled the amount that was on the table last time. Dolly, I don't need to tell you this is seriously good money and it's not likely to be matched by any other role.'

Cecil was right. She needed the money. She was just going to have to take a deep breath and deal with the Julian situation. They were adults, weren't they? Years had passed. Maybe they would be able to be professionals and have an amicable but detached relationship. Maybe when they saw each other there would be no sparks left.

'Okay. You can set up a meeting.'

●

'Why, Julian? Why did you insist on having me in the role?'

They were in a little coffee shop not far from the theatre, where auditions were in full swing. Cecil had almost talked her into agreeing to the deal, but she still had her reservations. She'd asked Cecil to get in contact with Julian and set up a meeting before she signed a contract. She needed to set some ground rules if she was to put her name to anything.

He held her gaze with those deep brown eyes and her stomach turned to water. The spark was still there. At least, it was for her. She pretended to stir her coffee so she didn't have to look at him.

'I owed you this much,' he said.

'Owed me? What do you mean?'

'Don't think I don't know what our split cost you. I know you haven't worked properly since. I feel terrible that you paid such a high price for our love and I got off scot-free.'

'Right. Yes, I paid a high price for leaving the way I did, but what other option was there?'

'I could have left the show. I would have happily done so for you. But you left and then it was done. I tried so hard to contact you, to tell you to come back and that I would be the one to leave, but you wouldn't have a bar of me.'

Dolly shrugged, wondering for a moment how things might have been these past few years if she'd relented and taken his calls. Perhaps if she'd been able to talk to Raymond . . . But it was no use speculating. What was done was done. 'Well, it's all water under the bridge.'

He nodded. 'I can't change what happened, but I can lend you a helping hand now.'

Dolly sipped her coffee slowly. 'I can't go there again, Julian. It's taken me too long to recover. I'll do the show if you can promise me we will be no more than colleagues.'

He held both hands up in front of him, a surrender. 'Whatever you want. You're the boss. It'll be strictly business if that's what it takes for you to sign. This isn't charity, you know. I might owe you, but you are still the best damn leading lady I've ever had the pleasure of working with.'

She appreciated the compliment. 'All right. If you promise.'

'I do.'

As she stood to make her exit, Julian touched her arm to stop her. 'I didn't, you know. Get off scot-free. Yours wasn't the only heart that was broken.'

Chapter Thirty-three

London
2019

Jane and Richard are looking at me quizzically, waiting for an explanation as to why I can't provide them with any ID.

I sigh. I've never fully explained my situation, and neither have they pressed me for details. But it's time to come clean and reveal just how I ended up in this mess. 'When Julian died, I was grief-stricken, as you can imagine.' I glance at Richard. Jane knows about my relationship with Julian now, through our work on the book, but I don't know whether she's relayed that part of my story to Richard.

'Julian Barrows was Dolly's life partner,' Jane interjects, for Richard's benefit.

'When he died, at first I was too upset to even think about my finances, but after a month or two I decided I'd better get things sorted. It was quite a challenge, because Julian had always taken care of the money side of things, you see.'

Jane raises her eyebrows, but Richard nods as if this makes perfect sense and I go on.

'I had my own little bank account and debit card. Julian used to transfer money into that each month and I could use it however I liked.

So, after he died, I still had access to that money and there was a fair bit in there. I'd been using that to pay for necessities but I started to worry that the balance was going down quite quickly. So, I thought I'd better see about getting access to Julian's main account. But that turned out to be impossible because Julian owned our flat and nothing – not even the electricity bill – had my name on it. I had no way of proving he and I were a couple. And, to make matters worse, I couldn't find any of my own identity documents.'

Jane frowns. 'But wouldn't you have used your passport to fly to LA for Julian's funeral?'

My breath catches in my throat. Two years have passed but the pain is still raw. 'I didn't go. Sondra asked me not to.'

'What?' Jane looks incredulous. 'But I thought you all got along?'

'Sondra and I do, yes. But Julian's daughter, Sammi, didn't want me there. You see, she and Julian had a big falling out before he died and I think she blamed me for that. She was in a bad way when Julian passed, and Sondra thought my presence at the funeral would only make things worse.'

'Oh, Dolly, I'm so sorry.'

'I didn't mind too much,' I say. It's a lie, but I can't bear Jane and Richard pitying me any more than they already do. 'I've never been one for funerals. I loved Julian and he loved me. I have no regrets. I didn't need to weep beside a hole in the ground to show him how much I cared. I only wish I'd been able to see him one last time before he left this world.'

Jane reaches across and squeezes my hand. I smile at her as I pull my hand back. I'm keen to finish explaining so I don't have to dwell on this part of my life for a moment longer than necessary.

'So,' I continue, 'I hadn't needed my passport for some time. I searched the flat high and low for it, as well as my birth certificate, but came up with nothing. I didn't even have a record of my National Insurance number. Eventually I remembered Julian saying something about keeping our passports along with all our other important documents in a safety deposit box at the bank. I tried calling the bank that had issued my credit card, but they informed me that the card was a supplementary card on Julian's account, which had been frozen due to his death. They couldn't tell me if Julian had a safety deposit box or not, and even if he did they couldn't give me access to it. They said I could apply to open my own account if I liked. I would just need to go to the bank and bring the appropriate identity documents. When I explained I didn't have them, and that's why I was calling, my call was passed around several departments before they put me in the too-hard basket. They told me I should probably apply for a new passport.'

'And did you?' Richard asks.

'Well . . . I did try, but it's not as simple as one might think. It's all online these days. I had a go, using Julian's computer in the study, but they wanted me to upload a passport photo and I couldn't work out how to do it. I'd planned on asking my friend's husband to help me, but before I got around to that a letter arrived from a lawyer in the US saying that I had to vacate the flat because it was going to be sold as part of the estate.

'Things just spiralled out of control from there. I had to move out quickly, so that was my focus.'

'Where did you go?' Richard asks.

'I know this will sound ridiculous, considering my current predicament, but I took myself off to The Savoy Hotel.'

Richard's eyes widen.

'I know, I know,' I say, 'but at the time it seemed perfectly reasonable. As I said, I hadn't had to think about money in years – not since I was a young woman. I knew it wasn't a cheap hotel, but I had no idea just how expensive it would be. I went through half the remaining money in my account in just over a week.'

Richard winces. 'Gosh.'

'What about all your things, Dolly? Did you have to put them in storage?' Jane asks.

I give a bitter smile. 'As it turns out, I didn't actually own much. The furniture and household items were insured by Julian and considered part of the estate, so I couldn't take them. All my worldly goods boiled down to my clothes, my cosmetics and my jewellery. Of course, that was still more than I could take to the hotel, so my friend Adnan offered to store some of it for me.'

'You haven't managed to sort out the identity documents, then?' Richard asks.

'No. Look, I didn't think the passport was a priority, at least at first. The lawyer informed me that I was a beneficiary of Julian's will, and that it might take a couple of months but I was to receive a substantial sum of money, so I figured my problems would be temporary.'

Jane looks confused. 'But Julian died almost two years ago. Has the money not come through?'

'Well, that's where it gets a bit complicated. Unfortunately, the next piece of correspondence I received from Julian's lawyers was to tell me his daughter was contesting the validity of the will and I would need to wait for the legal proceedings to take place before I received my share. Depending on the outcome, I might not get anything at all.'

Jane looks aghast. 'That can't be right! Richard?'

He shrugs. 'Not really my area of expertise. It's certainly possible.'

'Did you obtain legal advice, Dolly?'

I shake my head. 'I couldn't afford it. It's not the sort of thing that's covered by legal aid.'

Richard looks sympathetic. 'Was there no one who could help you?'

'Well, I really hate asking people for things, you see. It's just so humiliating. But I did end up reaching out to a few people. I was too proud to tell them how tenuous my circumstances were, so I pretended I was looking for a new flat to buy and that I just needed somewhere to stay for a short time. And, honestly, I truly believed that myself in the beginning.'

'So what happened? Surely your friends wouldn't want you living on the streets?'

'At my age, one's social circle tends to be small. Most of my closest friends have passed away. Still, I had a few people I thought I could count on. Friends I'd made through work or through Julian. More acquaintances than friends, really. People who I could ask for a favour but who I didn't want to burden for too long. And certainly not anyone I could trust with the truth of my situation. And I was mindful that people shouldn't think ill of Julian. This wasn't his fault, after all. So I moved around – couch surfing, I believe the young people call it – until there was nowhere left to go. Until people stopped taking my calls.'

'Oh, Dolly,' Jane says. 'I hope you know you will never be in that position again. Your welcome here will not run out.'

Richard, meanwhile, is wearing a businesslike expression. 'Do you know the name of the law firm that was handling Julian's estate?' he asks.

I nod. 'It's been a bit tricky keeping in touch, now that I'm of no fixed address – especially since I lost my phone – but I do call them every now and then to get updates.'

'No need to worry about doing that anymore. An associate from my firm will be representing your interests now.' He raises an eyebrow at me. 'With your permission, of course.'

'Thank you.' These two words are wholly insufficient to express my gratitude and relief, but they're all I can manage right now. I bite my lower lip to stop it from trembling.

'What about your pension?' Richard asks. He's got his phone out now and is typing notes. 'Was that paid into your account or Julian's?'

'Pension?'

'Yes. If you're a British citizen, you'd be entitled to one. Even if you're not a citizen but have lived and worked here legally for as long as you have, I think you can claim it.'

'Really? I had no idea. I am a British citizen, although I only got around to applying for that when I was working on *The Neighbour-hood*. In the early days it was easy to renew my work visa every couple of years, so I didn't bother with citizenship.'

'Nevertheless, you are a citizen now and entitled to claim welfare payments. Are you sure you never applied for a pension?'

'Not that I remember. I mean, perhaps I was informed that I was entitled to one. Julian took care of all our paperwork. Maybe he mentioned it, but I can't recall ever even talking about it. I wouldn't have applied for it, in any case. We didn't need the money when he was alive. He continued to work into his seventies and died a wealthy man. Neither of us would take welfare money we didn't need.'

Richard smiles. 'Well, I'm sure you could use it now, so I'll make it a priority to get that sorted.'

I shake my head and I can feel my cheeks burning. 'I know I must seem ridiculous to you. It feels as if this situation could have been easily avoided. I should have paid more attention to our finances. I should have planned for this situation, but it just never occurred to me that I would need to. I trusted Julian and took him at his word that if anything happened, I'd be provided for. Not that I blame him, of course. He wasn't to know that Sammi would contest the will.'

'Of course not,' Jane says kindly.

'I am ashamed that I let myself become soft in old age. It's not as if I was born privileged. I grew up knowing the value of a dollar. But somewhere along the way I lost sight of that. I was wealthy and I didn't even appreciate it. After a while, I took it for granted. And then, when my circumstances changed, I had no idea how to deal with it. I just didn't have the required skill set. Losing track of my identity documents made things even harder and I just kept coming up against roadblocks. The system expects everyone to understand and to have access to technology, which I admit is not my strong suit. And every official form you fill out requires proof of identity and a mailing address. Navigating it all just seemed impossible for someone like me. I'm afraid you must think me very foolish.'

'Not at all,' Richard says. 'If anything, this just demonstrates the holes in our welfare system. I expect many people fall through the cracks in a similar way. But you don't have to worry now. Jane and I, along with a couple of my colleagues, will make sure all of this gets sorted out.'

Jane reaches across the table and takes my hand, and this time I let her hold it. 'Dolly, whatever happens, you will never have to spend another night on the street. We will make sure of that.'

Chapter Thirty-four

London
1971

Once rehearsals started, Dolly and Julian fell into the same easy working relationship they'd had in New York. Their chemistry on stage was undeniable. Julian's skill as a performer had grown even further since they'd last worked together and she couldn't help but enjoy her time with him.

The entire cast was fabulous, and it didn't take long for them to become a tight-knit group. Dolly knew she had a reputation for being difficult to work with after the New York debacle, not to mention how horribly she'd behaved during *Hello, Dolly*, so getting along with her castmates on this show was important for her future career prospects. She tried to avoid Julian as best she could, given the situation, but it was tricky.

One night she found herself exiting the local post-rehearsal watering hole at the same time as him. 'Night!' she said brightly, walking quickly towards the tube station.

'Dolly, wait up.'

She knew she should keep going. She could duck her head and pretend she hadn't heard. But she stopped and turned. 'Yes?'

'How are you getting home?'

'On the tube.'

'I can't let you catch the tube alone at this hour.'

'It's fine, Julian. I do it all the time.'

'I'm getting a cab – it's going right past your place. Let me give you a ride.'

She shook her head. 'I don't think so.'

'Come on. What are you afraid of? You've given me your conditions and I've accepted them. I promise I will be a gentleman. Please don't risk life and limb when there's a safe, warm alternative on offer just to prove a point.'

She huffed out a breath of icy air. When he put it like that, it made it seem churlish not to accept. 'Oh, all right.'

He hailed a cab easily and, once it stopped, he held open the door for her. 'After you.'

She slid over as far as she could and Julian remained a respectful distance away when he got in.

At first they were quiet, but after a few minutes Julian asked what she thought of the latest changes to the choreography in the number they'd been rehearsing and before she knew it they were caught up in shop talk. Julian had her in stitches with his impersonations of the cast and crew, ending with a rendition of John Casey's exasperation at the chorus: 'Like herding cats, darlings!'

'Stop it!' she said, still laughing.

'See, this is nice, Doll. Isn't it?'

'Julian . . .'

'Don't worry, I'm not breaking my word. But couldn't we be friends again? At least while we're doing the show?'

Her head knew this was dangerous territory; that spending time with Julian could only lead to more heartache in the end. But it wasn't her head that answered. Her treacherous heart said, 'Yes.'

●

The next few weeks were reminiscent of their early days in New York, before anything romantic had happened between them. The only difference was that this time they were on her home turf. It wasn't as if Julian was a newcomer to London. He'd worked there often enough and, he reminded her, he'd been born in the city. 'I didn't move to the States until I was nine,' he said, proudly showing her his British passport.

'Goodness,' she said, laughing. 'You're more English than I am.' Even so, she delighted in showing him about town, finding special, offbeat places to take him. Second Act, Adnan's vintage and collectable clothing shop in Notting Hill, was one of these excursions.

He'd been sceptical. 'A clothes shop?'

'It's an institution,' she said as they climbed aboard the bus. 'Adnan has the most fascinating clientele. I can spend the whole day there just people-watching. You'll see. And, besides, I want to introduce you to my friend. He's utterly delightful and dying to meet you.'

'Me? Why? What have you told him?'

'Only the truth – that you're an egomaniac who's impossible to work with.'

His mouth dropped open as she took a seat next to an elderly gent reading the paper. Julian stood beside her, grabbing the handrail to steady himself as the bus took off. 'You didn't.'

She laughed. 'Of course I didn't. I'm teasing. You Americans take everything so seriously.'

'No we don't. It's just that the Brits have an odd sense of humour.'

'Hang on a minute, you were born here. Doesn't that make you one of us?'

'What do you mean, "one of us"? I thought *you* were Australian. Or is that only when you're watching the cricket?'

She winked at him then, and he laughed and rested a hand on her shoulder.

The old man folded his paper and rang the bell. When he got off at the next stop, Julian settled in beside her, his leg gently pressed against hers for the duration of the journey. She knew she should edge away from him, just in case he got the wrong idea, but she didn't.

When the bus finally arrived at their stop a good twenty minutes later, Julian trotted down the stairs in front of her and then turned and offered her his hand. Although she needed no assistance to alight the bus, she took it and smiled. 'Thanks.'

Julian squeezed her hand and didn't let it go for the whole ten minutes it took to walk to Adnan's shop in Portobello Road.

As predicted, Adnan was thrilled to see them. He took Dolly into his arms and kissed her on both cheeks. 'And this is the famous Mr Barrows I've been hearing all about, is it?' The words were friendly enough, but Dolly didn't miss the way Adnan looked Julian up and down.

'It is indeed.'

'Welcome, welcome. You'll stay for coffee, of course.'

Dolly grinned. 'Of course.' She turned to Julian. 'Have you ever had Turkish coffee?'

Julian shook his head. 'No, but I'd love to try it.'

'Better make it sweet, my darling,' she said to Adnan. 'This one's a virgin.'

Adnan laughed. 'Keep an eye on the shop, Doll. I'll be back in a flash.' He disappeared behind a red velvet curtain into the storeroom, from which there was a stairway that led to Adnan's family residence.

Dolly propped herself behind the counter and surveyed the shop. It was early and there weren't many people in yet, just a pair of giggling young women trying on hats at the back of the store. 'Take a look around. You'll be amazed by what you see. Adnan only takes quality garments; mainly vintage, but he also stocks one-off pieces from new designers who are trying to get a foot in the door. A lot of wardrobe and props managers shop here, so if a new designer gets a garment picked up that ends up being worn in a show, it can be good advertising for them.'

Julian stood in front of a glass display case featuring vintage cufflinks, tie pins and pipes. 'Wow. Some of this stuff is amazing. I can see why the wardrobe people would love it.' He bent to look at the price of a pair of gold cufflinks and whistled. 'Not cheap, though.'

Dolly shrugged. 'A lot of this stuff is rare. Adnan does deals for wardrobe managers he has a relationship with, though. He'll rent certain pieces out, but of course if the show runs for a long time, sometimes it's cheaper to buy the piece outright and sell it back to Adnan when the show closes.'

Their conversation was interrupted when a middle-aged woman dressed in a flamboyant orange caftan entered the shop. She approached the counter to inquire about a particular style of shoe that was popular in the 1940s, so Dolly left Julian in charge of the till while she directed the woman to the shoe section and assisted her to find what she wanted.

When she returned to the counter Adnan was back, pouring the coffee. 'Sweets for my sweet,' he said, nodding towards a tray of rose- and lemon-flavoured Turkish delight.

'My favourite!' Dolly exclaimed. 'Thank you, darling.'

As they drank their coffee (Julian downed his and pronounced it 'delicious', but Dolly noted he declined a second cup), Adnan excitedly told them about a new consignment that had come in the day before. 'A gorgeous haul from a deceased estate,' he said, as he dragged a trunk out from the storeroom. 'I've finished pricing all the items but haven't managed to put them out yet.' He flipped open the trunk's lid. 'Here, have a look.'

Dolly squatted beside the trunk as Julian and Adnan talked about how the rehearsals for *Godspell* were going. She sifted through the clothes, all elegant pieces, but too conservative for her taste. She was about to close the lid when she noticed a suit bag on the bottom of the trunk that she hadn't opened. She carefully unzipped it, pulled out the garment and instantly fell in love. 'Oh my stars, Adnan. I can't believe you have this.'

'I know. What a find, eh? Apparently it's never been worn.'

Maybe she could treat herself? The show hadn't started yet, but everyone kept telling her it was going to be a hit. 'What do you think?' she asked, holding it up for Julian's opinion.

He nodded his approval. 'Try it on and see.'

It was almost as if the peacock-coloured coat was made exclusively for her. She ran her fingers through the black faux fur of the lapel and looked up at Julian. 'Well?'

He took her hand and twirled her towards him, catching and dipping her dramatically once she got close. Their eyes locked and Dolly's heart raced. Was he going to kiss her?

He seemed to think about it, but in the end pulled her upright again and stepped back. 'Smashing, darling,' he said, adopting his version of an upper-class English accent. 'Seriously, the coat has "star" written all over it.'

'I think I'll get it. How much, Adnan?' Smiling, she glanced at the little price tag Adnan had pinned to the label of the coat and let out an involuntary gasp.

'It's pricey, I know,' Adnan said sympathetically. 'But it's Givenchy, darling. That's what it's worth.'

She shrugged off the coat and reluctantly returned it to the trunk. 'Out of this starving actress's price range, I'm afraid.'

Julian reached for his wallet. 'Allow me,' he said.

She shook her head. '*No*, Julian.'

'Please, Dolly, let me buy you this gift as a thank you for showing me around these past couple of weeks. I've discovered so many wonderful places I never would have found otherwise. Really, I insist.'

'Rules, Julian. Need I say more?'

Julian grimaced but put his wallet away.

Lunch was next on the agenda and Adnan recommended a cafe just around the corner, so after hugs farewell and promises to return soon, Dolly and Julian set off. They were at the cafe entrance when Julian discovered he didn't have his wallet. 'I mustn't have put it back in my pocket properly after I got it out at the store,' he said.

'Are you sure it's not there?' Dolly was certain she would have noticed if he'd dropped it.

'Quite sure.'

'Don't worry – if it's in the shop, Adnan will keep it safe. We'll go back.'

Julian nodded. 'Actually, why don't you go in and get us a table before it gets too busy. I'll run and grab it. I'll be back before you know it.'

Even though it was less than a two-minute walk to the shop, it took almost fifteen minutes for Julian to return, triumphantly holding the wallet aloft. 'Sorry to be so long, darling. Your friend Adnan is quite the chatterbox.'

She laughed. 'I was beginning to wonder what had become of you. I hope Adnan was playing nice. He can be a tad protective of me at times.'

'And he thinks you need protecting from me?' Julian looked bemused.

'He doesn't want to see me hurt again.' She shrugged. 'He thinks you have the hots for me.'

'He's wrong.'

Despite it being the only appropriate answer, Dolly's heart pricked with disappointment. 'Good.'

Julian reached across the table and covered her hand with his. 'Well, not wrong exactly, but not quite right either. You see, I don't have the hots for you, Dolly. I'm in love with you, and I have been from the moment you walked into that theatre on Broadway.' He leant across the table then and kissed her.

She couldn't help herself. She kissed him back.

•

The following morning, when Dolly awoke in her Clapham flat to find Julian already gone, she panicked. Had she just made a huge mistake? Was Julian already regretting what had transpired between them last night?

He'd been so convincing about his feelings for her, and adamant they could make this work, Dolly had been fooled into thinking maybe he was right.

'We're a brand, Sondra and I. A story, not a couple. You know that.'

265

'But you have a child.'

'Samantha's getting older now and the three-way parenting thing is . . . well, it's complicated. Let's just say Max and I aren't always on the same page, which can be confusing for Sammi.' His eyes softened. 'She's a clever little thing and she's learnt to play the two of us off against each other. It's difficult for all of us, but Sondra particularly – she seems to get caught in the middle.'

'I don't see how that helps us.'

'Sondra and I have decided we need to live more separate lives. We think that will be less confusing for Sammi. I'm away so much anyway.'

'You're getting a divorce?'

He blew out a long, slow breath. 'No. It's not that simple. We have too much tied up in the brand. It wouldn't be advantageous to either of us to let that go, especially not right now. I've forgone a few good film offers to keep working on Broadway, and to do *Godspell* here. That's fine while I'll still Mr Sondra Radley, but I fear a break-up might not go so well for me, career-wise. And Sondra is still perfectly happy with – and protected by – our arrangement. Nevertheless, we have decided on a more formal parenting agreement. We'll be together for Sammi's birthday and the main holidays, and then I'll have her for three weeks straight twice a year. It's time for me to step back and give Sondra and Max their space. Sammi might not get quite as much time with me, but when she does she'll have my undivided attention. We all agreed it's the best way forward.'

'And the press?'

He shrugged. 'We'll continue to stick to our story and make appearances together around the holidays. It's not unusual for me to be away from home for work, so hopefully we'll get away with it. Besides, there's always speculation about couples like us. So long as we keep denying it, we'll be fine.'

'So, you're suggesting you and I carry on in secret?'

He winced. 'It sounds so tawdry when you put it like that.'

'How would you put it then?'

'Keeping our private life private. We don't have to sneak around, if that's what you are thinking. London isn't LA. And besides, we're co-stars. It's only natural that we would be seen out and about together.'

'But this show will end eventually. What then?'

'I don't know, Dolly. All I know is that I love you and I want to spend the rest of my life with you. We will find a way to make it work. If you want to, that is.'

'I do.'

She'd bought in to every bit of it because she'd wanted to believe it. But now she'd woken up to an empty bed and wondered if she'd been a fool.

It wasn't until she threw back the covers that she discovered the box, wrapped in tissue, sitting in place of her lover.

She tore off the wrapping and lifted the lid, then gasped.

The coat.

She lifted it from the box and hugged it to her chest. As she did, a note fell from within the fabric folds.

For you, my darling, my one true love, because you should have all that your heart desires and more.

With love, J x

P.S. Just popped up the road to get croissants. Back soon.

Chapter Thirty-five

London
2019

Today feels cold enough for snow, although I know it's unlikely this early in December. Still, Jane and I have decided to play it safe and work from home rather than make the trek to the library in the icy conditions. Her office is toasty, and as I sip the tea she's just poured for me I say a silent prayer of gratitude that we found each other. I have no idea how I would have survived out on the streets on a night like the one just gone, and we're not even at the height of winter yet.

It's not just the shelter I'm grateful for. I'm quite settled here with Jane and Richard, and I think it's safe to say they've both become my firm friends. I can't stay here in this sanctuary forever, though. It's not fair to them. Their marriage still seems on shaky ground, even though the atmosphere has thawed a little since I first came to stay. My presence seems to have been a balm for their injured marriage; the two of them working in their different ways to reunite me with Jamie has given them a shared goal. It's a start, but I fear there's much work yet to be done to heal the rift between them, and they'll need time and privacy for that.

Fortunately, I will soon have the means to live independently, thanks to Richard's perseverance and meticulous attention to detail.

Six weeks have passed since I spoke to the adoption counsellor, and it's been more than a month since I received the records that I hoped would lead to me being reunited with my boy.

Richard helped me with the application process to obtain Jamie's adoption records. The first step in that was obtaining some identity documents. On his advice, I applied for a copy of my birth certificate from Australia, and once we had the birth certificate I was able to apply for a new UK passport. Not that I'm planning on going anywhere, but Richard said we might as well get as many forms of identity as we could, because one never knew when they would be useful.

Richard was sure I would have some pension entitlements. I've never had a head for money or bureaucracy and had no idea I'd qualify for this, but Richard pursued the matter and, lo and behold, he was right! I've just received my first payment. It's not a huge amount of money, but it'll be enough for me to rent a small bedsit, which is all I require. The past year has taught me just how little I need to be comfortable. Jane says she'll help me find somewhere suitable once we're finished working on the first draft of the book.

That time can't be too far away now. We've been working harder than ever. Jane is trying to distract me from the fact that, a week ago, I received some disappointing news.

After the adoption counsellor gave me approval to start the process of trying to track down Jamie, she explained that sometimes the records were incomplete or non-existent. If they did exist, I would be able to find out identifying information about my child, including his adoptive parents' names. She said that, if my son had sought information on me, a caseworker would be able to see that on his file. The caseworker would also be able to see whether he was happy for me to make contact. The counsellor warned me not to get my hopes up. She told me many adult children do not wish to make contact with their natural parents.

But hope is not an emotion one can control, and when, soon after lodging my application, I received an email from a caseworker saying she had located some records, I couldn't help but feel optimistic.

The first piece of information was that Jamie had been placed with Bethany Babies' Home. All of their records had been transferred to the Victorian Government, so they were easy to obtain. I received a copy of the adoption papers and the court order that made the adoption official. Jamie had gone to a Mr and Mrs Parker just weeks after I'd left for Sydney.

The caseworker asked if she could call me, and we organised a time that would work. That's when she told me the news that Jamie had also been searching for me.

'Now, Ms Ferguson,' she'd said, calling me by my legal name, 'I wouldn't read too much into that. The inquiry is years old. There is a note to say that your son welcomes contact from you, but it isn't recent and he hasn't inquired for some years. It's not unusual for people to change their minds.'

But this was the glimmer of hope I'd been looking for. The caseworker suggested I write a letter – nothing too personal or confronting, just something gauging how he felt about making contact. She said she could send me a template of how to set it out, if I liked. I was to compose the letter and email it to her and she would pass it on. She would let me know if Jamie responded.

Almost a month went by without a word, and then one morning last week there was a message in my inbox when Jane helped me to check it before we left for the library. It was from the caseworker.

Dear Ms Ferguson,

Yesterday I had a phone call with your son to discuss the contents of your recent letter.

I regret to inform you that at this time your son does not wish to communicate with you directly. He has asked me to pass on the following information:

He is well and wants you to know he had a happy child-
hood. He is married and has two daughters. He wishes you
well but does not wish to engage further with the process at
this time.

If this information causes you distress, I can arrange for you
to speak to a counsellor. Please let me know if you would like to
discuss this option further.

Your details will remain on file. We will advise you should
your son change his mind in the future.

Distress? That word didn't come close to expressing how I felt. Hopeless. Bereft. Broken. No, even those descriptors are not enough.

Jane was wonderful. She brought me tea and held my hand and didn't once tell me not to cry. When I had no tears left, she said, 'This is a setback, but we're not beaten yet.'

'What do you mean? It's done. We've located him, and, believe me, I'm grateful for that, but now the ball is in his court. He doesn't want to see me, and I have to respect that.'

'Yes, of course, but we still have our plan B. The book.'

I slumped back in the armchair in Jane's office. 'What use is the book now? We know where he is. We've found him, but he doesn't want any contact with me. I think that's game, set, match.'

'That's how he feels right now, but he doesn't know your story. And . . .' she taps the computer screen, 'this says he has daughters. Those girls are your granddaughters. Your flesh and blood. Don't they have a right to know something about their family history?'

This makes me sit up. 'Yes. Yes, you're right. Granddaughters, I'll be.'

'We need to get to work, Dolly, and finish writing this book as quickly as possible. Once we're done, I'll figure out our next step.'

We must be getting close to the end of the first draft now. I've told Jane most of the important things. She knows all about my child-hood, the beginnings of my career, my pregnancy and Jamie's birth, and of course the loss of my family. This past week I've revisited the start of my love affair with Julian, and finally, yesterday, I explained how we got back together after being apart for several years. That's all I've got. Our lives were remarkably normal once I moved into Julian's flat.

'Dolly?' Jane interrupts my musings. 'Are you ready to get started?'

I place my cup – a Royal Albert Old Country Roses teacup Jane reserves exclusively for my use – on its saucer and nod. 'Yes, let's get to it. Although, I don't know what else there is to tell you. Once Julian and I got together we were happy. We lived a pretty quiet life.'

Jane bites her bottom lip. 'Hmm, okay. I'm sure there's more to tell, though. Personally, I want to hear about the TV series, but we're still a few years away from that.'

'About twenty years, in fact. I was in my fifties when I started work on *The Neighbourhood*. We were like an old married couple by then.'

'But you never did marry. Why was that?'

I shrug. 'At first it was all about keeping up appearances. Julian and Sondra were a power couple – worth more together than they were apart – so it was important for Julian to keep up the facade. Remember, this was the early 1970s. It might have been the era of "free love", but people still took marriage seriously back then. And it wasn't just Julian's name he was concerned about.'

Jane doesn't look convinced. 'Oh?'

'Sondra was incredibly popular, and she and Julian had created an image of the perfect family. Julian knew if we went public, I'd be branded a home-wrecker. My career had already taken a huge hit after I left *Rose* in New York. Julian felt terribly guilty about that.'

Jane folds her arms across her body and huffs out a sound of disbelief, which prompts me to defend Julian.

'It wasn't his fault I left. I was young and impetuous. I knew he was married when I got involved with him.'

'Yes, but you didn't know there would be a child involved.'

'That's true, but neither did he when we started seeing each other. In any case, running away from the theatre was stupid. I should have talked to Raymond, or asked Julian to give his notice, but I didn't. I ran back to England and hid in my bedroom. Let me assure you, no good

272

came of that strategy.' I look at her pointedly, but she seems determined to ignore my inference.

'Right. Well what happened after you got the part in *Godspell*?'

I can't help but smile. That was such a happy time in my life. I launch into the opening bars of *Day by Day*, which brings a smile to Jane's face too. 'Those were the days,' I say. 'We had such a wonderful time on that show. It's not a traditional musical with big leads and a chorus. The whole cast is important. Well, I guess the Jesus and John the Baptist parts are the biggest – Julian played John the Baptist – but every cast member is important. We were all on stage for the entire show. It made us all very close.'

'And no one suspected you and Julian were an item?'

'More than suspected. Everybody knew.' I chuckle.

'Wasn't that risky?'

'Not really. The cast and crew were our mates, our gang. They had no reason to out us to the press. We trusted them. Besides, we weren't the only ones with secrets . . .'

'Ah, I see.'

'London isn't Hollywood. Julian was a star, but he wasn't as famous as his wife, and over here he was able to fly under the radar. My fame had faded by then, so we were able to live relatively normal lives. We spent a lot of time at the theatre, and when we weren't hanging out with the others we were happy just to be at home together.' I close my eyes for a moment and luxuriate in the memory. 'That first six months of *Godspell* was the happiest period of my life. Julian and I were working together every day and sharing the same bed each night.'

'That's a lot of time together. You didn't get sick of each other?'

'Not at all.' I shake my head, wondering how something that happened so long ago can feel so fresh in my memory. I can still conjure up his scent on the sheets, the feeling of the sun warming my face as we woke on those lazy mornings when neither of us had to work. We'd argue in the winter about whose turn it was to get up and make the tea.

'We were like newlyweds, I guess.'

273

Jane is recording our conversation on her phone, but she pauses to scribble down something in her notebook before she poses the next question. 'And what about Julian's wife and daughter?'

'He made regular trips back to LA to see Sammi and to fulfil his commitments to Sondra – accompanying her to premieres and other industry events. Sondra and Sammi came over here once or, actually, I think it was twice.' I pause to make sure my recollection is correct. 'Yes, twice. I remember now. They came for opening night at The Roundhouse and then again when we reopened the following year at The Wyndham.'

'And you all stayed together in the same apartment?' Jane asks incredulously.

'No!' I laugh at the thought. 'Both Julian and Sondra were very respectful of my space. Julian might have owned the flat, but it was my home. Whenever Sondra visited London, Julian booked a suite at The Savoy.'

'Did things stay civil between you all?'

'For the most part, yes. Occasionally Julian and Sondra would have a disagreement over Sammi, but I expect that's not unusual for parents.'

Jane nods her agreement.

'Otherwise, we all got along fine. Sondra and I genuinely liked each other, and she loved Julian in a platonic way and wanted what was best for him. It was actually a very good arrangement for us all.'

'I can see how it worked well for *them*, but what about you? Surely you would have preferred a less complicated relationship, one you were free to be open about in public?'

I shrugged. 'It honestly didn't bother me. At first it seemed important to keep it secret for both our sakes. The people that mattered to us knew and that was enough. As time went on, it seemed less important and it became kind of an open secret, where many people knew or at least suspected. As the years went by, the need to be discreet faded away.'

'No one ever outed you?'

'There were rumours, and sometimes these were published in the gossip mags – *Tatler* and so on – but Sondra, Julian and I always vehemently denied it, saying the three of us were close friends and had been for many years. In the early days I'd go on fake dates with fellow actors, who all knew about Julian and me, just to put the press off the scent. But as time marched on, people didn't care so much about what we were up to.'

'Why was that?'

'Of the three of us, Sondra was the real star. Julian was a good actor, a fabulous singer and a passable dancer, but his biggest claim to fame was being Sondra's husband. Once Sammi was born, Sondra worked less and less and eventually she wasn't such hot property in Hollywood. As a result, people became less interested in Julian's personal life.'

'But what about you? You worked plenty after *Godspell*. According to the details about your work history on the internet, you seemed to work consistently – at least until the end of the '80s.'

'Yes, I was lucky enough never to be out of work for long. But musical theatre was no longer in its heyday by then. I was able to make a good living and was well known among the theatre crowd, but it wasn't the same as being a movie star. It afforded me some anonymity among the general public.'

'But you shot to fame again later when you did the TV series.'

I laugh at this. 'Yes. It was quite odd to be back in the spotlight after years of flying under the radar. I remember I'd not long turned fifty. Stage parts were becoming more scarce as I was getting older. I was wondering if my career was completely dried up when Annie, one of the young actresses I worked with on *The Sound of Music* way back in the early '80s, contacted me. She had a major role in *The Neighbourhood*. I'd kept in touch with her sporadically for many years and she told me there was a guest part coming up on the show she thought I should audition for. I did and I got the part! I signed on for six episodes, but my character, Mrs Mackin, became such a hit with the viewers – especially in Australia – they wrote her in as a regular.

'I stayed with the show for fifteen years. When they finally wrote me out – at my request – I decided to retire. I wanted to spend more time with Julian. We were getting older, but with both of us working and him popping back and forth to the States every so often, it felt as if we never saw each other. Julian was still getting quite a bit of work back then, TV and some voice-over stuff for commercials as well as the occasional movie. I was happy enough just doing the odd TV special or talk show. Mrs Mackin remained a favourite of viewers long after she was written out of the show, so I got lots of invitations from people to be on chat shows, which was a lovely way to stay in the industry without having to work too hard. Honestly, Mrs Mackin turned out to be a godsend.'

'I started watching *The Neighbourhood* when Tom was a baby,' Jane says. 'I think that was why you seemed so familiar to me when we first met.'

'Look, it was just a bit of fluff – light entertainment, you know? Once upon a time I would have turned up my nose at such a thing, but I've come to realise shows like *The Neighbourhood* serve a purpose. They allow people to escape from whatever is troubling them for an hour or so. There's something to be said for that.'

'Yes, there is,' Jane says quietly, and I wonder if she's thinking back to the days when her son was a newborn.

'Anyway, *The Neighbourhood* provided me with good, solid work and a regular income for fifteen years, which I was grateful for. It filled in my time while Julian was working and gave me a whole new set of fans.'

'Julian did quite a few movies, didn't he?' Jane puts down her notebook and leans in, as if she's forgotten we're working on the book.

'He did, but he never really lived up to the promise of those early days.' That sounds disloyal and I don't mean it to be, so I elaborate. 'Not that he wasn't a great actor, he was, but the stage was always his first love, so he'd prioritise a West End or Broadway show over a movie. I think if he'd stayed in America he could have gone on to be one of the biggest stars of his generation, but once we moved in together Julian spent the bulk of his time here, so he preferred UK-based productions to US ones. He knocked back a few Broadway roles and, I suppose, as a result, he just wasn't as visible to American directors. Over time the offers for leading roles in movies became less frequent. But he still got some good supporting roles and was even nominated for an Oscar, for *Endless Sky*.'

'But he wasn't in the public eye as much as he'd once been?'

'Yes, exactly.'

'And eventually you were able to be together openly?'

'Pretty much. The older we got, the easier it got. The media is mainly interested in bright young things. Nobody cares who you're sleeping with when you're fifty . . . or older.'

Jane smirks. She knows this to be the truth.

'When Sammi was a child, Julian popped across the pond a few times a year to see her or to work over there, and while he was in the US he kept up the facade of being a happily married man. Once Sammi was grown, the visits to the States became fewer. He and Sondra were clearly living separate lives, but by that stage nobody cared.'

'He never divorced her?'

'We talked about it – Julian and I – and he discussed it with Sondra too, but by the time Sammi was in her late teens, which is when Julian first suggested it, it didn't seem to matter. It wasn't as if I was desperate to get married to him or anything. We were perfectly happy as we were, so I just couldn't see the point. Sondra wasn't overly keen at that stage either. Perhaps if Max had lived, she would have thought differently.'

'Maxine died?' Jane seems shocked.

This is all ancient history to me, but the people from my past have only recently come to life for her. 'Yes. Ovarian cancer, poor thing. Sondra was grief-stricken, of course. It took her years to recover – if one ever truly recovers from losing the love of their life.'

Jane's eyes mist with unshed tears and I regret my words. It's not as if she is a stranger to grief. She blinks a few times and then picks up her notebook. 'Let's talk about Sammi for a minute. What was your relationship with her like?'

My shoulders slump, weighed down by guilt; the one regret of my relationship with Julian. 'Non-existent. I rarely saw her.'

'Was that your choice?'

I nod. 'It was. And, looking back, it was a big mistake. Perhaps if I'd been more involved, things wouldn't have turned out the way they did.' My voice comes out in a wobble. I'm not ready to talk about Sammi yet.

Jane looks at me sympathetically. 'Do you want to take a break? It's just about lunchtime in any case.'

I rub my hands together. 'Yes, I think we've earned ourselves a sandwich and a brew. Why don't I go and pop the kettle on?'

Jane is staring at her phone distractedly. 'Good idea. There's pea and ham soup in the fridge if you'd rather that than a sandwich. You go on through. I just want to check my email. I'll be out in a jiffy.'

I amble into the kitchen, open the refrigerator and stare at its contents absent-mindedly. Sammi still occupies my thoughts. Her pain is the result of childhood hurts inflicted unknowingly by the adults in her life, including me. If I could go back and change things for her, I would.

'Dolly! Dolly, come back to the office for a minute, would you?' Jane's voice, breathless with excitement. 'There's something I need you to see.'

Chapter Thirty-six

London
2017

As Dolly sat down to breakfast, Julian lowered the newspaper and peered at her over his reading glasses. 'Dawn Duffield died.'

'Really?' Her shoulders sagged as she set her coffee cup down on the table. 'How sad. It seems like just the other day we were joking together at the BAFTAs.'

'God, that was decades ago, Doll.'

'I know, but it doesn't seem like it. What a shame. Dawn was a lovely person. It feels as if all our friends are being picked off one by one.'

'You weren't friends with Dawn, though, were you?'

She shook her head. 'No, not exactly. We were friendly, though. We were around the same age and our paths crossed from time to time. Makes you think, doesn't it?'

'Think what?'

'Life's short, old man. We should be living each day as if it's our last.'

'Pfft, we're not going anywhere. We're both fit as fiddles.' Julian grinned, and as he did the years melted away. He was still that handsome devil she'd fallen in love with more than fifty years earlier.

'Speak for yourself. These old bones are as stiff as a board in the mornings.'

'Ah, that's nothing a brisk walk won't take care of. Shall we head to the park after breakfast? It looks like a decent enough day out there. We should make the most of the mild weather. In a few weeks it'll be freezing.'

She nodded. 'If we're walking, I'll need to change my shoes.' She twirled a foot in the air to show off her black patent block-heeled shoe. 'I dressed for shopping.'

'Ah, you girls and your fashion. I'll never understand it.'

She smiled, loving the fact that he still thought of her as a girl.

'What are we shopping for?'

'I was hoping to drop by the food hall at Harrods and pick up a few things.'

'I thought Carmel got the shopping in yesterday?'

'She did, but she doesn't always get my order exactly right.' As a housekeeper, Carmel was the best. She came in three mornings a week to do whatever they needed – straighten things up, change the linen or do the laundry. On Fridays she did the grocery shopping, which was great, but she tended to bargain-hunt, even though Dolly assured her there was no need. She was only trying to help, Dolly knew this, but sometimes she needed to make an extra trip to the shops to get all the things Carmel had decided were unnecessary.

Julian raised his eyebrows. 'Carmel being thrifty again? Honestly, sometimes I wonder if she's worth what you pay her. It seems you're forever having to top up the shopping, and don't think I don't notice you rearranging all the knick-knacks after she's cleaned.'

'That's just because I'm a fusspot. And I can't blame her entirely for the shopping. I only decided this morning that I wanted to cook something special tonight.'

Julian rubbed his hands together. 'Chicken fricassee?'

'You wish. Did you not hear what the doctor said about your cholesterol?'

'I did. He said it was *slightly* elevated. Nothing to worry about, but to keep an eye on it.'

'To keep an eye on your *diet* is what he said.' Ed Freeman, Julian's personal physician, was almost as old as he was and tended to underplay things. The fact that he'd even mentioned the cholesterol worried her. Ed wasn't the type to mention anything that was insignificant. Dolly knew this because he was her doctor too. He came to the house once a year to draw blood and do a check-up on them both. This routine had started when Julian was at the height of his fame and it had been tricky to go to a regular clinic.

'I'm too old for dieting, Doll. I'd rather be dead than eat rabbit food.'

'Who said anything about rabbit food? I'm going to make something delicious and healthy. All right?'

He shrugged. 'You're the boss.'

'Seriously, Julian. You need to take care of yourself.' She softened her tone. 'I need you to stick around. I'd be lost without you, don't you know?'

He put down the paper and came to stand behind her, leaning forward so he could wrap his arms around her. 'I'm not going anywhere, my love. But don't you worry. If anything *did* happen, you'd be fine. I've provided for you in my estate.'

'Oh, Julian, it's not money I'm worried about. I mean, I'm sure I have enough of my own, don't I?'

He laughed. 'Stop worrying about it. Between us we are set for life. Now, enough of such maudlin talk. Go put on your walking shoes and let's get going.'

•

They'd had a lovely day. A stroll in the park followed by lunch in a new bistro Julian had been wanting to try. After that they ambled around Harrods and Dolly found all the ingredients she needed to make the stuffed chicken breast recipe she'd read about in one of her trashy magazines. (A habit Julian *still* complained about!)

Julian's phone rang just as they'd finished unpacking their purchases. 'Sammi,' he said looking at the screen. 'I'll take it in my study.'

Dolly set about chopping the capsicums and spinach, and tried her best not to eavesdrop. What went on between Julian and his daughter was truly none of her business. But even with the study door closed she could hear Julian's raised voice and frustrated tone. She wasn't surprised. Sammi never called unless there was a problem. After a few minutes there was silence. When he finally spoke again, his tone was subdued.

Good. Whatever had happened, he'd sorted it out, or at least come to terms with it. Dolly didn't doubt that Sammi would be the victor. She always got what she wanted when it came to her father.

Fifteen minutes later, Julian appeared in the kitchen, ashen-faced.

'Everything all right?'

To her horror, tears began to leak from his eyes as he shook his head.

Dolly raced to his side and clasped his hand. 'My darling, what's happened?'

'She's been arrested again. Back on the drugs.'

'Oh, Julian. I'm so sorry. What are you going to do?'

He looked up at her, defeated. 'Nothing. Nothing at all. Sondra and I agreed after the last time that we were done. Sondra's therapist says we're enabling her.'

Dolly kept her opinion about therapy to herself. 'So . . . you mean you'll leave her in jail?'

'No. She's already made bail. One of her friends put it up. But she's facing charges and there's a real chance she could go to prison if she's found guilty. She was calling because Sondra refused to pay for her lawyer. She thought I'd bankroll it, but I told her no.'

'Oh, Julian, I don't know what to say. Do you really think she'll serve time?'

He shrugged. 'Without a decent lawyer, it's possible. Hell, even with a good attorney, she might still do time. It's a miracle she hasn't already.'

Dolly rubbed his back. 'Are you sure about this?'

'No. But we've tried everything else. She's in her fifties, for Christ's sake. I don't know what else to do, Doll, and Sondra seems convinced this is the way forward. I just spoke to her a moment ago. She says her therapist believes Sammi needs to feel the consequences of her actions and to accept responsibility for her own life. The therapist says Sondra and I are blocking her way.' He pressed the heels of his palms against his eyes for a moment and then drew back and looked at her. 'What do you think?'

Dolly wasn't entering into this one. Even if she had an opinion, she wouldn't voice it. Right from the beginning, she been clear about her position. She wasn't Sammi's parent and she wanted no part of raising her. The child was now a middle-aged woman and Dolly wasn't about to change that stance. 'I think you and Sondra love Sammi very much and that you will do what you think is right. I love you and will support you no matter what you choose.'

Julian sighed. 'I'm just so tired, Dolly. Sondra is too.'

'Do you need to go over there to support Sondra?'

He shook his head. 'No. I offered, but she told me not to. She and Maxwell are heading to New York for a while. She thinks it'll be better for him to be away from his mother while this all plays out. I told her they're welcome to come here if she'd like. I hope you don't mind?'

'Of course not. Whatever you need. Do you think they'll come?'

'I doubt it. Sondra doesn't like to travel too far these days because of her arthritis. Even the flight from LA to New York is uncomfortable. But I'll tell her you asked. She'll be pleased to know she's welcome.'

'Is there a court date?'

'December.'

'Will you go?'

He nodded. 'Yes, I think so. I mean, just because we're withdrawing financial support doesn't mean we don't care. I want her to know that. I was intending to go for Christmas, as always, but I suppose I'll go a little earlier this year. Would you mind?'

'Of course not. Sammi is your daughter. You must put her first. I've always said that and nothing has changed.'

'Perhaps you could come. We can all have Christmas together. Sammi might not be joining us this year, but you, me, Sondra and Maxwell could spend the time together.'

Dolly shook her head slowly. Julian had stayed married to Sondra for all these years and she truly didn't mind that. At first it was to keep the press off their backs, but that hadn't been an issue for a long time now. They'd talked about divorce when Julian was in his late fifties but decided against it when they realised the main beneficiaries of such an action would be their respective lawyers. 'It's not as if I'm dying to don a gown and walk down the aisle,' Dolly had said at the time. 'We're happy as it is. Let's leave well enough alone.'

And it was true. She didn't need a piece of paper or a wedding band to know Julian loved her. And, it might be a technicality, but *not* being Julian's wife also meant she was *not* Sammi's stepmother. In all the years they'd been together, they'd managed to keep Julian's family life quite separate from his life with Dolly. It might be an unusual arrangement, but it had worked, and she saw no reason to change things now.

'I'd love to be with you, of course, but I think it's probably best if we stick to our normal arrangement, don't you? Whatever happens with Sammi, you and Sondra will have lots to discuss, and Maxwell will no doubt need support. I don't want to get in the way.'

'Yes, yes, of course.' There was a forced smile on his face now and Dolly's heart lurched at the sight. But she would not insert herself into Julian's family life, even at his specific request. It was for the best. She was sure of it.

'We'll have a wonderful New Year's Eve celebration when you return,' she said brightly. 'Just like always.'

Chapter Thirty-seven

London
2019

Jane ushers me into her desk chair and points at the screen. 'Read this all the way to the end and then I'll explain.'

She stands beside me silently as I begin to read the email she has open on her computer.

Dear Jane,

Thank you for your email. I'm glad you took the time to make contact.

I am thrilled to hear Rob's birth mother is so keen to get in touch, if not for Rob's sake, then for our girls.

We have two daughters, Alice and Clementine. Alice is a teacher, and she's just announced her engagement to Finn, who we all adore. Clem is still studying. She's not quite sure what she wants to do with her life yet but she's very artistic. I personally think she'd make a wonderful actress! (Her father is less enamoured of that idea.) The girls don't know about any of this just yet – Rob's not quite ready to discuss it with them – but I'm sure they'll be excited about the prospect of having another grandmother.

The situation with Rob is more complex, as you can probably imagine. I want you to know he harbours no anger or bitterness towards his birth mother. He knows she was very young when he was born and was possibly placed in a difficult situation by her pregnancy.

He was adopted as a newborn by Dulcie and Ken, and they have provided a wonderful home for him. People will sometimes remark how like his dad he is, so there's never been any hint to the outside world that he was adopted. For many years Rob did not know himself.

Rob discovered he was adopted when he was an adult, well after we were married, in fact. Alice was unwell and the doctors were having a hard time pinpointing what was wrong. Rob and I were both asked for detailed family medical histories and that's when Rob's parents came clean. Rob was shocked, and it made a difficult time even more distressing, but I guess we were so concerned about Alice that he didn't have time to dwell on the news. He registered his details with the adoption information service and found out what he could, but we weren't able to trace his mother from the information provided. Once Alice was diagnosed with coeliac disease and the medical need to trace his roots had passed, Rob seemed to put the whole adoption thing behind him. From time to time I'd ask him how he felt about it, but he would just shrug and say he had a mum and dad who he loved and that was enough for him.

The letter from Ms Ferguson (who I now know to be Miss Jamieson!) came out of the blue and I'm afraid Rob just wasn't ready to deal with it. I think it was simply the shock of it, because he's already having second thoughts.

After your message and subsequent email, I talked to him some more and he is tentatively open to contact. I can't promise he will be a good communicator just yet. He's still processing what's happened. I'm sure once he gets used to the idea he'll want to know more about his origins and will be keen to keep in touch.

If Miss Jamieson lived in Australia, I would suggest an in-person meet-up once Rob is agreeable, but obviously with her being in the UK that is not practical. Perhaps down the track we could organise a FaceTime or Skype call?

For the moment I am happy to act as a sort of go-between. If Miss Jamieson wants to write to Rob, I'll be happy to make sure he reads the letters and to reply on his behalf, if you think she would like that.

Thank you again for persisting and making contact. I do believe in time Rob will be grateful that you did. I know I am.

Warm regards,
Claire Parker

I read the email three times over with a hand on my heart, hardly daring to breathe, lest I accidentally wake myself from what must surely be a dream. Finally, I tear my eyes from the screen and look at Jane. 'I don't understand. The information we received said nothing about his wife. How did you track her down?'

Jane shrugs. 'It wasn't hard. I'd already started looking into Robert's background before you got that email last week. In fact, once we knew Robert's parents' names, I set about finding them. I guess I wanted us to have as much information about him as possible in case he made contact.

'It's amazing what Google can tell you when you have people's full names and an address to start with. I just searched for information and followed up every lead I could get. Robert was brought up in a reasonably small town on the coast.'

'Yes, the adoptive parents gave their address as Ocean Grove. I remember that from the court order.'

'Exactly. When I looked for information for Ken and Dulcie Parker of Ocean Grove, I came up with quite a bit. It seems they still live at the same address as they did when they adopted him. They're prominent members of their local bowls club – I found stories online from the local newspaper. Ken recently celebrated his ninetieth birthday – that was in the paper, too. Dulcie even has a Facebook profile. There wasn't much on that, but I was able to access her friends list. I wondered if I had the wrong people to begin with, because Robert wasn't listed as one of her friends, but then I found Claire and clicked on her profile. I couldn't see much because of the security settings and at this stage I didn't know what her relationship to the Parkers was, but I had a hunch she might be Robert's wife, so I kept digging.'

My head is swimming with all this information. 'My goodness, Jane. You're a real detective. I should have had you on the case years ago.'

She laughs. 'Years ago this wouldn't have been possible. Social media has changed the world. People are much more accessible these days.' She looks pensive for a moment but quickly shakes off whatever is troubling her and says lightly, 'Luckily for us, eh?'

'So how did you work out Claire is Jamie's – I mean, *Robert's* – wife?'

'She owns a gift shop in the town – I followed a link on Facebook to the shop's Instagram account and started following her. It didn't take long for me to find some personal photos on that account – none of her husband, unfortunately. There were plenty of references to "Rob", though. The evidence was circumstantial, but it seemed to add up. It was enough for me to risk getting in touch. I sent her a brief message on Instagram, explaining who I was and my connection to you. I asked if it would be okay to email her and she said yes. I contacted her without saying anything to you because I didn't want to get your hopes up, but when I saw her reply just now, I thought it sounded promising enough to bring you up to speed. What do you think?'

I have no idea about the Instagram and whatnot she's talking about. It sounds dreadfully complicated to me. But who cares? There is an email in front of me from my son's wife, offering to facilitate communication between the two of us. 'I couldn't be happier,' I say.

●

I'm too excited to concentrate on work after lunch, so Jane suggests we take the afternoon off. Richard has called to say he will be home for dinner, so Jane decides she'll make something a bit special. 'We'll have a bit of a celebration, in honour of your good news.'

While Jane busies herself in the kitchen, I try to distract myself with the historical romance novel I've borrowed from the library. I set myself up in the cosy sitting room and try to read, but all the time I'm thinking about what I might say in my first letter to Jamie. Should I tell him that's what I called him and why I chose that name? I wonder if he will want to know about his father, and how much I should say. The basic details will be in the book, but of course there wouldn't be anything that would identify Alan.

It was hard telling Jane about Jamie's conception, but I'm glad I did. She gently explained that these days what Alan did would be considered sexual assault. It took me a while to come to terms with that knowledge, but eventually it helped me to see that what happened wasn't my fault. Whether all that detail needs to be on the page, though, is something I'm still grappling with.

It's funny; all these months I've been focused on telling my story so that my son might know the truth, but now I am faced with the prospect of delivering the information to a real live person, not just an imagined one, I'm not sure how much he needs to know.

Maybe the book isn't such a good idea after all.

I bite my lip as I weigh up the pros and cons of all my secrets – even a sanitised version of them – being out in the world for everyone to read. And, more to the point, I think about how this knowledge might affect my son. The whole point of writing the book was for him to understand why I did what I did. But now I've made contact, I'm wondering if it's necessary for the whole, unvarnished truth to be out in the world. I don't want to jeopardise my relationship with him by airing things in public that he'd rather not have broadcast. Not that the book would identify him, either, but *he'd* know.

I'm already a bit nervous about the Sammi factor. She will not be pleased to see my relationship with her father spelt out so openly and she's already so angry with me over the falling-out she had with her father just before he died. I know she blames me for his withdrawal of financial support.

Jane and I have spoken about perhaps not revealing Julian's identity, but, as Jane pointed out, it was hardly a secret in the end anyway. She thinks concealing Julian's name will only make it more of a talking point.

Jane has worked so hard on the project. It would be cruel to pull the rug out from under her by giving up on the book – especially after everything she has done for me. And, I must admit, it has been cathartic, telling my story to her. Jane's insightful questions have helped me to see my life more clearly and I've been able to forgive myself for some of the choices I've made.

I realise I have my answer. I thought I was writing for Jamie, but now I realise this book is for *me*. I have to finish it. It's not about Sammi or Julian or even Jamie. This story has been told by me, for me, and I'm entitled to have my version of the truth out in the world.

●

The warmth of the fire and the comfort of the gentle world depicted in my novel combine to make my lids heavy, and before too long I drift off to sleep. When I wake, the light in the room is fading and it's clearly late afternoon. I get up and go in search of Jane.

There's a delicious aroma emanating from the kitchen but Jane is nowhere to be seen. I make my way to the study but she's not there either. I look at the computer on her desk and wonder if I could access the email from Claire Parker. It's not as if Jane hasn't shown me how to do it enough times. I just want to read those magical words once more. Make sure I didn't dream them. I take a seat at the desk and place my hand on the mouse. The large screen immediately comes to life.

A document appears before my eyes. I have no idea what I've done to make it appear, but now I've seen it I can't look away. It's a newspaper article and there's a large photo of Jane with her arm around her son. The photo was taken in Paris – the Eiffel Tower is in the background – and it's some years old. Jane is dressed in a navy frock and her hair is tied back with a jaunty red scarf. The boy – who looks to be around ten years old – is wearing navy shorts with a white T-shirt, and is holding an ice-cream cone. The clearly posed shot looks as if it was taken by a professional. The most striking thing about it, though, is how happy they both look.

My eyes flit to the headline below the photograph.

Lost in the Jungle:
The tragedy behind the downfall of a parenting icon
By Sara Langdon

As little as ten months ago the name Jane Leveson was synonymous with parenting.

Parents worldwide tuned in to her weekly podcast, read opinion pieces on her website, asked her advice and connected with each other through her various social media platforms.

Leveson dispensed her wisdom in a relatable yet authoritative tone, which made her irresistible to parents struggling with the everyday trials of modern parenting.

The 49-year-old mother of one began her blog, *Jane in the Jungle*, nearly two decades ago, after the birth of her son, Tom. Leveson's flair for aesthetically pleasing design coupled with her warm writing style quickly grew a following, and it didn't take long for the enterprising young mother to realise she was sitting on a potential gold mine.

Leveson quickly positioned herself as the 'go-to' expert on all things parenting. Initially her niche was babies and toddlers – she wrote articles with headlines such as 'Is co-sleeping bad for baby?' and 'Toddler tantrums? You're not alone' – but as her son grew, so did her expertise. At the height of her success, Leveson was regularly called on to comment in the mainstream media on a range of parenting issues – everything from teething to talking about sex to your teen. There was no child-rearing issue Leveson didn't have an opinion on.

After a tragic event on New Year's Eve involving her 18-year-old son, Leveson disappeared from the public arena.

(Click here to read our story: New Year's tragedy for parenting icon)

While some fans were initially sympathetic to Leveson's personal tragedy, as more details came to light about the incident, many began to ask themselves just how Leveson could have known so little about her own child.

What sort of a mother is Jane Leveson, really?

'Hello? Where is everyone?' Richard's voice floats down the hall and pulls my attention away from the screen. I shouldn't be reading this. I have no idea how to shut the screen off, so I simply leave it and head out of the study to make my way back to the kitchen, hoping it will turn itself off before Jane realises I've seen it.

All three of us converge in the kitchen at the same time. Richard pecks Jane's cheek and smiles. 'Something smells good.'

'Beef bourguignon,' Jane replies.

'Ooh!' Richard rubs his hands together. 'My favourite.'

She smiles. 'I thought it fitting for such a cold evening. Plus, we're celebrating tonight. Dolly has had some good news.'

'Let me guess.' Richard looks at me. 'You've found a publisher for the book?'

I shake my head. 'Even better.'

'Better than finding a publisher? I can't even imagine.'

'We've heard from Robert Parker's wife,' Jane says triumphantly.

Richard looks incredulous. 'His *wife?*'

'Yes,' I say. 'She wants to keep in touch on his behalf. Isn't it exciting?'

'Well, I didn't expect that.' There's an odd expression on his face as he glances at Jane. 'I'll be interested to hear how that came about. Are you sure it's actually her?'

'Relax, Richard. It's all above board. Go fetch a bottle of red and we'll tell you the whole story over dinner.'

Chapter Thirty-eight

London
2019

The inclement weather has kept us at home this week. We've been working in Jane's cosy office instead of making the icy trek to the library. Today dawns just as bleakly as those before it, despite my sunny mood. I'm still excited about Claire's email from yesterday, hopeful that in time she will be able to coax my son into communicating with me directly. In the meantime, Jane and I will get on with finishing the book.

Today we're talking about Sammi again and it's hard going. I've explained how she never really recovered from Maxine's death and how from her teens onwards she careened from one crisis to the next. First came the shoplifting, then the drinking, drug-taking and the subsequent arrests. She admitted to several abortions in her late teens but eventually gave birth to Maxwell in her early twenties. Sondra, who became responsible for raising her grandson as well as trying to help her daughter, was often overwhelmed and Julian spent a lot of time going to and from LA to support her.

'Did Sammi know about your relationship with her dad?'

I sigh. 'Yes. We never hid that from her.'

'But the two of you weren't close?'

I shake my head. 'When Julian and I decided to be together I was very clear that I didn't want to be part of Sammi's life. There were several reasons for that. The first was that Sammi already had three parents in her life at that stage, and I didn't think she needed another one. I also knew that if I were around when Sammi was visiting over here, it would mean she would have less time with her father. I didn't think it was fair to make her share that time with me.'

'That was very considerate of you.'

'Not really. If I'm being brutally honest, I was thinking more about myself than Sammi.'

'What do you mean?'

'I had given up my own child, and it felt disloyal to him to be taking on a parenting role with another child. In a way, Sammi was a reminder to me of all that I'd lost. I just didn't want to be around her. Looking back, I realise that was incredibly selfish. I wonder if things would have turned out differently if I'd allowed myself to be a part of her life.'

Jane's phone pings, halting my ruminations for the moment. She usually has the phone on silent when we're working.

'Sorry, Dolly,' she says, pausing the recording of our conversation. 'Do you mind if we break for a minute? I've been waiting on this email that's just come through and I need to attend to it.'

To be honest, I'm relieved. I'm not comfortable talking about Sammi, even though I know I must examine our relationship if I want my book to represent the truth. 'Must be just about time for morning tea,' I say. 'How about I go pop the kettle on and you can join me when you're ready?'

Jane nods distractedly. 'Yes, all right.'

The kettle has just boiled and I'm setting out Jane's favourite china cup when she comes racing into the kitchen, her eyes shining like an excited child's on Christmas morning. 'Rob has agreed to meet you in person!' she blurts out.

The saucer I'm holding clatters onto the marble benchtop. 'What do you mean?'

'I just got off the phone from Claire. She messaged to ask if I could talk. She says if we go to Melbourne, Rob will meet with you.'

Everything in the kitchen takes on a surreal appearance. Jane is talking and clapping her hands together, but I can't make sense of what she is saying. How can this be true? But surely Jane wouldn't tell me this unless she was sure.

'Dolly . . . Dolly! Did you hear what I said? Are you okay? Say something.'

I put a hand on the countertop to steady myself. 'I don't understand. He hasn't even written to me himself yet. Why would he agree to a meeting? It doesn't make sense.'

Jane's lips twitch into a knowing smile. 'Sometimes people don't know what they want until you put it in front of them. I might have given Rob a little nudge in the right direction.'

'What do you mean?'

'I've been researching all of your past productions, to verify the dates and so on. When I googled *The Rose of France*, I discovered there's a new production being staged in Melbourne early next year. It's previewing on New Year's Eve. I was thinking how lovely it would be for you to see the show again. Then I thought, why not? We could all go – you, me and Richard – it would make a lovely Christmas gift.'

'Jane, I couldn't accept—'

She shakes her head. 'Hear me out. I wondered whether, if you were going to be in Melbourne for a short time, Rob would snap up the opportunity to see you. So I mentioned to Claire we would be visiting over the Christmas period and asked her if she thought a meeting was possible. She was very enthusiastic about the idea, but of course she needed to run it by Rob. That was what the phone call was about. She wanted to let me know Rob has agreed. Now all we need is for you to agree. Just say "yes", Dolly, and I can make this happen for you.'

'Yes,' I say breathlessly, still not quite able to believe what I've just heard.

●

Over dinner it becomes clear Richard is not nearly as enamoured of the idea as Jane is.

He chooses his words carefully. I'm sure he doesn't want to dampen my excitement, but I can tell he's concerned. 'It's great news that Robert is open to a meeting,' he says, when Jane prompts him for his thoughts. 'I'm just worried things are moving a little too quickly.'

Jane shakes her head. 'Nonsense! Dolly has been waiting more than fifty years to see her son again. The meeting can't come a moment too soon.'

He smiles. 'Quite right, I'm sure, but even so, should we maybe do a bit more research before racing across the world? We don't really know anything about these people.'

'For heavens' sake, Richard, don't be such a killjoy. This is Dolly's son you're talking about. And I *have* researched them. Stop being, such a . . . such a *lawyer.*'

Richard looks hurt by this comment, so I cut in. 'I appreciate your concern, Richard, truly I do. I know there's some risk involved in this. Perhaps the meeting won't go as well as I hope. Even so, I want to give it a go. At least then I'll know I did everything I could to make our relationship right before it's too late.'

Jane folds her arms across her chest and gives Richard a smug look. 'Yes, of course. It's completely up to you, Dolly.'

I laugh. 'Well, not really. I don't have the money to fly to Australia. Jane has generously offered to gift me the trip, but I can't accept that. I could, however, accept a loan. I could pay you back over time. It might take a while, though.'

Richard looks aghast. 'Goodness, no. If Jane wants to gift you the trip, she absolutely has my blessing. I just want to make sure . . . well, I just don't want you to get hurt, that's all.' He's talking to me but looking at Jane, and her expression softens as he speaks.

'That's settled, then. I'll start making the arrangements tomorrow,' she says.

●

I excused myself not long after dinner, citing exhaustion due to over-excitement at the latest development as the reason for my unusually early retirement to my room. It's true enough, but that's not the only thing on my mind.

The events of the past week are swirling around in my head.

It's not just the trip Richard has had a lukewarm response to. His reaction to Claire's initial email yesterday was equally subdued, which took me by surprise. I thought he'd be delighted when he heard about Claire making contact – after all, it was his idea to search for Jamie using the adoption records, but he seemed perplexed by the news. 'I don't understand. How did she get *your* email address, Jane?'

'I messaged her first.'

'But how did you find her?'

'I tracked her down on social media.'

Richard frowned at this. Like me, he's a bit of a social media novice. 'Wasn't that a bit risky? I mean, the adoption services people said—'

'You're missing the point, Richard. It doesn't matter *how* it happened, just that it did. Claire has made contact and offered to facilitate communication between Dolly and her son. This is news to be celebrated.'

'Yes, I suppose so,' he said, but his agreement wasn't particularly convincing.

Things have moved on quickly from that initial contact. So much so, I'm finding it hard to take it all in. There's a been a flurry of emails between Claire and Jane. I sent a very cautiously worded message to Jamie (who I was careful to address as Rob), thanking him for being open to communication and telling him I was happy to answer any questions he might have. Claire responded saying Rob had read the email and would have a think about what he would like to ask me. I was excited enough with that progress, so today's development is overwhelming.

The news article I read about Jane yesterday is also on my mind. Part of me wants to surreptitiously access Jane's computer so I can finish reading the article, but even if I knew how to find it again, I'd feel bad sneaking around behind her back. I really should tell her I've seen it and give her the opportunity to explain if she'd like to, but she's been so happy and upbeat since Claire got in touch with us. I'd hate to do anything to shatter her good mood, especially because I know it's been a long time since she felt even slightly optimistic about anything. I'll leave it be for now. After all, what happened to Tom is none of my business.

I've given up on falling asleep any time soon. Despite a long bath and almost an hour's tossing and turning I still can't settle. My mind is churning and I need something to take me out of myself for a while.

I click on the bedside lamp and reach for my novel, only to find it missing from its usual place on the nightstand. I must have left it in the sitting room this afternoon. I hop up, slip on the fluffy guest robe that has quickly become mine, and head downstairs to retrieve it.

Jane and Richard are still up. I hear their voices coming from the kitchen as I make my way down the last few steps into the entrance hall. Their voices are terse, angry even, and I stop for a moment, trying to decide whether I should risk padding across the foyer to the sitting room.

'I don't understand what your problem is,' Jane says. '*You* were the one who instigated this whole process, remember?'

'Yes, but I didn't anticipate you would go outside the rules like that. There's such a thing as due process, Jane.'

'Oh, Richard, you can be such an old fuddy-duddy at times.'

There's a thud of a cupboard door being closed too hard.

'I thought you'd given all that social media nonsense away.' Even from the stairwell, I can hear the accusation in his voice.

Jane's voice drops to a lower volume, and I can only just hear her when she says, 'I have. I made new accounts just for this purpose, in my maiden name. I was careful. No one will know it's me.'

'I hope not. For your sake . . . And for Dolly's.'

'You're really not going to come?'

'No. I can't, Jane, not on such short notice. Christmas is only a couple of weeks away. I have cases that are ongoing.'

'The courts break over Christmas.'

'Yes, but not for long. And I have that big trial coming up in the second week of January. I need to prep. Besides, Felicity is expecting us for Christmas.'

This statement seems to enrage Jane even further. 'Ha, that's rich. Using your family as an excuse, when we both know you detest Christmas at your sister's as much as I do.'

'She's my family, Jane.'

'I thought *I* was your family. Besides, I can't believe you'd set foot in that house after the spectacular lack of support Felicity and Stephen showed us when Tom died.'

'Jane, be fair. It was a difficult situation for all of us.'

'He was their nephew. They couldn't even trouble themselves to attend his funeral. I'm frankly surprised we've even been invited to Christmas dinner.'

'Well, we have. I want to go. I think it will help to mend things between us. If we don't go, I fear the rift between us will become irreparable.' He pauses for a moment, but when there's no response he continues. 'I've mentioned that we have a house guest, and Felicity has said she is welcome to come too.'

'As if I would subject Dolly to that judgemental cow. No thanks.'

'I think you're being unreasonable. All I'm asking is that you postpone the trip, just a little bit. A month or two won't hurt, will it? It'll give Dolly time to build a bit more of a rapport with her son.'

'In case you haven't noticed, Dolly's no spring chicken. She's well enough to travel now, but who knows what the future will bring? What if she never gets another opportunity? We've lost our son, Richard, but Dolly's boy is alive and well. I'm going to make sure I do everything in my power to reunite them before it's too late.'

There's silence for a moment and then Richard speaks. 'All right, fair enough. But I'm sorry, Jane, I can't come with you. I've already told Felicity I'll see her at Christmas and I'm not going back on my word. Besides, I have told everyone at work I will hold the fort over the holiday period. I'm a partner. The firm depends on me. I can't just disappear to the other side of the world on a moment's notice. But you go, if you must.'

The conversation seems to be winding up so I pad upstairs as quietly as I can without bothering to retrieve my book. I'd rather risk a whole night of insomnia than be caught eavesdropping on my hosts.

Part Three

Chapter Thirty-nine

Melbourne, Australia
December 2019

I'd forgotten about the light here. Everything is so incredibly bright. It's five-thirty in the afternoon and there's not a hint of the sun setting any time soon. In fact, it could easily be mistaken for midday outside.

From up here on the thirty-seventh floor there's a spectacular view of the city, but you wouldn't know it's the day before Christmas. There's plenty of traffic – both vehicles and pedestrians – but the shimmering light makes it hard to see the city's festive decorations.

It's a different story on the ground. I took Jane to see the Myer windows early this morning. We were both up before the crack of dawn – still adjusting to the time change, I suppose. There wasn't a crowd there at seven o'clock in the morning, so we were able to get a close look at each of the scenes. It reminded me of my childhood.

When I was little, Granny and Grandpa used to bring me to Melbourne on the train every year as a special treat. We'd come early in December so we could see the windows before the city got too crowded. A photo with Santa and lunch at a restaurant was also included. I remember looking forward to that day each year, almost as much as Christmas Day itself. It all stopped once the little kids came along. Mum said I was too big for that sort of nonsense, but I knew it was because Granny wouldn't hear of taking my siblings and Mum didn't want them to feel left out. One year, she saved up and brought us all on the train herself. We couldn't get photos with Santa or eat in the fancy restaurant. We had sandwiches brought from home instead. Still, I remember that trip being the best one of all.

Jane loved the windows, but by eight o'clock she was already too hot and needed to come back here to the hotel for lighter clothes. She laughed at herself. 'Even though I knew it was summer here, I can't get my head around it being hot at Christmas time.'

The warm weather might feel wrong to those of us used to a Northern Hemisphere Christmas, but the frenetic energy of Christmas Eve shoppers here in Melbourne is no different to home.

Home.

The thought pulls me up. Once upon a time, *this* place was my home. I've only just realised I don't think of it that way anymore. I wonder, if things go well with Jamie – *Rob!* – could I make this country my home again?

I love London. Even after all that's happened recently, overall, the city's been kind to me. And, thanks to Jane and Richard, when we get back I'll be on my feet again. I'll have my pension, and Richard has spoken to a forensic accountant who seems to think I haven't been correctly paid royalties for the *Rose of France* cast album we recorded all those years ago. Perhaps that'll come to something. I don't need much – just enough to secure some sort of housing.

But there's no reason to think I couldn't be happy somewhere else. Australia is the country I was born in – maybe it's where my life should end, too. Don't they say home is where the heart is? If that's the case then my home has always been here, with Jamie.

But I'm getting ahead of myself. Let's not count our chickens, as Mum would say. Jane and I talked a lot about this yesterday. It was a funny sort of a day. We both slept a lot, even though we managed to sleep well on the plane. We woke late in the afternoon, ordered room service, and then went for a walk to see the Floral Clock in Queen Victoria Gardens.

We strolled for a while and then found a park bench so we could sit and enjoy the warm evening air. 'You mustn't expect too much from this first meeting,' Jane said, gently.

I smiled at her earnest face. 'Oh, darling Jane, you worry unnecessarily. It will be enough for me to see my boy in the flesh. Anything more is a bonus.'

'I just don't want you to be disappointed. It might take a while for Rob to feel comfortable with you.'

'I promise I'm not expecting him to declare his life is complete once he's seen me again. I understand how strange this will be for him. Honestly, don't fret. You've got me this far; the rest is up to me. If Jami . . . Rob decides he doesn't ever want to lay eyes on me again, I'll accept that. I just want the opportunity to tell him I never stopped loving him.'

I wasn't lying. Seeing Jamie and telling him I love him *will* be enough, but I can't help but hope for more.

First things first, however. The dinner tonight. I'm not ashamed to admit I've got the jitters. I've been ready for a good twenty minutes now, but I keep going back to the bathroom to check my hair and make-up. I scrub up okay for an old lady. Of course, the clothes and hairstyle help. A couple of months ago I looked like a bag lady. Huh – I *was* a bag lady. It doesn't take long to forget.

Jane gave me a manicure earlier and painted my nails a lovely shade of pink, which matches my new lipstick. I'm wearing a burnt-orange satin sheath topped with a pink-and-orange brocade jacket. These are two of the few remaining items in my collection, which I retrieved from Adnan when I went to collect my photos. Jane's hand-me-downs are lovely, but I wanted to feel like my true self when I met my boy. My pale-pink block-heeled mules (another early Christmas gift from Jane) are not quite broken in yet, but never mind. I only have to walk from here to the elevator. The restaurant is on the first floor of the hotel and we'll be sitting all evening. I'm as ready as I'll ever be. Now there's nothing to do but wait.

There's a tap on the adjoining door. 'Can I come in?'

'It's open.'

Jane enters the room, looking lovely in a floaty silk floral number. 'You look beautiful,' she gushes.

Beautiful is probably overstating it, but I smile at the compliment. 'Thank you. I was just about to say the same to you.'

'Shall we go? I know it's a little early, but I thought we could get settled at the table and maybe order a bottle of bubbly. That way the wine should arrive about the same time as Claire and Robert. A drink might be a good way to break the ice.'

Jane's such a clever girl. Always one step ahead. 'Marvellous idea.'

As we approach the elevator, I clasp Jane's hand. 'Thank you, my darling. No one has ever cared for me the way you have. I know I can never repay you, but I will never forget what you've done for me.'

She smiles at me with watery eyes. 'Hush. It goes both ways, you know. Now, we need to pull ourselves together. We don't want to be puffy-eyed when we meet this boy of yours.'

On the first floor the smartly dressed waiter walks us through a half-empty restaurant and shows us to our table by the window. As soon as we're seated, Jane orders a bottle of Dom Perignon and starts a conversation about the weather. She's saying something about how it doesn't feel like Christmas. I try to nod in the right places but I'm not really listening, and she knows it. We lapse into silence and I focus on the street below, hoping to catch a glimpse of my son as he enters the hotel. It's hard to see people's faces as they scurry past, so I'm taking stabs in the dark. There's a brown-haired man dressed in a suit, walking arm in arm with a smartly dressed woman. Perhaps that's him? But they don't stop at the hotel entrance, they hurry on down the street towards Federation Square. My eyes keep scanning.

'There's more than one entrance to the hotel,' Jane says softly, and I nod, but I can't take my eyes off the street.

The waiter arrives with our champagne, sets four glasses on the table and looks at Jane. She nods and he pours two glasses before melting into the background. Jane picks up her glass. 'Shall we have a pre-toast? A sip of bubbly might settle the nerves.'

I don't think I can stomach alcohol just now, so I shake my head. 'I think I'll wait for the others. But you go ahead and start.'

'Okay, I will. I don't mind saying I'm so excited that I feel a bit jittery.'

My eyes wander back to the street and that's when I see him. I drink in his image, thirsty for every detail. He's a middle-aged man in a navy-blue suit, holding his wife's hand. His hair is grey but thick and neatly combed. He looks quite dapper, in fact. A successful professional. My heart swells with pride. His wife has on a pink frock. She's slightly plump and very pretty. She has long blonde hair, which has been curled. I wonder if she's had her hair done specially for tonight. The thought of her going to this trouble pleases me.

They've stopped on the footpath outside the hotel and are looking towards the entrance. She says something to him and he shakes his head, and then she puts her arms around him and kisses him. My chest feels tight. My son has a wife who loves him. He lifts his head and glances up at the building, almost as if he can see me. My heart hammers against my ribs. It *is* him. There's no doubt in my mind.

A mother knows.

Jane senses something is up. 'What is it, Dolly? Are you okay?'

'I see him.'

'Are you sure? How do you know?'

'It's my son.'

She smiles. 'He'll be here in a minute, then. Are you ready?'

'I've been ready for nearly sixty years.' My gaze flits back to the street, but Rob and his wife have disappeared. The moment I have been waiting for for most of my life is upon me.

●

Ten minutes have passed since I saw my son on the street, but he hasn't arrived.

'Perhaps it wasn't him,' Jane says.

'I know it was.'

'Maybe they've had to make a stop to use the bathroom.'

I nod, not trusting my voice to speak.

He's not coming.

Deep down I know the glimpse I had of him is the last time I will see my son in this lifetime. I pick up my glass of champagne.

After another ten minutes have gone by, Jane's face is ashen. 'That can't have been them. Perhaps they're stuck in traffic. I mean, it's crazy out there, being Christmas Eve and all.'

I nod again and drain my glass. There's no point in trying to convince Jane she's wrong. She'll find out soon enough. The waiter returns to pour me another glass and I allow it. Perhaps the alcohol will dull the growing feeling of despair inside me. Jane makes a valiant attempt at keeping the mood light, talking about the Christmas lunch we've got booked and how much fun it will be. As much as I appreciate the effort, I find myself unable to provide her with more than the odd monosyllabic response. After a while she gives up.

'I might just text Claire. See where they're at.'

Jane focuses on her phone while I stare out the window, scanning the crowded footpath. There's no sign of them in the sea of people below. The restaurant is starting to fill up now. A new waiter approaches our table and asks whether we'd like to see some menus while we wait for the remainder of our party to arrive. I look at Jane and she shrugs.

'I think we'll wait a little longer,' she says to the waiter. He nods and moves away while Jane smiles at me. 'No answer from Claire, yet, but you know what people are like here. So laid back. They're only half an hour late, so I wouldn't worry yet. I'm sure they're on their way.'

I'm not sure how much longer I can sit here pretending every-thing is okay. I can feel tears pricking the back of my eyes, and there's nothing more unbecoming than crying in public. 'Jane, I—'

Her phone pings and she holds up a finger, indicating for me to wait. 'It's Claire,' she says. Her eyes scan the text and, although she tries not to show it, I can tell from her expression the news isn't good. Her thumbs move frantically to type a reply and moments later the phone pings again. She sighs and finally concedes defeat. 'I'm so sorry, Dolly, but something's come up and they're not able to make it.'

Chapter Forty

Melbourne, Australia
Christmas Day, 2019

I wake early. A crack of sunlight that has snuck through a gap in the heavy hotel curtains warms my face, and for a split second I'm happy. Then I open my eyes and see the envelope sitting on the bedside table, and the events of last night come flooding back. My chest aches under the weight of it.

I pick up the envelope, which was sitting on the floor inside my door when I arrived back at the room last night.

After we realised the Parkers weren't coming, Jane took charge of the situation as best she could. She made our excuses to the waiter, claiming I had a sudden onset migraine and would need to leave immediately. Then she ushered me back to the room, where we discovered the letter upon opening the door.

Jane retrieved it from the floor and handed it to me. I immediately knew it was from him, but I couldn't bring myself to open it in front of Jane. When I placed the unopened letter on the nightstand, she didn't mention it, instead offering to run me a bath while she ordered room service.

I stayed in the tub for ages and when I emerged from the bathroom there was a bowl of soup and a plate of scrambled eggs waiting for me. Jane was picking at a bowl of French fries and knocking back a large glass of white wine.

'I thought something light might tempt you,' she said.

I smiled and sat down in front of the meal. I managed a few mouthfuls of soup before pushing the bowl away. 'I'm afraid I'm just not hungry.'

Jane's eyes were glassy and her cheeks were flushed. 'There's a bottle of wine in the fridge if you'd like some.'

I shook my head. 'No, thank you.'

Jane drained her glass and headed to the mini fridge to refill it. 'I just can't believe this has happened,' she said. 'I trusted Claire. I thought she was telling me the truth. What I don't understand is why? Why would they do this to you? They know how far you've travelled. I just can't believe they could be so heartless.'

I smiled at her. 'To be fair, they think I'm here to see the premiere of a musical. They don't know I came all this way just to see Rob.'

Jane nodded, turning her anger on herself. 'It's my fault. I shouldn't have interfered. Richard was right. I so badly wanted to help but I've ruined everything. I'm sorry, Dolly. Can you ever forgive me?' A giant sob hiccoughed from her.

'Oh, Jane, darling Jane, there's nothing to forgive. You tried your hardest to make something wonderful happen. There's no shame in that.'

She covered her face with her hands for a moment and then looked up. 'Perhaps he'll change his mind. Maybe if I call Claire and speak to her . . .'

'Leave it for now,' I said. 'We'll think about it in the morning. I just want to get some sleep.'

'Of course,' she said. 'I'll leave you be.'

Before she opened the door into her adjoining room, I embraced her and kissed her cheek. 'I'll be okay, Jane. Please don't worry. Things will look better in the morning.'

Once Jane was gone, I got into bed and read the letter. Last night these words written by my son broke my heart. Once I was freed from the fear of causing Jane further guilt, I gave in to the desolation I felt and cried an ocean of tears. Sleep, when it eventually came, brought little relief. I was dogged by dreams of looking for lost items that would appear in the distance but evaporate like a mirage on a hot summer's day once I got near.

This morning as I read the letter again, my pain begins to ease.

Dear Miss Ferguson,

(Or should that be Miss Jamieson? My apologies for not knowing which title you prefer.)

I'm writing this letter in the lobby of your hotel, while you are no doubt waiting for me to arrive in the restaurant upstairs. I'm so sorry to disappoint you with my no-show, and this letter is both an apology for my lack of manners and an explanation of why I can't have dinner with you.

When I received your first correspondence a month or so ago, I was taken by surprise. I didn't know I was adopted until well into adulthood. When my parents eventually told me, I was shaken to my core. At the time there was a medical situation with my eldest daughter and I needed information, which is why I registered with the adoption information service and consented to being contacted.

Once the medical issue was resolved, I turned my thoughts to my adoption and what it meant for me. To be honest, I decided that other than the fact that I didn't know anything about my genetic make-up, it didn't matter much. I loved my parents, and it was abundantly clear they loved me. I was lucky to be raised by them. I decided to move on without pursuing contact and put the whole episode behind me.

I discussed this with my wife, of course, but my girls were little then and I decided this was information they didn't need to know.

I got on with my life and forgot all about the register. At that point you hadn't come looking for me, so I figured you were unlikely to.

Then, out of the blue, your letter arrived and I was forced to think about all of it again.

My wife was worried I would regret not getting to know you. We talked about it a lot. Claire and I are both only children and Claire's parents passed away many years ago. She's a very loving and family-orientated person who often laments the lack of a wider family circle, especially for our girls. She convinced me I should at least meet you and I, somewhat reluctantly, agreed.

But now I'm here I know I can't go through with it. I hope you will not take this the wrong way, but blood does not make us family. I say that not to shame or accuse you, but simply to state what's in my heart. My family are the people who took me in, who cared for me when I was sick, who cheered for me at endless sports days and football matches, and who wiped my tears when things didn't go my way.

Claire says love is infinite and my heart will expand to include you if I let it, and she's probably right. But here's the kicker. I don't want to. Not because I don't think you are worthy of love – I do. I understand you were probably in a terrible predicament when I was born. I don't blame you for any of the actions you took. You brought me into the world and gave me up so I could have a good life, and I will always be grateful for that. But I cannot risk causing my parents pain. They love me and will support me no matter what I choose, but I saw the fear in their eyes all those years ago when they had to confess I was not their biological child. I won't put them through that again.

My parents are old now, in their nineties. Dad's still strong as an ox, physically, but his mind is beginning to fail him. Mum had a heart attack two years ago and has never been the same since. When it comes down to it, I have two parents I love, and that's enough for me. I need to be focused on them, and them alone, in their final years.

Today, on the way to the hotel, I realised I had nothing to offer you, nor do you have anything to offer me. You gave birth to me, but you will never be my mother. That opportunity has passed and it's too late to go back.

I am not angry. Nor do I wish you any ill. But I have no desire to disrupt my life, or my parents' lives, by establishing a relationship with you.

I hope you understand and will respect my wishes.

Kind regards,
Rob Parker

On my second reading I realise I am blessed to have this letter in my hand. It should bring me relief, not pain. Because now I know for sure my son has had a happy life and was brought up in a loving home. How can I be unhappy knowing that? He's a good man who is putting the needs of his ageing parents before his own. I'm not sure if I have the right to feel proud of him, but I do.

It's Christmas Day and I refuse to feel despondent. Just a few months ago I was homeless, hungry and afraid for my future. I'd taken to scribbling down my memories in the futile hope that somehow the universe would deliver them to my son and I would be redeemed in his eyes. Now I know he doesn't need my explanations or justifications. He's alive, happy and healthy, and doing just fine without any of that.

And, as for me, I am safely housed, well fed and cared for. I have laid eyes on the child I gave up – if only briefly – and he has communicated directly with me. These are things I could have only dreamt of a little while ago. Rob is right. Family isn't always about blood. My grandmother deserted me when I needed her the most. And now Jane, a woman who was a stranger just months ago, has turned her life upside down to help me.

I will not let myself drown in self-pity. I am here, I am healthy and I am loved. That is so much more than so many other people have, and I plan to show my gratitude to the universe by enjoying myself.

313

When Jane tentatively knocks and then enters my room an hour later, she seems surprised to see me up and dressed. I'm wearing red linen trousers, navy sneakers and a crisp white T-shirt adorned with a koala sporting a Santa hat and the inscription *Beary Christmas* scrawled in bright red letters. I bought it on a whim in the duty-free shop at the airport while Jane was in the bathroom. I have a kangaroo one wrapped up for her.

'Merry Christmas!' I say with as much brightness and energy as I can muster.

Jane, who's wrapped in the hotel robe and looking very bleary-eyed, seems startled by my greeting. 'Yes, Merry Christmas to you too. You're up and about early. How are you feeling?'

'Grateful,' I say truthfully.

Jane frowns. 'Grateful? Why is that?'

'Because I'm here with you. Because I know my son is alive and happy. Because it's Christmas Day and I'm in a luxurious hotel in a sunny place, not alone, shivering on the street with nowhere to go.'

Jane's eyes fill with tears. 'Oh, Dolly, you deserve those things. You don't have to be grateful for them. And you don't have to put on a brave face for me.'

'I'm not,' I insist. It's a half truth. I am grateful, but equally I want to make sure Jane doesn't feel any guilt about what happened with Rob.

'I was worried about you last night. You seemed devastated.' Jane eyes me suspiciously. 'What's brought on this change of heart?'

I pick up Rob's letter from the nightstand and hand it to her. 'Read this.'

She takes the letter and sits in the armchair by the window. Her face clouds with concern as her eyes flit across the page. 'I don't understand. How has this made you feel better? He's asking you not to contact him.' Her shoulders slump. 'Please tell me this calmness isn't resignation. You're not going to just give up, are you? I'll try again,' she says. There's an edge of desperation to her voice. 'We still have another week—'

I shake my head to stop her from continuing. 'No, Jane. It's done. My son has only ever asked me for one thing in his life – to respect his wish – and I'm going to do that.'

'But—'

'No buts. I know you mean well, but this is my decision and I've made it. Rob knows how to contact me now. If he changes his mind, he'll get in touch.'

She looks bewildered.

'I know this might not make sense to you, but this letter has given me some closure. Until recently I had no idea what had happened to my baby boy. Now I have proof he is well and happy. He's had a good life so far and is a dutiful son to his parents. This is enough. I won't deny I'd hoped for more, but, truly, that was just me being greedy. I have answers to my questions, and I feel confident now that giving him up was the right decision for him. You don't know how grateful I am to have that knowledge.'

She shakes her head in disbelief.

I retrieve the wrapped T-shirt from my suitcase and hand it to her. 'Maybe this will put a smile on your face. Merry Christmas.'

'I thought we agreed not to exchange gifts?' Her crestfallen demeanour hasn't lifted.

'Oh, it's just a little something. A joke really. Go on, open it.'

She smiles half-heartedly as she removes the paper and then breaks into a grin when she sees what it is. '*Hoppy Christmas*? Where on earth did you get this?'

'At the airport, in duty free when you were in line for the loo.'

She stands up and comes to kiss me on the cheek. 'It's hilarious. Thank you.'

'I'm glad you like it. Now, go and get yourself dressed and we'll head out for an early stroll in the gardens. A walk in the sunshine always makes things better.'

Jane looks dubious, but acquiesces. 'You never cease to amaze me,' she says, as she heads back into her room.

Chapter Forty-one

Melbourne, Australia
Christmas Day, 2019

Our early morning walk was as restorative as I'd hoped. It's hard to feel glum out in the fresh air, especially on Christmas morning when every person you meet along the way is full of warm wishes and good cheer. Even Jane seems a little happier by the time we've returned to the hotel.

After a light room-service breakfast, Jane and I went our separate ways to prepare ourselves for the lunch we booked weeks ago. Jane has sacrificed being with Richard at Christmas to bring me here. Things might not have turned out as we'd hoped but I'm determined to enjoy this day as much as possible, for her sake as well as mine.

I'm now dressed in my special Christmas Day outfit – the one Jane helped me pick. 'It's quite sparkly,' she'd said, back in that fancy store on the high street.

I'd run my hands over the red chiffon dress and turned slightly to admire its sequin-adorned sleeves in the mirror. 'If there's ever an occasion to sparkle, it's Christmas Day. Don't you agree?'

She looked unconvinced. 'I suppose so.'

I made my expression serious. 'If you are going to be my lunch date on Christmas Day, I think you should get yourself something with a little pizzazz too.' I didn't want to say so to her face, but Jane's whole wardrobe is dreadfully beige. She's a real beauty under all that washed-out mediocrity; she just needs a little glitter to bring out her natural shine.

After a great deal of encouragement from the young salesgirl and from me, we talked her into a drapey white pantsuit woven with strands of metallic gold thread. It's subtle enough for Jane not to be too terrified of it, and shimmery enough to please me. A fitting compromise. I only hope she hasn't changed her mind at the last minute and dressed herself in one those oversized linen outfits she favours.

I take one last look in the mirror and, after a touch-up of the lips, I'm satisfied I look suitably festive. After a light tap on the door that separates our rooms, I push it ajar. 'Can I come in?'

'Of course,' she says in a voice completely without verve. She's sitting on the edge of the bed and not even the lovely pantsuit – which she is wearing, I'm happy to see – can lift the sombre mood in the room. I'm keen to be downstairs in the restaurant, where I hope the fine food, carols and some very decent champagne will help cheer us both.

'Jane, come on now. It's Christmas. The show must go on.'

This elicits a smile from her. 'You truly are incredible, Dolly. I thought I'd be lucky to get you out of bed today, and yet here you are trying to cheer me up. How can you be so upbeat after what's happened?'

'I've lived long enough to appreciate that each day brings its own rewards, if we care to see them. Do I wish things had turned out differently? Of course I do. But I also know no amount of moping will change things. Now, let's get downstairs and make the best of things, shall we?' My tone is a touch brighter than I feel, but that's one thing showbiz has taught me. Sometimes you just have to smile when you don't want to. More often than not, you'll feel better for it.

Jane stands and smooths down the pantsuit. 'Ready when you are.' She looks lovely but her carefully applied make-up doesn't quite conceal the dark circles beneath her eyes. Her disappointment at my bungled reunion with Rob seems excessive and, even though I know she feels responsible, I'm not sure it quite accounts for her demeanour. Perhaps being away from Richard at Christmas time is bothering her more than she thought it would.

Downstairs, ice sculptures of reindeers, boughs of mistletoe and a truckload of fake snow have been added to the restaurant's Christmas decorations, transforming the space into a winter wonderland, which seems ironic considering the temperature outside. Perhaps it's an attempt to lessen the culture shock of Christmas in a warm climate for the hotel's many visitors from the Northern Hemisphere.

Last night's waiter is working again, which I think is dreadfully unfair, but he's young and perhaps is enjoying the boost to his wages working on Christmas Day will bring.

He smiles at me. 'Welcome back, Miss Jamieson, Mrs Leveson. Merry Christmas to you both. I trust you are feeling better today, Miss Jamieson?'

I bat away the shame of last night's events and return the smile. 'Quite well, thank you. And Merry Christmas to you too!'

He leads us to a table by the window, thankfully a different one to where we were seated last night. 'Can I bring you ladies a drink? Champagne, perhaps, to start?'

Jane seats herself wordlessly, so it's up to me to reply. 'That would be lovely.'

Once the waiter has left us, I retrieve Jane's gift from my handbag and pass it across the table to her.

'Dolly!' she says. 'You shouldn't have. I didn't . . . The little T-shirt was more than enough. I don't want you spending your pension on me! I don't have anything for you. I didn't think—'

'Stop that nonsense right now. You have given me numerous gifts already. This trip and this gorgeous outfit I'm wearing, for starters. Not to mention that you've housed me, fed me and cared for me for months now.'

For the first time today, Jane smiles with her whole face. 'You know, I can't remember the last time I had a surprise Christmas gift. Richard is so obsessed with getting the perfect gift that I usually end up giving him a list to choose from.' She takes her time undoing the ribbon and carefully removing the wrapping paper without tearing it. 'Ooh,' she says when she sees the small navy box with the hotel's logo embossed on it.

'Don't take any notice of that,' I say. I got one of the staff here to wrap it for me.

She lifts the lid and gasps when she sees the pendant inside. 'Oh! Dolly! How . . .? This is too much. I mean, it's just gorgeous, but I can't let you. Where did you even . . .?' She flushes pink then and I know she's embarrassed by what she was about to ask. How could I afford such a thing when my only income is a small and very recently acquired pension?

'It's okay.' I smile at her. 'It was my mother's. She gave it to me when I moved to the city. I would like you to accept it as a token of my appreciation for all you have done for me.'

She places a hand on her chest and her eyes are shining with tears. 'Thank you. That is so, so kind of you. But I can't accept a family heirloom.'

'Please. I want you to have it. Who else am I going to give it to?'

Her mouth opens and then closes again. Then she shrugs. 'I don't know, but it should stay in your family. I know things don't look good right now, but Rob might have a change of heart. And he has daughters. Perhaps you could leave it to one of them.'

'I planned to give you this irrespective of what happened last night. I had it boxed and wrapped on the day we arrived here. I know this will seem strange to you, but I feel we've become close enough these past few months for me to speak my mind. I realised something about you a little while back. Since my mother died, there's been no one in my life who has liked me just for me – apart from Julian, of course. What I'm trying to say, my darling Jane, is you took me in – maybe out of charity at first – but it didn't take long for me to see that we are kindred spirits indeed. Please wear my pendant and know that you are as dear to me as it is. One day, when I am gone, I hope it will remind you of the good times we've shared.'

Her hand moves from her chest to lift the necklace from its box, and I see she's blinking back tears. 'It's beautiful.'

'Put it on. One of the reasons I encouraged you to buy that pantsuit was because I knew the necklace would look good with it.'

She grins at me as she unclasps the chain and brings it to her neck. 'You really did have this all planned out, huh?' She fastens the necklace and looks to me for my approval.

It looks just as I imagined it would. 'Perfect.'

Before either of us can say more the waiter appears with our champagne. He pours quickly and disappears after telling us our first course will be along soon.

I lift my glass. 'A toast,' I say, and I wait for Jane to join me. She raises her glass too. 'Here's to us, Jane and Dolly. A perfect pairing. Merry Christmas!'

'Hear, hear. Merry Christmas to us both,' Jane agrees as she clinks her glass against mine. She takes a large sip and sets her glass down before reaching across the table and squeezing my hand. 'Thank you,' she says. 'For everything.'

●

The meal is delicious and the atmosphere festive, and for a while Jane and I are caught up in the spirit of it all, enjoying ourselves, even. But as the afternoon wears on Jane's cheerfulness wanes. I'm sure she thinks I haven't noticed, but all the happy families around us seem to be affecting her mood. There's a large group seated nearby, and Jane's eyes keep flitting to a woman sitting next to a teenage boy. They appear to be mother and son. Right now, the woman's arm is draped casually on the back of the boy's chair, and Jane can't seem to take her eyes off them.

Oh my stars, what a selfish old woman I am! I've been so wrapped up in my personal melodrama, I haven't even thought about the fact that this is Jane's first Christmas without Tom. No wonder Richard was so unhappy about her travelling so far away at this time of the year. I wonder what on earth possessed her . . .

My thoughts are interrupted by the appearance of another diner behind Jane's chair.

'I'm so sorry to interrupt, but I was wondering if you are Mrs Mackin?' she says in a shaky voice.

Jane turns her head to respond to the woman, but I get in first. 'Yes, I'm Dolly Jamieson and I played Mrs Mackin on *The Neighbourhood*.' I sit up straight in my chair and smile at her, with what I hope is an appropriate amount of enthusiasm for a once-upon-a-time TV star.

The woman, who is at least as old as Jane, presses both palms to her cheeks and begins to babble. 'Oh my god, oh my god. I can't believe it. Can I get a selfie? No, wait. Do you mind if I get my daughter? We're huge fans of the show. We've seen every episode from the start.' She looks behind her, presumably to where the daughter is sitting. 'I'll bring her over, if that's okay?'

My smile doesn't falter. I'm excited to be recognised all these years after my time on the show has ended. 'Of course, my dear. I'd be delighted to meet her.'

The woman hurries off across the restaurant and I look at Jane, who is frowning. 'That was kind of you, but you don't have to say yes, you know. If it bothers you, I can ask the woman to leave us in peace.'

I clasp a hand to my chest. 'Good gracious, Jane, don't be silly. It's important to give the fans what they want. Without them we actors would be nothing.'

Jane sighs and looks as if she wants to say something, but before she can the woman returns with her daughter. 'I'm Judy,' she announces breathlessly, 'and this is my daughter, Tracie.'

Tracie looks mildly embarrassed but smiles, nevertheless.

While this pair take their selfies and share their thoughts on the show, others in the restaurant begin to take note and soon another couple of fans have wandered over to our table.

'Sorry,' I mouth at Jane, who shrugs and gives me a smile. I don't want to ruin our lunch, but it's such a thrill to be treated as a star again that my desire to revel in the moment is irresistible.

Ten minutes pass before the last fan heads back to their table. I look up to find Jane staring at her phone. I suddenly feel like a heel.

'I'm so sorry, Jane. That must have been tiresome for you. It's just . . . well, it's been ages since anyone recognised me. It used to happen all the time. At the height of my fame on the show I was stopped often – I'll admit that got a bit annoying. But over the years, after I'd left the show, it started to settle down and become less intense. I'd still get recognised at least once a day at first, then it slowed to once a week and then sometimes even less than that. The more sporadic the attention became, the more I valued it. In the months before I met you, nobody gave me a sideways glance at all – unless it was accompanied by a command to move along.'

Jane sips her wine and looks pensive. Eventually she says, 'There are worse things than being invisible.'

I want to ask her what she means but we're interrupted by the wait-staff, who clear our pudding plates and bring a pot of tea and some shortbreads to the table. When we're alone again, I say, 'When I was living on the streets, you know what was worse than the biting cold, worse than always being dirty, even worse than the fear of being robbed or violated?'

She shakes her head.

'The worst thing for me was feeling as if I didn't matter to anyone. That my existence was of no consequence to any other human being. On the days I didn't go to the library – if it was closed for one reason or another – I could go for hours, even the whole day sometimes, without having any meaningful contact with another human being. I'd smile at people on the street, and they'd avert their eyes. It was as if they thought I was contagious. As if, by acknowledging me, they'd be at risk somehow.'

She considers this for a moment. 'Maybe people don't know what to say.'

Once upon a time I would have accepted this as a decent excuse, but not anymore. 'Homeless people are just the same as everyone else. They've had homes and families. They have hopes and dreams. People don't seem to realise how close they are to living that life themselves at any given moment. It only takes one disaster to start things snowballing. One minute you're in a lovely townhouse in Belgravia, the next minute that life is gone. It can happen to anyone. Well, lots of us anyway. So, you can say the same things to a homeless person that you'd say to any other stranger. "Hello" is a good start.'

'I've never thought about it like that.'

I smile awkwardly, embarrassed to realise I've been lecturing Jane – the last person on earth who needs to be given lessons in kindness. 'I suppose that's understandable. There's a lot we don't think about until it happens to us.'

'Yes,' she says, wistfully. 'You are so right about that. I'm certainly guilty of judging others, only to realise how wrong I was when I was thrust into a similar situation. I guess that's why I crave invisibility. It's the shame of having got it so wrong. Every judgement I've ever made about another mother, every confident statement about what constitutes "good parenting", every superior thought about my ability to raise a child has mocked me these past twelve months. All the stupid, judgemental things I've said come back to me in the middle of the night, twisting my gut and keeping me from sleep. Now I stand in solidarity with all the broken mothers of the world.'

'Jane.' My voice comes out in a whisper. 'You poor darling. That is too much weight for any person to bear. I haven't asked you this before because it's not my business, but maybe it would help you to tell me what happened to Tom.'

Chapter Forty-two

Melbourne, Australia
Christmas Day, 2019

It's late afternoon and we're back in the botanical gardens. We've changed out of our finery and are walking silently. Jane has agreed to talk about Tom, but said she couldn't do it in the restaurant, surrounded by all those happy families.

We've been walking for about ten minutes and she's yet to speak. I'm beginning to wonder whether she's changed her mind when she says, 'The day Tom was born was the happiest day of my life.'

I nod, not wanting to interrupt her, but I'm not sure she notices.

'All I'd ever wanted was to be a mother. It's probably not very politically correct to say so, but I wasn't very ambitious growing up. I just wanted a secure family life and to have a child of my own. I wanted to give my child the world, be the mother I wished I'd had.'

'You weren't close to your mum?' I venture when she pauses.

She laughs. 'My mother was hard to pin down. She didn't enjoy being constrained by silly things such as working for a living or caring for a child. A real "free spirit", was our Christine – sorry, Crystal, as she took to calling herself in her final years.'

'And your dad?'

She shrugs. 'I never knew him. Mum told me dozens of different – and conflicting – stories about him over the years, but I've never had any contact with him. I have no idea who he is, or even if he's still alive.' She stops for a moment and looks at me. 'That's why I can't understand your Rob not wanting to meet you. I'd give anything to meet my dad, even just once.'

I don't know how to respond to this, so I gently steer her back to Tom. 'How old were you when you had Tom?'

She begins to walk again. 'Almost thirty. Richard and I were married when I was just twenty-three and we started trying right away. It took us years and three cycles of IVF to have him. So, when he was born it was as if we'd been gifted a miracle. We felt blessed.'

'I can only imagine.'

'I gave up my job as a legal secretary to be a full-time mum. Richard was already working as a barrister by then, so it wasn't as if we needed the money.'

'Did you enjoy that?'

She looks at me with her eyes glistening. 'Oh, Dolly, I have never admitted this to anyone, but I hated it. Here I was, with everything I've ever dreamt of, and I felt somehow . . . unfulfilled.'

'I don't think that's anything to be ashamed of. There's nothing wrong with wanting more from life.'

'I felt like a failure. I had this beautiful little baby, but he wasn't enough for me. I made extra efforts to be the perfect mother – cloth nappies, homemade organic food, once he was starting to wean from the breast, attachment parenting . . . You get the picture.'

I have no idea what attachment parenting is, but I nod, and she continues.

'I took him to the library and to swimming lessons, to baby music lessons, for god's sake. People commented on what a wonderful mother I was. But it was all an act. Inside, I was suffocating.'

'What did Richard have to say about all this?'

'Richard? I couldn't tell Richard. He had been worried about me giving up my job, wondering if I'd be bored. He suggested a part-time nanny. I made such a song and dance about how no child of mine would be raised by a nanny.' She exhales audibly. 'As you can imagine, it was hard to come back from that.'

'Are you saying you were unhappy for all those years without telling anyone?'

She shakes her head vigorously. 'No. I wasn't. I found something to fill my cup and it was pretty much perfect.' She sighs and stops again. 'We've been walking for ages. Are you okay? Should we find somewhere to sit?'

'I wouldn't mind a bit of a spell.'

She slips her arm through mine and leads me to a nearby bench, shaded by a large oak tree. We take a seat and Jane continues. 'It was the late '90s, and up until then I'd not really used the computer for much other than data entry and word processing. The internet was a bit of a mystery to me, and I wasn't interested in it, to be honest. Richard had installed a computer and a dial-up modem in the study in case he needed to send emails after hours. He gave me a crash course on how to use Internet Explorer to find information. He was quite enamoured of the whole thing and kept saying, "It's amazing, isn't it? Like having a whole library right here in your own home." One afternoon, while Tom was sleeping, I started thinking about his first birthday party and I was looking for inspiration. I thought I'd start up the computer and give the world wide web a go. There was so much information online, I couldn't believe it. I mean, it wasn't a patch on what we have today, but still . . .'

'I'll have to take your word for that.'

She smiles momentarily and then a more serious expression comes over her face. 'I was hooked almost immediately. At the time blogs were very popular. You know about blogs, right?'

I nod. 'I'm familiar.' That's probably overstating my knowledge, but I don't want her to get sidetracked.

'I couldn't get enough of them. I loved reading the mummy blogs written by women just like me. Everyday I'd hang out for Tom's nap time so I could read them. It wasn't long before I joined their ranks and started my own blog.' She sighs. 'Looking back, that's when the trouble started.'

'What do you mean?'

She launches into a long description of how her blog became popular and how she soon realised she could make money from it. I let her explain without telling her I already know this part of the story from reading that awful newspaper article.

'Soon it was a fully-fledged business. I was a parenting expert in charge of a small media company. I had staff – including an au pair. The woman who was hellbent on being a perfect mother was now advising others how to do the same, while outsourcing the mothering of her son to a series of twenty-something nannies.' She shakes her head in disgust.

'I think you're being hard on yourself. A lot of mothers work.'

She continues as if she hasn't even heard me. 'I was such a hypocrite; telling people how to bring up their children *and* quietly sitting in judgement of them, when, all the while, my own son was suffering from a lack of my attention.'

'I'm sure that's not true.'

She shrugs. 'I'm afraid it is. And, because of my inattention, not only is my son dead but two other mothers are without their children this Christmas too.'

I've been looking out across the park to a calming pond but now my head snaps around to look at her.

Jane is crying silent tears. 'Tom killed his ex-girlfriend and her new partner on New Year's Eve last year.'

I can't help but gasp. This isn't at all what I'd imagined.

I place my hand on hers, but she shakes it off and keeps talking; the words pouring out of her now in an avalanche of pain.

'He mowed them down in the little hatchback Richard and I had given him for his eighteenth birthday. Richard was worried that it was extravagant, that we were spoiling him, but I told him not to be ridiculous. What were we earning all this money for if not to spend it on our son?' She swipes the tears away with the back of her hand.

I fish around in my pocket for the pressed hanky I put there earlier and hand it to her. She accepts it and smiles weakly through a fresh bout of tears.

'Not in my wildest dreams did I imagine my child would be capable of taking another person's life. He was such a beautiful baby and a sunny-natured little boy. He did okay in school. I mean, he wasn't a genius, but he tried hard and got reasonable marks. He was just an average kid. He struggled a bit to make friends in high school at first, but he got over that. There were a few little bumps – a fight with another boy at school that led to a suspension – but nothing out of the ordinary. Well, I didn't think so, but obviously I was very wrong about that . . .'

'Could it have been an accident?'

She shakes her head. 'I don't think so. I don't know. Apparently, he and April's new fellow fought inside the pub on New Year's Eve. The police believe he went back to his car and waited for them to leave the pub and then followed them. Whether he meant to kill them, just frighten them a bit, or whether the whole thing was an unfortunate accident is something I'll never know, because he ran from the scene of the accident into the nearest tube station and jumped in front of a train.' She's stopped crying now and her words are flat and emotionless. Nevertheless, they hit me with the force of a physical blow.

'Jane, I'm so sorry. I don't know what to say.'

'There's nothing you can say. There are no words to make sense of what happened.' She laughs a hollow laugh. 'Although plenty of people have tried.'

My thoughts turn to the article I read online. 'Oh, Jane, you poor thing.'

'Don't feel sorry for me. It's what I deserved. How could I have not seen this in Tom? How could I not know? The online world was quick to judge me and I don't blame them.'

'That's the downside of being successful and of having a public profile. People think they have a right to an opinion about your life.'

She shrugs. 'In this case, they had every right. I mean, I'd been lecturing the public for years about what makes a good parent. Who did I think I was? The YouTubers went to town and Twitter was downright ugly.'

'I don't know much about Twitter, but you mustn't let the opinions of strangers define you, Jane.'

'But they were right. I'm a hypocrite and a failure. What sort of mother doesn't see such violent tendencies in her child?'

'How could you have known? If he'd never been violent before, what hope was there of predicting this? Besides, from what you've said, you don't know what happened that night and you never will.'

'Maybe I just wasn't paying enough attention. If I'd been a better mother . . .'

I shake my head. 'Nothing you have told me makes me think you were a bad mother. In fact, quite the opposite. You put everything into raising your child. Yes, you worked. So what? You raised your child in a loving home and constantly thought about his needs. You were there and that's what counts. That's more than what I did for my son, and yet I don't see you sitting in judgement of me.'

'You made a sacrifice for your child. I'm not sure I sacrificed enough for mine. *He* should have been enough. If I'd been more concerned about his needs and less concerned about being "fulfilled", maybe this would never have happened.'

'And maybe it would. You don't know that. You did your best, Jane – that's all any of us can do. Tom was raised by two loving parents. That's so much more than many other children have. And what about Richard? I don't see anyone blaming him. Not that they should, of course, but why is everything always the mother's fault?'

'To be fair, Richard didn't ever claim to be a parenting expert. Me, on the other hand . . .' She sighs and shakes her head. 'My business died almost overnight, which was devastating. I mean, of course I deserved to be taken down, but I had to let go all my staff. It wasn't just Tom I failed . . .'

'Jane, none of this is your fault. You're being too hard on yourself. I'm sure your staff understood. The person most affected by this has been you, and frankly I think you are coping remarkably well considering all you've been through.'

She deliberates for a moment and nods. 'I don't know about "remarkably well", but I am starting to feel as if it might be worth hanging around on this planet for a bit longer.'

Her words take me by surprise. 'Was there a time you didn't feel this way?'

'Many, many times.' She blows out a breath. 'In fact, I've spent the best part of the past year thinking about the easiest way to end it all.'

I'm shocked. 'Oh, Jane, no! You don't feel like that now, do you?'

She shakes her head.

'What changed your mind?'

She smiles then and says, 'I met you.'

•

We stay on the park bench for at least half an hour, sitting in quiet meditation, before Jane finally says, 'Shall we head back?'

I'm not sure if it's wishful thinking, but she does seem a little more at ease with herself now she's talked openly about that terrible night. I didn't say much in response to her story, just that I knew in my heart she was a good and kind person, and nothing she had told me today had made me think she was a bad mother. I didn't labour the point, because, as I well know, no words can ease a mother's guilt. It's a burden we each must deal with in our own way. I hope that in time Jane will come to see that Tom was an adult, wholly responsible for his own actions, and nothing she did or didn't do was a factor in that one terrible decision he made, and that there is no such thing as a perfect mother.

As we get closer to the hotel, our conversation has turned to the rest of our stay here. We had originally planned a visit to the Great Ocean Road, but the weather has been scorching hot and there are bushfires cropping up in parts of the state.

We're not due to go back home until the second of January, but now I know it's almost the anniversary of Tom's death, I can't help but wonder if we should see whether we can book an earlier flight. Jane and Richard shouldn't be apart on such a night.

My business here with Rob is done. I would like to see the production of *The Rose of France*, especially as it's being staged at the theatre where I had my start in show business, but Jane's marriage is much more important than a sentimental trip down memory lane. As we round the corner to the hotel's entry, I suggest an early return to London, but Jane gives me such a vague, noncommittal answer I wonder if she's even heard me.

I steal a glance at her and realise she's staring at something ahead of us. When I follow her gaze, I see a tall man getting out of a cab in front of the hotel. He's wearing a rumpled business suit that looks ridiculously out of place in this heat, and I'm about to say as much when he turns to face us.

'Richard!' Jane cries, her voice breaking with emotion.

He opens his arms, and she runs into them.

Chapter Forty-three

Cordelia Cameron Theatre
Melbourne, Australia
New Year's Eve, 2019

The hotel has organised a car to drive us to the theatre, even though it's within walking distance. Normally, I would refuse the offer but neither Jane nor I are wearing shoes suitable for walking, so we accept gratefully. And thank goodness for that, because it is smouldering hot outside.

As we get closer to the theatre, I realise there's a crowd gathered either side of a roped-off red carpet.

'Wow,' Jane says. 'Look at that. Seems as if this is a big deal.'

'Good grief!' Richard taps Jane's shoulder and points. 'Is that Cate Carnegie? What on earth is she doing here?'

'Well, she is Australian, darling. Even movie stars are entitled to visit their families at Christmas,' I reply.

Richard sits up straight in his seat and adjusts his tie. 'Looks as if we're in for a very interesting evening indeed.'

The driver pulls up as close to the red carpet as he can manage. He gets out and opens the car doors, assists me from my seat and then presses a card into Richard's hands. 'Call this number when you're ready to leave, sir. I'll come to collect you.' He touches his cap and looks first at Jane and then me. 'Have a lovely evening. Happy New Year.'

Several other guests are making their way up the red carpet. Cate Carnegie has just disappeared inside with a regal wave, but the young couple trailing her seem to be causing almost as much fuss among the crowd amassed behind the velvet ropes. I have no idea who they are – perhaps the stars of a local drama or reality TV show. Whoever they are, the fans seem to be loving them.

As we step onto the red carpet, a smartly dressed young woman wearing a headset and carrying a clipboard approaches us. 'Good evening. Could I have your names, please, so I can check them off the guest list?'

I smile at her. 'Miss Dolly Jamieson – and these are my guests, Mr and Mrs Leveson.'

The usher gives us a bored smile and then casts her eye over the list. 'Oh!'

Richard clears his throat. 'Is there a problem?'

She shakes her head and bestows a more gracious smile upon us than the last one. 'No. No problem at all.' She looks at me. 'In fact, Mr Garibaldi, the theatre manager, has asked me to alert him to your arrival, Miss Jamieson. He wants to greet you personally. If you wouldn't mind stepping to one side for just a moment while I make the call.'

'Of course,' I say, surprised the theatre manager would have any clue who I am. The three of us step to one side as the usher beckons forward the next group and checks them off, all the while talking into her headset.

After a quick conversation, the young woman returns to us. 'All sorted, Miss Jamieson. Please make yourself known to the usher just inside the entrance. She will escort you to Mr Garibaldi. Have a magical evening.'

Richard offers an arm each to Jane and me and we make our way up the red carpet. We take our time, partly to ensure I don't trip over in these new heels, but also to savour this special moment. Coming back here after all these years feels surreal. In some ways it's hard to believe that I'm the same person as that naive young girl who came to Melbourne with stars in her eyes – and left with a baby in her belly.

We're about halfway along when a voice calls, 'It's Mrs Mackin from *The Neighbourhood*! Oi, Mrs Mackin, over here. Can we get a selfie?'

Adrenaline fizzes in my veins but I don't want to make Jane feel awkward or exposed. I turn to face her. 'Do you mind, darling?'

'Of course not,' she says. 'Go mingle with your adoring public.' She drops Richard's arm and he escorts me to the rope, where half a dozen people vie for my attention.

'Relax, my darlings,' I say, in my most regal voice. 'I'm happy to have photos with you all.'

After a few minutes, it becomes apparent we are causing a traffic jam on the red carpet, and Jane wanders over. 'I think perhaps we should keep moving.'

'Yes, of course.' I blow kisses in the direction of the fans. 'Goodbye, darlings! Lovely to meet you all.'

Inside, the theatre is buzzing. The foyer is filled with beautifully dressed patrons, most of them holding champagne flutes. The usher just inside the door is waiting for us. 'Miss Jamieson?'

I nod. 'The one and only.'

The usher smiles. 'Lovely to meet you. I'm Sarah. I'll be looking after your party tonight. If there's anything at all you need, please let me know. But my first job is to take you to Mr Garibaldi.' She smiles at Richard and Jane. 'Welcome, Mr and Mrs Leveson. We're delighted to have you as our guests this evening, along with our esteemed VIP, Miss Jamieson. If you would all like to follow me, now.' She takes me by the arm and gently steers me through the crowd, with Richard and Jane following close behind. Soon she stops outside an office with a sign reading *Private* on the door and briefly knocks before peeking inside. 'Mr Garibaldi, I have Miss Jamieson and her guests to see you.'

'Lovely. Bring them in.'

Bruno, as he insists we call him, greets us all warmly, kissing Jane and me on both cheeks, European style, and shaking Richard's hand when I introduce him.

He turns to Jane. 'Now, Jane, I hope you don't mind, but we've had to do a bit of a reshuffle to accommodate the extra ticket for Richard. With your permission, I'd like to steal Dolly away from you for the night. I have reserved seats for you and Richard in the dress circle, but if you can spare her, I'd like Dolly to come and meet a few people backstage.' He looks at me. 'That is, if you'd like to, my dear?'

I can barely contain my excitement. 'I'd be delighted.'

'Excellent. I also have a special seat set aside for you, Dolly, but Sarah will be able to bring you back to Jane and Richard when the show is done. Does that sound acceptable to you all?'

'Wonderful,' I say.

Jane thanks him profusely for finding a ticket for Richard, but he waves her thanks away. 'No, thank you all for coming.' He looks at me as if I am the greatest star on earth. 'We're honoured to have a former leading lady of the show with us tonight.' He turns his attention back to the usher. 'Sarah, if you'd kindly escort Richard and Jane to their seats, I'll take care of this lovely lady.'

I kiss Jane and Richard quickly. 'Goodbye, darlings. Enjoy the show!'

•

I haven't been backstage in a theatre for more than twenty years, but the familiar frisson of elation hits me the moment we arrive.

The atmosphere might be familiar, but the architecture is not. I'm surprised to find the bowels of the theatre are nothing like I remember. I'd expected some modernisation, of course, but there's nothing recognisable here. There are wide walkways leading to wood-panelling and glass rehearsal areas, offices and dressing rooms. It's all rather plush. Bruno explains that, after a fire back in 2010, the theatre had been gutted and rebuilt from the bottom up. The public areas have been restored to incorporate as much of the original theatre as possible, but down here it's all modern.

After I recover from my initial shock at nothing being as I remember, I am impressed by all the comforts and conveniences the designers have included. This would be a beautiful theatre to work in.

'The director has specifically asked if she can meet you,' Bruno says, glancing at his watch. 'We need to hurry, though. It's getting close to curtain up.'

'Lucinda Carroll wants to meet me?' Surely Bruno is being kind. Lucinda Carroll is an esteemed director, known for her avant-garde interpretations of classic plays. She takes the essence of the classics and is true to their spirit but uses her fresh approach to appeal to modern audiences. Some of the old purists don't care for her work – Julian was not impressed by her 'meddling', as he called it – but I think she's simply wonderful.

'Yes,' says Bruno. 'She is very excited you are attending tonight's performance.'

'I feel a little strange coming backstage before the show. In my day, visitors were discouraged this close to showtime.'

'That is generally the case here too, but they're making a special exception. Director's orders.'

'How lovely of her. I feel quite chuffed.'

'Oh, there's Sevda, the assistant stage manager.' He waves at a small dark-haired woman walking towards us. 'Hey, Sev, this is Dolly Jamieson. Lucinda wanted to see her before lights up.'

The young woman breaks into a huge smile and holds out her hand for me to shake it. 'It's an honour to meet you, Miss Jamieson. We were all so excited to hear you were coming to watch us tonight.'

I'm beginning to think this is some kind of set-up. Has Jane organised a 'grant a granny a wish' experience, like the ones they do for the sick kiddies? 'Really? I'm surprised that any of you young people even know who I am.'

'Goodness, Miss Jamieson, we all know. Miss Carroll is so excited that you're visiting us tonight. She's told us all how she much she admires you. It's truly an honour to meet one of the women who played Amethyst in the play's very first production.'

It's been sixty years since I performed in this theatre. I wasn't even Dolly Jamieson back then; I was plain old Margie Ferguson. Obviously, some theatre historian has made the connection. Or perhaps Jane has come right out and told them. I wouldn't put it past her. Maybe she's even paid someone to give me the full VIP experience. How mortifying! Nevertheless, I am here and it is lovely. The least I can do is be gracious. 'How kind of you to say.'

She smiles and comes to a stop outside a door with a gold-painted circle on it and knocks.

'Yes?'

Sevda opens the door. 'Miss Jamieson for you, Ms Carroll.'

'Oh, fabulous! Please send her in.'

Sevda smiles at me and opens the door wide. 'I'll leave you to it.'

Lucinda Carroll jumps up from where she is sitting and rushes over to me, taking both of my hands in hers. 'Miss Jamieson, I am truly honoured to welcome you here tonight.' She squeezes my hands and lets them go.

I smile at her. 'You are too kind. I am the one who is honoured. I'm excited to be here and feel blessed to be backstage to soak up a little of the pre-show buzz, but I'm a little perplexed as to *why* I'm here. I do hope I'm not intruding, especially this close to curtain up.'

'Intruding? Absolutely not, far from it. When I heard you were coming to the show, I just had to meet you. I feel very privileged to have this opportunity. I'm a huge fan of your work. Please, won't you sit down.' She gestures to an emerald-green velvet couch.

'Thank you.' I lower myself onto the couch and she takes a seat beside me. 'You'll have to forgive me, my dear, but it's hard for me to believe a young woman such as yourself would even know about me, let alone be a fan of my work. I mean, I would have retired from the stage before you were born, I imagine.'

She laughs heartily. 'You flatter me, Miss Jamieson. I'm in my sixties and I can assure you I have seen you on stage quite a few times.'

'Oh, my! I did think you were a tad younger.' We both laugh. 'When you get to my age it's hard to tell. Everyone starts to look like a teenager. So, tell me, what shows have you seen me in?'

'I was just a little girl the first time I saw you on stage. I was nine years old and in London visiting my grandparents. My nanna took me to the theatre as a special treat. To see this show, in fact. It was a magical experience. I loved everything about it – getting dressed up in my best clothes, going out at night like a grown-up, seeing all the men in their tuxedos and the ladies in their finery. But, oh, the performance itself . . .' She presses her palms together as if she's praying. 'Oh my goodness, I had no idea it would be so moving. It was a wonderful show. And you . . .' She closes her eyes momentarily. 'You were out of this world.' She opens her eyes and looks at me again. 'Sorry, I'm gushing.'

'Gush away, my dear. It's lovely for an old lady like me to be praised by such an esteemed director.'

She brushes the compliment away with a wave of her hand. 'Anyway, with this being an anniversary performance, I did a little digging to find out who played Amethyst in the original cast. I was keen to have the original leading lady here for opening night. Cara Beecham is listed on the program but, as I'm sure you know, she passed away years ago.'

'Yes, that was tragic.'

Lucinda nods. 'Yes, very sad. In any case, I knew she'd only played the role for a short time so I started to look for the performer who took her place during the original run after she had to bow out. I'd never heard of Margie Ferguson and no one seemed to know what had become of her. But, then, when I looked at the photos we have from that show I realised that Margie Ferguson and Dolly Jamieson are the same person! I asked my assistant to see if we could find you, but no one had any luck getting in touch with you, so we'd given up on having you here. Then, your friend Jane called the theatre to say you would be in town and would like tickets . . . well, I couldn't believe our luck!'

'I'm absolutely thrilled to be here,' I reply.

She smiles broadly. 'I'm so pleased. Now, the reason I wanted to see you before the show is that I have something I'd like to ask you. It's actually quite audacious of me – please don't think I'm unaware of that – but I just couldn't pass up the opportunity while I had you here.'

'I'm intrigued,' I say.

What Lucinda Carroll asks me next takes my breath away.

Chapter Forty-four

Melbourne, Australia
New Year's Eve, 2019

The show's spectacular finale brings the audience to its feet, and after several curtain calls, the director joins the cast on stage. She is given a microphone and steps forward to address the audience.

'Thank you,' she says, as the applause quietens. 'Ladies and gentlemen, my name is Lucinda Carroll.' She's interrupted by more thunderous applause, but she gestures for the audience to stop, and they do. 'Thank you again, but I'm not standing out here for your applause, as lovely as that is. I'm here because I have a very special guest I would like to introduce to you tonight. The actor I am about to invite to the stage has had a long career in show business; in fact she started her career in this very theatre more than sixty years ago. I first saw her perform in London when I was a young girl. I'm utterly thrilled to introduce you to the woman who made the role of Amethyst Rose her very own.

'Ladies and gentlemen, please welcome to the stage the one and only Miss Dolly Jamieson.'

The theatre breaks out in fresh applause as I stride out to take my place at centrestage. Lucinda welcomes me and asks me how it feels to be treading the boards once more.

I take a moment to look around the theatre. 'Marvellous.' And I open my arms out wide, as if to embrace the room. 'It feels like coming home.'

The audience bursts into spontaneous applause and this time it's harder to get them to stop. When the applause dies down, Lucinda begins to speak. 'Dolly, we are so thrilled to have you back here at The Cordy. I know I'm being presumptuous, putting you on the spot like this, but I was wondering if we could ask you to sing for us, while you are here?'

I place my hand on my chest and bow slightly. 'I'd be honoured.'

For a moment, before the orchestra begins to play, I feel a prickle of fear. Doubt seeps in. What on earth am I thinking? I am an old woman. I have not sung in front of a proper audience in years – the rush-hour crowd at the underground station notwithstanding. I don't know if my voice is up to it. But then the spotlight hits the stage and the music begins. I no longer question my ability. In fact, I no longer think, I merely feel. I'm operating on instinct now as I step into the light and begin to sing.

I am performing *Nothing I Wouldn't Do*, the central song from this show and my signature piece. Of course, my performance is not as spontaneous as Lucinda has made it seem in her very generous introduction. She asked me backstage if I would be willing and, after I agreed, she informed the other directors and the cast of her plan for me to sing after the first curtain call. During the second act I was given access to a rehearsal room, and after a couple of tentative run-throughs I decided I didn't want to overthink it, so I joined the residual cast in the green room. There was a big screen in there, showing the action on stage. Technology has made the theatre a whole new world to me. But when I close my eyes and listen to the music, I realise the important things always remain the same.

My voice does not fail me. I have the audience in the palm of my hand now; they are holding their collective breath, riding the crest of the wave with me until I reach the song's stunning climax. It takes all my strength and concentration to reach that final high note, but I get

340

there and, as I do, the crowd rises, cheering and clapping, their appreciation forming new music to fill this beautiful building.

There are no words to fully describe my elation at this experience. It is more than coming home, it is a return to self. This is who I am, who I've always been, and I feel damn lucky to be reminded of that truth.

•

Afterwards, at the party, I am a celebrity again. Everybody wants to talk to me, to tell me how much they loved the song, how they'd seen me in the West End years ago, or (their voice dropping to a conspiratorial whisper) how they'd watched *The Neighbourhood* entirely for my performance in it. I'm thoroughly enjoying myself, but there's something missing. I'm desperate to find Jane. I want to know what she thought. Did it really go as well as I think it did, or are people just being kind?

I'm also aware the hours are ticking by. It won't be long before *that* time. Not everyone would understand the significance – the power – of that hour, but I do. It's been more than half a century now, but I still remember the moment I discovered my mother and siblings had died. At that time every year, I pause and a chill comes over me. And usually I feel the same way on this evening, too, at the time I discovered Julian would never be returning home. Tonight, I have been too preoccupied to dwell on it.

Maybe Jane won't want or need me by her side when that hour comes. Richard is here now and maybe it's best if they're left to their own devices. I don't want to intrude, but I want to be close by in case she needs me. After all, that's what friends do.

Lucinda has introduced me to a boorish man – his shirt is half untucked and droplets of red wine stain its front. He's paying far too much attention to Lucinda's chest for my liking. Apparently he's a patron of the arts and he expects us to listen appreciatively to his dull little anecdotes as repayment for his financial generosity. This is where being my age is advantageous. I pretend to be hard of hearing and, after repeating himself several times, the bore gives up. He makes his excuses and moves away. Lucinda laughs at me. 'You imp! I wish I could get away with that. He corners me at every one of these events.'

'Darling, just be rude. You're the director. People will just chalk it up to your artistic temperament.'

She laughs again. 'Sound advice.'

'Lucinda, dear, I don't want you to feel you need to babysit me. I'm sure there are people you need to schmooze, and I'd like to catch up with my guests, if they're still here.'

'On the contrary, I'm honoured to be in your company, but let's see if we can track down your guests for you. Although, I'm not sure how much help I can be, seeing as I don't know what they look like.'

At that moment I see Sarah, the young usher who'd greeted us when we'd first arrived. I wave at her and when she nods, I beckon her over.

'I saw your performance, Miss Jamieson. You were absolutely wonderful,' she gushes.

'Oh, hush, darling, you're far too kind. Sarah, dear, I wonder if you might do me a favour.'

'Yes, of course.'

'Do you remember Jane and Richard? They were with me when I arrived.'

'I do. I've been looking after them this evening.'

'Excellent. Do you know where they are now? I'm keen to catch up with them.'

She nods. 'You wait right here, and I'll bring them to you.'

'Would you? Thank you, darling. I'm ever so grateful.'

Sarah smiles and disappears into the crowd. Lucinda is deep in conversation with one of the cast members, a delicious-looking boy with startlingly perfect teeth. A passing waiter offers me a glass of champagne, which I accept. I'm left to my own thoughts for a moment as I sip my drink and wait for Sarah's return.

Being on stage tonight has made me think about my life, about my achievements, in a different way. I came here to Australia to find a missing piece of myself – to find my family, my flesh and blood. It might not have worked out the way I'd hoped, but I did find something I needed. At least I know my son is alive and well and is living a happy life. He doesn't need me or want me to be part of it, and I think I'm okay with that, because, tonight, I've been reminded of who I am. Performing has brought me the purest joy I've ever known in life. It's where all my faults disappear and I am perfect. My relationship with the audience is the most satisfying I've ever had. I love them and they love me back. It might not be lasting, it might not be monogamous, but in the moment it is true. I am blessed to have known such love.

'Dolly!' Jane's voice cuts into my thoughts. She winds her way through the crowd towards me, with Richard and Sarah trailing behind. She reaches me and uncharacteristically throws her arms around me. 'Oh my god! You were magnificent! I cried! Truly. You can ask Richard.' She turns now to Richard, who has just caught up.

'Ask me what?'

'Whether I cried or not.'

He grins. 'Like a baby. She was so proud. We both were.' He steps forward to kiss my cheek. 'Well done, you. You were wonderful.'

Jane has loosened her grip on me now but still has hold of my free hand. Lucinda finishes her conversation and steps forward. 'Hello,' she says extending her hand for Richard to shake. 'I'm Lucinda Carroll, the show's director.' She turns to me. 'Is this your family, Dolly?'

It's then I realise there is one person in the world who I can count on no matter what. A person who I truly love and who loves me back unconditionally. Jane is my person.

'Yes,' I say proudly. 'It is.'

Chapter Forty-five

Three years later

'It's quite a good turnout, isn't it?' Richard says, eyeing the crowd as they pour into the events space in the library. 'I'm not sure there's going to be enough chairs.'

'Don't worry, I'm sure Stacey has it sorted. She's very efficient like that,' Jane says.

Emily, the publicist from our publishing house, taps Jane lightly on the shoulder. 'Excuse me, Jane, a few media representatives have arrived. It would be great if you could come to meet them.'

'Media?' Richard raises his eyebrows. 'Wow, that's impressive.'

Emily smiles. 'We had a very enthusiastic response to the press release.'

'You'd better take me to them,' Jane says.

Ten minutes later I am sitting in an armchair on a raised platform in front of a packed room. Jane and the interviewer, Kathy someone – apparently she used to be a big deal in morning television and now has a big following on YouTube – are seated to my right. All three of us have microphones clipped to our clothing.

Jane and I have had our hair and make-up done professionally for the event, and despite the stylist trying to talk me into wearing my hair in an 'elegant' chignon, I chose to wear my long silver tresses loose, but pinned back off my face with two sparkly red hair clips. I'm wearing an ankle-length, pale-blue silk dress and a bold red-and-pink geometric patterned coat, with cherry-red Doc Marten boots on my feet. Huge, dangly red earrings and matching red-framed glasses complete my 'author' look. Jane has ignored my suggestions of something a little more 'show business' and gone with a navy trouser suit. Despite everything that's happened these past couple of years, she's still not comfortable in the limelight.

Stacey stands in front of us with a microphone. She's incredibly chuffed that Jane and I chose to have the launch here, but, truly, where else would it be? This is the place Jane and I met and where we first conceived the idea for the book. This little library changed both our lives.

'Ladies and gentlemen,' Stacey begins. 'It is my great pleasure to welcome you all to the official launch of *The Life and Times of Miss Dolly Jamieson*, co-authored by Dolly Jamieson and Jane Leveson, who are our very special guests. Both ladies are well known to us here – Dolly in particular has been a much-loved patron of the library for many years – and we welcome them both warmly today.' There's a pause for applause and I smile at the audience, too scared to look at Jane, lest I laugh at Stacey's newfound appreciation for me.

Stacey continues to introduce Kathy and, after what seems like a never-ending list of housekeeping items (toilets at the back of the library to the left, emergency exits are on both sides of the building, the book will be available to purchase at the end, and so on) she finally takes her seat in the front row.

Kathy begins with an enthusiastic endorsement of the book, saying how she was unable to put it down, and then she begins her questions. 'Dolly, you have had such an interesting life. What made you decide to write about it now?'

'Well, it was Jane's idea actually.' I look across at Jane and she smiles. 'One never thinks one's own life will be interesting to others, but Jane here was always asking about my career and my life, and she convinced me other people might be interested in reading about it too.'

Kathy interrupts. 'It wasn't just that, though, was it? You wanted to record your life story for someone special.'

I nod. 'Yes, that's right. I'd been trying to jot down my thoughts for a while, because'—I pause and look out to the audience for dramatic effect—'there is someone very dear to me from whom I've been parted for many years. I wanted that person to have the opportunity to know about my life, and why I made the choices I have.' I tap the side of my nose. 'That's a hint about what's in the book, but Jane has made me promise not to give away any spoilers. So, if you want to know more, you'll have to buy a copy.'

'Or borrow one from the library!' Stacey interjects from the front row.

The audience laughs and Kathy directs her next question to Jane. 'And how did the two of you meet? I believe it was in this very library, is that right?'

'It is! I wandered in here one morning when I had time to kill. Dolly struck up a conversation with me, and I was instantly fascinated by her.'

'So you became friends?'

'Not immediately,' I pipe up. 'Jane didn't know what to make of me at first. I was in a bit of a mess back then.'

'Well, I was too,' she says. 'We were both struggling somewhat with life at the time.'

Kathy nods. 'I'd like to hear a little more about that, if you don't mind. Dolly, what do you mean you were "a mess"?'

'I was homeless when I met Jane.' Even though this fact has been well publicised in the media, a couple of audience members still gasp. I smile to reassure them. 'Hush now. It's all turned out all right.'

'But now you live with Jane?'

'Yes,' I say. 'Jane and her husband took me in. I've been living with them for three years. It was supposed to just be a temporary stay, while I sorted myself out, but Jane and I went on a trip to Australia together – something we talk about in the book – and when we arrived home it was the beginning of the pandemic. Jane and Richard were concerned about me living alone while all that was going on, so they convinced me to stay. I guess somewhere along the way we all got used to each other.'

Kathy looks at Jane. 'That was very charitable of you, Jane, inviting a near-stranger to come and live with you.'

'It wasn't charitable at all, actually. I met Dolly at the darkest time of my life. Right from the first moment I saw her, she brightened my world. Despite our age difference, I found we had a lot in common. I guess you could say we're kindred spirits. Dolly was there for me at a time when many other people had abandoned me,' she says pointedly, and I wonder if this Kathy was one of those in the media who shamed Jane after Tom died.

Without batting an eyelid, Kathy goes on to talk about women supporting women. I don't know whether she's being genuine or not, but the words ring true. I have two women, Jane and Sondra, to thank for ensuring I wouldn't have to live the last years of my life in poverty.

After what happened with Rob, I decided it was time to let go of the past and look to the future. With Richard's help (and against his advice), I contacted the lawyers to tell them I wanted to withdraw my claim on Julian's estate. I didn't need the money anymore, thanks to my pension and the safety net provided by Jane and Richard. Sammi could have my share. Maybe that would ease her pain. The minute it was done, I felt free.

A month later I got a beautiful letter from Sondra, thanking me for doing my bit to give Sammi closure. She told me how much Julian loved me and how she knew he would want me to be cared for, and that was why she was sharing her portion of the estate with me. You could have knocked me over with a feather!

I could have bought myself a little townhouse, but Jane and Richard convinced me to stay on with them. I used part of the inheritance to pay for a little extension on the back of their house. Now I have a downstairs bedroom and private sitting area.

Jane is looking at me. 'Having Dolly in our home just feels right,' she says. 'She's very much part of our family now.'

The audience lets out a collective 'aw' as I reach across the gap between us to pat Jane's arm.

'How lovely,' says Kathy, smiling broadly before redirecting the conversation. She asks if I have plans to write any more books.

I laugh. 'No. I'm not an author. Jane's the one with the writing talent. I don't see any more books in my future, but I am keeping busy. I've started mentoring at a local theatre school. I'm teaching singing and stagecraft to a group of very talented young people, and that is filling my time and my mind these days.'

'What about you, Jane? It's been a few years since you closed down your social media empire. You mentioned earlier that you were going through a hard time when you and Dolly first met. I think what you and your family went through is no secret to most people. Is there any chance we might see you writing about that in the future?'

Jane's eyes narrow and my heart begins to thump, but she handles the question beautifully. 'No,' she says decisively. 'I don't want to revisit that dark time, but, in any case, it's not my story to tell. I would never do anything to make things worse for the victims' families, so I won't be writing or talking about that subject in the future.'

'Right. I can understand that. I imagine it's quite confronting for you to be in the public eye again after what you've been through. In fact, I believe when you took on this project initially, you didn't want your name on the cover, preferring the idea of being a ghostwriter. Is that correct?'

'Yes, that was the original agreement.'

'What made you change your mind?'

'Dolly was keen for me to take credit for my work. And, frankly, I was inspired by her honesty in the book. She's taught me there's power and redemption in owning our stories. Her example has made me want to be braver.'

There's a lump in my throat now and I have to blink hard to keep my tears at bay.

'What's next for you?' Kathy asks.

'Right now, I'm running an online support network for families of young offenders.'

'Goodness, that sounds as if it would keep you busy.'

'It does.'

'So, no more books from you, then?'

'Actually, I did enjoy the writing process. Part of that was working with Dolly, of course, but I also loved the research process, and taking the raw information and making it work as a story. I enjoyed it so much that I've decided to write a novel. It's early days yet, so I'm not sure if it will ever be published, but I'm having fun with it.'

Kathy flashes her chemically whitened teeth in a disingenuous smile. 'Lovely.'

She wraps it up then, thanking us and the library staff, and reminding the audience that Jane and I will be available to sign books purchased from the bookseller who is waiting to serve them at the back of the room.

Emily rushes up to the stage area. She thanks Kathy and then ushers Jane and me to the signing table. 'You were both wonderful,' she gushes.

I grin at her. 'That was a hoot. It takes me back to the old days when I would do publicity for a new show.'

'I'm glad you enjoyed it, considering we have several more of these to come over the next few weeks!' She turns to Jane. 'How was it for you?'

'Not as bad as I'd feared. Especially as it was the first time I've spoken in public since . . .'

Emily knows Jane's story. 'I thought you handled yourself beautifully. Well done to you both. Now, sit yourselves down. Here are some signing pens. I'll go fetch some water for you and will be back in time to be in charge of crowd control. Just sing out if there's anything you need.'

While Emily's away fetching water, Richard arrives and places a glass of champagne in front of each of us. 'Well done, you two. I'm proud of you both.'

'Thank you, darling,' I reply. 'Isn't our girl clever? This is all her doing.'

Richard winks at me, but there's sincerity in his voice when he says, 'She is indeed.'

A line of eager fans has started to form already so Richard wanders off to mingle with the champagne-drinking, canape-eating crowd. Jane and I get busy signing and, despite Emily's best efforts to keep the line moving, it seems to go on forever.

After what feels like hours we are finally at the last person in line. 'Who should the ladies make the book out to?' Emily asks, pen at ready to write down the correct spelling on a sticky note for us.

'Clementine,' she says, and I don't have to look at her to know who she is.

'Clementine Parker?' I ask tentatively, in case I am mistaken.

'Yes, that's me,' she replies and now I can hear her Australian accent.

I scramble to my feet and open my arms to the young woman – my own flesh and blood.

When I finally let her go, Clementine begins to speak. 'Granny,' she says, trying out the word. 'Can I call you Granny?'

'Oh, my darling, I would love nothing more.'

Author's note

In April 2019 I was on holiday with my family in the UK. Although it was officially spring, the weather was freezing! My teenage son was thrilled to see snow for the first time, but it made me worry to think about the large number of homeless people we encountered on our travels enduring that weather.

One night, while I was waiting outside a grocery store for my husband, I struck up a conversation with a homeless woman about the book she was reading. When my husband returned, the woman thanked me for talking to her. She said most people didn't even make eye contact, let alone take the time to chat, and that she appreciated the opportunity to feel normal for a little while.

Afterwards, I couldn't stop thinking about her words. I tried to imagine what it would be like to go through life feeling invisible.

When we were back home in Australia, I came across an article in *Good Weekend* that described the increasing problem of homelessness among older women. The article featured the personal stories of some homeless older women, and I was particularly moved by one woman's story. She'd worked in TV in various roles, eventually rising to the position of associate producer. Her lifestyle was one that many would envy – a good income, lots of overseas travel and a home in Sydney's well-to-do Northern Beaches. After a change in her health ended her career, she suffered many financial setbacks and eventually found herself without secure housing. This was an outcome she could never have imagined.

As I read her story, I knew that this was a topic I needed to explore further.

I began to research and was confronted by what I found. In Australia, homelessness is growing faster among older women than in any other demographic. In the five years from 2011 to 2016, census data showed that homelessness increased among women in the 65 to 74 age bracket by 51 per cent.* This is a trend that is occurring in other countries, including the United Kingdom, where we meet Dolly.

The reasons for the rapid increase in homelessness among this cohort are complex and varied, but systemic issues such as ageism in the workplace, the gender pay gap and lower average superannuation balances at retirement for women all play a part. Then there are factors such as the impact of 'grey divorce', the death of a spouse or an unexpected change in health.

As dire as the statistics are, unfortunately they don't tell the whole story. The full extent of this problem is hidden because many older women who don't have secure housing are 'couch surfing', or relying on family and friends to put them up. Embarrassment can prevent these women from categorising themselves as homeless.

I was shocked to learn that many women who, prior to a change of circumstances, identified as middle-class find themselves financially vulnerable as they age. Perhaps because of their limited experience with the welfare system, these women can struggle to access services to assist them. Lack of access to technology and/or an inability to navigate online resources sometimes compounds the problem.

Homelessness can be difficult to overcome. The absence of things that many of us take for granted – for instance, a permanent mailing

---

* Sharon Bradley, 'House Call', *Good Weekend* (*The Age*, *Sydney Morning Herald*), 8 February 2020, p. 20

address – can create unforeseen obstacles to gaining employment or even receiving welfare benefits. Shame and guilt can prevent some women from seeking help, and a shortage of age-appropriate and gender-appropriate services also has an impact on outcomes for older homeless women.

These are some of the issues that inspired me to write this book. I wanted to explore what might happen when an older woman without family support finds herself in a difficult financial situation. I also wanted to examine the impact of lack of social contact, or 'feeling invisible', on people who are sleeping rough or on the streets. Finally, I wanted to highlight the fact that homelessness is a problem that could affect any of us.

As a character, Dolly Jamieson is many things – fierce, talented, proud and vulnerable. Most of all, she's a fighter who never gives up hope. I hope you loved reading her story as much as I loved writing it.

Book club discussion notes

1. In Australia, homelessness is growing faster among older women than in any other demographic. Other nations, such as the US and the UK, report similar trends. Why do you think this is?

2. Can you imagine how Margie Ferguson's life might have been different if her father, James, had returned from the war? Do you think she still would have gone on to become Dolly Jamieson?

3. One of the things that Dolly hates most about her current situation is feeling as if she is invisible. Why is this so painful for her?

4. Dolly and Jane quickly become friends. What is it that draws them together? Why do you think their friendship works?

5. Richard is clearly grieving; however, he is not burdened by guilt and shame the same way Jane is. Why do you think this is? Do you think men are judged on their parenting in the same way women are?

6. Dolly's travels take her to cosmopolitan locations of the 1960s and '70s – Melbourne, Sydney, London and New York. Which one of these cities would you most have liked to visit during Dolly's era?

7. When Dolly makes contact with Rob/Jamie, things don't go to plan. Can you understand Rob's reaction to her presence?

8. Although Jane and Dolly are in very different financial situations when they meet, they are both dealing with loneliness, isolation and shame. What are some of the aspects that you think contribute to this sense of loneliness in today's society, particularly for older women?

9. Dolly is a proud woman who hates to accept charity, but she is grateful for the kindness of strangers. What do you think makes the difference between the two?

10. There are a number of events in the book that show how people's lives can change in an instant. Which of these events did you find the most shocking or did not see coming?

Acknowledgements

Some books are a dream to write. The words flow onto the page effortlessly, the story taking shape as if by magic.

This was not one of those books!

I'd had the idea percolating away for a while before I started to write it during the long months of lockdown in 2020. The first draft was awful, and I was frustrated because I desperately wanted to do justice to Dolly's story.

Enter my generous publisher, Beverley Cousins. Bev, your encouragement, patience and thoughtful comments made all the difference when I was struggling to make this book work. In many ways, Dolly's final story is as much yours as it is mine. Thank you. I am truly grateful.

Thanks also to Kathryn Knight, whose keen eye and insightful remarks in the copyedit elevated the manuscript well beyond what I could ever achieve on my own. Kathryn, thanks for always being so kind when you are correcting my many, many mistakes! I'm also grateful to Lauren Finger for her meticulous proofread. Thanks, Lauren, for making me look good!

Thanks to the whole team at Penguin Random House Australia, who are always a delight to work with. A special shout-out to Lisa Brewster from The Brewster Project for creating Dolly's gorgeous cover.

One of the things I love most about being a writer is that I get to hang out with other writers. Sometimes I still pinch myself when I realise this is my life!

Sally Hepworth, Jane Cockram and Kirsty Manning, thanks for the lunches, the road trips and, most of all, the laughs. Thanks also to the Writers' Camp crew – Amanda Knight, Emily Madden, Rebecca Heath and Rachael Johns. I can't believe it's been a decade now since we first met! Tess Woods, Delwyn Jenkins, Nina Campbell and Kylie Ladd, thanks for always being in my corner. To my Geelong crew, I miss you all so much! And to my new crew, Wellington Women Writers, thanks for welcoming me to Gippsland. There are so many other wonderful writers who I connect with on a regular basis. Please know I appreciate you all.

Special and heartfelt thanks to Kelly Rimmer, for reading many drafts and for educating me about musical theatre. (And also for our daily chats!)

I'd like to give a shout-out to all the wonderful writers I've mentored over the past couple of years. Working with you has been such a pleasure, and I'm sure you've helped me to grow as a writer as much as I've helped you. I'm so excited to watch your careers develop.

Thanks to all my friends for understanding why I never answer the phone when I'm writing! An extra special acknowledgement to my lifelong bestie, Fiona Newman, for sharing her dance expertise with me.

As always, thanks to my family. To Charlie, Will and Alex, thanks for your support and for being the people you are. And David, thanks for everything, but especially for doing all the cooking and washing while I play with my imaginary friends.

Finally, and most importantly, I'd like to thank my readers. Without you I would have no reason to write. Thanks to everyone who follows me on Facebook or Instagram, or subscribes to my newsletter, and a huge shout-out to my online reading group, The Reading Couch. I absolutely love connecting with all of you.

You can connect with Lisa at:

lisairelandbooks.com

Instagram: @lisairelandbooks

Facebook: facebook.com/lisairelandbooks

The Reading Couch: facebook.com/groups/149288140312440

After working for many years as a teacher (and a brief stint as a professional organiser – before Marie Kondo made it cool), Lisa Ireland is now a full-time writer.

Lisa lives with her husband in a small town in Gippsland, Victoria. When not writing, she spends her days mentoring aspiring authors, drinking coffee and playing minion to her incredibly spoilt dog, Lulu.

The One and Only Dolly Jamieson is Lisa's seventh novel.

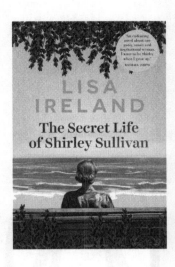

Elderly. Is that how the world sees me? A helpless little old lady? If only they knew. I allow myself a small smirk.

When Shirley Sullivan signs her 83-year-old husband, Frank, out of the Sunset Lodge Nursing Home, she has no intention of bringing him back.

For fifty-seven years the couple has shared love, happiness and heartbreak. And while Frank may not know who his wife is these days, he knows he wants to go home. Back to the beach where they met in the early 1960s.

So Shirley enacts an elaborate plan to evade the authorities – and their furious daughter, Fiona – to give Frank the holiday he'd always dreamt of.

And, in doing so, perhaps Shirley can make amends for a lifelong guilty secret . . .

'An endearing novel about one gutsy, smart and inspirational woman. I want to be Shirley when I grow up.' Rachael Johns

'Beautiful, breathtaking and heart-wrenching.' *Australian Women's Weekly*

Discover a
new favourite

Visit **penguin.com.au/readmore**